Under

Different

Stars

The Kricket Series
Volume 1

By
Amy A. Bartol

47NORTH

Text copyright © 2014 by Amy A. Bartol

Published by 47North, Seattle

www.apub.com

Amazon, the Amazon logo, and 47North are trademarks of Amazon.com, Inc., or its affiliates.

ISBN-13: 9781477821121
ISBN-10: 1477821120

Cover design by Regina Wamba of Mae I Design
Cover Photo by Aaron Draper

Library of Congress Control Number: 2014948392

Printed in the United States of America

For Tom, Max, and Jack, my stars

Contents

Chapter 1 – Chicago

Chapter 2 – Lumin

Chapter 3 – Strangers

Chapter 4 – Waking Up

Chapter 5 – The Pool

Chapter 6 – Follow Your Eyes

Chapter 7 – With Every Mistake

Chapter 8 – What's It Gonna Take?

Chapter 9 – Split the World in Two

Chapter 10 – Transport

Chapter 11 – Comantre Crosses

Chapter 12 – Processing

Chapter 13 – The Palace

Chapter 14 – My Next Deal

Chapter 15 – Come to Ruin

Chapter 16 – Tell the Truth

Chapter 17 – No Future

Chapter 18 – One of Us

Chapter 19 – Bend or Break

Chapter 20 – Swanks and Tanks

Chapter 21 – Never Enough

Acknowledgments

About the Author

Chapter 1

Chicago

Flipping a coin into the air, I watch as it arches toward the cascading water of the fountain. "Home," I whisper to myself as it breaks the surface, causing ripples to race toward the lapis tiles.

"That's a waste of money," Enrique says after pulling the earbud from my ear. "Why do you continue to throw your money away when you know that Lou is gonna get it at the end of the month?" he asks. I glance at Lou, who's leaning against the mahogany front desk of the City Insurance Building, reading the *Chicago Tribune*, his distended belly straining against his janitorial jumpsuit. He absently uses a rag to polish the desk's surface that he's gone over a thousand times already.

"He doesn't get to keep my wish, does he?" I ask, looking back at the fountain before pulling my coat on over my own khaki janitorial jumpsuit. I pull the other earbud from my ear, press "Pause" on my iPod, and tuck my headphones in my pocket.

"You can stop wishing for Prince Charming to come and rescue you," Enrique says with a grin, watching me wrap my scarf around my neck and put on my mittens. "I'm right here, Kricket. Enrique and Kricket Rodriguez . . . that sounds chill. We can put the announcement in the *Trib*." His teeth look stark white in contrast to his honey-toned skin as he smiles at me.

"I think finding Prince Charming is your wish. Mine is still Northwestern University," I reply, picking up my backpack and throwing it over my shoulder.

"Just think how happy my mom would be if I told her I was marrying you. She'd flip out, seriously," he says half-jokingly.

"Enrique, that's a really tempting offer, but since I'm only seventeen, I'm gonna keep my options open," I reply, putting my hat on and trying to sweep my mass of blond hair beneath it.

"I thought you heard back from U of M," Enrique says, zipping his coat and putting on his hat. His thick, black hair sticks out beneath it.

"I did. The University of Michigan liked my test scores. I just can't afford it, even with a partial scholarship. Plus, what am I going to do in Ann Arbor?" I ask, trying not to sound disappointed. "I don't know anyone there."

"You don't really know anyone here, either," Enrique replies. "It's not like you have to stay for your family." He nudges me with his elbow.

"No . . . you're right." I try to smile to cover the stab of pain his comment causes.

"You have no idea how good you have it, Kricket. It must be total freedom not having cousins, aunts and uncles, and parents on your back all the time about what you're doing," he says. "Being on your own must be nice."

My shoulders slouch forward as I try to hide my face. "It's better than foster care," I say softly. "I only have to stay below the radar for a few more months. Then, when I'm eighteen, they can't touch me. No more under-the-table jobs. I'll be able to get a real job, for real money. You know Bridget, my roommate?" I glance at him and see his nod. "She works at the Mercantile Exchange. She thinks she can get me a job verifying trades on the currencies floor in the spring. If

I get accepted to Northwestern, I can take classes at night and work at the Merc during the day."

"Your ambition makes me feel like I gotta take a nap." Enrique holds the door for me as we step out of the corporate offices of the City Insurance Building. It's still dark out at five in the morning, but the streetlights in the loop illuminate the entire area. The softly falling snow looks magical as we walk by the Christmas holiday displays in the downtown windows.

"I need to have goals. If I thought that I'd be emptying trashcans for the rest of my life, I'd lose it," I admit.

"You could do a ton of other things. Like . . . modeling. You're a giant, sister," Enrique says, his feet make crunching noises as he walks over the snow on the salted sidewalk.

"Five-ten is not that tall."

"C'mon, you look like a Viking. Those modeling agents would freak for your hollow cheekbones, and I bet they've never seen a natural blond walk through their lobby doors." He stops at the end of the block and waits for the light. "But when they see your freakish eyes, they'll beg you to sign with them."

"My eyes are not freakish!"

Enrique makes a derisive sound. "I've never met anyone with violet eyes," he replies, raising his eyebrows. "If I had eyes like yours, I'd be in New York making some serious cash."

"Yeah, and the minute they enter my Social Security number into their agency computer, the Illinois Department of Social Services will show up and haul me back to some juvenile detention center. No thanks," I say, feeling a shiver tear through me. "I've spent too many years trapped in their hell. I'm not going back—even if they can only hold me for a few more months. When I'm eighteen, I can do whatever I want, but until then, I'll sweep up coffee grounds, empty trashcans, and listen to my iPod."

Enrique's smile fades. "It couldn't have been that bad—"

"No, it was worse," I counter, unable to keep the edge out of my voice.

"Of course it was bad," he says, looking guilty. "You didn't know me then. Now you have family. My mom wants you to come over for Christmas dinner next week. She's making the enchiladas you love," he says in a singsong voice.

"Mmm, enchiladas sound great. What time?" I ask, feeling my throat tighten a little at the thought of not spending Christmas alone. I was going to spend the holiday with Bridget in our apartment, but she's going to go to her boyfriend's parents' house in Northwood. I know that she's feeling guilty about leaving me alone. She invited me to come with them, but it's hard enough for her to try to fit into Eric's family without having to tote me along too, so I told her that I'd rather stay in the city.

"I don't know. I'll ask and tell you Monday," he says.

"Wouldn't you rather invite Michael?" I ask.

He shoots me a sidelong glance. "Uh, definitely not," he replies.

"Why not?" I ask. "They're your family. They'll love you no matter what."

"Where are you from, Kricket? Either you're really naïve or you've really never had a family, 'cuz if I bring Michael to Christmas dinner, you'll be getting a new roommate."

"Families are supposed to love you no matter what," I say softly, looking into his dark brown eyes.

"You've really never had a family, have you?" he asks rhetorically.

"No . . . not one that ever lasted," I admit, stopping beside the stairway to the El station.

"You're lucky, trust me. Anyway, what're you doing this weekend?"

"I'm going to see if they need any help at the bar—they sometimes let me bar-back when they're really busy. If not, then I have a date with William." I smile, watching the plumes of my breath curl and dissipate in the air.

"William? You met someone?" he says, narrowing his eyes suspiciously.

"I did. His name is William Shakespeare. He's British and has a funny accent," I smirk, watching Enrique's slow smile.

"You're gonna read all weekend? You should come out with Michael and me. We're checking out a new club in Wrigleyville," he says.

"Uh, you know I have that rule." I hold up my finger.

He frowns. "What rule?"

"You know, the rule about people."

"What rule about people?"

"The one about never getting involved with them," I explain.

"What about me?" he asks. "You're involved with me. We're friends."

"You're the exception that proves the rule." I turn away before he can hug me goodbye. "Say 'hi' to Michael for me. I'll see you Monday." I hurry for the stairs.

"Call me if you change your mind," Enrique shouts as he walks backward toward the bus stop that will take him to the south side.

Giving him a cursory wave goodbye, I climb the stairs to the El platform. I walk under the heating lamps on the platform, grateful for the warmth. Seeing Pete asleep, propped up against the wall of the station, I walk over to him. Bending down, I open my backpack and pull out half of a peanut butter sandwich I have left over from dinner. I put it in his lap, hoping he'll see it when he wakes up. "You need a shower, Pete," I mutter under my breath.

The train makes the sound of scraping metal as it slows down to enter the station. I straighten, looking over my shoulder. The platform that was empty only a second ago now has three new occupants. Startled, I stiffen and face the tracks again. Normally, I'm the only one here this early, going north. Plenty of people are headed downtown, but not many are leaving at five o'clock—not unless they've spent all night in a nightclub.

Putting a hand on the shoulder strap of my backpack, I pull my hat down, trying to hide my face and hair as they come closer to me. Not turning my head in their direction, I strain my eyes to watch their movements on the platform, hoping the really tall one in the middle doesn't take an interest in me. *He's buff.* I assess him quickly. *Steroids?* I wonder to myself. *Tailored clothing—expensive. Maybe I'll be invisible to them, dressed in my baggy jumpsuit and coat.*

Holding my breath as the train comes to a stop in front of me, I approach the doors as they open, stepping into the fluorescent-lit car. Holding on to the metal railing, I take a seat on the bench immediately to the left of the door.

Glancing down the aisle to the other door, the three men from the platform enter the car. The tallest one, dressed in a tailored, black trench coat, enters first, and his eyes immediately search for me. Angling my face away from him and putting my earbuds in, I look down, trying to be invisible. I scroll through my playlist, feeling tense. Something's wrong. I know it instinctively. As a kid, I learned to read the room well as a survival technique. Alarm bells are going off in my mind. I can tell when someone wants something from me; it's in the body language.

Exquisite black-leather dress shoes stop in front of me, causing goose bumps to rise on my arms. Not looking up, I vaguely hear a male voice speaking to me over my music. Continuing to ignore him, I feel the earbuds being tugged gently from my ears.

"There. That is better, no?" a very masculine voice asks. "Can you hear me now, Kricket?"

Moistening my lips and feeling my heart pounding in my chest, I slowly trail my eyes over the massive form in front of me. Seeing the expensive cut of his coat and the cashmere scarf hanging loosely from his collar, I can rule out that he works for the DSS. No one who works in social services wears shoes that expensive. My eyes pause for a moment on his neck, seeing thick, black tribal tattoos covering one side of it.

My eyes drift over his slashing cheekbones and sculptured mouth to his black hair; it's not military cut, but it's short nonetheless. But I lose my breath when my eyes connect with his. His irises are a lovely shade of violet, a similar color to mine.

His mouth twists in an ironic smile. "Ah, Kricket, I've found you," he murmurs, crouching in front of me while pulling my hat from my head, causing my long, platinum-blond hair to cascade around my shoulders. Reaching out, he gently touches my hair, letting it spill through his fingers.

Some harsh, ingrained lesson from my past makes me respond. "Who?" I ask, raising my eyebrows. *Deny everything until you know the score. That's rule number one,* my mind whispers to me. "My name is Jane." I push his hand from my hair.

"Jane? I don't think so. No, you're Kricket for sure. Your eyes have already told me who you are," he states, smiling and showing all of his beautiful teeth. "But I'm impressed that you can read the situation—the need to lie—it's intriguing. What else do you know?" he asks, tilting his head to the side and smirking. I look at his friend standing to the right. He's completely massive too, with the same black, tribal tattoo on his neck and the same black hair and violet eyes.

Temporarily mesmerized, I gasp as strong fingers grip my chin, forcing my gaze back to the man in front of me. His eyes have narrowed, making him look a little older than I first thought, maybe mid-twenties. "Do not look at him. He's not important right now," he says.

"Does he know he's not important?" I ask, my mouth dry with fear.

Looking surprised at my response, a small smile breaks through his arrogant expression. "Jax, do you know that you're not important?"

"Yes."

I frown. "If you're not important, then who is, Jax?" I inquire, watching humor flicker in the eyes of the man in front of me.

"Trey," Jax answers.

"You're Trey, right?" I ask, feeling my heart racing.

"I am."

My fear builds to an unacceptable level as my hands begin to shake. "Why are you important, Trey?" My eyes dart quickly around. *There's no way out of here until the train stops.*

"I'm important to you because I hold your destiny in my hand," he replies, watching my response.

"You mean Kricket's destiny, don't you? I'm Jane," I reply, trying to look calm.

"Your name is Kricket Hollowell. You're the daughter of Pan Hollowell and Arissa Valke—"

"My parents are James and Sally Klume. Sorry, you have the wrong girl, and this is my stop, so—" Trey interrupts me as his hand shoots out to keep me in my seat when I try to get up.

He shakes his head. "I can't let you do that. My job is to take you back," he states, not taking his hand from my arm.

"Take me back where?" I ask.

"To your home."

"Springfield?" I say the name of the first city that pops into my head.

"No," he frowns, looking irritated. "Ethar."

"Kandahar? I'm sorry, but I've never even been to New Jersey," I say, purposefully misunderstanding him.

"E-t-h-a-r," he says, drawing out the word like I'm feebleminded.

I moisten my lips. "Okay, listen to me carefully, so there's no misunderstanding here," I say, speaking slowly like one would to a child and looking into crazy Trey's eyes. "I'm Jane Klume—of the Springfield Klumes—so I'm not going anywhere with you, or Jax, or him." I indicate the other freak on his right.

"I can understand your position. If I were you, I might not want to return home either, but the time for cowardice is over. You need to face your family and pay for your crimes."

My mouth drops open as I search his face. "My crimes?" I ask after my mouth snaps shut again. *He's insane.*

Trey nods as both his eyebrows come together. "Desertion, among others," he replies, tightening his hand on my arm, like he severely disapproves of me.

"You're mental . . ." I trail off, seeing the serious expressions on all of their faces.

"We're quite sane," he replies easily.

Slipping my gloved hands into my pockets, I notice the train slowing. The automated voice begins announcing our arrival at the Fullerton station. Trey's eyes focus in on my hands.

Slowly, I pull one hand from my pocket. Opening it, I ask, "Mint?" and extend my hand, filled with cellophane-wrapped red-and-white-striped candies.

He lets go of my arm. "No," he frowns, looking at the mints in my hand like they're poison.

Pulling my other hand quickly from my pocket and pressing the button, I ask, "Pepper spray?"

Jumping up on my seat, I continue to spray Trey, Jax, and the other thug with my can of pepper spray. Seeing them clutch their hands to their eyes as they moan in pain, I fit myself between the handrails on my right and run out the door of the train, dropping the can as I go.

I run down the snow-covered stairs and clutch the handrail before jumping the last few steps to the sidewalk below. Looking around frantically, I spot a cab parked across the street. Not looking for cars, I step off the curb, hearing squealing tires as I do. Reaching the cab amid viciously honking horns, I open the door, diving onto the backseat. "Lincoln Park—Diversey and Clark," I say, panting the cross streets to the driver. "I'm in a hurry," I add, pulling a twenty from my wallet and flashing it at him.

The taxi peels away from the curb. Looking out the back window, I scan the area for Trey and his buddies. I don't see them, so maybe they didn't get off the train. Sitting back in my seat, I close my eyes as I tremble in fear.

Chapter 2

Lumin

I pay the taxi driver as he pulls up at the corner of Diversey and Clark. I jump out of the cab, looking rapidly up both sides of the street for anything suspicious. Seeing nothing, I hurry past the drugstore, bookstore, and drycleaner. I pull my keys from the pocket of my backpack and open the outer door next to the drycleaner.

I make sure the door locks behind me after I step inside. I take a deep breath to try to calm the ache of fear in my chest. I haven't been this scared since I climbed out of a second-story window and jumped from the run-down apartment where I once lived. I hadn't felt the impact of hitting the ground then. It'd been nothing compared to the beating I'd just received. But I remember the fear. I just can't remember if it was fear that I'd die in the fall . . . or fear that I'd live.

I bypass the elevator because it's slower than a cab in rush hour and walk to the stairwell. Climbing the stairs to the third floor, I peek out, looking at the door of my apartment near the end of the hall. The hall's empty. Taking a deep breath, I walk to my door and unlock it. Pushing it closed behind me, I turn the dead bolt and secure the chain to it. Leaning against the door, I close my eyes, running my hand through my hair and feeling dampness from the melted snow.

"Kricket!" Bridget calls from the end of the hall that leads to the one room of our studio apartment. I jump, not expecting Bridget to be up so early on a Saturday morning.

"Bridge," I say, exhaling and trying to calm my racing heart. "What're you doing up?" I ask, seeing that she's dressed nicely in a designer skirt and top that we found at the Salvation Army. It looks great on her because she has a bangin' body.

"I'm packing. Eric talked me into going to his parents' house a couple days early since I don't have to work this weekend. I'm so glad you're home. I need your opinion. Do you think I should take this skirt, or is it too short for the suburbanites?" She tucks her long dark hair behind her ear before holding up a small, black-leather skirt to her slim waist.

"Honestly?" I shake my head. "I mean, you're meeting Mom and Dad . . . Dad might like it, but Mom. Will. Freak."

Biting her lip, she stomps her foot and whines, "You're right. Are you sure you can't come with me?"

I shake my head slowly. "You're gonna be fine. They're going to love you, Bridget."

Her fingers twist in agitation. "Yeah, until the long silence comes after they ask me what my parents do, and I tell them my dad's doing a mandatory twenty for armed robbery," she replies, grimacing.

"Maybe you don't have to tell them. Maybe you can just say you haven't seen him lately because he's upstate," I reply.

Bridget flails her arms. "You see, I need you there. You're like a diplomat or something."

"You'll be okay, just keep your eyes open. Watch what his mom does, and follow her lead. If she eats her soup with a fork, then you eat your soup with a fork," I advise her. "Just like we used to in juvie."

"Who eats soup with a fork?" Bridget asks, looking confused.

"Not the point. I'm just saying, when in Rome . . ." I trail off.

Bridget's brow wrinkles. "They eat soup with a fork in Rome?" she asks, and I laugh.

"Uh, forget the soup. Just have a good time and relax. Hipster Eric likes you." I peel off my jumpsuit and throw it in the hamper. Finding a pair of pajama bottoms in my closet, I put them on.

Bridget's dark eyes narrow, "You should stop calling him 'Hipster Eric' 'cuz you're gonna slip one of these days."

"You really like him, huh?" I ask, seeing her try to hide it.

"He keeps asking me to move in with him," Bridget replies with a faux-casual shrug, watching my reaction. "But you've been to his place. It's completely ridic. I'm not the kind of girl who can live somewhere like that. It's too . . . *nice.*" She wrinkles her nose, like "nice" is a bad thing.

Something in my heart twists. Bridget is my only family. I want her to be happy. She deserves nice —she deserves love. But if she moves in with Eric, I'm completely screwed. I can't live here without a roommate. "I don't know, Bridge, I think you'd do all right with 'nice.' Enrique thinks he might be looking to move out. He might need a roommate," I say casually. It's only a half lie because he did say that Michael would get him tossed out.

"Really?" Bridget asks, looking happy as she tucks her brown hair behind her ear.

"Yeah." I nod, trying to smile.

She tries to hide her relief from me by lowering her eyes. "Well, I'm still thinking about it. I want to see how this week goes. I may not be able to handle being with his family," she says honestly. I nod absently, my mind tumbling over itself with the ramification of what this means for me.

A knock sounds on the door, making me jump. "That must be Eric. He wants to get on the road before the traffic hits," Bridget says, heading for the door.

"Wait!" I flinch before running in front of her to the door and blocking her from opening it. Seeing the alarm on Bridget's face, I put my finger to my lips. Then I say in a deep voice, "Who is it?"

"Uh . . . Kricket? It's me, Eric." Eric's muffled voice sounds through the door.

Feeling relief, I look through the peephole before opening the door. "Merry Christmas, Kricket," Eric says, shoving a beautifully wrapped package in my hands and kissing my cheek. As he walks past me, I close the door behind him, locking and chaining it.

Bridget watches me closely, only distracted when Eric picks her up off her feet for a huge hug. "You smell great," he says in her ear, causing her to smile and her hazel eyes to sparkle.

"Thanks," she murmurs before turning her eyes on me. She narrows them as she asks, "'Sup with you?"

I shrug, noncommittal. "Just some guys on the El giving me static. I thought they were DSS for a second, but maybe they're just random."

"What's DSS?" Eric asks, looking confused.

"Dipshit sailors," Bridget lies. "Did they follow you here?"

Shaking my head, I explain, "I don't think so. I got off at Fullerton and took a taxi."

Eric pulls his snowy hat from his head. "You should call the police, Kricket." Eric's blue eyes widen in concern. "You can make a report." I smile. He doesn't know anything about me.

Bridget understands my dilemma. She knows I can't go to the police because they'll take me into custody, and I won't be able to get out of juvenile detention until I turn eighteen. I probably have zero chance of applying to be an emancipated minor because I broke out at sixteen and have been dodging them ever since. But once Bridget aged out of the system and got a job in the city, I finally had somewhere to go. We'd spent a year together as roommates in one of the worst juvenile centers in Chicago. We had each other's back there. When she wrote me and told me where she was, it was only a matter of time before I found a way out during a rare fieldtrip.

"It wasn't a big deal. They were probably coming home from the club . . . you know how it is," I say, downplaying it. I catch the look in Bridget's eyes. She's worried.

"Maybe I should stay for the weekend," she says. She wants details, but she won't ask me now. Not with Eric here. She'd never put my freedom at risk, and so she'll never expose to Eric that I'm a runaway from DSS.

"No. I'll be fine," I assure her. "They can't possibly know where I live." I use a P.O. box for my mail, making sure that no one gets my real address here, just in case I get an investigator assigned to my case who doesn't suck. Since I'm paid under the table at work, I don't have to worry about any payroll checks being printed in my name.

"You're sure?" She doesn't look at all convinced.

"I'm sure," I reply, trying to appear confident.

"Okay, come here and sit on my suitcase so I can get it to close," she orders.

I do as she asks, and she pushes the latches closed. Eric picks it up off the bed, carrying it while I walk with Bridget toward the door. "Call if you need me."

"I will," I agree, feeling choked up. I stop her at my closet, pulling out a present for her and one for Eric. "Merry Christmas, Bridge."

"I mean it—I'll come right back if you need me," she says, taking the presents from me. "Your present is on your bed."

"Thanks," I say, trying not to let my eyes get teary.

"Merry Christmas, Kricket," she says gruffly as she tries to do the same. Impulsively, she gives me a quick hug.

"Ready?" Eric asks, unlocking the door.

"Yeah," Bridget says, following him into the hall. "Lock this," she orders, pointing at the door.

"I will," I reply before closing it. I throw the bolt, latching the chain. Walking to my bed, I pick up my present.

Sitting down on the worn coverlet, I slowly unwrap the present from Eric. It's a very expensive-looking espresso machine. Looking for a gift receipt so I can take it back, my shoulders slump when I can't find one. *Maybe the pawnshop will give me something for it,* I think. I set it aside on the floor near my bed.

I open the little cardboard box from Bridget and find a delicate gold bracelet that has a thin gold plate with the word "Sister" etched in the metal. Smiling and blinking back tears, I put it on, shaking my wrist so that "Sister" sits on top.

Pulling the blinds down over the window, I set my alarm clock so that I'll be up in time to eat and relax before I go to the club downstairs to see if they need me. Laying my head on my pillow, I pull my blanket up to my chin. As I close my eyes, I try to blot out the images of Trey and his pals that invade my head, making my heart pound against the wall of my chest like it did when I was on the train. It takes awhile before I finally sleep.

Dreaming of lush fields, running barefoot under an azure sky that contains not only a brilliant sun, but also another moon on its infinite horizon, I awake drenched in sweat. My alarm clock is blaring, reminding me that I have to get ready for another Saturday night in the trenches.

After eating a quick meal, I take a shower. Combing out my hair, I braid it in two long plaits that fall well past my shoulders. Wrapping a black hair tie around the end of one braid, I pull a loose strand of hair from the end of it. As I hold the blond strand in my palm, it turns black immediately, then curls up and turns into a speck of dust. Letting my hand drop, I glance at the mirror.

"Who are you?" I whisper to my reflection, knowing that she doesn't have the answer either.

I give up and go to my closet to get dressed. Putting on my jeans and a black, short-sleeved T-shirt with the words "Boys lie" emblazoned in white letters on the chest, I lace up the secondhand black boots I just picked up at the Salvation Army. They're perfect because the leather is soft, having been broken in just right. Shrugging into my coat and backpack, I check the hallway outside through the peephole in my door. Seeing no one, I step out and lock it behind me. I take the back stairs and exit into the dark parking lot behind our building.

"Luther." I smile, seeing my favorite bouncer sitting on a stool, guarding the back door to the trendy nightclub called *Lumin*. "'Sup, Sherlock?" I ask, using the nickname I gave him because he has an uncanny ability to sniff out the fake IDs from the real ones.

"Nothin' but my rent," Luther replies, smiling broadly as he fidgets with the black permanent marker in his hand. "You workin' tonight?" He gets up from his seat to give me a brief hug.

"If they need me. You been working out?" I ask, squeezing his bicep that's the size of my thigh.

"Always," Luther says, showing me his muscles with a broad, gold-toothed grin.

"Nice," I admire. "Don't be giving the girlies that gun show, or you'll never get rid of them."

"You know that you're the only one I want. Just a few more months till you're legal, right?" he says with a wink.

Pointing to my shirt, I frown. "No way, Luther. I've seen how you operate."

"That's harsh, Bug. You're calling me a boy and a liar?"

Smiling and backing down the hallway, I ask, "Where's Jimmy?"

"In the kitchen, probably. Come and talk to me if things aren't too busy," he says, watching me head down the hall.

Approaching the bar, I can see that the bartenders are getting slammed already. The place is at near capacity, and it's not even ten o'clock yet. Jimmy's talking to the wait staff and begins rapidly nodding his head as he sees me approach. Over the noise of the crowd, he yells, *"Go to the bar—they need you. Fumblin' Frank didn't show again."*

I nod, turn toward the bar, and see the look of relief on Tina's face when she sees me. *"We need ice—and a case of Heineken . . . it's Corporate Asshole Night!"* Tina yells, and I nod again. I rush to the kitchen, filling two large buckets with ice. I haul them through the crowd to the bar, dumping them in the ice bins. Taking the steep stairs leading to the basement behind the bar, I run down to the refrigerators. Locating a case of Heineken, I take off my coat and backpack, stowing them. I climb the stairs to the bar and begin stocking the small refrigerators. The night progresses quickly, and I'm sweating from running up and down the stairs, keeping the bar stocked. I watch Tina and Sean work, making sure that whatever they need is refilled and available to them before they have to ask for it to be done.

Sipping a glass of water, I glance at the world beyond the bar. It's a crush of people, and I'm glad that I mostly get to stay back here and don't have to venture out there except when we need ice. Drunken people make me nervous. I dislike their predictable unpredictability— the emotions that are so intense and seem to turn on a dime. I've been subject to too many drunken people in my life. Once I get out of my situation, I plan on staying away from bars and nightclubs . . . and drunken people.

"Hey, Heidi . . . HEIDI." I hear a male voice slurring behind me. A handsome man dressed in a dark suit is hailing me. His tie has been loosened rakishly at the neck, and his short, brown hair is falling artfully over his brow. He's leaning over the bar between us. Seeing that he has my attention, he shouts, *"I don't lie, Heidi. Hey, where are you from? Sweden or some shit? Hey, come over here."* He crooks his finger at me, trying to get me to approach the bar.

I shake my head and continue sipping my water.

"Heidi, I like your braids. C'mon—I won't bite. I don't lie! I swear I'm telling the truth when I say that you have the sweetest ass I've ever seen," he calls with the look of drunken earnestness.

Glancing down the bar, Tina approaches the man calling to me. *"You need something?"* she yells above the din, throwing down a napkin in front of him.

"I need her." He points to me, leering.

Before Tina can answer him, an enormous man behind the drunk reaches down and pulls him off his feet by his necktie. "Apologize to her," I hear him say, just above the noise of the crowd. The look on the corporate man's face would've been comical if I wasn't so absorbed by the sheer size of the man holding him. He's at least a half-foot taller than the man he's holding. In this light, his hair looks blond—platinum, the same as mine. It's long, to his shoulders, pulled back from his face and tucked into his black leather jacket.

"I'm sorry!" the drunken man shouts hastily. I give him a mute nod, accepting his apology. The giant blond man in front of me lets go of the drunk's tie, dropping him to the floor. The intoxicated man fumbles backward away from the bar, disappearing into the crowd behind him.

"Thank you," I sigh in relief to the tall stranger, beginning to step forward to speak to him. Then I see his neck. Large, inky tribal tattoos shoot up one side of it. I stop and my eyes widen. Two other blond men, each around the same size as the one in front of me step forward to flank him, their eyes focused on me.

As I step back, Tina gets closer, dropping a new napkin in front of each of them, intending to take their orders. Backing up farther, I put my hand on the wooden doorframe leading to the basement. Feeling like I just hit the tripwire of a trap, I place my foot on the top step leading to the basement and see what I don't want to see. The tall, blond man tenses and begins to spring over the bar.

Pounding down the stairs, I dash toward another set of stairs that leads up to the cargo doors. My braid is seized from behind, and my head snaps back brutally, knocking me off my feet. A meaty arm goes around my waist, pulling me back into a treelike chest.

"Kricket, you can't outrun me," he whispers in my ear.

"Who's Kricket?" I ask, clenching my teeth against the pain from the whiplash he just gave me. "Let go of me, freak!"

"You're Kricket," he says lightly, turning me around to face him. "Daughter of Arissa Valke of Alameeda clan."

Holding my neck and staring into his blue eyes, I retort, "I'm Jane Klume . . . of the White Sox clan, so let go of me before I scream, you piece of sh—" He shakes me roughly.

"You're a little rebel and you're definitely Etharian—I'll prove it," he says sternly, pulling out a knife from a shoulder holster. Holding my braid in his hand, he slashes the sharp edge over my hair, severing it. Immediately, the hair in his hand turns black and becomes dust while the stub of hair that's still attached to my head begins to lengthen and grow until it's the exact same length it was before. I'm not shocked. It has been doing that since before I can remember. He smiles. "Greetings, Kricket."

"Who are you?" I ask, watching the stairs as the other two men tread cautiously down toward us.

"My name is Kyon, and this is Forester and Lecto. We're your friends," he replies, attempting a smile that looks more like a shark showing its teeth. Visions of every social worker I've ever been assigned to bounce rapidly through my head. They are all very different, but they all have one common thread. They always claim to be my friend right before they leave me in the deepest pit of hell.

"What do you want?" I ask, trying to buy time so I can figure out how to get out of this.

"We want to return you to your family." He watches my reaction.

Feeling a deep sense of déjà vu, I try to think of what to do next. "What family? What are you talking about?"

"The family from which you were stolen. You're a very important member of our clan." The shark smile comes back to his face.

"Is that right?" I ask sarcastically, not believing a word he's saying. "What am I, royalty?"

"No, you're much higher than that. You're the daughter of a priestess, which makes you a priestess, too," he replies, his eyes assessing me.

I laugh, but not with humor. "Okay . . . glad we cleared that up. This is a joke, right? Did you and your buddy Trey get together, pick me out—decide to play with my head or something? It's not funny, freak!" I try again to pull away from him.

Kyon's eyes shrink to slits. "You've spoken with Trey Allairis of Rafe clan?" he asks angrily.

"The conversation was really one-sided, kind of like this one," I reply, flinching as his grip becomes even tighter before he shakes me hard again.

"What did he tell you?" Kyon demands.

"I don't know—something about taking me back to my family so that I can pay for my crimes," I retort. "It didn't appeal, so I had to say no."

He flashes me a lightning-fast smile that dies just as quickly. "He has no idea what you're worth." Somehow I know he's being truthful, or at least he believes what he's saying is true. "It's a pity . . . your eyes—they're Rafe, but you have your mother's face—her hair. You look Alameeda, too." A shiver escapes me.

"You knew my mother?" I ask, seeing the cold calculation in his eyes. I've always known that I'm different. My first haircut made that shockingly clear and is the very reason one foster family returned me to DSS the next day. The caseworker didn't take my foster mother seriously, and I never let anyone cut my hair again after that. I'd scream and cry and make a huge fuss until they'd give up.

"Your ignorance makes you less appealing. You should try not to speak," he says, ignoring my question about my mother with an arrogant twist of his lip.

I ignore his suggestion. "So, what are you going to do now?" I can't see any way out of this because not only does Kyon have a death grip on my arm, but his friends, Forester and Lecto, are flanking us.

"Now I—" Kyon doesn't get a chance to finish because the sound of a shotgun racking cuts him off.

Chapter 3

Strangers

Bug, you okay?" With a deep voice Luther calls from the stairs behind, pointing the shotgun directly at Kyon. He inches down the basement stairs toward us, watching my eyes. Shaking my head, my eyes drift to Kyon, trying to read what my defiance will cost me. Kyon's murderous scowl speaks volumes.

"We called the police," Jimmy yells from behind Luther on the stairs. He's near Scott, the beefy head bouncer.

"That is a shotgun, is it not?" Kyon directs his question to Luther.

"You're damn right it's a shotgun, and it's liable to tear a hole clear through you if you don't let go of Kricket," he replies, clenching his teeth.

Kyon smiles down on me, tightening his fingers on my upper arm. "Kricket," he grins. I close my eyes briefly, knowing my lie has been exposed. "It's such a powerful name," he breathes. Not taking his eyes from me, he says to Luther, "You fire that weapon, and you will hit Kricket as well." Kyon turns, hauling me again toward the cargo door.

"Shit!" Luther says behind us. "Scott, hand me your piece." An instant later, the sound of a slide being engaged echoes behind us. "That's the sound of a Glock 22PT pistol, black, 40 S&W, 15 rounds, polymer full-size frame with a 4.49-inch barrel and night sight. Personally, I would've gone with something that has more bling, but Scott here has a hard-on for law enforcement."

"Am I supposed to be frightened?" Kyon asks, turning back to Luther and grinning.

"That's the general idea," Luther says, matching his grin, except his is capped with gold teeth. "Now, let her go before I see how many rounds it takes to drop you."

Holding my breath, I wait to see what Kyon will do next. Deliberating for a moment, Kyon lets go of my upper arm abruptly. Feeling his gaze on me, I want to hide from him, as he's memorizing everything about me. Slowly, I take a step back from him, watching his blue eyes follow me.

"Don't go far, Kricket," Kyon says softly, smiling his shark smile at me again. I grimace, seeing the look of confidence in his body language. A second later, Kyon strides menacingly toward Luther.

Luther tightens his grip on the gun. "Blondie, you're about to get capped. Stay where you are!" Luther stresses the last few words, but Kyon continues to cut the distance between them. Not thinking at all, instinct takes over when the loud report from the gun sends a burst of adrenaline through me. Running out the cargo doors, I look over my shoulder just in time to see Kyon stagger back from the bullet entering his shoulder. Pausing, my heart lurches painfully in my chest as Kyon reaches Luther, picking Luther up off his feet and throwing him back into Jimmy on the stairs.

Seeing Forester and Lecto look in my direction, I don't waste any more time, but run full out into the alleyway between the buildings. Running down the dark, snowy street, the sounds around me muffle. All I can hear is my heavy breathing. Entering the busy sidewalk, I cut through the crowd of people waiting to get into the club. I run like a butterfly, dodging between parked cars and traffic to get to the other side of the street. Glancing over my shoulder, Forester emerges from the alley, spotting me.

I whimper before darting down the street and turning onto Clark, where I come to the corner. Ducking into a head shop, I look wildly around for a place to hide among the racks of T-shirts and shelves of old vinyl records. The clerk doesn't even look up from his comic book as he sits on the stool behind the counter.

"There's a back door—straight through, behind the black curtain," he says in a bored, monotone voice.

"Thanks," I breathe. I find the back door leading to a parking lot. Sprinting to the next street, I go north toward Wrigleyville. Running flat out for about a mile, I have to revert to a fast walk as I pinch my side, trying to relieve the stitch in it while looking over my shoulder. Seeing nothing out of the ordinary behind me, I enter a diner that has a pay phone. Pulling change and a wad of singles from my pocket, tips from my job tonight, I insert the change into the pay phone and dial Enrique's cell.

"Yeah?" Enrique answers.

"Enrique? It's Kricket. Listen, I need your help. I'm at Leo's Diner in Wrigleyville. Can you meet me?" I ask, hearing the desperation in my own voice.

"Yeah . . . okay. What's the 411, Kricket? You sound like you're trippin'," he replies.

"Just . . . can you hurry, Enrique? Please?" I plead, trying to remain calm.

"Yeah, of course. This new club is filled with Abigails any-way . . . lame. Can I bring Michael?" he asks.

"Yeah, just hurry," I repeat, peering through the glass doors of the diner.

"Okay. I'm on the way," he says. Hanging up the receiver, I walk into the diner. Finding a place near the back, away from the doors, I sink onto the bench seat, picking up the menu and hiding my face behind it. When the waitress comes over, I order a coffee.

Glancing at my watch every few seconds, relief pours through me when Enrique and Michael push through the doors. When Enrique sees me, he grasps Michael's hand as he leads him to my booth.

"Two coffees," Enrique says. He holds up two fingers to the waitress before turning to me, "Girrrl, 'sup with you?" Enrique asks, his eyebrow rising in question. "You got a braid on one side and your hair's just hangin' loose on the other side. I gotta say that I'm not lovin' this look—it's very Cher meets high school cheerleader." He's dressed for the club; his dark eyeliner makes his brown eyes appear almost black.

"And never the twain should meet, in my opinion," Michael adds, sitting next to Enrique on the opposite side of the booth. He shrugs out of his Burberry coat, keeping his meticulously wrapped scarf in place. "Where's your coat? It's arctic out there. All we need are penguins and Nanook of the North."

"I know, right?" Enrique agrees, not letting me answer. "I should get one of those Russian fur hats, but faux fur, not real fur 'cuz did you see what they do to those poor animals?"

"Enrique, you're wearing leather boots. That's cow." Michael points this out with an eye roll.

"But they're Gucci!"

Pulling the braid out from my hair, I run my fingers through it to unbraid it. "Your sense of moral outrage is well placed, Enrique, but I'm about to join your furry little friends if you don't help me," I cut in, causing them both to look at me in question.

"What?" Enrique asks, his eyes going wide.

"Three guys tried to jump me on the train on my way home from work this morning, before I ran from them. Now, three different guys tried to take me at the club tonight," I explain in a stream of words. "I think Luther might have shot one of them before I bailed." Silence greets my explanation as Michael looks at Enrique. "I need a place to crash for a few days. I need to figure out what I'm going to do."

"Luther shot someone?" Enrique asks, his jaw dropping open.

"Yeah . . . this big one, Kyon. He's like a giant, and he was trying to make me leave with him," I say breathlessly, feeling a burst of adrenaline at the memory.

"What happened? What did they want? Were they DSS?"

"They're definitely not social serve-thy-selves and I don't know what they want exactly—it's something to do with my family—the ones on the train were—they were like really beautiful—tall, like dark-haired athletes—with these warrior, tribal tats on their necks and eyes the exact shade as mine," I explain, wrapping my hands around my coffee cup and seeing the ripples on the surface of it from my trembling.

"Your family? But I thought . . ." Enrique's question fades.

"They knew my parents' names and everything, but they could've gotten that out of my file at DSS," I continue. "The other ones at the club were blond, blue-eyed, but otherwise they could've been from the same mold as the guys on the train . . . except . . ." I trail off.

"Except what?" Michael asks.

"Except the ones on the train didn't try to lie to me. They said they were going to take me to my family where I could 'pay for my crimes,'" I tell them.

"Pay for your crimes?" Enrique's voice gets higher with agitation. "What's that supposed to mean?"

"I don't know, but they were being truthful," I state, feeling my mouth go dry, so I take a sip of my coffee.

"How do you know they were being truthful?" Michael asks, looking from me to Enrique.

"Ah, you gotta show him, Kricket. I can't explain it 'cuz he won't believe me," Enrique says to me before he turns to Michael. "She has like a radar for bullshit. Here—tell her some things about you, and she'll tell you if you're telling the truth or if you're lying."

"Serious?" Michael asks as his eyebrows go up.

"As camel toe," Enrique replies.

"Um . . . okay . . . hmm . . . I'm a Young Republican." He watches my face.

"True," I reply, hearing Enrique choke on his coffee.

"You're what!" Enrique scowls at Michael, wiping his mouth with his napkin. "Oh my Gawd, why?"

"I support the NRA," Michael continues, ignoring Enrique's derisive tone.

"True," I reply. Enrique's eyes widen even further.

"I'm out," Michael says, looking in my eyes.

"Lie."

"I have a sister named Beth," he says.

"Lie," I reply.

"I'm for real about Enrique," Michael says softly, looking down.

"True," I reply, watching Enrique's frown soften.

"How do you do that?" Michael asks me, sounding awed.

I shrug. "I could always do it, but it's not absolute. I can't tell you *why* you're lying. I also have trouble discerning a lie from someone who is drunk because the signals fluctuate; it messes me up. And I only know *if* you're lying, not whether what you're saying is really the truth. You can *believe* something to be true, but you could be wrong . . . you see what I'm saying?"

"Yes, it's still a little subjective," he replies, and I nod my head in agreement. "So the men on the train were telling the truth?"

"Yes, Trey was one of the ones on the train, but the one in the bar, Kyon, lied," I say, paling.

"What did he say?" Enrique asks, his brows pushing down.

"He was truthful when he said they wanted to take me to my family, but he lied when he said they were my friends," I explain, feeling ill.

"So, no glad tidings from home?" Michael asks. I shake my head slowly. "When did your parents die?"

"When I was young—five . . . I remember them a little, but it was just us, no one else." My mother's beautiful platinum hair flitters through my memory. "I can't recall any other family. I don't know what these men are talking about." I drop my chin, not looking at them, because I've always hidden my odd characteristics from others. I've never told Enrique about how my hair regrows instantly because there's been no good explanation for it.

Enrique's expression becomes one of resolve. "Kricket, you're coming home with me, and we'll figure out what to do. Do they know where you live?"

"Yeah, Kyon—that's the one at Lumin—he must've known, because I live right above there," I reply in a raspy voice. "Luther shot him." My throat begins to close as the shock of what happened is now wearing off. "The police are probably looking for me. I left my backpack there. They'll find everything I've worked so hard to hide." I think of the keys to my apartment. Someone from the bar will tell them where I've been living, believing that they're helping me.

Tears that I can't hold back fill my eyes. Reaching across the table, Enrique takes my hand. "Maybe we should go to the police station. Maybe you'll be safer with them."

Pulling my hand back from his grasp, I wipe my eyes with the back of my fists, feeling embarrassed by my tears. "It depends on where they put me. Since I'm a runaway, I'll probably be put into corrections. If that happens, I probably won't last until my birthday," I say honestly.

"Why not?" Michael frowns.

" 'Cuz I look like Barbie." I reply, knowing they can connect the dots.

"Bad girls don't like Barbie?" Michael asks, both his eyebrows rising.

"No. Bad girls want to rip Barbie's head off and flush it down the toilet," I state emphatically with a half grimace. "I might have a chance in a fight if it's one on one, but that rarely happens. Usually, it's a pack, and they have someone distract the guards. You can see it coming and have no way to stop it."

"What do you mean?" Enrique's mouth is open in shock. I lift up my shirt, exposing my abdomen and show them the scar on my side. Enrique gasps, putting both his hands to his mouth.

"Shank," I say, running my fingers over the ugly crescent scar, "made from a plastic comb that was sharpened to a knife's edge. They cornered me in the rec room after the social worker left with their friend who pretended to be sick. I can't go back. I really need your help," I plead quietly.

"You got it, sister," Enrique assures me, looking from me to Michael with a "holy crap" expression on his face. "Listen, I'll pay for the coffee while Michael goes and hails a cab. You just sit tight here."

Tears brighten my eyes at his words. Unable to answer him, I nod my head. Reaching across the table, he grasps my hand and squeezes it before letting it go. Michael and Enrique rise from the booth, moving toward the cashier at the front of the diner.

Following Enrique with my eyes, I watch him walk casually by a booth at the front of the restaurant that contains two men. Feeling the hair on the back of my neck begin to rise, I recognize the violet gaze from the man on the train—Jax. Feeling like I'm moving in slow motion, I get up from my seat, backing away from the front of the restaurant.

Jax and the other one from the train immediately follow me. I glance at Enrique, who smiles reassuringly from the cashier's register, but his smile falters as he sees the fear on my pale face. Turning, I almost knock over the waitress as I run for the back door. Pushing the glass door aside, I run into someone directly in front of me, because I was looking over my shoulder. Arms wrap around me, pinning my own arms to my sides as my feet leave the ground.

"Don't struggle, Kricket," Trey's deep voice says in my ear, causing a shiver of fear to fly through me.

"Let go!" I say breathlessly, struggling against Trey's massive chest. "Everything has to be difficult where you're concerned. So be it." Trey sighs with regret as he shifts me in his arms. Squeezing me tight with one arm, he brings the other hand up to my face, covering my mouth and nose with a cloth that reeks like ammonia. My eyes water as my fingernails dig into his wrist, trying to make his hand move so I can breathe. "Don't fight—we won't hurt you," he says softly, but I continue to struggle. My vision blurs as spots dance in my eyes, and then everything goes dark.

Chapter 4

Waking Up

The unfamiliar scent of man and leather, combined with the tinny taste in my mouth, makes me realize that I probably shouldn't be wherever I am. Not opening my eyes, I listen to the sounds around me while the soft leather beneath my cheek sways in a gentle motion.

"What's the first thing you'll do when you get back, Wayra?" A male voice asks from ahead of me.

"You mean after we give our report?" Wayra asks.

"Yes," The male voice responds.

"I'm heading straight to Sequelle's and eating an entire venish."

"No one can eat an entire venish."

"Is that a challenge, Jax?" The swaying beneath my cheek gets more pronounced.

A stern voice next to me says, "Watch the road, Wayra." Peeking through my eyelashes, long legs in tailored pants stretch out next to me in the backseat of the limousine. I recognize his voice. *It's Trey's,* I think, feeling the blood leave my face.

"I'll take that wager. No Etharian can eat an entire venish," Jax replies. "I'll lay thirty-two fardrooms on it. Are you going to get in on this, Trey? Wayra's giving away his money."

"No." Trey sounds bored.

"C'mon. You have more money than the Regent. That's probably why you're here now. He probably despises royalty with wealth."

"I've seen Wayra eat an entire venish before, and Manus didn't send me to do this mission. I volunteered," Trey replies evenly.

"You volunteered for this? Are you cracked?" Jax asks.

"I'm getting there," Trey says with a sigh.

"Why would you volunteer to leave Rafe? Was Charisma pressuring you? You know, all those girls only want one thing: a commitment ceremony," Wayra says the last part like they're dirty words.

"No, they all want a title," Jax counters.

"I'm not the one to inherit. Victus will. I'm minor royalty. I get invited to the swanks, but no one seeks my favor," Trey begins to explain.

"No one but the ladies seek your favor, you mean," Wayra cuts in. "I've been with him to a few of his obligatory parties. His military status goes over well with the blushers."

"Hey, you have to take me to a swank when we get back. I could use a few blushers hanging on to my every word," Jax says excitedly.

"Just make sure that's all they hang on to, Jax," Trey responds. "Anything else will get you a commitment ceremony in those circles."

"I'm just a Jarhead. They'd probably string me up before they allowed a commitment ceremony to take place," Jax replies, not sounding too concerned about it.

"What's a Jarhead?" Wayra asks.

"Oh, that's what the humans call Cavars. It's their military soldier—a Marine."

"Where did you learn that?"

"Their Internet," Jax says. "You didn't think I was working the entire time we were here, did you?"

"If you had been, maybe we'd have bagged her months ago," Wayra replies, sounding irritated. "I could've been eating venish by now."

There is silence for a few moments until Jax says, "What do you think they'll do to her?" My heartbeat increases, knowing that he's talking about me.

"Not this conversation again, Jax," Wayra growls. "They're gonna do whatever they do. It's not our concern."

"Yeah, I know, but . . ."

"But what?" Trey asks quietly.

"But she's just so . . . small and alone. You read her human files; they read like some grim tragedy. Maybe she's already paid for her desertion," Jax says with a note of concern.

"Maybe you should represent her, Jax," Wayra teases him, making my heart twist a little. "You can tell Skye she's been punished enough—that because of her, we weren't all thrown into a global incident."

"Maybe I will," Jax says. "Maybe I can get her a proper representative. I can hire a wigg for her."

"Where are you going to get the money for a wigg?" Wayra laughs.

"I'll start by taking yours, chester," Jax counters.

"Don't call me a chester. I've never forced myself on a woman in my life . . . although, I have been with a couple of westers," he replies, sounding like he's grinning.

"When have you been with a wester? What woman would try to force herself on you? I've seen more attractive faces on sloats," Jax laughs, and Trey joins him.

"I get plenty of blushers," Wayra replies, not sounding as irritated as I would have thought. Silence fills the car for a few moments.

"How many circas of vista did you give her, Trey?" Jax asks, sounding concerned again.

"Two." Trey answers. "Why?"

"Because, she should be awake by now. She's so little . . . maybe two was too many," Jax says slowly.

Feeling a gentle hand rest on my neck, I try to remain calm, but my heart is racing. "Her pulse is rapid," Trey says. "Can you hear me, Kricket?"

I remain silent.

"Kricket?" Jax asks a little louder than necessary.

"She's awake," Trey says derisively, and a moment later a hand comes down hard on my butt, making my eyes jerk open as a squeak escapes from me.

"Don't touch me, chester," I hiss, turning to Trey and narrowing my eyes at him. His violet eyes narrow back at me. Wiping the back of my hand over the corner of my mouth where drool has collected, I straighten in my seat. Glaring at Jax, who's in the front next to Wayra, I test the handle of the car door, but it won't open. I push the switch of the automatic window, but it won't open either. My head crashes against the window as dizziness overwhelms me.

"Whoa! Easy now!" Jax says from the front, looking like he's about to crawl over the seat to get to me, but there's little chance of him fitting through the narrow space. Jax is almost as big as Trey, at least six feet five and all brawn.

Leaning back against my seat, I hold up my hand to stop him from coming to me. "I'm fine," I lie, closing my eyes for a second and trying to regain my equilibrium.

"You don't look fine. You look like you're about to boot," Jax replies. "Stop the car, Wayra. I want to get out and check on her."

"She looks fine," Wayra says, peering at me through the rearview mirror. I hold up my middle finger to him, and he just stares at me like he doesn't know what it means.

"Yeah, but it's my job to make sure that she is fine. I'm the medic," Jax says adamantly.

"Ah, c'mon and admit it. You wouldn't be half as concerned if *she* had a face like a sloat," Wayra counters with a smirk.

"Wayra, if she turns up dead, they're not going to send you to face Skye—that'll be me because I'm the medic. I'm trained to patch up combat wounds. This should be simple," he grumbles. "I'm responsible for her health—let me do my job."

"Pull over, Wayra," Trey orders. The car immediately slows, pulling to the side of the road. The door locks click open. Opening my door on the passenger side, Jax crouches down by my side as cold air seeps in around him. I can't tell what time it is because it's gray and overcast outside, but it's definitely daylight. I must've been out for a while.

Opening a case, Jax withdraws a set of glasses that look like something someone would wear after eye surgery—grandma goggles. Trying to put them on me, I fight off his attempts, pushing the glasses away.

"These don't hurt . . . see?" he demonstrates, putting the glasses on and looking like a complete tool. "They just check your vitals—synapse firing rate, dendrite chemical composition, reuptake rates—just standard stuff," he explains, grinning and taking off the glasses.

"All that and they're *so* fashionable," I reply sarcastically, continuing to pull back as he attempts to put them on me. "Let me just break it down for you, Jax. My head feels like one of you smashed it with a rock. I need some water and maybe an aspirin, and I'll be super. Oh, and if you could just let me off at the next town, that'd be even better."

"Water I can do. Aspirin is . . . what's aspirin?" A small smile touches his lips as his eyes scan mine.

Seeing that he's being truthful, that he really doesn't know what aspirin is, my breathing increases, choking me. "I . . . can't," I manage to say, as I begin hyperventilating. Looking around wildly, I feel like the walls of the car are caving in on me.

Trey's warm hand goes to the back of my neck, making me bend forward, while he murmurs, "Breathe slowly . . . calm . . . even . . ."

He strokes my back gently, his voice soft and silky. Jax jumps in the car, having to duck his big body as he goes to the bar on the side.

Slowing down my breathing, I accept a glass of water from Jax. Sitting up and sipping from the heavy barware, my hand comes up to touch a tender spot that is throbbing behind my ear.

"Careful." Jax warns me as he touches my hand and directs my fingers away from the small bandage they felt. "Your incision is still healing."

"My what?" I feel like I might be sick.

"I inserted a translator implant into your temporal lobe," he says, smiling at me until he sees my ashen expression. "It's okay," he explains quickly, holding up both of his hands. "It's just a translator. You'll be able to understand a host of languages now without any difficulty. Some words may still be foreign, but it will work well for the most part. Now I don't have to speak English for you to understand me." He smiles, like he did me a favor by shoving something into my brain.

"Take it out," I whisper, feeling my hands shake as I raise my fingers to the bandage again.

He glances at Trey, who shakes his head. Jax looks back at me. "I can't."

"You can't, or you won't?" I ask in growing panic.

"He won't." Trey answers for Jax.

Jax frowns. "You need it, Kricket. Everyone has one. See?" He turns his head and folds his earlobe away so that I can see a tiny scar behind his ear. "All it does is translate. That's all. I promise."

"Who told you that you could do that to me?" I ask as anger replaces distress.

"I did," Trey says beside me. Lifting my eyes to Trey's and seeing how exquisitely the shade of violet fits with the darkness of his brows and sun-kissed skin, I manage to whisper, "Thank you for telling me the truth."

His eyes soften a little at the corners right before I hit him in the side of his head with my heavy water glass. As water and glass shatter outward, I hurl myself through the open door of the car, striking the ground and running across an open field covered with a thick blanket of snow. Stumbling a couple of times, I manage to stay on my feet by putting my hands into the drifts.

Trying to increase the length of my strides, I nearly fall on my face when my feet are kicked out from under me. Trey's arm snakes around my waist, catching me up and hoisting me over his shoulder. He jogs back to the limo, shoving me inside and shutting the door behind us. He pushes me onto the seat beside him. The doors lock immediately as Trey barks out the word: "Drive!"

Feeling the car pull away again and breathing in shallow gasps, I swallow hard, looking at Trey in the seat next to mine. The side of his face is bleeding from a cut near the hairline, and his brow is already beginning to turn an ugly shade of purple. A little of his blood has dripped onto his dress shirt, marring the crisp, white fabric. Jax extends a cloth to Trey, who presses it to the side of his face while he watches me coolly.

"Kricket," Trey says, speaking my name like a warning, and I flinch, "every choice you make will affect you. So, think hard before you make your next move. There will be consequences to your actions."

"All actions come with consequences," I murmur, attempting to mask my fear.

"Painful consequences." He restates his meaning.

"I'll shoot for the other kind," I reply, raising my chin a notch and trying to look aloof.

"You won't escape," Trey says sullenly, leaning forward in his seat. Opening the small refrigerator and pulling out an ice tray, he dumps a few cubes in the cloth, pressing the cold compress to his face.

"Fortune favors the brave," I reply, raising an eyebrow. Leaning forward, I take one of the remaining cubes of ice from the tray. I touch it to my tongue and watch him watch me.

"That sounds like an argument for doing whatever you want," Trey growls.

"It's cause and effect and . . . I'm just sayin'," I let the melting ice cool my tight throat as I try not to pant from the exertion of my last failed attempt.

"You're just saying, what?" Trey scowls at me, not letting it go.

"I'm just saying that when there is little left to lose, the consequences of one's actions don't carry the same weight—painful or otherwise."

"She has you there, Trey," Jax replies, grinning at me.

A smirk crosses my lips. "And maybe you should worry more about the consequences of your actions, *chester*," I add, nodding toward the television screen mounted near the front of the limo. An awful, grainy photo, taken of me when I was around fourteen, flashes up on the small screen as a scrolling marquee runs beneath my photo. "That's an Amber Alert, making you officially *wanted* perverts."

Trey doesn't seem to flinch, watching the screen as my hideous, unsmiling face stares back at us. "That doesn't even look like you," Jax says, and my heart sinks a little. "It looks like a mug shot."

"It's me," I mumble, remembering being processed back into the system after another failed foster home. Quickly, I stuff that memory back down, looking out the window as snow-covered cornfields slide past.

"Ho! Did you see that?" Jax bursts out, scrambling in his seat for the remote to turn the volume up on the television. "That was—"

"Kyon!" Trey finishes for him, sitting forward in his seat, riveted to the screen.

"What?" Wayra calls from the front, the car swaying a little.

"It *is* that knob knocker, Kyon!" Jax swears under his breath, as the newsreel replays me approaching the bar in Lumin before I began backing up and running. Then it shows Kyon leaping over the bar to follow me. The footage from the camera behind the bar must've been turned over to the police and news agencies. The image freezes on Kyon's face as the anchorman implores his viewers to report any information to the FBI or the Chicago Police Department.

"That means Kyon got away, doesn't it?" I ask Jax, not taking my eyes off Kyon's shadowy image.

Both Jax and Trey turn and stare at me. "What happened?" Trey demands, his ice lying forgotten on the seat next to him. "Did he try to hurt you?" He quickly scans me for anything out of the ordinary. His concern throws me for a second.

My eyebrows pull together. "No, he was super nice—we're besties now. In fact, Forester and Lecto are my new BFFs, too," I reply, watching Trey's face turn from concern to a scowl.

"They're no friends of yours. You're Rafe and they're—" Trey grinds his teeth, looking very muscley all of a sudden.

"Knob knockers?" I ask, trying to fill in the blank he left with what I had heard earlier.

"Alameeda," Trey hisses. Turning to Jax, he says, "Please refrain from teaching Kricket things she shouldn't be learning."

Jax frowns. "She should know a knob knocker when she sees one—it's a life skill."

"What exactly is a knob knocker?" I ask Jax, seeing that it's really irritating Trey. "Shouldn't your translator tell me what it is?"

"Kyon is a knob knocker," Jax replies, a grin of approval on his lips. "And I'll upgrade you with slang later."

"No you won't," Trey says abruptly. "Kricket doesn't need to know that."

I scowl at Trey before turning to Jax. "I see. So a *knob knocker*," I emphasize the words to irritate Trey, "is a liar who accosts women for his own gain?" I ask. Jax's grin grows broader as he nods his head.

"What did Kyon say to you? What did he want?" Trey grasps me by my upper arm so that I'll look at him.

I clamp my lips and Trey's frown deepens. "You refuse to answer me?" he asks, his voice quiet—deadly. Goose bumps rise on my arms. I know that I've just crossed some invisible line with him; I know it because I've crossed them many times in the past and usually end up paying heavily for it. Stiffening, I straighten in my seat, bracing myself for the consequences that'll probably be very painful.

"How far are we?" Trey barks out the question as he drops his hands from me.

"Fifteen—twenty fleats maximum, sir," Wayra answers in the clipped tone of a military soldier.

"Any sign that we could've been followed?" Trey shoots back.

"No sign, sir."

"I could've taken care of Kyon here," Trey murmurs to himself, his hands balling into fists.

"I take it you two aren't friends," I surmise. Trey's unfocused pupils contract as I interrupt his thoughts. When his eyes meet mine, it's clear by his intense expression that he'd been plotting something deadly.

Jax laughs mirthlessly, "That's an understatement—"

"No one answers her questions," Trey orders, his stare pinning me to my seat. "Our information is more valuable to her than hers is to us."

"Ooooh, I guess I'm going to have to put on my anthropologist's hat for this one, then."

Trey ignores me, sitting back in his seat and watching the news on the television as it replays my flight from Kyon. The newscaster breaks in, announcing that there is new information to this story. An interview featuring Enrique with a microphone shoved near his mouth begins rolling. He's describing the scene at the diner last night.

"It's Enrique!" Jax grins, causing my head to snap in his direction. "Wayra, that reminds me—you still owe me 12 fardrooms for Enrique. He led us right to her."

"I didn't say he wouldn't. I just didn't think it'd be so fast," Wayra counters over his shoulder.

"That wasn't quick. If one more male asked me to dance last night, someone was getting hurt," Jax mumbles.

"You must've looked at them too long," I state absently, hearing Jax's comment.

Both his eyebrows rise. "What?" he asks.

"Usually, a man will only ask you to dance when you've made the appropriate amount of eye contact," I answer. "If you make eye contact for three seconds or longer with a man, you've basically invited him over."

Trey and Jax both stare at me like I've unlocked a mystery. "But then again," I continue, eyeing them both, "I bet they'd ask you to dance even if you only looked at them for a couple of seconds."

"Why?" Jax asks in confusion.

"Er . . . you're all über-man types," I falter. I'm not going to tell them that they're eye candy.

A composite sketch of Jax flashes up on the screen with the name "Trey" written beneath it. Jax's mouth drops because it looks almost exactly like him. "He only saw me for something like five or six seconds," Jax says.

"And yet he managed to capture your smoldering eyes," I reply grimly, trying to quell the tears forming in my eyes for what Enrique is doing to help me.

"You told Enrique about us?" Jax asks, and I shut up again, refusing to answer his question. Seeing the fear in my eyes, Jax says, "We're not going to hurt him. We were just following him to find you. I promise, he can't come where we're going."

"He'll know that we have you now. He'll follow us," Trey says with satisfaction, looking at the television.

"Enrique?" I ask.

"No, the knob knocker," Jax says absently. "Do we wait for him?"

"No, we finish our mission," Trey says with a hint of reluctance in his tone. "If he manages to catch up, though, then it's really not our fault that we had to take him out, is it?" Trey smiles at Jax.

"No, we'd just be protecting our prisoner," Jax grins back.

"We're here," Wayra announces, slowing the car in an empty parking lot in what looks like the middle of absolutely nowhere.

Chapter 5

The Pool

Trey's eyes lock with mine. There is anticipation in them and . . . happiness. I glance at the window, seeing that we've pulled up to some kind of defunct tourist attraction—a "mystery spot," as the falling down billboard indicates. It's also closed for the season.

Parking the car, Wayra unlocks the doors. Trey and Jax exit the limo, along with Wayra. I can hear them pulling things out of the trunk. Not moving from my seat, I wait, figuring that they want me to get out because they left all the doors open.

The smell of gasoline assails me as I watch Wayra through the window take a gas can and spill the liquid over the front seat.

"Kricket," Trey says in a gentle voice, bending and peering at me from outside the car. "We're going to burn the car. You might want to get out before we do that."

Fear and confusion prey on me. I drop my chin, shaking my head.

"You want to stay in the car?" he asks, frowning.

I shake my head no again, looking at him.

"Listen, Kricket, I just want to take you home and finish my mission. If you comply with me, I promise that I won't hurt you," Trey says truthfully, extending his hand to me.

"Do I have a choice?" I ask, looking at his hand warily.

"No," he replies. I deliberate for a few moments, but he's right. There's really no choice. The gasoline is making it almost impossible to breathe. Reluctantly, I ignore his hand and slide to the opposite side, getting out of the car and walking toward where Jax is standing by the hood.

Stuffing my hands under my armpits and feeling the frigid wind on my exposed arms, I hunch my shoulders against the cold. Trey carries a black duffle bag with him to my side. Standing close to me, his body heat radiates out, making me inch closer to him. He's really tall; my head only reaches to his shoulder. He didn't bring his coat with him. His dark gray, woolen dress pants and tailored, white button-down shirt would make him look corporate if the thick, black tattoos on the left side of his neck didn't make him look like some kind of ancient gladiator.

"Why are we here?" I ask Trey, while Wayra lights a match, tossing it into the cab of the car. Flames burst to life as Trey grips my upper arm, ushering me up a wooden plank walkway, leading to another wooden causeway.

"Was that a question?" he asks, raising his brow. "That's funny because I thought we agreed that neither of us was answering questions." I grit my teeth while Trey pulls me along next to him through the deepening snowdrifts.

Approaching a gated wooden fence, secured by a padlock, Wayra jogs ahead. Pulling wire cutters from his duffel bag, Wayra easily removes the lock, pushing open the gate leading to a limestone cave. The sign outside the cave says that while surveying this spot years ago, workmen discovered that their equipment could not be leveled, as the plum-bob needle seemed to always skew to the right. It was theorized that gravity does not affect this particular spot in the same way that it does elsewhere.

Fear threads through me. Until now, I'd been hoping that this was going to somehow turn out to be a horrendous reality show prank, but now, I'm beginning to fear that this is far from staged. Pausing for a moment, Trey, Jax, and Wayra each don a headlamp before Trey grasps my arm again, leading me inside the cave.

Wayra jogs ahead of us, deeper into the winding, dark tunnel. When we finally catch up to him around several twists and turns, he's securing climbing ropes over a sheer drop. He flashes his light over at the wall, saying, "Alameeda. They came through this way. The wackers didn't even have the decency to use decomposing lines." Pulling the Alameeda lines out of the wall, Trey lets them fall over the edge. I wait to hear them hit the ground, but I never hear a sound. Paling, I look at the inky darkness where the world seems to just fall away.

I begin to back up, putting my hand against the wall. Looking over my shoulder, I can't see anything behind me. It's completely dark. I won't get very far without a flashlight or a headlamp. Turning back to them, I'm nearly blinded by their lights as they all focus on me. Putting up my arm to shield my eyes from the light, Trey says, "Kricket, come here."

"I'm not going down there," I reply quickly, taking another step back from them.

"Yes, you are. Come here now," Trey orders sternly.

"I want to go home!" I demand, hearing my voice echo off the wall and feeling like I'm going to burst into tears, which is something I never do. I rarely allow anyone to see me cry, especially strangers.

"This is the way home," Trey replies.

"*No!* I want to go to *my* home—Chicago," I retort, taking another step back and feeling cold, rough stone against my fingertips.

"You cannot thrive under the wrong stars, Kricket," Trey says in a calm, soothing voice. "The stars here are in opposition to you . . . can't you feel it? You are foreign to them. You have no ancestry here—no lineage. Let us take you home."

"Where I can 'pay for my crimes'?" I ask with a scowl. "No thanks!" I turn and run blindly for a few steps before the light behind me tells me I'm caught. Trey picks me up, swinging me over his shoulder again. Carrying me over to the edge, he says, "We're going down there, Kricket. I can tranquilize you and take you, or you can come willingly; the choice is yours, but you will go." He drops me from his shoulder and stands me in front of him, angling his light up so it isn't shining in my eyes. "Which will it be?" he asks in a soft, deadly tone.

Knowing that if I'm tranquilized, there will be absolutely no chance of escape, I look at the ground, saying, "That's not really a choice because the result is nearly the same." Seeing Trey reach for his pocket, I straighten. "Okay, I'll go!"

Wayra steps nearer to me and begins strapping me in a rock climber's harness, securing a line to it. I'm sure he notices that my entire body is shaking, but I'm hoping he's attributing it to the cold and not the fact that I'm completely terrified. "Have you rappelled before?" Wayra asks, his violet eyes looking concerned.

"Yeah, at the Y a couple of times," I say, thinking of the comfortable, fake rock wall in the comfortable, urban environment.

"The Y?" His brow arches in question.

"Never mind," I growl, shaking my head. "I just hold this line loosely, letting it slip through, and the tension gathers here, right?"

Wayra gives me a crooked smile, saying, "That's all there is to it. That . . . and stepping off the edge."

"Is that all?" I ask.

Trey nods. "Jax will go first. Then you and I will follow. Wayra, you cover our eight," Trey orders, stepping into his harness.

"You mean our six?" I ask, giving him a funny look.

"What?" Trey asks, not looking at me.

"Wouldn't it be our six? If Wayra is covering our back—our rear—then it's our six," I say, seeing him grin. I blink, completely distracted by the way his eyes tilt up appealingly when he smiles.

"On a human clock, it would be six. On an Etharian timetable, it's eight," he answers, and my mind whirls with the implications of what he just said.

"Thirty-two? Are there thirty-two hours in a day there?" I ask, "Or, do you just have cycles of sixteen? Is it even hours? When you say 'eight,' what do you mean?"

"Those sound like more questions," Trey murmurs, looking at me smugly. "Did you misplace your anthropologist's hat?"

Narrowing my eyes at him just makes him grin wider. Jax cuts in then, saying, "See ya at the bottom. Baw-da-baw," before he steps off the edge of the precipice.

"Can I at least ask what 'Baw-da-baw' means?" I ask Wayra, seeing him grinning, too.

"It's military. Cavars say it before going into battle—it's a war cry," Wayra answers. I nod to him, feeling my knees go weak as Wayra guides me to the edge of the crag.

Placing my heels over the edge, my stomach twists as my hands tighten on the line strapped to my harness. Closing my eyes, I take a deep breath and say, "Well then . . . Baw-da-baw . . ."

Several moments pass before Trey clears his throat. I open my eyes again. "You can go now, Kricket," Trey says, looking like he's trying really hard not to smile.

"I know," I shoot back. "I'm going."

"Do you need me to hold you?" Trey asks with a smirk. Seeing that he's making fun of me, my spine straightens.

"Baw-da-baw," I bite out, stepping off the edge. I immediately begin to rocket toward the bottom of the abyss, because the ratchet on my harness is failing to tension the rope; it's sliding through too quickly.

Sliding past Jax on his rope, I try desperately to hold on to my line as it pulls through my fingers, burning them through my gloves. Looking up, light blinds me again as Trey reaches out, clasping me to his huge body and squeezing out what little air is left in my lungs.

Wrapping my arms around his chest, I almost lose my grasp on him when the tension in his line catches, slowing us down. "Don't let me go!" I try to scream, but it comes out as a raspy whisper.

"I won't," Trey promises in a low tone by my ear, squeezing me tighter. "Hold tight. We're almost to the bottom."

Hitting the ground softly at the bottom, Trey doesn't let me go right away, but continues to hug me to him as I shake in his arms. "Are you hurt?" he asks as my cheek rests against his neck.

"That wasn't supposed to happen, right?" I ask, hearing the quiver in my own voice.

"No," he admits grimly, setting me on my feet and checking my harness. "You're too light. This harness is designed for someone with more weight than you. I should've checked this myself. You need a smaller ratchet. How many turks do you weigh?" he asks me seriously.

"What's a turk?" I ask, hearing Jax touch down behind us.

"You trying to stop her heart, sir?" Jax asks in a concerned tone, coming to me and checking me for injuries.

"No, she's stopping mine," Trey replies softly, watching Jax examine me.

Swatting Jax's hands away, I say, "I'm fine. Just my hands hurt."

Trey reaches out, taking my hands in his. He pulls off my gloves gingerly and turns my hands over. His face darkens at the bloody marks left on my palms from trying to hold the rope.

Wayra hits the ground hard behind us, releasing his clamps and running to me. He stops when he sees my hands. His mouth goes slack jaw for a moment, and I try to pull my hands back from Trey to hide them. "I'm fine," I murmur quickly, seeing the fierce look that Trey is giving Wayra.

"She probably weighs less than a hundred turks," Trey says in a low voice, piercing Wayra with a scowl.

"I should've used a smaller ratchet. I'm sorry, Kricket," Wayra says before grasping the back of his neck with his hand as he frowns grimly.

"Uhh . . . okay," I say softly, not sure how to handle an apology from one of my kidnappers who almost accidently killed me but is still going to hold me against my will. "Next time, we'll make sure I weigh more turks," I stutter, nodding my head like I'm not still freaking out inside over what just happened.

Jax begins to laugh beside me while pulling a pouch out of his duffle bag. "We'll make sure Wayra takes you to Sequelle's with him. That ought to put some turks on you." Opening the pouch, he extracts a spiky plant limb that looks like aloe. "Hold out your hands for me palms up," he orders.

Doing as I'm told, I flinch when Jax squeezes the plant leaf over my palms, extracting its salve and rubbing it onto my cuts. "Ahh, that burns!" I hiss, pulling my hands back from him.

"Does it burn more or less than pepper spray?" he asks with an ironic twist of his lips.

"You *so* deserved that pepper spray, and if I had any more of it, we wouldn't be having this conversation now, Jax," I reply, entirely unrepentant.

"You have the confidence of someone who is at least a couple of crikes old," he says, pulling my hands back to him and beginning to wrap them in soft bandages.

"How much is a crike?" I ask, watching him.

Squinting his eyes, he says, "Hmm, about fifty years or so."

"How old are you?" I ask suspiciously, gauging him to be around 23 or 24, like Trey and Wayra.

"Two crikes and a floan," he replies casually. Hearing me choke, he looks up in question, "What?" he asks, not understanding why my eyes are so wide. If a crike is fifty years, then he's over a hundred years old. "Oh, you think I'm too young to have been given a mission like this one. Well, you wouldn't be the first to say that," he grins.

My eyes widen further. "How old are they?" I ask, nodding toward Trey and Wayra, who are packing the harnesses back in their bags and winding up the lines.

Jax shrugs, "About the same as me . . . give or take a speck."

"How long do you—I mean, do *we* live? On average?" I ask, feeling completely weirded out.

"A few jamarch, and before you ask, a jamarch is about a thousand years, give or take."

"So, like three thousand years?" I ask, my mouth feeling really dry.

"More like four and sometimes, if you're really lucky, five."

"Five . . . thousand," I breathe, having a "holy crap" moment. Jax nods, unwrapping the bandages he had just wrapped around my hands. Pulling them off, I have another freak-out moment, seeing that my palms are almost completely healed.

"Ready?" Trey asks, examining my hands and touching my skin gently.

"How did you do that, Jax?" I whisper. Putting one hand to Trey's cheek, I turn his head so that his headlamp shines on my other hand more brightly. I stare at my hand in fascination.

"I didn't do it. It was the hordabus plant," Jax gives me an ironic smile.

"Did you see this?" I ask Trey in awe, still resting my hand against his cheek when I look in his eyes.

"Yes. It's better. Let's go," he says gruffly, looking at me strangely while reaching up and pulling my hand from his cheek. Taking my arm again, Trey begins ushering me toward the mouth of another tunnel. A golden, luminescent glow shines from the tunnel as we near it. Stalactites, towering above our heads, drip condensation into the vast underground pool below them, making the pool ripple from thousands of tear-shaped drops.

The pool itself is aglow, as if it's being lit from far beneath its surface. The light is reflecting off the walls and ceiling in jeweled patterns, making everything seem enchanted.

Nearing the edge of the water, Trey removes his shoes, shoving them in his duffle bag. Next, he reaches up, unbuttoning his shirt and shrugging it off. Sitting down on a huge rock, I ask, "Taking a swim?"

"You could say that," Trey replies, his eyes twinkling in the glow from the water.

"I've never seen anything like it," I breathe, gesturing lamely toward the incandescent water, avoiding looking at Trey and his bare abdomen. I can feel heat flushing my cheeks; I'm not at all used to being around men like Trey—or any half-naked men in general.

Glancing around, I see Wayra and Jax are also taking off their shirts. I avert my eyes from them, too. "You're all going swimming?" I ask rhetorically, feeling really uncomfortable now.

"I wouldn't call what we're about to do 'swimming,'" Jax says, frowning. "It's more like . . ." he trails off, thinking.

"Trying not to drown," Wayra fills in the blank.

"*What!*" I shout, my voice reverberating throughout the enormous space.

"This is the way home," Trey says, watching me look from him to the water in front of me in complete horror.

"But I can't swim," I say, paling.

"*What!*" All three of them shout at once, making me cringe.

"Of course you can swim, Kricket," Trey says exasperatedly. "Everyone can swim."

Shaking my head, I croak, "I can't—no one ever taught me—I grew up in the city." I jump up from the rock and pace along the waterline. "I've been to North Beach a couple of times, but we basically just wade along the shore! You don't actually expect me to go in there, do you?" I argue, fear entering my voice again.

"A Rafe that can't swim. It's unfathomable," Wayra utters, looking completely shocked. "Those humans should be flogged—how could they not teach her to swim—it's like robbing one of one's soul," he rants, grasping the back of his neck with his hand again in agitation.

"We'll go together," Trey says, looking at me in an assessing way. "I'll hold you. You won't drown."

Jax's eyebrows knit together. "Trey, there's force; you cannot be expected to successfully hold her."

"Then bind us together," Trey replies, looking at me. "She weighs less than a hundred turks. It'll be less than my gear."

"He has a point, Jax," Wayra says, seeing Jax's skeptical face.

"It'll work," Trey states, loosening his belt.

I quickly turn to Jax, trying to garner his support. "This is stupid, right?" I say. "He's an idiot to do this."

"No, he has a point. If we tie you two together, you should be able to make it," Jax says, shifting to the ground and rummaging through his duffle bag. "We can separate your gear, Trey. I can take some in my bag, and Wayra can take the rest. Here," he says, coming up with a pair of scissors. "I'm going to modify your clothing, Kricket." Not hesitating, he leads me to a rock and sits me down on it. Cutting my jeans, he makes them into shorts—really short shorts. "Less drag," he explains.

I glance at Trey; he looks like an advertisement for Calvin Klein. Wearing only dark, athletic boxers, he's something out of a catalog or a warrior movie. Blushing deeply, I want to crawl under the rock I'm on. "Wade into the water together. We should tie you two so that you're face-to-face with both your heads above the water," Jax says. Trey nods, extending his hand for me to take.

Avoiding looking at him, I stand up, walking to the water's edge on my own. Dipping my toes in the water, I pull them back sharply. "It's freezing!" I glower at them, hearing my voice echo off the walls again.

"It is," Trey agrees, scooping me up in his arms and wading out quickly into the water before I can object further. When he is chest deep, he says softly in my ear, "Breathe."

Clinging to him tightly with my arms around his neck, I inhale deeply before muttering, "Shh . . . you're interrupting me plotting my revenge."

"If you survive this, I'll insist you learn to swim," he says, sounding annoyed as Jax wades to us with a line, circling us.

"If I survive this, I'm killing you," I reply dryly, feeling the rope tense, drawing me tighter against Trey's warm body.

A small smile touches his lips at my comment. "How do you propose to do that?" He gazes into my eyes as Jax knots us together.

"I'll let you spend some sleepless nights worrying about that," I reply, my teeth beginning to chatter as the cold water is chilling me to the bone.

"You're as securely tied as I can make you," Jax says next to us. "Kricket is becoming hypothermic, Trey. You should go now—we'll follow close behind."

"Look at me, Kricket," Trey orders. When my eyes meet his, there's something in them that wasn't there before, an intensity that he hasn't shown before now. "Inhale as much air as you can, then let it out. Do that a few times."

Nodding my head, I take in a shaky breath before letting it out.

"Again," he says, encouragingly. I do it again. "The next big inhale I want you to hold it, then we go," Trey says, breathing with me.

"Okay," I say, feeling every fiber of my body shaking in his arms.

Breathing in, he lets the ropes and my arms hold me to him as he dives us under the water, swimming down to the light beneath us. I gaze around in wonder as creatures that I've never seen before swim around, emitting light. A current begins to develop, weak at first, but in just moments it catches us, pulling us both with unbelievable force and propelling us forward. Wrapping his arms around me, the water tears at us, beating us as we spiral like a corkscrew.

Feeling like an earthworm in a flash flood, I'm hoping to hit a sidewalk soon, even if it will probably mean that I'll be squashed by some kid's bike tire. My lungs burn as the urge to inhale is warring with common sense. Bright, intense light is shining through my eye lids, making them almost red. But black spots are slowly blocking out the light.

Hugging Trey to me desperately, I shake my head, trying to force myself not to inhale the water all around me. But I can't hold on. Inhaling deeply, the water chokes me. Digging my nails into Trey's back, I struggle against him, knowing that I'm drowning. The current is slowing down as the light is fading around us. My entire body begins to relax as I open my eyes, seeing Trey staring back at me beneath the water, and then everything just goes black.

Chapter 6

Follow Your Eyes

I hear his voice calling my name in the dark as pressure on my chest turns into a burning agony in my lungs. I cough and a gurgling sound emits from me as my eyes flutter open. I'm being pushed on my side while I retch water onto the sandy ground.

I inhale a deep breath and cough again; my wet hair clings to my neck as my entire body shakes from trauma. Intense, violet eyes peer down at me from above as Trey says my name again.

"So lost," I whisper, closing my eyes and feeling like the tide is going to sweep me away, back into the water. Trey picks me up in his arms, pulling me to his chest. He strokes my back hypnotically.

"Here, Trey, put her down. I need to—okay, take it easy," Jax says defensively. "I just want to make sure . . ." Jax trails off. "At least let me cut the rest of the rope off you two."

I feel a gentle tugging on my abdomen, and the rope eases away from me, allowing me to breathe more deeply. My eyes flutter open briefly. My cheek rests against something warm and solid. I look up from Trey's chest to his chin. He sits down wearily, leaning against a rock with me on his lap.

"What *was* that?" I ask in a low, gravelly voice.

"Thin spot," Trey says, touching my cheek with the back of his fingers.

Jax sits next to Trey and eyes me, clearly wanting to snatch me from Trey to examine me. I gaze back at him from my position on Trey's lap. Jax says, "It's what some humans call a wormhole. It's a link between your Earth and our Ethar."

I just continue to stare at Jax's concerned face. Then I murmur, "Oh," but only because he seems to be looking for a reaction from me.

"Your universe and Earth are our closest dimension—well, right now they're the closest," Wayra chimes in, digging through his bag. Finding a canteen, he hands it to Jax. Jax twists the cap off, extending it to me. I shake my head, feeling like I'm waterlogged. "In another few of your millennium, Quixar will be closer."

Jax nods, "He's right." He hands the canteen to Trey, who drinks like he has been in the desert.

I feel drunk. "Is this the only thin spot?" I ask. My mind is still hazy, but I know that I need to find out all I can about how this works if I ever hope to get back home.

"No," Jax replies, handing me some kind of protein bar that Wayra handed to him.

"Are they all in water?" I feel ill. I never want to repeat what I just went through. Nearly drowning while being flushed to another world is probably the worst torture ever—in either place.

"No, there's another gateway just a few clicks north of . . ." he trails off, looking at Trey's face. "Uh . . . no. Some are located on the ground, but you wouldn't want to travel through a few of them."

"Why not?" I ask.

"They drop you at the poles. It's a little colder than Chicago, even in winter. Aren't you more interested in Ethar?" he asks, his eyebrow tilting up.

Raising my head off Trey's chest, I gaze around curiously at the panorama. We're at the edge of a basin, facing an enormous mountain. The clear water is a mirror's reflection of the imposing mountain, looking like it could indeed be an alternate universe. "Holy . . . mother of . . ." I breathe, looking up at the sky and seeing a waning sun and a moon so close it looks like I could reach out and touch it. Not only that, it's blue.

"Eat, Kricket," Trey says softly, pushing the protein bar in my hand nearer to my mouth. "You'll need your strength for what's ahead."

"Why?" I ask. "You mean there's more?"

"We need to get to Rafe," he replies, accepting a protein bar from Jax.

"This isn't it?" I blanch, taking a small bite of the protein bar and immediately fighting the urge to spit it out. "Ugh! What is this?" My face distorts in disgust. "It tastes like bark!"

"Oh, there's bark in it, and protein." Jax smiles while chewing his bark bar. "It's from the grumrell tree, and it contains enzymes that ward off parasites and insects, but it tastes like—"

"Cat poop," I state, trying to fight my gag reflex and hearing them all chuckle.

"Eat it," Jax replies, "or when we travel through the Forest of Omnicron, you'll get an intestinal worm the size of those hot dogs they sell at Wrigley Field." He takes another bite of it.

"Eewwww," I whisper, feeling a shiver go through me. I nibble on the bar again, having absolutely no appetite. "When are we going to the Forest of Omnicron?"

"When you're finished with that bar," Trey says, "we'll leave."

"How are we getting to Rafe? Is it far?" I ask, feeling like I need to lie down for at least a day before I move again. My muscles ache, and even though it's really warm here, deliciously warm, I'm still shaking like I was when we were in the frigid water of the underground pool. "Can't we stay here for a while?"

"No," Trey replies. "This is a water source for every creature within twenty clicks of here, and most of those creatures are bigger than us."

"Excuse me?" I ask, hoping I misunderstood him.

"This is wilderness, Kricket," Wayra admits, pulling out clothing for Trey and Jax and tossing it to them. "This is not our territory."

"Whose territory is it?" I ask. "Someone needs to give me a really good explanation for why I have to move from here after I literally almost drowned a few minutes ago."

"No one owns this territory—or everyone does; depends on how you look at it," Jax explains.

"It belongs to every Etharian, but no one can alter it or attempt to annex it. It's protected land," Trey says.

"So, basically, don't try to build a summer home here because you'll never get a building permit?" I ask.

"Not only can you not build, you can't employ a vehicle on this land or in its airspace," Wayra expounds.

"So . . . no limo?" I ask.

"No roads, Kricket." Trey's tone is soft as he rubs my arms, like he's trying to improve my circulation.

"How large is this territory?" I ask.

"Hmm . . ." Jax scratches his chin. "About the size of South America, wouldn't you say, Trey?" he speculates. Trey nods.

"So, we're supposed to *walk* across South America?" I ask.

"No!" Jax exhales, holding both hands out to me, like he wants to stop me before I freak out. "We're not too far from the borderlands of Rafe territory. We're really close to the Comantre clan, too."

"Too close," Wayra adds, looking tense.

"The way you're all acting—it's like we're in danger or something." My voice sounds hollow. I watch them look at each other.

"We're not in danger, exactly," Jax replies. "It's more like we're not very comfortable with our current position."

"Oh," I reply nervously, glancing around. Trey sits forward, easing me off his lap. He stands up quickly and dons a pair of sleek, dark, utilitarian-type pants and a shirt that doesn't hide just how perfect his physique really is.

After fastening his belt, Trey flips open a small panel on the thigh to reveal a tiny row of buttons. Pressing one a few times, the fabric of his pants changes from dark shades of brown, to camouflage, to white, to sand, to a watery-pattern that looks like actual water wavering on his body. Selecting a chameleon setting, the pants begin to blend in with his surroundings, taking on the shades and shapes of whatever is nearby. He does the same with a panel hidden in the lining of his shirt, and then he looks up, eyeing me critically.

I self-consciously put my hand to my hair, running my fingers through it to try to smooth out the tangles. "Did we bring anything for Kricket to wear?" Trey asks Wayra.

"Uh, no. She's a prisoner. I didn't think it mattered," Wayra says. Trey frowns at Wayra before he glances back at me. I stiffen, hearing just how insignificant I am to them.

Jax nudges my arm, trying to make me take another bite of my bark bar. "Eat that and I'll give you this," he says, holding up a small leaf in his palm.

"What's that?" I ask suspiciously.

"It will refortify your enamel and take away the taste of . . . cat poop," he says, trying not to crack up.

"So, it's good for my teeth?" I ask for clarification.

Jax nods, putting on his clothes that are just like Trey's. Feeling pissy now, I shove the whole bar in my mouth at once, trying really hard not to gag on it. I need to remain strong if I'm going to find a way to get away from these tools and get back home. Reaching for the canteen, I swallow several mouthfuls of water. Afterward, I hold out my hand for the leaf Jax had promised. Popping it into my mouth, the taste of mint quickly dispels the awful aftertaste.

A terrifying shriek sounds from beyond the basin, echoing off the rocks and making every hair on my body stand on end. Bolting to my feet, my eyes the size of saucers, I whisper, "What was that?"

Before anyone can answer me, a deeper, more gut-churning roar comes from the same side where the shriek sounded.

"Ready, Kricket?" Trey asks, reaching his hand out to me grimly.

I stumble toward his hand, taking it like a lifeline. "Let's go!" I reply. Taking his duffle, he drops my hand for a moment, threads his arms through the bag, and then grabs my hand again. He leads me rapidly away from the water, toward the cover of enormous trees.

Under the canopy of leaves, the light dims as trunks and branches tower over us, higher than some of the buildings in the loop. I've seen pictures of large trees—redwoods in national forests that are so large that one could drive a car through their trunks. These trees are bigger. You could drive a cross-town bus through one and traffic could pass you going the opposite way. Another roar sounds behind us.

"Can you run?" Trey asks me, frowning.

Paling, I nod, "What is this place? Jurassic Park?" I ask, picking up my pace. Trey matches it as Jax and Wayra flank us.

"I saw that movie!" Jax says, excitedly. "How did they do that?"

I don't answer him but fall into the quick pace that I always use to run for the El when I'm late.

"Those sounds were definitely mammals," Trey says. "The first one was a mastoff, and the second was a saer."

"Describe," I insist. Trying to keep my breathing easy and steady, my boots are pounding the dirt beneath me, making squishing noises because they're still wet.

"A mastoff is an enormous, hairy mastodon with long tusks," Trey says.

"That's prehistoric," I say, narrowing my eyes. "And a saer?"

"Scary cat," Wayra fills in.

"How scary?"

"You see me running?" Wayra counters grimly.

Looking around me, I can see the scenery whipping by me faster than it should be. I stop for a second, confused by what's happening. Everyone pauses with me. "Kricket?" Trey asks. "What's wrong?"

"I—did you see how fast we were going?" I ask, searching their faces in confusion.

"Yes, but we need to go faster," Wayra urges, looking over his shoulder.

"No—I—how fast do you think we were going?" I ask.

"*Oh!*" Jax says, catching my meaning. "Gravity is different here, Kricket. It exerts a little less force on Ethar. We have roughly the same size planet as Earth, but it turns a fraction slower, creating slightly less gravity. It's not that different from Earth, but enough to make everything grow larger. You'll probably be able to jump higher, too."

"And that'll come in handy if we don't go now," Wayra reminds us. Seeing his distress makes me move again. Picking up the pace and plowing ahead, we eat up the terrain in no time.

Running, we leap over huge, fallen branches as if they aren't there; but after about an hour, I begin stumbling over unseen roots because the twilight is turning to darkness. Catching me before I stumble again, Trey halts us beneath another huge tree that looks like every other tree in this vast woodland. Pushing away from him and bending over, I grasp my side, trying to work out the cramp. My face feels flushed as sweat drips from my jaw.

"Here, Kricket," Jax says, handing me the canteen. Thanking him, I put it to my lips.

"Up or down? Wayra asks Trey, breathing heavily from running.

"Definitely up," Trey says with a grin, pointing to the high canopy of branches above our heads.

Wayra grins too. "How did you spot that?"

Trey shrugs, still smiling. I look up and see nothing unusual.

"How do you feel about heights, Kricket?" Jax asks, staring up, too.

"Don't ask me that. Why are you asking me that?" I shoot back, narrowing my eyes at him.

"We need to rest, and we need a safer place to accomplish it," Trey says. "How well can you climb trees?"

I just stare at him for a moment before I say, "Let me put it to you this way, Trey: I've never had a backyard in my life . . . that I can remember." My hands go to my hips defensively, waiting for his disapproving scowl.

Shaking his head, he mutters, "Add climbing to the list with swimming."

"Do we put her in a harness? Hoist her up?" Wayra asks.

"No," Trey says, shaking his head and sounding annoyed again. "I'll take her up. Kricket, get on my back."

"Why?" I ask tiredly.

"Because I gave you an order. This isn't Chicago, Kricket, where you can do whatever you want. Here, there are consequences when orders are disobeyed," he replies, glaring at me.

Feeling hot and sticky from running for my life through the jungle, my chin rises militantly. "I'm sorry, I don't recall joining your army, so your orders don't apply to me."

I see Jax cringe. "Kricket—" Jax says quickly, but Trey cuts him off by holding up his hand. Then, he turns to me and the menace in his eyes is unmistakable.

Bracing myself for whatever is coming, I watch as Trey approaches me and leans down until he's an inch from my face. "This is your draft notice, Kricket. You're in *my* army now. You no longer think for yourself. *I* will think for you. *I* will tell you what to do and when to do it. Do you understand?" he asks.

Allowing a small smile to grace my lips, I reply, "By your logic, I guess I should ask *you* if I understand." I look beyond Trey's scowling face and see Jax close his eyes as his face falls. I look back to Trey.

"Wayra, hand me the rope," Trey says softly, his eyes never leaving mine. Feeling myself pale a little, I fidget, shifting from one foot to the other as I wait with my heart in my throat for what is going to happen next. As the rope is put into Trey's hands, he asks, "Feel like changing your mind?"

Shaking my head, my chin comes up. "No."

I watch his expression sour, like he tastes something he despises, right before he lunges toward me. I cringe involuntarily as my face turns away. My arms come up to protect me, knowing his fists will probably hurt more than I'm used to. He surprises me, though, when he doesn't hurt me. He merely grasps my wrists, tying the rope around them as I tug against him to get free.

Trey looks almost alarmed, like seeing me flinch and realizing that I thought he intended to hit me wasn't the reaction he'd expected from me. His voice is gruff as he says, "I'll treat you like a prisoner until you learn to follow my orders. I can't have you disobeying me here. It could get us all killed, Kricket." I remain silent. "Wayra, put her on my back. We've wasted enough time," Trey orders, watching my reaction. I try not to have one as Wayra picks me up, looping my arms over Trey's neck as he settles me on Trey's back.

"She's on, sir," Wayra says in a clipped tone.

"Try not to choke me, because it'll be a long way down," Trey advises me over his shoulder. He doesn't waste any more time but begins climbing the huge tree in front of us. I have to wind my legs around Trey's waist as he climbs the bark like a monkey. Glancing up, I can see a wooden platform above our heads. When we near it, Trey slips through an opening. He sits on the lip of the deck, ducking under my arms so that I'm no longer attached to his back.

Leaning against the massive trunk, I gaze around, seeing rope railings leading to rope bridges connecting several of the trees together hundreds of feet above the ground. Darkness is descending, making it difficult to see very far.

"What is this place?" I ask Trey, as Jax crawls through the hole in the wooden planks.

Trey frowns at me, but doesn't answer my question. *He's still pouting,* I think, shifting my eyes away from him.

"It's a base. A place to stop and rest," Jax answers soothingly. He leans forward to untie my hands.

"No. Leave it tied," Trey says, watching my reaction as Jax reluctantly drops his hands. I close my eyes, resting my head against the tree. Weariness makes my body droop, and I wave off the canteen before giving in to fatigue.

I must have slept, because when I open my eyes again, it's much darker. The only light is coming from the enormous moon above my head and a galaxy of stars surrounding it. No one has touched me, I think, because I'm still in the same position. My hands are numb, as the rope around them is cutting off my circulation. Flexing my fingers, I try to get the blood flowing back into them.

"She's not at all what I expected," I hear Wayra say from around the curve of the tree.

"What did you expect her to be like?" Jax asks.

"I don't know—whiny. I thought we'd have to listen to her crying the whole way back, but she hasn't cried once," he says, sounding confused.

"She's fiery," Trey's voice says easily. "Wild."

"My mouth almost dropped open when she stood up to you, Trey," Jax says, sounding amused.

"Mine, too," Trey replies ruefully. "I didn't know whether to wring her neck or . . ." he trails off.

"Can someone please tell me what that little pink, lacy thing is that I keep catching a glimpse of when she bends down?" Wayra asks.

"I don't know what it is, but I have to say that I like it more than I should," Jax replies, sounding amused, and Trey and Wayra grunt in agreement before the conversation lulls.

"How did Pan and Arissa die?" Wayra asks, causing my face to lose color.

"Pneumonia," Jax says. "That's what was listed on the medical records."

"Pneumonia? What's that?" Wayra asks.

"Best I can tell, it's a human type of Crue," Jax replies.

"But Crue is treatable—no one dies of Crue," Wayra says, sounding confused.

"Pneumonia is a virus that humans contract. We may have been able to treat them with our medicines, but they had no resistance to it—no antibodies to protect them from it, and without our medicines . . ." he trails off.

"It makes me nervous. Kricket grew up on Earth. She hasn't been exposed to any of our germs. The first thing we have to do when we get her back to Rafe is a battery of inoculations," Jax says. My heart twists in my chest, hearing that my parents might be alive today if they had stayed here.

"You mean, she could get Crue and die?" Wayra asks, sounding nervous.

"Not if I can help it. We keep her away from everyone until she gets vaccinated; after that, she should be fine," Jax says in a determined tone.

"Do you think the knob knocker knows all this? She talked to them. There's no telling what kind of diseases she can get from Kyon," Wayra says with irritation in his tone.

"We have to keep her away from them," Jax says. "Whatever they want, it can't be good. Her mother was one of their priestesses—that's higher than royalty there."

"Makes you wonder what made her run from them," Trey says softly.

"Or what Pan possessed to make her run to him," Jax counters in a contemplative tone.

"Hmm?" Trey asks.

"What makes one run into the arms of one's enemy?" Jax poses the question.

"I cannot fathom," Trey answers, sounding puzzled.

"Love," Jax replies, and Wayra chuckles.

No longer able to hold still without my legs cramping, I stir from my position. Sitting up against the tree, a small groan escapes me as I try to stretch, only to be inhibited by my bound hands.

"Kricket?" Trey asks softly, and getting up, he comes to my side, kneeling down. "How do you feel?" he asks, hovering like he's not sure of what to do. It seems uncharacteristic of him because he's always so confident. Jax follows him, hovering too.

"I have to go to the bathroom," I say, dropping my chin and resting my wrists on my raised knees. I'm grateful that it's dark because I can feel heat flushing my cheeks.

"Oh!" Trey says, like I've said something extraordinary. "But other than that, you feel healthy, right? No fever . . . cough . . . rash?" he asks. I raise my head a notch, holding out my wrists to him mutely.

As I watch Trey untie the rope, Jax springs away, coming back with a small package. "Here, this is for . . . uh, there's a diagram, if you need help," he says.

"I need a light," I say, curiously taking the soft bag from him that looks like it came from a day spa. When Jax returns with the light, I get to my feet. I feel lightheaded, and it causes me to sway a little. Trey's arms go around me, steadying me.

"Jax, get the visor," Trey orders. "We need to check her vitals—something's not right."

"I'm fine." I push away from Trey, but he doesn't let me go completely; his hand remains on my elbow. "Just had a head rush . . . stood up too fast. Stop hovering," I scold him.

"I'm not hovering," Trey retorts with a frown. "I don't hover!"

"You're hovering. He's hovering, isn't he, Wayra?" I ask, seeing Wayra watching us.

"You are hovering, sir," Wayra replies with a smirk.

"I don't hover," Trey growls, scowling at Wayra, who holds up both his hands.

"I need some privacy," I say softly, looking at his hand on my arm. He immediately lets go of me, turning away.

Taking the package, I go further away from them, around the other side of the enormous tree. I scan the contents of the satchel; it's full of toiletries. It has wipes that are like wet naps and a sponge, that when I unwrap it and squeeze it, contains a soapy solution for washing my body.

Quickly, I take care of my pressing needs. Then, I use the sponge, cleaning myself as quickly as I can. After I put everything but the comb back into the bag, my stomach growls loudly. Knowing I have to keep my strength up, I move back around the wooden deck of the tree, finding Trey, Wayra, and Jax sitting with their backs to the trunk, speaking quietly to each other.

"I'm not quite sure what to do with this," I say to Jax, holding up the bag he had given me.

"I'll take it," he says. Thanking him, I hand it back along with the headlamp. They have a long sticklike lamp that's glowing dimly near the turn of the tree. Its light isn't yellow, but ice blue, and it doesn't seem to be attracting any bugs. I sit near them and let my legs hang over the edge of the deck while holding one of the woven rope spindles of the railing.

I can't help marveling at the night sky, the immensity of it. No lights mar its perfection. Goose bumps rising on my arms make me realize that the lack of light means there aren't any cities around, no civilization that I'm accustomed to for survival. Feeling myself panicking, I begin combing out my hair, trying to calm myself. *I have to stay with them until I can find some sort of civilization. I don't know how to survive here.*

The conversation behind me slowly dies. Glancing over my shoulder, I pause, seeing them all watching me. I narrow my eyes at them, and Jax straightens, saying, "Are you hungry, Kricket?" Nodding slowly, I see him get up. Rummaging through his pack, he produces something packaged in a clear wrap. He hands it to me. "I think this one is pheasant."

"Mmm, pheasant," I say sarcastically, and see him grin.

"It's like . . . hen," he says, "with bread . . . uh, dough?"

Opening the package, I extract a small pie from it. "Does it taste like cat poop?" I ask, sniffing it suspiciously.

"Just try it," he says before returning to his seat. I take a tentative bite and find it tastes like a chicken potpie. My stomach growls again as I take a larger bite, chewing it hungrily.

"I think the pheasant is the best one—better than the quiche," Wayra says. "I once traded four quiche packs for one pheasant. That was the day I got this," Wayra holds up his arm and shows us a long, thick scar. "Sactum amp tossed by an Alameeda who snuck into the compound at chow time."

"You're supposed to get out of the way when someone throws an amp at you," Trey says with a sarcastic grin.

"Oh really?" Wayra fires back.

"Why didn't you get it wrapped?" Jax asks, looking at the scar.

"Because it looks tough. The blushers love scars. I'm not going to get it removed either—it's a badge of honor," he says, flexing his arm and showing off his powerful muscles.

Jax rolls his eyes. "You think that's tough, check this out," he says, lifting his shirt and showing us a deep scar across his back. "That's from a squelch tracker."

"How did it just skim over your back like that and not rip you to pieces?" Wayra asks, looking at Jax's scar admiringly.

"I was laying face down in mud." He grins at his explanation. "The heat seeker couldn't find all of me to rip apart. So, the next time you dig your trench, go deep," Jax says, with a cheeky smile.

"You're a cautionary tale," Trey says. "Remind me to use you when we're training the new gits."

"Where are all your scars, Trey?" Jax asks curiously. "Did you get wrapped?"

"Yeah . . . I don't remember it, though," Trey replies softly, looking down. "One moment I was in a battle; the next thing I can remember is waking up at an outpost."

"Did they do regeneration?" Jax asks, definitely interested.

"Yes, extensive regeneration, so they tell me. They almost had to go to my brother, Victus, for DNA, but they managed with what was left of me.

"That's so crystal," Wayra says in awe.

"No, it's not. Regeneration is disturbing," Trey says honestly.

"Did you watch the regrowth?" Jax asks.

"I watched my hand reattach, but they put me out for the rest. When I woke up, I didn't have a scratch on me," he replies, grasping his hand and flexing it. Looking up, he catches me watching him.

Jax follows Trey's stare to me. "What about you, Kricket? Any skinned knees or broken bones?" Something in his eyes tells me to be careful. I stiffen before trying to pull off a casual shrug.

"You know," I say quickly, "the usual."

"No . . . I don't know. What counts as 'usual' on Earth?" he asks doggedly, like he knows something.

"I once had a paper cut, right here on this finger. That hurt a lot." I hold up my little finger and wag it in the air.

Wayra and Trey both grin, but Jax frowns. "I read your medical files," Jax says in a low tone.

"Oh?" I ask, pretending that I don't know what he's talking about.

"Broken clavicle, dislocated shoulder, broken radius, three broken ribs, and a stab wound to your abdomen. There was more," he continues, watching my reaction. "What was that all about?"

"Would you believe I'm clumsy?" I ask in an offhanded way, watching all of them scowl at me.

"You're as nimble as a cat, Kricket," Trey replies.

"Perhaps I have a problem with authority."

"A very dangerous problem to have."

"Isn't it just?" I agree, quirking a brow.

"Why was I not informed of this abuse?" Trey asks Jax in a low tone.

"Because the parameters of our mission did not include stalking and killing humans, sir," Jax replies in an even tone.

"We could've made exceptions; it is a special case," Trey replies. "Do you still have her files?"

"Of course, sir," Jax replies. My face flushes, knowing what must be in my files.

I grit my teeth as anger flares up in me at their intrusion into my life. They have no right to look at those files—at *me*, like I'm some sort of criminal deviant. "You say you were wounded in battle? Are you at war?" I ask, attempting to change the subject.

"No. Not now. This was almost a crike ago," he replies.

"Fifty years ago?" I ask, seeing him nod. "Was it just the Alameeda clan that you fought?"

Trey shakes his head slowly, his eyes never leaving mine. "No. They had allies. The houses were divided."

"Houses?" I ask in confusion.

"Clans. There are five clans of Ethar," Trey explains. "Rafe is but one."

"Alameeda is another . . . and the Comantre clan?" I ask, remembering that they had mentioned that we are near their territory.

Surprise flickers in Trey's eyes at my words. "Yes. Comantre is a house—an ally to Rafe," he says, scanning my face.

Wayra gives a snort, saying, "When it suits them." His sarcasm is not lost on me.

"When you say 'house' or 'clan,' do you mean 'nation' like America or Great Britain?"

"In a way, you could make that sort of connection," Trey replies. "But the scale is not the same."

"Scale?"

"A nation implies vast multitudes. Our population is . . . smaller."

"How small?" I wonder, not sure why since they have superior medicine. Regeneration for a race of people that can live thousands of years must be vast—enormous. I would think their cities would tower over Chicago.

"So many questions. I have one for you, Kricket. What did Kyon tell you when you met?" Trey asks.

I pause, realizing I'll need to give some information to get more from them. Turning back to look at the darkness, I say, "He said I look like my mother, but it's a pity about my eyes, that they make me look like I'm from Rafe." I glance at them again and see the scowl on Trey's face. "I have a question. Why come looking for me? I'm half Alameeda, your enemy, as I am half their enemy. What can either of you possibly want from me?"

"Why do you think we want something from you?" Trey asks, his eyes narrowing at the accusation.

"Everyone wants something, Trey. Some are up front about it, and some, well . . . some just lie," I say, slowly looking at each one of them.

"You are one of us; you belong here," Trey replies, like that is all there is to it.

"That's almost sweet . . . and I see that you believe that, but you're just doing your jobs, right? What I want to know is, what's the politics behind the decision to send someone to look for me?"

"I can think of several. You are Etharian, living among humans. We do not want humans to become aware that our race exists," Trey replies.

"Why not?" I ask.

"Hundreds of reasons. Human greed is legendary. Their need to consume and to waste and to destroy their environment is prevalent to me in the very air I had to breathe while I was there among them," Trey replies, looking annoyed.

"So, you were afraid I'd tell your secrets?" I ask, not at all convinced. "But I didn't even know about Ethar until you came for me."

"That was not known to us. We didn't begin looking for you until recently. We were looking for Pan, but his trail led us to you."

"Why were you looking for him? Was he a criminal?" I pray that he'll answer my question. My need for information about my parents is a burning thing.

"He was a hero," Trey replies abruptly. "A brave soldier from a very prominent family. No one understands why he would throw that all away to . . ."

"To what?" I ask, holding my breath.

"To commit himself to an Alameeda." Trey's eyes go to my hair, scanning its length. For just a second, it feels like he's touched my hair. A shiver runs through me at the sensation.

"Is that a crime?" I ask, feeling defensive about my mother.

"It's not just that he committed himself to an Alameeda. It's that she was a priestess in their clan," he replies, his mouth twisting in a small frown.

"Is that bad?" I feel my heart accelerate.

"It's said that the priestesses of Alameeda are endowed with . . . gifts." Trey watches me, like I'm supposed to know what he means.

"I don't . . . gifts?" I wrinkle my nose at him.

"Other senses, senses that go beyond the five that are common in us all."

"Like ESP?" I ask. Trey's eyebrow rises in question. "You mean some of them can see the future or something like that?"

"Yes," he nods. "Pan committed to Arissa and she to him. It's the Alameeda who objected the most. They threatened to go to war with us again unless she was returned to them."

"What! Why would they go to war over one woman?" I ask in complete disbelief, even when I can see he's being truthful. He, at least, believes what he's telling me.

"They say Arissa was very powerful. Perhaps they didn't want their enemies to benefit from her knowledge," he says, watching me like a skilled interrogator.

"What knowledge? Could she predict the future?"

"I don't know what her gifts were, Kricket. It was never common knowledge."

"Someone knows—the Alameeda for sure. Kyon said that I'm the daughter of a priestess, making me a priestess, too. Is that why they want me?"

"Without a doubt," Jax states, looking grim. My extremities seem to go numb then, and my fingers weaken their hold on the rope spindles.

"They can't have you. You have Rafe blood in you. You're part of our ancestry, a Rafe citizen. They cannot take you from us," Trey replies, like he wants to reassure me.

"Kyon said you have no idea what I'm worth," I reply, thinking of all the ramifications of his statement.

"If you're a priestess, too, then you have gifts," Wayra says, as if the thought just occurred to him.

"I . . ." I trail off, thinking.

"What can you do?" Wayra asks. Jax and Trey both lean forward a little, studying my every move. "Do you know? Have they developed yet?"

My survival instincts kick in. "I'm tired." I fake a yawn, stretching my arms above my head before yawning again loudly. "I'd like to rest now. Is there somewhere I can sleep?" Easing back from the edge of the deck, I stand up, looking at them for direction.

"You're avoiding the question," Trey says, his gaze running over me slowly. Despite my fear, something warm ignites in me at his gaze, confusing me. Raising my chin a notch, I avert my eyes, but I still feel a raw awareness of him.

"It's been a long day for me," I say honestly, putting a shaky hand to my forehead and rubbing it. Seeing my hand tremble, I bring it down, putting it in my other one and watching them both shake now.

Trey notices my hands; his eyebrows come together as he watches them. "It will be even longer tomorrow," he says softly. "We should all try to sleep now." Jax and Wayra both rummage through their packs, coming out with bedrolls.

"Here," Jax says, handing me a bedroll. Jax spreads his out where he had been sitting, perpendicular to the tree so that if he rolls in his sleep, he won't roll off the edge. I spread mine next to his and see a small smile form in the corners of his mouth.

Trey spreads his bedroll next to mine so that I'm between them. Trying to ignore them, I lie down on the blanket, resting my head on the pillow. I close my eyes and take a few deep breaths as I attempt to slow my racing heart. It takes me a second to figure out that what I find the most frightening in this moment is the silence. I'm lost in it. No horn honks or sirens or passing El trains disturb the night. No trace of my home exists here.

As I hold back tears that threaten to slip from beneath my closed eyelids, a thought occurs to me: *They were real. My parents weren't just some made-up dream that I conjured late at night in my bed in the dark. My sketchy memories of them are real.* Piercing elation crashes into and vies with crushing grief. I find it hard to breathe. There are people in Rafe and Alameeda who know a lot more about them. I can find out the truth. I can finally know who my parents were. *But at what cost?* I wonder.

My body is weary, but sleep eludes me. I open my eyes and gaze at Trey next to me. He has his arms crossed behind his head as he stares up at the brilliant stars in the clear, night sky. He seems almost ethereal, bathed as he is in the bluish glow of the light stick. The warmth I felt earlier comes back, slipping through me and filling me with another kind of glow that calms my fear. Feeling his radiating body heat, my breathing slows. *He's too perfect looking to be real. This has to be a dream after all.* With that thought, I relax enough to sleep.

Chapter 7
With Every Mistake

Curled on my side, my fingertips glide softly over warm, supple contours on their way to my face. Tucking my hair back from my eyes, I open them, focusing on the thick, inky line of Trey's tattoo. My fingers return to rest on Trey's chest again, and then I still, suddenly wide-awake. I cringe, seeing that I'm snuggled up against Trey's warm body like he's an oversized teddy bear. My head is just below his chin, and his arm is resting on my hip as we're turned toward each other like . . . lovers.

Stiffening, I close my eyes, mouthing the words "holy shit" before trying to ease back a little from Trey. Inhaling a breath, I smell his scent all around me. My eyes fly open again as a pulse of desire shivers through me. It surprises me and makes me want to hide from him. I have to quell my impulse to run. Instead, I ease my hand off Trey's chest, trying really hard not to wake him as I begin to roll away.

"Where are you going, Kricket?" Trey whispers softly, opening his eyes and watching me freeze like a criminal.

"Uh—nowhere—um, bathroom?" I ask, my heart pounding like I did something wrong. Feeling my face flushing as I move back to my blanket, I see now that I had invaded his space, not he mine.

"There are personal totes in Jax's gear. Take one with you. Come back when you're finished. We're going to rest until the sun is fully up," I nod, not meeting his eyes. Hurrying over to find a tote bag of toiletries, I take one with me around the bend of the tree.

Closing my eyes and leaning against the trunk, I fight the urge to completely fall apart. *I'm still here in freakin' Etharian hell,* I think. I'd been hoping that this was all some weird delusion that would go away in the morning, but it's definitely real because I can smell Trey all over me.

My hair tickles my nose; I inhale, feeling another twinge of desire tear through me at Trey's scent. "Ugh," I groan. *What's wrong with you? He's the enemy, and he's completely old!*

Taking my time because I'm in no hurry to go back to my blanket, I use all the toiletries in the bag. I carefully wash my body before combing out my hair. After braiding it in one thick plait, I tie it with a leather string I find in the bag.

Chewing on one of those minty leaves, I creep back around the tree to my blanket. None of the guys have moved an inch. Wayra is snoring softly on his blanket as I step around Jax. I sit down before lying back and staring up at the leafy canopy above my head.

"I thought I was going to have to come and find you," Trey murmurs next to me, making me jump at the sound of his voice.

"Oh?" I ask, not looking at him.

"You took your time."

"I wasn't aware that it was a timed test," I shoot back, glancing at him and seeing the corners of his mouth tip up at my response.

"Do you always rise so early?" he asks.

"Do you always sleep so late?" I counter.

"Days are longer here. There are thirty-two parts in a rotation. You're probably used to Earth time," he surmises, stretching his long arms. "The transition will be brutal for you. You're going to want to sleep when you should be awake and be awake when you should sleep."

"So, noon is at . . . sixteen o'clock?" I ask, feeling my heartbeat pick up.

"Yes," he grins, showing his perfect teeth.

"Eight more hours in a full day?"

"That's right," he replies. "But we call it a 'rotation' not a 'day.'"

"How long will it take to adapt to the time change?"

"That depends on you. How adaptable are you?" His eyebrow arches.

"I'm a chameleon," I reply in a clipped tone, looking straight up at the leaves above. "I'll survive."

"Really?" he asks with surprise in his tone.

"Yes." I nod once.

"All alone?"

"Yes."

"It will take a very hard, very determined personality to survive what is ahead for you without help."

"Got it," I growl through clenched teeth, anger flaring up in me at the sympathy in his voice.

"You're tough?"

"I'm stone."

"Stone can be broken."

Tilting my head toward him, I meet his eyes. "Don't worry about me. I'll be fine. I'm used to holding on to nothing as tight as I can."

Wayra snorts irritably from his position on his blanket. "Ah, you gotta stop talking, because she's breaking my heart!" He sits up and glowers at Jax next to me. "Okay, we'll hire her a wigg, but that's it! After that, I'm out."

I frown. "I don't need your charity. If you want to help me, then let me go home," I say softly, not sure what they're talking about, but fairly certain that it's charity.

"We *are* taking you home, Kricket," Trey says. "Ethar is your home. You should know that by the way they abused you on their planet," he says, looking angry all of a sudden.

"It wasn't all bad," I mutter, defending my home. "I had friends there—friends that are probably worried about me now." I begin to panic as I think about Bridget and what she'll do when she finds out I'm gone. *Maybe she'll move in with Eric and he'll take care of her,* I think. *Enrique will be okay. He'll miss me, but he has a huge family and maybe Michael will help him.*

"If that wasn't all bad on your scale, Kricket, then I definitely don't want to see you define really bad for us," Jax says next to me. He moves from his blanket, crouching to smooth and roll it before stowing it back with his other gear.

"It was almost over. I was almost free." I sigh with exasperation. "If you take me back, things will be different for me there. I can go to school and be somebody. I can have a life in a couple of months. I won't have to hide anymore."

"You'll have a life here, Kricket," Trey says. "After you pay your penance, you can be whatever you want."

I still, staring at Trey. "Excuse me? Did you just say 'pay my penance?'" I ask, wide-eyed.

"Yes," he replies, frowning. "But the most they can give you is a few floans. It will actually work out well for you since you don't have anywhere to live; it will be provided for you."

"Like jail?"

"No! Not jail! Penance . . . uh . . ." He looks to Jax for help. "Like public service . . ." he trails off at my scowl.

My eyebrows slash together. "You're going to make me pick up garbage on the side of the road?" I ask, putting my hands on my hips.

"You won't have to pick up garbage—I don't think—depends on where they place you," Jax says, and he has the decency to blush a little.

"How long is a floan?" I ask, crossing my hands in front of me as my foot begins to tap.

"About a year, give or take a speck," Jax replies, watching my foot.

"*A few years!*" I glare at them. "*Are you outta your minds?*"

"I said give or take a speck—a month. That's really not that long," Jax says, sounding defensive.

"Jax, you're telling me that someone wants to punish me for being born. It doesn't matter if that is for a day—uh, a rotation or a floan—it's insanity," I retort, trying to rein in my temper.

"Technically, no one petitioned Skye to relocate or to trespass on Earth. You can be held accountable for violating our encroachment laws regarding Earth," he says, looking a little embarrassed, but I'm not sure if he's embarrassed for me or for the idiots at Skye.

"Well, Jax, I don't really understand any of this, but I *think* that I was probably a fetus when all this went down!" I pace the deck, thinking. "That'll probably give me some legal recourse," I say softly to myself, biting my thumbnail. "It sounds like a lame excuse to come looking for me. Someone needs a pawn for something—"

"What did you say?" Trey asks, his violet eyes training on me.

"Pawns," I repeat absently.

"We're pawns?" he asks intently.

My lips twist in an ironic smile. "Oh, you're a pawn—soldier—Cavar—whatever you want to call yourself." I wave my hand in a dismissive gesture. "You follow orders but don't go thinking for yourself because you're in *their* army now." I point in the general direction where I think *they* might be. "Should we go?" I drop my hand and go to my blanket. Rolling it up, I hand it to Jax. "I'm interested in meeting with your Skye—whoever *they* are."

Jax says, "Skye is the military branch of our government . . . uh, sort of like—"

"The Army?" I ask.

"No."

"The Navy?"

"Uh-uh."

"Marines?"

"The Cavars are like the Marines. Skye is like—"

"The Defense Department," Trey says, handing his bedroll to Jax.

"But I thought Skye was like your judicial system."

"You violated encroachment laws—a global violation, which falls under defense. They have their own judicial subsection. Defense isn't accountable to any other branch of government; they're autonomous.

"They're self-governing?" I ask with dread.

"Yes."

"And you think that's okay?"

"It's worked so far," Trey replies.

I put my hands on my hips. "For who?"

"There's no way she's only seventeen floans," Wayra mutters, pulling his gear together. "She looks like a blusher, but she acts like a saer."

"Me-ow," Jax says next to me, grinning.

"How long will it take to get there?" I ask them, dropping to one knee and tightening the laces of my boots.

"That depends," Trey says, lifting his gear. "We can only go as fast as our weakest link—a few days if we move."

"Did you hear that, Wayra?" I ask, looking at him. "You'd better keep up."

Heading toward the hole in the planks, I hear Wayra say, "I think I'm in love."

"You're taking all of this well," Jax says, joining me.

"Am I?" I ask, brushing off the concern I can see in his eyes. "Well, the thought just occurred to me that I might as well hang out on Ethar for a few months. Take in the scene. I've been in worse places. I'll see what Skye has to say for itself. If it reeks, well, then I only have a few months—er, specks—until I'm eighteen, right?"

"You plan to go back to Earth—to escape?" he asks, looking concerned. "Um, that's not a very good idea. Everyone will have learned about you by then. The Alameeda will know everything—"

"So," I shrug, "what do you care? Your job will be over. You'll have delivered me to my . . . penance. I won't be your problem anymore."

"Yes, but it will be okay. We can help you—"

I interrupt, holding up my hand. "Look, I get the guilt thing. You'll check in on me, you'll make sure nothing really bad happens to me, blah, blah, blah. Don't sweat it, Jax. In a couple of weeks, you won't even remember my name. Now, how am I getting down from here?"

Trey grasps both of my arms, before turning me and making me look at him. "What Jax is trying to say is that going back to Earth will not be a viable option for you. Ever," he says, unsmiling. "The Alameeda will follow you. Kyon will follow you."

"Oh . . ." I trail off, thinking. "He is a total . . . what's the word I'm looking for, Wayra?"

"Wacker?" Wayra replies, and Trey narrows his eyes at him disapprovingly.

I point my finger at Wayra. "Yes, he's a *total* wacker, but now that I've met him, he can be avoided. I'll just have to look out for huge blonds."

"What about us?" Trey asks with menace. "How will you avoid me?"

"Why would you come looking for me if I vacate? Skye will probably send someone else and I can play shy with him, too," I say stiffly, not liking his tone.

Amy A. Bartol

"I'll volunteer," Trey counters.

"No, you won't. You'll move on to the next one," I say, blowing off his words.

"On to the next what?"

"On to the next goal, ambition—the next thrill," I retort with heat. "You think I should follow their rules? Well I'm going to do what's right for *me*, not what *you* think is right for me."

"This is the problem with authority that you alluded to last night?" Trey asks, leaning his face close to mine.

"No, this is survival, Trey. I'd love to coach you, but I charge for babysitting."

"I have a feeling that you'll be the navigator for my next thrill," he replies, loosening his grasp on my arms with a scowl.

"Request permission to carry her down, sir." Wayra says, staring at me.

"Denied," Trey barks with a clipped tone, making me climb on his back before he easily picks his way down from our treetop haven. He lets me go when we hit the ground, and for the next few hours, it's an endurance test as we run at a fairly steady pace through the woodland terrain.

The terrain is amazing though. Our path is carrying us near sheer cliff drops that overlook canyons with rock that contains striations of red, orange, brown, and silver. Everything is big, massive, like it could swallow us up. Feeling very small, I push myself to keep up with them. I'm trying to focus on the simple problem of continuing to move, instead of the fear of what lies ahead.

Trey, running beside me, scans me critically before signaling to the others to stop. Sinking to a rock beneath a shady tree, I pant, fighting the urge to double over from the cramp in my side. Sweat is pouring down the sides of my face, not only from the exertion of running through the woods, but also from the heat. It's tropical here, and I'm still used to winter temperatures. Jax tries to hand me a protein bar, but I push it away from me, shaking my head. The smell of it right now is enough to make me gag.

"You have to eat it, Kricket," Jax says cajolingly, crouching down near me. "It will keep you healthy."

"It will . . . make me . . . hurl," I pant. "Give me a . . . second. I might be able . . . to eat it . . . once I . . . catch my breath." I lean over, feeling cold, even when I know that I'm as red as fruit punch. Closing my eyes and opening them, my whole world tilts, making me slip off the rock to the ground. From far away, Trey says my name, but I can't seem to answer him.

ॐ

Water swirls around me as I open my eyes. I shiver, realizing I'm in Trey's arms. He's standing chest deep in crystal blue water, with Wayra pacing on the bank only steps away. Clutching Trey closer to me, my cheek remains on his shoulder. Watching a bead of water slip down his powerful neck, I hear Jax say, "She's waking up."

Trey, cupping his hand in the water, pours some of it over my hair. It drips down the sides of my face, cooling me. "Let's get her out. I'll get the visor, and we can check her vitals."

As Trey wades out of the pond with me in his arms, I try to lift my head from his shoulder. It makes me dizzy so I lay it back. It's then I notice that I'm only in my bra and underwear. A blush creeps into my cheeks as I hug Trey tighter to me. Wayra meets us on the bank, draping a blanket over us. Trey sits down with me on his lap. He leans against a tree trunk, holding me securely to his chest. Peeking at his face, he seems angry as he smoothes my hair back from my face.

Hurrying over with the visor that looks like grandma goggles, Trey sets them on my eyes. Everything is green as I gaze around at the water in front of us. Flashing green lights and readouts occupy the peripherals of the glasses, but the information is running faster than I can possibly read it.

"Ho!" Jax exclaims next to me.

Immediately, Trey's arms tighten on me as he barks out, "What? How bad is it?"

"Naw, it's not bad . . . it's just . . . Kricket . . ." Jax breathes, like he's in awe. "Look at this brain activity. It's massive."

"What do you mean?" Trey asks with relief in his tone.

Jax grins. "She's lighting everything up. Look at her frontal lobe—it's off the charts."

"What does that mean? Is she healthy?" Trey growls.

Jax nods enthusiastically. "She's healthy! We didn't fry her with heat stroke, that's for sure. Or if we did, she's got more brain activity than anyone I've ever seen to compensate for it," he replies, sounding seriously geeked about it.

"Those things aren't broken, are they?" Trey asks speculatively.

"No . . . here." Jax pulls them off my face. "Wayra, come here."

Wayra walks over and Jax puts the glasses on his eyes. "See! He's normal—well, normal for him. See how it doesn't light up in these areas?" he points out to Trey.

"Yes."

"Now watch this," he says, taking the glasses off Wayra, he places them back on my face. "See? It's like Christmas in Chicago with all those lights," Jax says proudly.

"So that means she's smart?"

Jax beams. "Yeah, she's smart! She's brilliant! There's no telling what she can do."

"If she's so smart, why did she run until she almost popped? Why didn't she just tell us she needed to rest?" Wayra asks derisively.

"Personality flaw," Trey replies. "She's going to show us that she's not weak."

"She's sitting right here," I murmur, pulling the glasses off my face and handing them to Jax. "Where are my clothes?" I ask, still shaking as I pull the blanket closer to me.

Wayra points to the branch of the tree where my T-shirt and shorts are hanging, dripping wet, from being rinsed off. "Don't you know that you're supposed to be slower?" Wayra scolds me, frowning and sounding irritated, like I've scared him. "You're small and you're female. We're trained to be fast, so we don't know when we're going too fast for you unless you tell us."

"I've trained, too," I reply, frowning back. "I run up and down stairs for a living. It's just that it's hot here."

Jax hands me the canteen and says, "Drink this until it's gone. You have to be rehydrated."

"Okay," I agree, having a hard time holding the canteen because I feel weak. "Sorry. I'm not usually this lame."

"You should be sorry," Trey scolds me. "You're old enough to know when you need to rest. Don't make us treat you like a child."

"I'm not a child," I reply, lifting my chin.

"Then don't act like one," he says with his eyebrows coming together. Looking at Wayra, he orders, "Find us shelter. We have to rest now. We can resume tonight."

"Yes, sir," Wayra says, turning and running off.

I sigh. "I'm going to be okay soon; then we can go." Trey's jaw just gets tighter as he ignores me. Jax presses the gross protein bar into my hand.

Jax tries to soften Trey's anger. "She's looking better. I just can't figure out what's wrong with her feet," Jax says, looking stumped.

"My feet?" I lift my feet so that they're peeking out from beneath the blanket. They look normal to me, but Jax still has a concerned expression. "There's nothing wrong with my feet."

"Uh, your toenails are a stunning shade of pink," he replies, and at first I think he's joking, but concern is still there in his eyes.

I struggle to suppress a smile. "Jax, that's nail polish." I wiggle my toes demonstratively.

Jax's eyebrow quirks and it's accompanied soon after by a crooked smile. His eyes narrow as he gives me a sidelong glance. "What's nail polish?"

"Paint . . . for your toes," I murmur, grinning.

"Why?" he wonders, looking intrigued.

"Uh . . ." I shrug. "I don't know . . . because it's pretty?" He glances back at my feet again, his brow wrinkling in thought.

"Yes . . ." he says distractedly. "It does have a certain allure . . ." He trails off when Trey reaches down and covers my feet with the blanket again, scowling at us both.

"*Sir!*" Wayra barks, running back to us. "You gotta see this!"

Trey tenses before lifting me in his arms as he stands. "Report."

"The knob knockers, sir—they're close and they're breaking every restriction ever enacted," Wayra reports, sounding anxious. "They have E-Ones and ALVs. It's a good thing we stopped here, or we would've run right into them."

"How close are they?"

"Two, maybe three clicks to the north, sir." He leads us to a sheltered break in the trees. It takes me awhile to see the almost silent, hovering, helicopter-like vehicle skimming the trees on the horizon. It's followed, not far behind, by a larger, black aircraft that resembles a bullet. Seeing it, my heart pounds in my chest, because the black one looks more like a spaceship than a plane. There is nothing like it on Earth that I know of.

Trey speaks softly, "The Alameeda know where we came in, and they know where we're going."

"They seem willing to risk a global incident by violating airspace to get what they came for," Jax says, and then everyone turns to stare at me.

"Oh, c'mon!" I grumble, feeling fear course through me. "I can't be *that* important. Maybe they're just here to pick up the knob knockers. Here, let me down," I add, wiggling in Trey's arms.

Trey sets me gently on my feet, but he holds me tightly to his side, making sure I don't fall down. "Not a very fair fight," Jax mutters under his breath, looking at Trey. "They gotta know we didn't bring any real weapons with us. Just the archaic, legal kind."

Trey rubs my arm absently. "We'll have to evade for now. I hate running from them."

"I hate being tortured, so evasion sounds absolutely acceptable to me," Jax replies.

"*What!*" I gasp, breathing faster.

Trey shoots Jax a look full of censure. "They won't torture you, Kricket," Trey assures me.

"But they'll torture you?" I ask as my eyes go wide.

He shrugs. "They may just kill us. They can't afford to have witnesses."

I straighten as adrenaline pumps into me. "Right. Okay, let's go," I urge them sternly, holding his hand and tugging him back as hard as I can. Glancing at my hand in his, Trey's eyes move up to my face. "Move it!" I repeat as I grasp his wrist and tug him in the direction away from the ships. "Let's go!"

"Are you scared?" Trey asks, frowning at me. "I—"

My eyebrows slash together. "You bet your *ass* I'm scared, so let's *move* before someone gets *tortured*!" I yell at them, tugging harder on Trey's arm.

Jax smiles despite my fear. "We're wagering now?" Jax asks. "What's an ass, and how many fardrooms do you think it's worth?" Ignoring Jax, I pull on Trey's hand again.

"They don't know where we are yet, Kricket," Trey assures me gently. "We'll find shelter and stay down. Tonight, when it's dark, we'll change our trajectory and travel toward the Comantre territory," he explains in a soothing tone. "They won't expect it because they don't know that we've seen them."

I stop tugging on his arm; it's futile anyway—I haven't managed to move him at all. "Okay," I nod, with my grip easing on his hand a little. "Can we find that shelter now? And can we go this way?" I point away from the terrifying ships.

"Yes," Trey replies as he takes my hand in his. His grip is tight enough to be reassuring. To my relief, he allows me to lead him away as the Alameeda ships continue their search for us.

Chapter 8
What's It Gonna Take?

Trey scoops me up in his arms again, carrying me back to the small pond to collect their gear and my clothes. As I shrug back into what's left of my jeans, Wayra says, "You'll have to explain those pink garments to us later, Kricket." Blushing, I pull my damp T-shirt on over my head.

I look around at the trees anxiously, feeling as if Kyon is going to jump out at us at any second. When I meet Wayra's unwavering stare, I reply, "Wayra, if we get out of this alive, I'll give them to you."

"Promise?" he asks me, looking excited.

"Yeah, I pinky swear," I reply with sarcasm, holding up my little finger to him.

"Excellent!" he breathes. Looking away from Wayra, Jax and Trey are both frowning at me.

"What?" I ask, feeling jumpy. "You want them, too?"

"Can you walk?" Trey asks, holding his hand out for me to take.

"Yes," I say with a worried frown, taking it immediately.

"You haven't eaten your protein bar," Jax scolds, pointing to it in my other hand.

"Are you serious? Kyon, Forester, and Lecto are probably out there somewhere and you're worried about my protein bar?"

"Yes," Jax gives me a stubborn nod.

I open my mouth and shove the entire thing in it, chewing it quickly. "Hop-py?" I mumble around the mouthful.

"Yes, now we can go." Jax extends his hand, offering me a mint leaf. I snatch it from him, chewing faster so I can pop it in my mouth.

Moving west, we're careful to remain under the thick canopy of branches. It's creepy how quiet the aircraft are. No rotors propel the helicopter, or as they call it, the "E-One." It hums and is creating a rustling of branches that has quieted the wildlife around us. As it slinks along, the E-One makes sweeping passes, missing us by what I consider fractions, but the distance doesn't seem to be concerning either Trey or Jax.

When I notice that Wayra is no longer with us, I panic and pause. "Where's Wayra?"

"He's right behind us covering our tracks," Trey answers calmly, squeezing my hand reassuringly. He smiles at me with a puzzled expression, causing my heart to pick up a little more. He's probably the most attractive person I've ever met, and I'm starting to find the way he makes me feel when he smiles irritating.

"Okay," I fumble nervously.

"Are you worried?" Trey asks.

"Uh—*yeah*," I reply with a hint of sarcasm because "worried" is an understatement.

Trey's eyes soften. "Why? I said that the Alameeda wouldn't torture you." Trey squeezes my hand lightly. It's meant to be reassuring.

"Yes, I heard you say that." I scan the sky above us to see if I can locate the E-One.

"Do you believe me?" Trey asks.

"You're telling the truth."

He gives me a sidelong look. "That's an odd thing to say. How do you know I'm telling the truth?"

I shrug. "I just know." I lower my eyes from his as I drop my chin.

"Well, if you just know, then you can stop worrying."

"Right," I mutter and suppress the impulse to roll my eyes. "Just because you *think* they won't torture me, doesn't mean they won't. So for now, I'm safer with you."

Trey pauses and frowns. "Why do you think they'd torture you?"

"I met Kyon. I know the look," I reply, not sure why I'm being so honest with him.

"What look?" His jaw grows perceptibly tighter.

My eyes shy away from his. "The look of someone who sees me as a means to an end."

"Have you encountered that look often?" he asks in a quiet way. His expression is unreadable.

"Often enough."

"And I don't have that look?"

"No. You're indifferent; that makes you safer. You have no need to lie to me."

"How do you know that?" he asks while holding back a tree branch for me as we move on.

I bite my lower lip before I reply absently. "You've always been honest with me." I watch the sky. "You don't want anything from me except my cooperation, so you can do your job and get rid of me. You don't even care if I know it. That makes you very different from Kyon. The first thing that Kyon did when we met was lie."

"Sir, check this out," Jax says ahead of us. Peering into a dark cave, I see that it's partially shrouded by winding vines and vegetation.

Dropping his gear, Trey rummages through his bag, pulling out a small case. He flips it open and quickly assembles a wicked-looking crossbow with metal-tipped projectiles that resemble notched, elongated spikes. He extracts a very sexy pair of sunglasses from the case. As he puts them on, he orders, "Wait here."

"You're wearing sunglasses into a dark cave?" I ask with a skeptical expression.

"They're night vision."

"Why didn't you use those in the cave on Earth?" I ask, thinking the headlamps are ridiculous if you have *très* chic night vision.

"Because there are very specific rules for using our technology while on Earth." He hoists the crossbow up.

"Do you always follow the rules?"

"Yes."

"Ugh, you're a Boy Scout."

"I'm not a boy. I'm an adult."

"Good for you. Where are you going, old man?" I ask, not at all sure why I feel so anxious about him leaving me.

"I'm going to investigate this cave—make sure the only saer in it is you," he replies, and Jax laughs.

"Good luck. Don't get eaten—or do, whichever," I reply sarcastically, but my heart is pounding in my chest because he's going in there alone. Trey smirks before walking cautiously into the cave. Jax efficiently assembles his crossbow, raising it quickly and aiming it as Wayra steps through the break in the trees.

"It's me," Wayra says in a low tone, watching Jax lower the weapon.

"Did they shadow you?"

"My shadow didn't even shadow me."

"Crystal," Jax says, tossing the crossbow to Wayra. He rummages through his bag again, coming up with two pairs of sunglasses and handing one pair to me.

"Where's my crossbow?"

"What?" Jax smiles his crooked smile.

"My weapon?"

"You want a recurve?" he asks, while assembling another crossbow.

"Crossbow, recurve, whatever you call it. Do I get a weapon?"

"No," Jax replies, smiling at Wayra and nodding toward me, like he thinks I'm adorable.

"Why not?" I put my hands on my hips.

"I can think of a few reasons: you're a female; you're not trained to use it; you're our ward; I don't want to be shot; and if you end up killing Kyon, we'll be laughed out of the Cavars," Jax replies, grinning.

"What does my being a female have anything to do with it?"

"You're small and weak," he replies, like he's never heard of the feminist movement.

My mouth hangs open for a moment before I snap it shut. "I'm not small," I say between my teeth.

"You're tiny," Jax counters.

"Runt," Wayra agrees.

"I'm five foot ten."

"See, you're not even a link," Jax states.

"What's a link?" I ask, closing my eyes and rubbing my forehead.

"About six feet," he replies. "Don't get me wrong, it's polar to be a female your size—absolutely polar—"

"Positively polar," Wayra agrees.

"Polar?" I growl.

"Attractive . . . alluring . . ." Jax says, thinking.

"Sexy?" I ask, feeling heat in my cheeks.

Nodding adamantly, Wayra agrees, "Sexy. Polar."

Continuing to assemble his weapon, Jax smiles. "But you're deceptively strong. It must be because you're used to more gravity. Your muscles are stronger. You can run farther with more endurance than the average female on Ethar."

"Is that it?" Wayra asks Jax. "I was wondering. She was keeping up with us for so long, I couldn't figure it out."

"If I promise not to shoot you, will you give me a recurve?" I ask again, getting back to them arming me so I can defend myself.

"No," they both say in unison.

"Clear," Trey says, emerging from the mouth of the cave, startling me. "Gather the gear." Looking at me, Trey says, "Good, you have glasses. Let's go." Grasping me by the elbow, he leads me deep into the cave to a rounded-out cavern, where he instructs Wayra and Jax to drop the gear.

Taking out a bedroll, Trey hands it to me, saying, "Here, try to get some sleep. We're staying here until it gets dark. Then we'll head west." I nod, spreading out the blanket. I lie down on the hard ground, but every little sound makes my eyes fly open. When Wayra comes back from his patrol to report that the E-One and ALV have headed north, I see them all visibly relax. My eyes droop then, and even though I'm freaked, I'm also completely exhausted, so I sleep.

❧

Waking up, I see Jax smile at me from across the small fire, asking, "Kricket, are you hungry?"

I sit, stretching my sore muscles. "I'm starving," I admit.

Jax hands me a wrapped package. It's another small pie, but this one tastes like eggs. "It's quiche," he says, helpfully.

"It's good. Thanks," I murmur, taking another bite. Trey watches me eat. "How long did I sleep?"

"About six parts—and before you ask, a part is roughly an hour," Trey replies. "But we still have a few parts before we can leave."

"Okay." I finish my food. "Any sign of the knob knockers?" I see Trey cringe, and Wayra smothers a laugh.

"Kricket, 'knob knockers' is not proper language for a young female such as yourself," Trey says, sounding old. "And no, they continued north."

I grin at Trey. "You don't think my saying 'knob knockers' is *polar*?" I ask, hearing Jax and Wayra crack up.

"No, I don't," Trey replies, looking sourly at Wayra, who suddenly finds the ceiling interesting. "I think you'll fit in better if you refrain from using those kinds of words."

"Who said I want to fit in—or that I even *can* fit in?"

"Why wouldn't you fit in?" Both Jax and Wayra look down because they *know* I won't fit in.

"Because I'm a realist and this is *my* life you're playing with, Cavar," I reply. "You think you're delivering me home. I disagree."

"You can fit in; you just have to try," Trey insists.

"How do you propose I do that? Are you going to teach me etiquette?" I laugh.

"Yes. Why not?" he responds, staring back at me like he has just agreed to a dare.

Smiling at him, I ask, "What makes you think I'm uncouth?"

"I didn't accuse you of being uncouth, just easily influenced by others." He glares at Wayra, who looks unrepentant.

"Okay, this should kill an hour—uh, a part," I amend. "Where would you like to begin teaching me to be a proper Rafe citizen?"

"Let's start with salutations," he says, standing up and offering me his hand to help me up. Ignoring it, I rise on my own, facing him. "How would you greet someone?"

"Depends. Are you a friend, an acquaintance, a business associate, a teacher, a family member, or a boyfriend?" I ask.

"A boyfriend," Wayra says.

Trey scowls at him, and then he turns to me and answers, "In a formal situation."

I hold out my hand to him. When he doesn't take it, I take his hand in mine, shaking it firmly, saying, "Hello, Trey, it's very nice to meet you."

Jax mimics me, taking Wayra's hand and saying, "Wayra, it's very nice to meet you."

Wayra pushes Jax away, saying, "Get off." Then he shivers, like his skin is crawling.

"What's wrong?"

"He touched me," Wayra says, frowning.

"So?"

"So, he's going to get hurt if he does it again," Wayra replies, and Jax grins.

"You don't shake hands?"

"No," Trey says. "Males rarely touch each other."

"Really?"

"And females rarely touch males they don't know or who aren't a part of their family," he adds, making me feel awkward all of a sudden. *I've been holding his hand all day,* I think, feeling stupid.

"Okay, so touching is bad. What do I do?" I ask, letting go of his hand.

"If we are peers, then you incline your head, like a nod, but pause for a moment before you lift your head," he demonstrates.

I try to suppress a giggle, mimicking him. He sees it and grins, asking, "What?"

"It's just the opposite of the hood greeting. In the hood, you lift your chin up and say, ''sup,'" I explain. "Do I say anything when I incline my head?"

"'Greetings' is standard. If you know my name, you may say it."

"Ah, just like Kyon, but he touched me," I murmur. Trey frowns at my words. "How do you greet someone who's not a peer?"

With his eyebrows still together, he answers, "If you're greeting royalty, then you drop to one knee and incline your head, bringing your right arm up to your shoulder." He demonstrates, looking extremely elegant and poised.

I follow his lead, asking, "How do I know the difference between a peer and . . . er . . . royalty?" I try to match the refined sweep of his arm with mine.

"You should be introduced to royalty. You will not greet them unless you're introduced," he explains as we both stand again.

"Ah-ha—snobs. So, you're royalty, right?" I ask, and his eyes go wide, not understanding how I know this about him. "Victus is the one to inherit, but you're minor royalty—no one seeks your favor." I repeat almost verbatim what he'd said in the limousine.

"You were listening to us—in the car," he states, frowning.

"I'm always listening—chameleon, remember?" Sinking to my knee again, I incline my head while bringing my hand up to my shoulder, saying, "Greetings, Trey Allairis."

"How do you know my last name?" Trey grasps my upper arm and pulls me to my feet.

"Kyon mentioned it," I reply, looking at his hand on my arm. "Uh, no touching. It's impolite," I scold him prudishly. "Now, how would you greet an Alameeda priestess? Would you take a knee for her?"

"You mean, how would I greet a delegation from Alameeda?" he corrects me. "She would be accompanied by an entourage, and I would kneel. Victus would not. He would incline his head. But I wouldn't kneel if I were a Cavar in the capacity of protection."

"Interesting."

"You're a Rafe citizen, Kricket. Your affiliation with the Alameeda will only make you seem less like one of us," he warns.

"I'm both. To deny my mother would be wrong."

"There may be some who will want to see you crawl because of your heritage."

"I'm stone, remember?" I ask, quirking my brow. "I can't be afraid to fail, or I'll be stuck wherever you leave me. I can't hide what I am and there's always a way around those people—or through them. Don't worry about what I'll do next. You won't be there to see it."

"She's got you there, Trey," Jax says. He stands up. "You'll be at the swanks with the blushers. I need you to get me into one."

Trey is silent for a moment, not taking his eyes from mine. Then he says, "I don't know, Jax . . . I'll be responsible for you, if I get you in. Do you even know how to comport yourself at a swank?"

"Yes," Jax replies. He goes down on one knee before me. Rising up, he asks, "Would you care to comport with me?" He stands at my side holding his arm out in front of him with his other arm behind his back.

In my most arrogant tone, I say, "Indeed."

Jax raises his chin. "You may lay your hand on my arm, and I will guide you to the floor."

"The floor? Like the dance floor?" I ask, laying my hand on his arm.

"Mmm," he agrees with an arrogant nod, looking straight ahead.

"How does one dance on Ethar?" I ask, extremely curious as he leads me a few steps away from the fire. "Is there touching involved?"

"Some."

I bring my fingers to my lips. "Scandalous," I reply. I drop my hand. "Are you going to break it down for me?"

Jax looks a little less arrogant. "Well, I could use some instruction, too. Trey, can you demonstrate?" he asks.

"But you were comporting so well," Trey replies sarcastically.

"Oh, you gotta show us your moves, Trey," I say.

"Why must I?"

"Because you'll ruin my first kidnapping if you don't," I reply, quirking my eyebrow challengingly. "How will I be able to compare it to any future abduction if you don't at least attempt to show me how you dance?"

"You're not being kidnapped. You're being remanded," Trey replies, but his eyes soften in the corners.

"Well then, the least you can do is entertain me before I get *remanded*."

Trey holds up his finger and says, "I will show you *one* dance, if you promise to show me one that you know."

"Deal," I agree immediately.

He positions me to face him. Then, he asks, "Do you know any music with stringed instruments?"

"You mean, like orchestral music?" I wrinkle my nose.

"Yes."

"Um . . . 'Ode To Joy' . . . Beethoven," I reply, unsure. "But I only know the refrain."

"How does it go?" he asks.

Humming the classical music as best I can, he smiles. "Yes, that's good, keep humming. Now," —holding his hand toward me above our heads, he continues— "touch your fingertips to mine . . . no, left hand to left hand." I do so as he instructs, and he adds, "Make sure you keep eye contact with me. Now, we will turn so that you will be standing where I am and I will be in your position."

"Half turn—got it." I back around as he moves forward.

"Now, we switch hands and repeat the same movement."

After we do, he says, "Now, we drop our hands, and you curtsy and I bow to you."

"Curtsy?" I falter, grinning. "How does one curtsy?" Jax, standing by us, demonstrates a curtsy, which I attempt to imitate.

Wayra chimes in, "Why are you so good at curtsying, Jax?"

Ignoring him, Trey says, "Then we both face the far wall. I will extend my hand up to you again and you will meet it with yours, just allowing our fingertips to touch again."

"Then, what?" I feel the heat of his fingers on mine. A slight blush begins coloring my cheeks while I gaze in his eyes.

Trey's expression is serious. "Then we drop our hands and look straight ahead, taking a step." We do as he says. "Then, we turn our heads toward each other again, make eye contact and our hands touch again."

"So, this is a weird kind of line dancing," I say, continuing to follow his moves.

"Hmm?" he asks, raising his brow.

"Never mind." I wave my hand.

"Those are the basics for that particular dance."

"What's it called?"

"The revel."

"Well, no one will accuse you all of being b-boys," I murmur, smiling at him. "I'm almost afraid to show you how we dance. You might have a heart attack."

"Why? Is it dangerous?" he asks, looking confused.

"Uh . . . you could say that. What can I show you that won't totally freak you out?" I ask rhetorically, thinking. "Oh! I know. I'll teach you salsa! My roommate, Bridget—her real name is Brigida; she's Cuban-American—she changed it to Bridget because she thinks it helps on job applications," I explain. "She makes me dance with her all the time."

Spinning around him, I show Trey how to turn and then to shift me in his arms so that I will spin away from him. "Once I'm out here, pull my hand to bring me back to you," I instruct, feeling him pull me back. Winding inward on his arm, I end up pressed to his chest. Smiling and looking up at Trey, I say, "And that's basically how you . . . salsa . . ." I trail off, my fingers curling on his chest at his intense expression. He drops his chin down, his face coming close to mine.

"I'm next," Wayra says behind me, coming closer.

"No way. I'm next," Jax counters.

Trey freezes with his face very close to mine. "No one's next. It's time to go," he says softly, letting go of me and turning away. "Pack up the gear, and put out the fire. I'll scout the area before we leave. We'll move silently tonight. No talking once we exit the cave. Do you understand?" Trey asks in a tight tone, turning back to me. He looks angry, like I did something wrong. "We need to complete the mission, so we can get back to our lives."

Raising my chin a notch, I say, "Got it."

Trey nods, leaving immediately for the mouth of the cave. I follow more slowly, mentally kicking myself for being so stupid. These guys aren't my friends—not even close. They're being paid to do a job.

They're delivering me to some kind of scary institution where I'll be subject to someone else's whims. My heart twists inside my chest because I can't help feeling as if they're betraying me. *I'm stone. Nothing touches me—nothing,* I repeat in my head. I put on my night-vision glasses and walk into the darkness.

Chapter 9
Split the World in Two

Running through the night, I'm dodging between trees and over terrain that's as magical as it is dangerous. I'm directly behind Trey; he's blocking branches for me while maintaining an easier pace than before. We stop before a clearing that's carpeted with wildflowers and singing insects, and I accept the canteen from Jax.

As I gaze around, everything is clear to me, almost as crisp as daylight. My night-vision glasses allow me to see the colors of the flowers: brilliant vermilion and fuchsia, with intoxicating fragrances. I lean down and bring my face close to the beautiful red bloom near me. Inhaling its scent, I feel the petals brush against my cheek, like the silk of a scarf my mother once owned. I pluck the bloom, tucking it behind my ear.

In seconds, Trey grasps my arm, tugging me to him and pulling the flower from my hair, throwing it on the ground. Grasping my chin painfully, he turns my head as his fingers sweep the place where the bloom had rested. "Are you trying to kill yourself?" Trey asks in a low, harsh tone. He turns my chin so that I'm forced to look at his face, and his eyebrows shoot together as he scowls at me. He points his finger in my face. "What's wrong with you?"

"What?" I ask feebly.

"Don't you know what lives on those flowers—what kind of poisonous insect inhabits them?" I can't read his eyes, because his glasses are blocking them, but his mouth is stretched in a grim line.

"Uhh—" I breathe, not able to think because he's right in my face, looking furious enough to hit me. My heart jumps into my throat. I want to run, but I can't because he's still holding my chin. "I won't —touch anything. I'm sorry—" I stutter in a low whisper, feeling all of the color leaving my face. I hate myself in this moment. I misjudged him. He's more dangerous than I'd thought.

His tirade is far from over as he continues to question me. "Why would you put something like that in your hair, so close to your ear?" His grip tightens on my chin. I try not to flinch or pull it away from him.

"I . . . thought it was . . . pretty."

His hand on my arm tightens, "You think a turbine worm drilling into your ear would be pretty?" he asks me, like I'm the dumbest person he's ever met.

"*Sir!*" Jax yells in an agitated tone behind Trey. "Can I speak with you?"

I hold my breath, hoping he'll let me go. Slowly, Trey's grip eases as he drops his hand from my chin. "Report," Trey barks, still glaring at me.

"In confidence," Jax replies, frowning at me, too. Trey lets me go completely, and I immediately back up from him, putting some distance between us. Trey continues to scowl as he gestures Jax toward the woods behind them.

I perch tentatively on a large rock and wrap my arms around my body. I scan the ground for anything that could possibly resemble a turbine worm. My chin aches a little, but I refuse to rub it or show any sign that what just happened had hurt me in the least. *Never show weakness.*

"Kricket." Jax says my name and I duck my head like a guilty criminal.

"What?" I answer, rising from my rock to face him. Trey is only a few steps behind.

"How often do you see flowers growing wild in Chicago?"

"Uh . . ." I clear my throat because it feels tight all of a sudden. "Well, corporate buildings sometimes have small terrariums," I mumble.

"Are those flowers wild?" he asks, frowning.

"No," I reply, feeling like an idiot as my face gets redder.

"And if you picked one of those flowers, what would happen?"

"Um, I'd probably get fired, and security might escort me out of the building."

"You wouldn't be worried that it could kill you?"

Shaking my head, I drop my chin a little more, feeling stupid again. Tears burn my eyes, but I refuse to give into them, forcing them back down.

"Because you've never seen any flowers that can kill, right?" he asks in a gentle tone. "And there has been no one in your life who stood by you—protected you by warning you about things like dangerous plants?"

I try to appear casual as I shrug. "My friends weren't concerned with botany."

"No, it was all about urban survival, and if we were in Chicago, you could show us what not to touch." He smiles at me.

I shrug again. "That, and maybe a free meal at happy hour—I know a place in the loop that serves free pasta marinara, and you only have to buy a coke."

"I'd bet a thousand fardrooms that you do," Jax says sadly. "We should go. We have a lot of ground to cover."

I nod, keeping my shoulders back and my eyes averted as I walk by Trey. We move more slowly through the open fields. Trey and

Wayra are both leading the way now and using the scopes on their recurves to scan the surrounding woods. Skirting a herd of what looks like horses, my skin prickles, noticing that each one has two long, wicked horns growing out of its head just behind its ears. Shivering, I ask, "What are those?" because I'm learning that everything here should be treated with the utmost caution.

"Spixes," Wayra answers me.

"Friendly?"

"Not particularly. Those are wild ones," Wayra replies, nodding toward the herd. "But they can be trained and ridden."

"Yeah?" I ask, watching a beautiful brown and white spix rise up on its hind legs, pawing the air when it sees us moving past the herd. "Do you have a spix?"

"No," Wayra smiles. "Trey's family has some. I've ridden with him at his family home."

Not wanting to hear anything about Trey or his stupid family who know all about stupid flowers and riding spixes, I say, "It's kind of sad to think that some people would want to tame something that is meant to be wild. Maybe there ought to be a law against it."

Looking up, I see Trey try to suppress his grin. "You only say that because you're the wild thing we've been sent to tame."

"Like you could tame me," I scoff, and Wayra laughs.

"She's a fire woman," Wayra says, grinning at me.

"That she is," Trey mutters. I ignore them because I'm not sure if I was just complimented or insulted.

An agitated nicker from a spix makes Trey's head snap up. He scans the area behind us just as the spixes begin surging forward, looking wild and deadly as their hooves rattle the ground like thunder. But that's not half as frightening as the roar that tears the very air around me.

In the next moment, my elbow is seized by Trey. He pulls me forcefully in his direction, making me veer out of the path of the spixes as they pour around us, screaming like wildly fleeing people from a burning building. He positions me in front of him and urges me to run with his hand on my back toward a shallow ravine. When we reach it, Trey pushes me down into it, covering me with his body. Turning my face as a louder roar sounds, a huge, gold-and-gray-striped feline pounces on a spix a few feet from us, tearing the spix's neck open and shaking it wildly with its saber-toothed jaws.

I struggle to get Trey off me so that I can run. "Don't move," Trey breathes in my ear. I still as a low, long growl sounds behind us. A second cat, the size of an SUV, slinks nearer to the one eating the spix.

"They're going to fight over their dinner. When they do, we're going to get up and run to the trees to your left," Trey instructs me in a calm tone.

"Can't you just shoot them?" I ask, looking desperately at the recurve on the ground near us.

"No," he says grimly. "I can't kill saers with a recurve. Their pelts are too thick."

"You stupid Boy Scout!" I hiss at him in a low whisper. "You come out here with saers and bring a cap gun? You should break the rules just once, Trey. You might enjoy it!"

"You can give me your opinion if we make it to those trees. Now, let's move!" he says, hauling me up with an arm around my waist and pushing me to run ahead of him in the direction of the trees. Loud snarling sounds come from behind us as my heart drums in my ears. I stumble, but Trey's arm grasps my waist again, helping me regain my balance as we continue to retreat.

Making it to the trees, Trey pulls me behind a rock. Kneeling, we both pant, turning to see if we're being pursued. "They didn't notice us," Trey says, breathing hard next to me, sounding surprised.

"You sound like . . . you didn't think . . . we'd make it," I pant, turning toward him, feeling adrenaline coursing through me.

"I didn't," he admits, clutching me to his chest and hugging me tight. Kissing my hair near my temple, he whispers against it, "You're so brave."

"I'm not brave." I twist out of his embrace and turn to look at him. "I'm just going to hang on long enough to kill you."

"Is that right?" he asks, grinning in amusement.

"Yes, and that's the third time you've tried to kill me." I push against his chest as anger erupts in me. His grin falters as his eyebrows come together.

"Third time I've—what are you ranting about?" he asks, looking almost offended while holding me away from his chest so he can peer down at me.

I hold up one finger. "First, you nearly drowned me!" Another finger joins the first. "Then you made me run until I about died of heat stroke!" A third finger completes the trio. "And then—*then*, you take me across a field *teeming* with *saers* just *waiting* to eat us!" I rant at him, shaking in the aftermath of nearly being a meal for vicious saber-toothed tigers.

Trey's grin is totally gone now as his frown deepens. "I didn't try to drown you. I was the one who had to swim with your limp body in my arms and pound on your chest to get you to breathe," he counters, looking sullen. "And I didn't *make* you run; I stopped you when I noticed how red you were getting. And it was either take our chances with the saers by moving at night or let us all fall prey to the Alameeda. It was a calculated risk, one that has paid off so far," he says in a softer tone.

"So far? *So far? Trey!*" I yell at him. "What are our chances of actually making it to Rafe?" I ask, still breathing hard.

"With you, better than I thought. You keep up and you follow orders fairly well—when you choose to—and you're smart—when you're not trying to kill yourself with flowers and cranium-boring insects," he adds sarcastically.

"You thought that I was trying to kill myself with a flower?"

Amy A. Bartol

"What was I supposed to think? Znous are known to be swarming with turbine worms and when you put it next to your ear, I thought you had become suicidal."

"Trey, I thought that the Znou was beautiful and I wanted to keep it," I say, explaining myself to him. "I wasn't trying to kill myself. If I get suicidal, you'll know 'cuz I'll be dead. The only thing I'm feeling right now is *homicidal*, so watch your back."

Trey's smile comes back all of a sudden, like my anger toward him is amusing. "Why is it that you're only angry with me?" Trey asks, getting to his feet.

"What?" I ask sullenly.

"You aren't angry with Jax or Wayra, just me." He extends his hand to help me up.

Ignoring it, I get to my feet unassisted, dusting dried grass off me. "Because you're the one who's driving this mission. And maybe they're more likable." *Take that, egomaniac,* I think to myself, watching him stiffen as he picks up his gear.

"We need to move if we plan to locate your *likable* Cavars," Trey replies, looking stern.

"They're not mine. I plan on giving you all back when we get to Rafe." I follow him as he weaves a path through the trees.

"Why? We can help you—"

"Yeah!" I scoff. "You've helped enough. Any more help from you guys and I'll be dead."

"If it was not for us, you'd be with Kyon now, and you would be . . ." Trey doesn't finish.

"I'd be what?"

"Their prisoner," he says softly.

"Oh, as opposed to *your* prisoner," I say sarcastically. "I'm starting to think there isn't a very big difference."

"It is a big difference!" Trey replies, and he believes what he's telling me.

"Really? Why?"

"Because, they'd consider you a priestess. You'd never have a life of your own. Every decision would be made on your behalf, without your input. You'd be taken care of—worshipped almost, but never free—never able to live as you choose. You'd be their property. If they want to align with a family or a house, they can barter your services, or even you, to gain it."

"You mean, they'd treat me like chattel—a possession?" I ask, feeling ill.

"Precisely."

"What kind of services would they have me perform?"

"Depends on what you can do—what gifts you possess," he replies. "They're secretive about their priestesses, but word leaks out. It's said that some can move things with their minds."

"Like telekinesis?"

"Yes," he affirms, "and some are persuasive. They can make you believe any lie."

"Handy," I say, shivering.

"And some can see what the enemy is planning," he murmurs, unconsciously flexing his hand that was reattached. "A strategic edge."

"How do you combat something like that?"

"You make your plans and then, at the last second, you do something random," he says, looking grim. "Sometimes it works."

Paling, my head feels like it's spinning. "So they were bitter when my mother left their little party?"

"They threatened war," he replies. "I remember it; it was all anyone spoke of for a while."

"So my parents left because they were afraid of causing a war?"

"Maybe. Or maybe they wanted to protect something far more important to them."

"What?" I ask, not getting it.

"You. The Alameeda didn't know about you, and maybe your parents wanted to keep it that way. They could've stayed on Ethar—in Rafe. We don't turn over our citizens to anyone, not even the Alameeda, not even if they threatened the peace we enjoyed for more than thirty years."

"How did you know about me—where to find me?" Goose bumps rise on my arm and I rub them.

"I was sent—I'm special Cavar—elite branch. We were told of an important mission to Earth, and I volunteered."

"So, they knew about me—your superiors?"

Trey frowns. "You were not unexpected, if that's what you're asking. No one named you, but offspring was discussed," he admits, still frowning.

"What?"

"I felt then that they anticipated a child . . . that offspring was a . . . certainty. I was surprised when Jax was assigned to the mission."

"He wouldn't normally come?"

"Not to remand prisoners. It's like you were a special case from the start."

I shake my head. "I'm so dead," I whisper, feeling like I'm going to hyperventilate. Stopping in my tracks, I lean against a tree. "Trey, you have to take me back. I can't—I don't know how to survive here. You're talking about politics on a scale that I can't navigate. This isn't like dodging DSS or about how bad someone will hurt me in some foster care hell. This is—this is about whether or not I can tell if the next person I meet is going to want to kill me for what I can or cannot do, or what I might or might not know, or how I can influence . . ." My eyes fill up with tears. I squeeze my hands into fists, trying to force them back down.

Trey faces me. "Kricket," he says soothingly, "I can't take you back. They'll find you on Earth. You can't hide anymore. It would be like trying to dodge raindrops. You believe me, don't you?"

Wiping my cheek with my fist as a tear slides down it, I say ironically, "Of course I believe you. I'm a priestess. I know when you're lying. It's my special *gift*." My throat aches from trying to stop my tears.

His eyes go wide. "You'd know if I were lying?"

"Yes," I admit wearily, feeling completely depleted.

Trey's jaw tenses. "We'll keep that a secret just between you and me. Promise," Trey says adamantly, putting his hand on my hair and stroking it gently.

"Who am I gonna tell?"

"Promise," he says again. His hand moves to my cheek. He uses his thumb to wipe away a tear.

"Sure, I promise," I agree, feeling a surge of desire at his touch. I resist the urge to rest my cheek against his chest.

His thumb rubs my cheek again, lingering there before his hand drops from me. "We need to get you to Rafe. You're our citizen. We'll protect you," he says. "You know I'm not lying."

"You may not be lying, but you could be totally naïve, Trey."

His eyes soften. "So, you aren't infallible?" he asks with a smile in his tone.

"You wouldn't want to play poker against me; I'd know when you're bluffing."

"What's poker?"

"A card game," I reply, looking up at him. His hand brushes my hair again, tucking it behind my ear.

"Diverting?" He takes my hand in his.

"Lucrative . . . I can earn a stack doing it. I just can't let anyone suspect that I'm playing them, not the cards," I explain, allowing him to lead me as we begin to walk again.

"That sounds dangerous," he says.

"Depends on who gets played."

"Can you predict the outcome? What card will be laid next?" he asks, stepping over rocks and helping me traverse them.

"I don't know," I answer, thinking.

"You're young. I wonder what else you'll be able to do," he says offhandedly.

"You think there will be more?" I feel my heart race.

"I wouldn't bet against it," he answers, but seeing me drop my chin in fear, he quickly changes the subject. "We need to keep moving. Jax and Wayra will scout the territory west, looking to pick up our trail. They're probably ahead of us now, but when they don't find our trail, they'll double back."

Moving quietly together, Trey and I make it to a precipice where uneven, moss-covered limestone overlooks a spectacular view of a valley below. As we near the edge of the crag, my breath catches in my throat as decaying skyscrapers appear below us. Hollow frames with crushed and fallen-in rooflines scatter the horizon like some ancient civilization long abandoned.

"What's this?" I ask, feeling goose bumps rising on my arms.

"Amster. Some people refer to it now as the 'Amster Rushes' because the ruins look like the stems of plants growing in a wetland. It was a great city a century ago," he says.

"Looks like it has hit a recession," I reply, rubbing my arm with my hand.

"Its demise was not brought on by any economic force. It was a pandemic that destroyed this city—and just about every other city in Ethar a thousand years ago."

"A plague?" I repeat, as a shiver runs through me while I follow him along the rocky path.

"Yes, things changed here very quickly. It's reported that the virus, named 'Black Math,' developed into a pandemic in less than two rotations. Incubation of the disease was rapid—less than a rotation from contracting it until it annihilated the person's vital organs."

"How many people did it kill?" I ask, horrified.

"Billions. I don't know the exact death toll, but it nearly wiped out the entire population."

My jaw hangs open for a moment. "It almost killed everyone?"

Trey nods sadly. "We have a cure for it now, and we have laws."

"Laws?" I ask, not knowing what laws could do to stop a pandemic.

"Yes. We strive to maintain a balance on Ethar now. We try to control ourselves. We don't pollute the environment because that could cause microorganisms to mutate and wipe us out."

"You think something like that can be controlled through environmental precautions?"

"It's a start," he replies. "In the wake of the pandemic, the five houses of Ethar developed from the survivors."

"What are the names of the five houses?" I see light dawning on the horizon and shining on the rusty skeletons of the Amster Rushes.

"Rafe, Alameeda, Comantre, Peney, and Wurthem," he states, pulling his night-vision glasses from his face.

"Who's the most powerful?" I ask, seeing him grin. I pull my glasses off as well, handing them back to Trey, who pauses to put them in his bag.

"You have to ask?"

"I mean, besides us?" I roll my eyes. He pauses, looking at me and taking my hand again.

His smile deepens. "Finally," Trey mutters.

"Hmm?" I ask, confused as he squeezes my hand.

"You said, 'us,'" Trey replies, his eyes softening in the corners.

"I did?" I stiffen. "Well, I meant to say, 'besides Rafe.'"

"But you said 'us' instead," he replies triumphantly, causing a small smile to twist my lips. We begin walking again while his smile only broadens.

"Fine," I mutter, *"besides us."*

"Alameeda is as large as *us* and their technology is keeping pace with ours. The other houses are smaller. They're all powerful in their own ways, though."

"So, our ally is Comantre. Who aligns with Alameeda?"

Trey's eyebrows rise. "You don't act your age. You ask questions that I'd expect from someone older than you."

I wrinkle my nose. "Really? Don't be too awed by the profundity of my mind. I just find it important to know where everyone stands. I hate stepping on land mines. It's messy."

"The Alameeda are aligned with the Wurthem clan," he replies, looking serious. "Making them the largest in numbers."

"What about Peney?"

"They like to remain neutral."

"Ahh, they're Switzerland," I muse. "You said that together Alameeda and Wurthem are the largest? How large?" I wonder, trying to gauge whether we're talking a population like China or something like the U.S.

"Together, they have a population a little smaller than Chicago," Trey replies, and then he pauses when I stop walking beside him.

"What?" I breathe.

"Alameeda has almost a million citizens—Wurthem is a couple of hundred thousand short of that. They're big, but—"

"Trey, if they're the biggest, then that means there are less than five million people on Ethar," I breathe. "That's—"

"Black Math," he replies grimly. "Now you see why it's important that we don't allow humans to become aware that we exist? We have more advanced technology than humans, but they'd have sheer numbers."

"And your defense department—Skye—doesn't like those odds?"

"No, especially not when coupled with Alameeda's recent aggression. We don't need problems with humans, too."

"Alameeda is causing trouble?"

"The Alameeda Brotherhood is no longer adhering to our global treaties and laws. You just witnessed their airspace violations firsthand."

"So . . . the Brotherhood is like Skye?"

"Not exactly. Rafe divides power mainly between Skye and our monarch, who is the Regent. That's not the case with the Brotherhood; they're the ruling faction. Period. There are at any one time around twenty males from the most powerful Alameeda families who comprise the Brotherhood.

"Just males?" I ask, wrinkling my nose when Trey nods. "I'm annoyed already."

"Really? Because it gets worse. These males are bred for the Brotherhood. Whenever a brother is lost, they meet to choose candidates to fill the vacancy."

"How do they choose?"

"It's a secret," Trey smirks.

"And the priestesses?"

"They're owned by the Brotherhood—controlled by them. Most are given to a Brother as a consort—a wife."

"She has no say in it?" I ask in disgust.

"No."

We walk together in silence; I'm trying to process what I've just learned. Hearing moving water ahead, the rocks twist around a bend, exposing a small, shimmering waterfall. Water is collecting in a pool nearby before it flows to the edge of the stone, pouring off the ledge, creating another waterfall to the valley floor far below.

"We'll break here," Trey says, pulling me along to the water's edge.

"Is this water safe to wash in?" I ask, eyeing the water suspiciously.

Grinning, Trey pulls off his shirt and runs toward the water, jumping in and disappearing in its depths. Surfacing, he says, "It's perfect."

Tentatively, I walk to the edge, dipping my foot in. It's just cool enough to be refreshing. Easing into the water, I grip the rocks near me, leaning my head back to submerge my hair, rinsing it off.

Splashing water on my face, I try to wash the dirt from it, using my hands.

Peeking at Trey, I see that he has his back to me, running his hands through his hair. Beads of water are trickling down his skin, flowing over the sleek contours from his broad back to his narrow waist. Feeling heat creep into my cheeks and spread throughout my body, I forget what I'm doing for a second.

"Kricket?" Trey asks, making my eyes shoot to his face as he gazes at me over his shoulder.

"Hmm?" I feel my face flush hotter.

"I asked you if you're hungry," he says, looking puzzled.

"Uh . . . yeah," I reply, turning and wading out of the water, while running my fingers through my hair to smooth the tangles in it. I'm beginning to feel like a crunchy granola girl. It's not a look that I favor.

Going to his pack, Trey returns with his bedroll and spreads it on the ground. He hands me a protein bar. I scowl at him, watching him smile. "What?" he asks before saying, "Jax and Wayra have all the good food. I just have these."

I sit down next to him on his bedroll. Taking a bite of my protein bar, I can't help cringing. "You know what I miss?" I ask.

"No," he replies, lying back with his arm behind his head, chewing.

"Pizza—and not that crappy New York style pizza. No, I'm talking Chicago deep-dish. The kind that's so thick, it's impossible to eat more than one piece."

"Talk to Wayra. He ate a large one of those by himself," Trey says with a smile.

"Yeah?" I ask, amazed.

"Yeah," he says softly as I lay back next to him.

Yawning, I eat the rest of my disgusting breakfast and accept the minty leaf from Trey to cleanse the taste from my mouth.

"Is a large pizza as big as an entire venish?" I close my eyes wearily.

"No," Trey murmurs with a smile in his voice.

"Oh," I reply before falling asleep with Trey's warm body next to mine.

Chapter 10

Transport

"Kricket," a soft whisper breathes in my ear as a masculine cheek grazes mine.

A warm hand strokes my side, and I mumble, "Sleepy." Turning over, I snuggle against him, feeling his chest resting against my back, spooning me.

"I should get hazard pay for this," Trey groans as he dislodges his arm that's trapped beneath me. Pulling away from me, he sits up.

"You're looking alert, sir." Jax's voice is full of mirth. Opening my eyes, I see Jax and Wayra standing beside the water, watching Trey and me.

"Took you long enough," Trey mutters sullenly, not getting up. I sit up next to him, rubbing my eyes and smiling at Jax and Wayra.

"You didn't get eaten by the saer," Wayra says, sounding jazzed about it.

"That's debatable," Trey replies next to me, frowning.

"You get much sleep, sir?" Jax grins.

"No, something crept into my bones—my blood."

"Are you sick?" I ask, concerned. His frown deepens, but he doesn't answer.

"Sir, go walk it off," Jax says sympathetically. "We'll feed the little silver-haired siren."

"Yeah . . . okay," Trey mutters, getting up and walking away from us.

"Is he okay?" I ask Jax, completely confused.

"He's a *very* healthy male." Jax comes nearer to me and hands me breakfast.

"Thanks." I accept a quiche from Jax. "How did you get away from the saers?" I ask and take a bite, watching for Trey to come back.

"The spixes forced us to the opposite side of the field from you," Wayra says. "We saw you break for the trees! Kricket, that took courage!"

"That wasn't courage. I was following orders," I reply.

"You should join the Cavars." Wayra holds up his wrist horizontally, with his hand balled in a fist, like a weird salute.

Mimicking him and watching him grin, I hear Jax ask Wayra, "Can you imagine her in our regiment?"

Wayra frowns. "On second thought, it's too dangerous for you, Kricket."

"Did I just get dishonorably discharged?" I grin and finish my quiche.

"No, you're just, you know . . . small."

"You keep saying that," I reply, rolling my eyes like he's crazy.

Snapping branches make us all look toward the trees. "We've got Comantre Syndics—units on our eight and thirteen," Trey says, creeping near us. I stiffen, seeing Wayra and Jax jump to their feet.

Trey heads directly for his gear. He pulls out clothing and then shrugs into a long, tunic-style jersey that reaches to his thighs. The fabric is like supple leather in drab green, with black inset darts running through the material on either side. As the tunic falls into place, it makes him look like a modern, urban version of a medieval Knights Templar. The hood attached to the tunic is black, and it's sleeker than a medieval cowl, more chic. The sleeves look like a lightweight form of chainmail, hugging the curves of his arms that are protected by more black fabric. His black pants are overlaid with the same type of armor. Trey pushes his hood back and turns to me in an assessing way.

He takes another uniform from his gear and brings it to me saying, "Put this on."

Wayra and Jax have dressed in uniforms, too. I start to pull it over my head. "No," Trey orders, "We need to get rid of your human clothes. We're not giving them any information about our mission. Don't speak unless I say it's all right."

I nod, blushing and turning away from him. Taking off my T-shirt, I hand it to Trey before pulling the tunic on over my head. This one is dove-gray with deep, intricate crimson lines running like darts through the torso of the garment on either side. Soft sleeves that lack armor are attached to it, making it more of a dress uniform than a combat one. The tunic reaches below my knees, making me look waifish.

I unbutton my jeans and step out of them. I toss them to Trey who throws them in the water. They float away and disappear over the edge of the cliff. Pushing and rolling the blousy sleeves, I allow Trey to wrap a crimson scarf around my waist like a belt, cinching the garment to me more securely. Stepping back from me, Trey's frown deepens.

"Well, that didn't work," Wayra says next to him, looking at me critically.

"What do you mean?" I try to see what I look like.

"He was trying to make you look like you've spent your entire life on Ethar."

"At least her boots cover her toenails," Jax says under his breath.

"Try putting up the cowl," Wayra suggests, and Trey flips up the hood, covering my hair with the soft gray leather.

"No, it looks like we're trying to hide her hair," Trey says, flipping the hood back down.

"We *are* trying to hide her hair. It makes her look Alameeda."

"We'll be treated with suspicion no matter what," Trey says. "No one speaks of the mission. We spotted Alameeda violating the treaties while on holiday in the Forests of Omnicron. We are seeking safe passage as citizens of Rafe."

Only moments later, a unit of well-armed, enormous soldiers crash through the brush, pointing weapons that look like tricked-out machine guns at us and shouting orders for us to surrender and kneel. Trey, Wayra, and Jax slowly drop to their knees, putting their hands behind their heads.

Weapons swing toward me, training on my heart with blue beams of light. I raise my chin, balling my hands into fists and putting them on my hips.

Scowling at Trey, I say between my teeth, "Honey! Are you going to let them speak to me like that?"

Wayra and Jax's eyes become rounder. Trey's eyes narrow as he says in a soft tone, "Kricket, these are Comantre soldiers—"

"I see them, and they're ruining my holiday, sweetness," I whine in a grating tone, trying to keep my hands clenched so no one sees them shaking. "Tell them that you told me that if I agreed to a commitment ceremony with you, that you'd take me to the Forest of Omnicron where I could see wild saers and herds of spixes!" I sneer at Trey, gesturing with a flick of my hand toward the soldiers who look stupefied in front of us. "*Then*, you can tell them how *your* men lost all *my* luggage! Just because they saw some Alameeda thingies flying around."

Turning to the soldiers in front of me, their pure pleasure at the spectacle I'm creating gives me the courage to continue. "They lost *everything! Look at me!* I have to wear his clothes," I complain, pulling at the beautiful tunic like it's a rag.

"Kricket—" Trey tries again, but I cut him off.

"I'm telling my father—you know how important he is in Rafe. He's going to be *very* upset." I burst into tears and hide my face in my hands.

"Kitten—" Trey plays along.

"Don't you 'Kitten' me!" I hiss, taking my hands from my face. "I just want to go back to Rafe!" I stamp my foot. I peek at my tunic and notice blue laser beams are no longer dotting the front.

One of the soldiers walks over to Trey, motioning for him to get up. Trey rises, along with Wayra and Jax, who are averting their eyes from me. The soldier asks Trey in a low tone, "Is this your first consort?"

"We're from Rafe. We only get one consort," Trey responds sourly, scowling at me.

"She's part Alameeda," the soldier says. It's not a question.

"Yes, she is."

"Only the good part!" I sneer at them, like a true waspish princess.

Hearing the Comantre soldiers cracking up, the one that seems to be in charge says in a low tone to Trey, "You poor wacker," while looking at me and shaking his head. "You can't commit to the young ones, no matter how beautiful they are."

"I know, but look at her," Trey says, gazing at me like I'm the most beautiful creature he's ever set eyes on.

"Well, that's the trap, isn't it? No one told you that they change the instant you commit, did they?" He smirks. Trey shakes his head. "Ah well . . . you'll have to make it up to her then. No going back now."

"No going back now," Trey agrees, almost to himself. I make a derisive sound, crossing my arms and looking at the sky.

"So you've had a hard go of it on your holiday?" the soldier asks.

"You could say that. We spotted Alameeda violating airspace. It made us cut our plans short. Our transport out isn't supposed to arrive for another three days. Can't understand what they were doing there."

"Yeah, we saw them, too," the soldier says. "That's why we've doubled our patrols on the border. They haven't acted aggressively toward us, but knowing them, that could change in an instant."

"Trey Allairis of Rafe," Trey introduces himself with a nod.

"Gideon Santis of Comantre," the soldier replies by way of an introduction, inclining his head. "Looks like you could use a transport."

"We would be in your debt," Trey replies, smiling gratefully.

"We could take you back to Comantre Crosses. You'll have to arrange something from there."

"We have friends there. It should be no trouble arranging something."

"You have identification?" Gideon asks, narrowing his green eyes at Trey.

"We do, but my consort has lost hers with her gear," Trey lies easily, while producing metal tags that he detaches from the wide black belt on his waist.

Examining and scanning the tags with a handheld device, Gideon nods before handing them back and saying, "Well, come with us then." He pauses, looking at me while shaking his head and muttering, "You poor wacker."

Wayra and Jax collect the gear while Trey walks to my side, putting his arm around my shoulder and pulling me to his chest. Pressing my face to his uniform, I cry real tears, feeling my body shaking against his.

He whispers in my ear, "What did you call me?"

Searching my mind, I respond, "Sweetness?"

"No, before that." I can hear the grin in his voice.

"Honey?" I reply, sniffling and pulling back to look in his eyes, seeing them soften as he looks at me.

"Yes, honey; you'll have to tell me later what that is," he says softly, pulling me back to his chest and rubbing my back soothingly. "Please let me take it from here. If you say more, your human upbringing may slip out."

Nodding, I whisper, "I'm all tapped out. It's your show now."

"Good . . . I think."

"We have an ALV on the ridge," Gideon says, beckoning us to follow him. Trey nods, leaving his arm around my shoulder and pressing me to his side as we walk with the soldiers.

An enormous, black, bullet-shaped ship, the length of three El cars and the width of two, is poised on a rocky ledge. Its large cargo door is open on one side, acting as a ramp to enter the vehicle. Jump seats line the walls on either side of the ship. Leading me to one, Trey indicates that I should sit.

Gazing around like a tourist, I sit in the seat. Instantly, belts crisscross my chest, pinning me to the seat back. Gasping loudly, I look down wildly at the belts. I can see that I've drawn everyone's attention when I look up again.

"She's used to Hover Crims," Trey says, excusing my behavior to the Comantre soldiers. Sitting down next to me, the belts on his seat instantly wrap around him, securing him to the seat back.

"Oh," I say with a nervous smile. When I begin to wring my hands, Trey covers them with his own, squeezing gently. Jax sits on my other side, and Wayra sits directly across from me, like sentries.

Gideon watches Trey and me from his seat across from Trey's. His eyes rest on our hands clasped together. He's studying me with a fascinated expression, like he's never seen anyone who looks like me before. "You're such an odd mix—Alameeda and Rafe . . . almost impossible to believe."

"Her mother was an ambassador of Alameeda, and her father is royalty. He always says that he's never met a more intriguing woman in all of his rotations than her mother," Trey replies easily. "They committed to each other, and they now live in the Valley of Thistle."

"I hear that Thistle is grand," Gideon says while still studying me. "They hold the spix races there, don't they?" he asks.

"They do. You should come with your family. We'd love to host you," Trey says, wrapping his arm around my shoulder familiarly as I lean my cheek against his chest. "Wouldn't we, Kitten?"

"Mm," I nod. "That sounds like a dream."

"Is that where you held your commitment ceremony? In Thistle, Kricket?" Gideon asks me kindly.

"Yes, Thistle. It's very lovely this time of . . . uh, now," I end, aware that I almost said "year." Trying to cover my near slip, I add, "You know, I studied human culture; it's a little obsession of mine, so I wanted to model my commitment ceremony after a traditional human wedding."

"Really?" Gideon's rust-colored eyebrows rise in question. "What did you do?"

"Oh, well, it was magical, wasn't it, Trey?" I ask him, peering up at his eyes and seeing him nod slowly. "We wanted to keep it simple, so we hosted it in the backyard of our estate. My mother said that the gazebo in the garden would be a perfect place to say the vows. We decorated it with wildflowers, but we didn't use any Znous because they have turbine worms in them."

Several of the soldiers sitting near us laugh, like I made a joke. Realizing that they're listening too, I blush a little, before continuing. "I wore a white gown, and Trey wore a black suit, and we wrote our own vows to each other."

"What do humans promise, when they say their vows?" he asks, seeming to be enjoying my story.

"Ah, well, traditionally, the bride—that's the female, would promise to love, honor, cherish, and obey her consort, but Trey knows I'm *way* too independent to *obey* all the time." I hear the soldiers around me cracking up again, probably remembering the scene by the waterfall. Looking next to me, I see Jax trying hard to keep a straight face.

Straightening in my seat and seeing the cargo door closing, blocking out any hope of escaping, I continue, "Trey knows what an oddball I am—how I don't seem to think like other females my age. So instead of the traditional vows, I told him that when we first met, I felt like a butterfly trapped in a net."

The door closes with a loud thump. I close my eyes briefly before opening them and gently laying my hand on Trey's, trying to cover the fact that fear is making me shake again.

"But I told him that the more time that I spent with him, the more I began to realize how much he means to me. I told him that since it seems to be my destiny to dodge raindrops, I was grateful to be dodging them with him. So, I promised him that it would always be his name on my mind when I start my rotation and when I go to bed each evening and every quiet moment in between. It will be his name savored on my lips, stretched across my heart, worshipped by my body, and branded in my mind until death do us part and forever after that."

I feel Trey take my hand as he raises it to his lips, kissing my fingers gently.

"Do ya have a sister?" the soldier with the fiery-red hair near Wayra asks, getting nudges and laughs from his friends around him. I shake my head, feeling a blush stain my cheeks right before the entire compartment lurches upward like an insane carnival ride, making me feel like my stomach dropped to my feet.

"Ugh," I groan, closing my eyes.

"What's wrong?" Gideon asks with concern.

"Nothing, I just hate that part," I reply, trying to make it sound like I've done this before. Then, the compartment walls begin contorting, caving in on us like a garbage compactor. My heart lurches into my throat, feeling my seat move forward toward Wayra and Gideon, like some ugly, funhouse ride. It stops a short distance in front of Wayra's seat. He winks at me, and my eyes shoot from his as a rumble like thunder shakes the craft. I pull my hand from Trey's, gripping the straps of the belts crisscrossing my body.

When the noise dissipates, Trey whispers in my ear, "This is normal."

"For who?"

Hearing his deep laugh, I clench my teeth. As I glare up at him, he's watching me with a sexy glint in his eyes that I haven't seen there before. My body reacts to his sultry stare, as a heightening awareness of him makes my skin feel electric.

Feeling the craft rocket forward, it's only a few minutes before the ALV begins a rapid descent. Like an elevator whose cable had been cut, we plummet toward the ground; the vehicle trembles and shudders from the velocity and force being exerted on it. I squeeze my eyes shut, and Trey rests his enormous hand on my thigh, distracting me momentarily from the fact that we're going to be flattened when we hit the ground. Peeking at Trey, I try to pry his hand from my leg, but he's not letting me.

The craft distorts again, widening and taking me back away from Wayra, who winks at me again as the wall and seats straighten out to their original positions. As we touch down, I notice that I have a death grip on Trey's finger, one of the ones resting on my thigh. Easing my hand away, I say quietly in Trey's ear, "Do you mind?"

"Do I mind, what?"

"Your hand is on my thigh. You're touching me. Isn't touching bad?" I ask, remembering his etiquette lesson.

"You're my consort. I'm supposed to touch you," he replies in a low tone, his cheek brushing mine. Heat flushes through me at the caress.

Glancing at the soldiers around me, they're all watching us like cats watch a birdcage. "You don't have to oversell it."

"Hmm?" Trey smiles at me as the cargo door opens, releasing air and pressure from the interior of the craft.

"Shh," I hush him, holding my breath in anticipation of the first sight of my new civilization.

Chapter 11
Comantre Crosses

As the ramp deploys from the ALV, I scan the exterior, seeing that we're in some sort of military compound. The first thing I notice, stepping out of the transport, is that the air is cooler. The sticky, tropical atmosphere that I've grown accustomed to in the last few days has lost the sweltering edge. It's like this area is climate controlled, not too hot or too cold or too humid.

Although the weather is temperate, the very air is electric with activity as soldiers file here and there on their way to whatever duty they have to fulfill. Enormous vehicles with long clawlike, robotic arms are off-loading cargo from airships in the same area where we are debarking. Facing the gaping, retractable door to the fortress, a small shiver escapes me. The architecture is sleek and high-tech, modern with old world accents like space station meets medieval gothic fortress. Windows, like arrow slits, line the exterior walls, forming crosses in the perfectly mortared, metallic gray façade. Defensible parapets tower above our heads, patrolled by more well-armed Comantre Syndics.

Pressing nearer to Trey's side, I walk with him through the bay doors and into a military checkpoint. Mounted guns on the walls raise threateningly the instant I approach the threshold to the interior. Blue pinpoints of light dot me again while flashing lights begin to whirl around as loud, terrifying sirens blare throughout the area. I freeze when an automated voice rises above the din, saying: "Unauthorized personnel present in bay Acrom, Peston, Florna-Zero, Nine, Nine, Hertza." Trey steps in front of the blue dots, shielding me from them.

Gideon immediately barks out, "Authorize visitor." Looking at my ashen face as the sirens cease and the guns idle again, he says, "I apologize. I should've alerted them to you prior to landing."

Smiling grimly, I try to pull off a casual shrug. "I get that a lot."

"I would wager that you do," Gideon replies, grinning.

Frowning, Trey asks, "Are you okay?" When I nod, straightening my shoulders, he reaches out, taking my hand and holding it tight.

Ushering us through the main gate, Gideon leads us down wide hallways with illuminated floors and ceilings. Passing by bustling soldiers, I'm beginning to feel uncomfortably like a carnival sideshow freak. Everyone is giving me a second look, even the super-tall, willowy females who are nearly as statuesque as their male counterparts.

Pausing at an administration desk and glancing around, I see that everything is big, not just the people. Chairs are taller and wider, tables are higher, and door latches are mounted so that I'd have to reach up to open them. Listening absently, Trey begins answering a barrage of questions put to him by the Comantre soldier in charge, as Jax stands by us, filling in when asked a direct question. Wayra is lingering on my other side, staring down anyone who ventures too close to me.

Seeing that my job here is to keep my mouth shut, I study the females milling around. They look like tall, exotic birds; their limbs are exaggerated and lithe. Some have long, rust-colored hair, like Gideon, but others have hair of varying shades between light brown and tawny. No one has platinum hair like mine. Neither do they have dark hair like Wayra, Jax, and Trey. Eye color is different, too. Comantres that I can see have varying shades of green and blue eyes. No violet eyes, like us. I'm realizing that I'm like a genetic anomaly here. I'm short, blond, and violet eyed: freakish.

"Wayra, am I a freak?" I ask him softly, seeing soldiers by the far door eyeing me.

"Yes," he answers honestly.

"What makes me a freak?" I see him smile.

"You're different. You look like the enemy, Alameeda, but . . ."

"But what?" I look up at his face.

"But any male soldier here would have a pinup of you in his footlocker, if he could," he says with a cheeky grin.

"What? Why?" I feel my face go red at the thought of them hanging a picture of me in their lockers.

"You don't know?" Wayra asks, his eyes going wide along with his grin.

"No!"

"You have dangerous curves—you are very female in all the right places, more hips, more glutes, breasts," he rattles off, breaking down my physical attributes and making me grit my teeth. "You have a beautiful face, too. And the way you move—stealthy, like a saer, is *so very* polar."

"You like my swagger?"

"You have presence—magnetism," he looks me over from head to foot. "And that part you said on the transport, about worshipping your mate with your body, I doubt that there was a male there not jealous of Trey in that moment."

Seeing a Comantre soldier slow down, staring at me as he's moving past, Wayra says, "Keep walking."

I feel a hand on my elbow, and Trey says, "We're being detained, Kitten, until we can arrange for your identification. They've offered to give us space to rest and clean up."

"Oh," I see soldiers collecting in front of us. "That's kind of them. I need a sho—to clean up." I stop myself before I say "shower" because I have no idea what cleaning up here entails.

We're led down a labyrinth of hallways until we finally make it to a room. "This room is for the committed couple. Your men can lodge across the hall," a soldier says, ushering Trey and me into the room. "The doors will be locked for security purposes. If you need anything, there is a com link by the door."

"Thank you for the accommodations," Trey replies graciously. "As soon as I can arrange for identification for my consort, I will notify you."

"Do you need a communicator?"

"No, I have my own with me," Trey says with a smile. The soldier nods, gesturing to Jax and Wayra to enter their room, before allowing a door to drop from the ceiling, locking us in. Studying the room, I see it contains a bay of bunk beds built into the wall on one side and a small commissary and dining area on the other side. The far wall has a window like the crossed arrow slits that I'd seen earlier.

Walking to the window, I gaze around at the world outside, feeling my heart beat wildly in my chest. We're in a city, but it's like no city I've seen on Earth. There are streets of green, made of well-manicured grass. Vehicles like hovercrafts speed along the thoroughfares near the ground; some look like elongated hover cars, and some like small versions of Stealth Fighters. Glorified one-passenger vehicles that resemble motorcycles are speeding by faster than any I'm accustomed to.

Pressing my hand against the window, I see clean sidewalks of cobblestone that are alive with moss, and small white flowers like a sprinkling of confetti, paralleling the grassy streets. Residences that resemble brownstones line the sidewalks, with slate steps that lead up to enormous double doors. These buildings are three and four stories high. But this is just one level of the city. Another tier is over this one, like a graduated step; it rises above the street as aircraft zip past, adhering to traffic laws that are completely unfamiliar to me.

This second level appears to be residences as well. Heliports line the front stoops of these residences. Rooftop gardens rise like lush oases on this tier, making them look enchanted and unreal. Mesh, metallic sidewalks, like catwalks, line this level and are equipped with intricate wrought-iron railings to prevent someone from toppling over the edge accidentally.

Looking up, I see at least four more graduated tiers of buildings and traffic towering over my head. Goose bumps rise on my arms at the unfamiliarity of it. I squeak as Trey's arms wrap around my waist, pulling me against his chest. Leaning down, he nuzzles my ear while whispering in it, "We're being monitored . . . you're still my consort."

"Where?" I ask, while turning in his arms and wrapping my hands around the back of his neck seductively.

Leaning closer to my face, his cheek brushes mine, and my skin ignites. "Thermal detectors on the wall near the door." His lips trail featherlight kisses over the column of my neck. "Audio in the vents, digital in the lights."

"Ohhh," I breathe, but I'm not sure if it's in response to his kisses or to what he just said. "What should we do?"

"We might need to sell it a bit more. I think they're having a problem believing our match," he murmurs between kisses as he's working his way over the contour of my cheek.

"Why?" I feel breathless.

"I'm a Cavar and you're half Alameeda," he replies right before his lips meet mine for the first time. His kiss is soft and sweet at first, just a teasing of his lips, eliciting small shivers of desire from me. But in a few moments, it changes, becoming heated and urgent. Responding instinctually to his touch, desire is rising fiercely within me, and with it a ripple of fear is running through me as well because I've never felt passion like this before. It's burning me, consuming me, and leaving almost no room for thought.

Picking me up off my feet, Trey's lips find mine again as he carries me across the room to the attached bathroom. He shuts the door by pressing a button on the frame before he sets me on my feet, reaching into a glass enclosure and turning on the jets of water. Steam immediately pours from the enclosure while Trey unties my belt, letting the red scarf sink to the floor. Tugging the tunic over my head, I wait silently for him to kiss me again, but instead, he's looking around at the ceiling and shoving me into the hot shower.

Although getting pounded by jets of water feels pretty good right now, it's not nearly as good as kissing Trey. I poke my head out of the shower, raising my eyebrow in question. Trey groans like he's in pain, mumbling, "You're so polar, Kitten . . . yes, do that—ahh, that's so good." Leaning against a small vanity, he crosses his arms over his chest, averting his eyes from me. He's creating an audio picture for those who are monitoring us.

My face turns several shades of red. I groan too, but mine is in embarrassment. *He was only kissing you for the cameras,* I think, feeling stupid and . . . disappointed.

Biting my bottom lip, I close the door between us, letting the steam make it opaque. Then, I close my eyes, groaning louder than before as water cascades down my hair. "Ohhh, Trey . . . *Trey!*" I call out in a raspy tone, like I've heard Bridget do in the middle of the night when Eric sleeps over. Finding a dispenser of shampoo, I pour some in my hand, lathering it in my hair. Eliciting what I hope is a sensual sounding gasp, I let my voice strain as I murmur, "Ahh . . ." Rinsing my hair, I try the other dispenser that smells like coconut. Hoping that it's conditioner, I gasp a few times breathlessly. Taking off my undergarments and cleaning them with shampoo, I sling them over the top of the shower to dry off.

Hearing Trey groan with desire, and then say, "Kricket," a shiver of raw desire filters through me again harder, stunning me with its force and making me feel like he has touched me. My trembling fingers touch the glass between us. "Kricket." He says my name again, and it has an even more powerful effect on me.

I pull my fingers away from the glass like he has burned me as I bite my bottom lip again. "Trey," I call out, letting my voice become hoarse and raspy as I lean back against the tile wall, "I need you . . ." I trail off because what I just said sounds too honest, even to my own ears. The water is the only sound that greets me as I listen for his response. Thinking that Trey might have left, I crack the door, allowing steam to pour out of the shower.

Trey is leaning against the wall of the bathroom, looking like he's in pain. Sweat has collected on his brow as he's staring at me with dark eyes. "Can you hand me a towel?" I mouth with no sound, so I won't be overheard.

Just staring at me, like he has no idea what I just asked him, his eyes dart to the wall of the shower. Glancing at myself, I see the outline of my body clearly through the glass. "Oh!" I say, pulling back and just reaching my hand out for a towel. Feeling the cloth touch my hand, I pull it in, wrapping it around myself before stepping out.

Ignoring me, Trey steps into the shower before flinging his clothes over the door and turning the water to cold. The steam soon dissipates and I have to avert my eyes from him because the shower becomes completely transparent again.

Finding a hairbrush on the shelf, I use it, pulling out all the snarls from days of being dragged through the Forest of Omnicron. I examine my reflection in the mirror for the first time in days. I can't believe that I look almost the same. Apart from a tan, I can't even tell that I've just been pulled through the universe to another one where I'm the enemy to just about everyone, and the only three people I know just want to hand me over to someone else.

I hear the water turn off before Trey steps out and takes a towel from the shelf behind me. Wrapping it around his hips, he touches the wall behind me. Air begins blowing at him from above, drying his hair. "How did you . . . ?" I begin to ask, but I stop when he lifts my hand to touch the wall where he'd pressed it a moment ago. Air begins blowing down on me from above. My eyes widen, looking at the point on the wall where all the magic happens and not seeing anything to indicate what it is.

Trey's arms go around me from behind. He nuzzles my neck near my ear, and I melt against his chest. "I need to make a connection," he whispers in my ear. "Do you think you can refrain from touching anything or looking like you don't know how anything here works?" His eyes scan my face.

I stiffen in his arms, realizing he's just acting. "I'll try not to be a tourist," I say, straightening and feeling insulted, not even sure what he means by "make a connection."

"Good, just stay near me, and don't be like you usually are."

Narrowing my eyes at him, I whisper, "How am I usually?"

"Unpredictable," he replies, holding my hand and leading me out of the bathroom. He collects something that looks like a phone from his gear, then goes to the bottom berth and lies on it, pulling me down next to him. As I snuggle against him and rest my head on his chest, he says in my ear, "I'm going to take your picture."

He holds the phonelike communicator away at arm's length and pushes a button to snap my picture. He brings the communicator back down and looks at the photo of the two of us. We look like lovers. "Send optical to seven Key Griffin Indie. Message: Trey Allairis requests identification for Kricket Allairis, travel tags for transport to Rafe—Isle of Skye to Violet Hill, to the Valley of Thistle. Current position Comantre Base—Comantre Crosses."

Dropping his hand, he rests the communicator on his chest, rubbing his eyes with his other hand. "Are you hungry?" Trey asks me wearily.

"No, I could use some clothes, and, maybe you can show me how to . . . I don't know—there was no toilet in the bathroom," I whisper in his ear.

His arms wrap around me and pull me closer. He groans. "How are you going to survive, Kricket? You don't even know the basics. Any child knows more than you do!" he whispers harshly, like he's angry about it.

"I'm not a child," I hiss in a whisper. "You only have to show me once and I'll get it. You know what? Forget it. I'll figure it out."

I pull away from him and rise from the bunk. I walk back to the bathroom, dropping the door shut by pressing a small button on the frame like I'd seen Trey do. "Okay, if I were a toilet, where would I hide?" I whisper to myself, wondering why Trey is being a *total* knob knocker. I touch the wall, and the hair dryer turns on again. Trying another spot, a heat lamp comes on, too. Touching the wall again, as the need to find the right spot is becoming more and more of a priority, makes a compartment open.

Picking up a silver box that resembles a viewfinder, I put it to my eyes, pressing the button. A click sounds and dust flashes in my eyes. Feeling blinded, I pull it back from my face and glance in the mirror. The viewfinder has applied some makeup to my eyes. Studying the viewfinder, I gasp as the door opens and Trey frowns at me.

He pulls me gently from the bathroom. "Kricket, this is the lavare and this"—he steers me to a door next to it, pressing the button on the frame to open it—"is the commodus. What happened to your eyes?" he asks, still looking irritated. "They're all red."

"I think I was supposed to close my eyes before I pushed the button on this thingy." I hand the automatic makeup artist to him. Entering the commodus and finding a toilet, I quickly close the door and use it. Flushing the toilet, an automated feminine voice speaks to me from above, "You are calcium deficient. Please acquire a calcium supplement at the commissary."

"That's *totally* creepy," I breathe, washing my hands. Rewrapping the towel around me, I step out of the commodus, finding Trey already dressed in his uniform again.

"I've ordered you some clothes," he says, eyeing my towel.

"How?"

"Com link," he states, pointing toward the door.

"Of course," I reply, trying to cover my ignorance.

"Here," Trey hands me a paper-thin square.

I look at it in the palm of my hand and don't know what it's for. "Thanks, you shouldn't have gotten me this cute, little piece of paper. I didn't get you anything."

"Just eat the calcium, please," he says, ignoring my sarcasm.

"Oh, you heard that?" I'm embarrassed that my calcium deficiency was broadcast by a creepy fem-bot.

"I'm a chameleon. I'm always listening." A reluctant smile twists his lips.

I smile, too. "I'm rubbing off on you."

"You're doing something to me," he agrees. "Kricket, I—" he begins to say something, but the door opens to reveal a Comantre soldier waiting outside the entrance to our room. Trey retrieves a package from him, bringing it to me as the door closes behind him again.

"Here, Kricket," he says, handing me clothes bundled in tissue paper.

Taking the clothes from him, my fingers dance over the soft, silky fabric. "It's been a long time since anyone bought me clothes," I murmur, hugging them to me. "I'll pay you back." I hate the thought of owing anyone anything, and I especially hate the thought of owing Trey anything.

"You're my consort," Trey says, giving me a meaningful look. "What's mine is yours."

I close my eyes briefly, knowing I just messed up. "Of course," I reply, trying to cover up for my slip. Tentatively, I rise up on my tiptoes and give him a light kiss on the cheek. "Thank you."

Turning, I go to the lavare to change. After I unwrap the package, I lift a pair of form-fitting black pants and hold them up to me. I pull them on, and they fit as if they're tailored to my exact measurements. Next, I slip on an ultra-stiff white cami with built-in support that feels like a corset. It pushes everything in and up, making my curves even more dangerous. A long, tailored white jacket is included. It has two rows of black buttons down the front and a slim black belt at my waist; the collar is straight and stiff, reaching to just below my ears. A cowl-like hood that can be worn to cover my hair is attached to the collar.

Looking at myself in the mirror, I whisper to my reflection, "Who are you?" because I look urban glam. Leaving the hood down, I brush my hair again before stepping out of the lavare.

"Who's this?" Jax asks when he sees me. His eyes scan me like he's never seen me before.

"They let you out!" I say, seeing Wayra next to him as he studies me, too.

"*Kitten*, we'll be able to leave soon," Trey says, using his nickname for me to remind me that we're still being monitored. "The consulate has stepped in to facilitate replacing your lost identification. They've sent an escort."

"That was fast," I murmur, feeling goose bumps rise on my arms.

"Yes, it was very quick," Trey agrees, looking concerned.

"I had expected it would take longer. We must be very lucky," I add, thinking of all the bureaucratic red tape humans have to juggle when creating new documentation for someone.

"We're more important than we thought," Trey replies, making me shiver.

Gideon arrives then, stepping into the room and saying, "Well, everything checks out now. Your escorts from the consulate have arrived with your identification, Kricket." He hands me tags with my assumed name and numbers on them. Holding them in my fist, I smile, feeling my heart racing. "Your father must be a very powerful man in Rafe to have expedited all of this."

"He is," I agree, feeling my hands shake, "very powerful."

Gideon smiles at me, nodding. Trey intervenes then, "Remember, Gideon, if you're ever in the Valley of Thistle, please visit my family. Just ask for Trey Allairis."

"Yes, I'll do that. Many thanks, Trey. And by the way, I was wrong. You're a very fortunate Etharian," Gideon says with a smirk. "Well, this way then." Seeing Gideon smile at me, I blush, thinking maybe he was listening to us in the shower.

As we're led from the room, Gideon shows us to a cavernous main lobby that's bigger and more ornate than Union Station. Amid all the chaos of really tall people going about their business, five elegantly uniformed men with dark hair and violet eyes stand by the outer doors, waiting silently for us to come to them.

"Regent secret police," Wayra whispers to Jax. "What are they doing here?" he asks grimly.

"I don't know," Jax whispers back. "They look like a bunch of knob knockers to me."

"Shouldn't they have sent more Cavars? Why do I feel like I'm about to deliver a sloat to the butcher?"

They look as ominous as crows to me. Their tunic uniforms are black, emblazoned with a gray shield. An intricate, violet saer rearing on his hind legs and breathing fire is embroidered on the shield.

Feeling someone take my hand, I look down to see Trey's warm fingers entwined in mine. He squeezes them gently, but he's looking straight ahead at the men by the door. As we approach them, they all go down on one knee, using a sweeping arm gesture before rising again. The slender one in the middle says, "Trey and Kricket Allairis. We're here to escort you back to Rafe. Your transport is just outside."

"Fine," Trey says in a dismissive tone, walking right by them and ushering me through the doors. Just outside, in a diplomatic parking area, sit two gleaming, white crafts that resemble smaller versions of Stealth Fighters.

Ushering me to one, Trey places his hand on the small of my back as I climb the stairs. Inside, the cabin looks like a posh living room equipped with sofas and large recliners. Trey leads me to a seat near a window. I sink into the large chair, and Trey sits next to me.

Pulling out his communicator thingy, Trey begins barking weird words into it, like a code. Then he says, "Ateur Victus Allairis, message: Need to speak with you. Urgent. Contact immediately."

Jax and Wayra sit in the chairs directly facing ours so that we occupy our own area. Ignoring the thinner Regent agent across the aisle, Trey continues to use his communicator, tapping on it like he's typing something.

In frustration, the agent by our chairs clears his throat loudly. "I'm Ustus, the agent assigned to the Hollowell case. You are to take the other transport. Your mission is over. You have successfully delivered Hollowell to us. We'll deliver her to the corrective court for processing."

Trey glances at me and raises one eyebrow in question. I nod; the agent is telling us the truth. Trey frowns at Ustus. "I have received no such orders from my superiors; therefore, my mission is not complete."

"Your orders are here," Ustus counters, snapping his fingers. Another darkly clad agent appears, handing him a digital tablet. Trey takes it from the officer before plucking a silver bead from the tablet. Placing it in his ear, he touches the face of the tablet with his hand. It scans his hand and Trey listens to whatever is being explained in his earpiece.

He pulls the earpiece from his ear. "They said I'm to turn her over to you upon our arrival in Rafe." He's not being truthful.

"Listen again: My orders were clear. We handle it from here," Ustus replies in a frustrated tone.

"You know, the thing about these messages is that they only play once," Trey replies casually, handing it back to the officer.

"If you refuse to get off this transport, then I'll be forced to take her to the other one." Ustus is determined not to back down.

"You can try," Trey replies with menace in his tone, standing up. Wayra and Jax stand too, looking very muscley again. "But I wouldn't recommend it."

Ustus's nostrils flare, but he takes a step back, nodding to his men behind him. "I will remain on this trift. We'll take possession when we reach Rafe." The other agents nod, exiting the sleek aircraft to board the other one. Turning to Trey, he says in a stilted tone, "I hope that your lack of cooperation does not adversely affect the commendation you're to receive from Skye for this service."

Sitting down in their seats again, Trey's frown deepens as he looks at Jax and Wayra.

Ustus walks to the front to sit with the pilot. I try hard to smile at the Cavars. Pulling off something just short of a grimace, I roll my eyes and say, "You can *try*." All their eyes turn to me as we burst out laughing. Feeling the trift lift off the ground slowly, like it's levitating, everyone sobers quickly.

I moisten my lips that have suddenly gone dry. "Once we get to Rafe, you have to hand me over to those Regent guys, right?" I see Trey's eyebrows pull together.

"Yes," he states, almost sullenly.

"How long do I have?" I ask, feeling anxiety creeping in.

"It should only take a quarter of a part," Jax says with what looks like regret. Since a part is a little more than an hour, I do the math and figure I have about twenty minutes until I get handed over.

"Who are the Regent police?"

"They're a special branch that takes care of palace affairs," Trey says.

"Palace as in a royal family kind of thing?"

"Er . . . maybe like Secret Service?" Jax responds, looking at me to see if that's a good enough explanation.

"So, this is no longer military and it's not a civil court situation, like you were led to believe."

"This is completely wacked," Wayra growls in a low tone, looking between Jax and Trey.

"Who knows about me besides you guys?"

"Our superiors," Trey replies, looking grim.

"That phone thing takes pictures, right?"

"Yes."

"Okay, take my picture," I say, running my hand through my hair. "Then I want you to send it to all of your e-mail accounts or whatever it is you guys have here. Send it to your brother, too."

"Why?" Wayra asks, looking at Trey's smile.

"Deniability—it's hard to deny something when there is proof that it exists," I explain. "Oh, I think we should send a picture of Trey and me to Gideon, too. You know, to thank him for his hospitality." Seeing Trey's smile deepen, I hold still for the pictures.

Snapping a few photos of me, Trey hands the phone to Jax, who takes a couple of pictures of us together. Then I still as something occurs to me. "Wait! Uh—wait a second! Don't send that! Here, can we erase these?" I ask, panicking and trying to reach for the communicator.

Pulling it back from me, Trey asks, "What's wrong?"

"Not such a good idea for you guys." I reach for the phone again. "You need to erase them."

"Why?" he asks again.

"Because this will get you in trouble."

"No, this is insurance," Trey replies. "We keep it."

"You shouldn't be involved," I say, thinking about what could happen to him if he used those pictures to help me.

"I'm involved," he states, like that's the end of the discussion.

My frown deepens. "Don't be stupid. This feels like a 'sacrifice the pawn' move to me. If that's the case, then you can be included in that if you have these pictures."

"Or it can elevate me to queen," he replies, unruffled.

My lips twitch at the mental image of him as a "queen." "This is not queen material—knight maybe, but not queen," I reply, chewing my bottom lip.

"I'll take the upgrade." His eyes soften a little. "Here, memorize this."

He holds his communicator up to me; there is a serial number on the back with fifteen letters and numbers. "What is this?" I ask, trying to commit the code to memory.

"My number."

"Oh," I murmur, feeling myself blush. "Okay."

Everyone falls silent then. I gaze out the window at the blue sky dotted with ultra-white clouds. Glancing at Trey, I see his jaw is tense, like he's on edge. His hand on the armrest next to mine moves so that it's just touching mine. The knot in my stomach eases a little and is replaced by his presence and the feeling of being protected.

From my seat, I watch the trift make a rapid descent and touch down on a manicured lawn. The lawn is incredible; it's laid out with intricate cascading water features that make the Buckingham Fountain in Chicago look like a birdbath. In the distance beyond the gardens, I can see structures that look like porticoes leading to beautiful, ornately sculptured buildings—like something you might see in Versailles.

"Where are we?" I ask.

"The palace," Jax says, looking nervous.

"Oh." I feel ill. "Okay, I have something for you guys." Reaching inside my sleeve, I pull out two small packages wrapped in the tissue my new clothes came in. Handing one to Wayra and one to Jax, I smile at their startled expressions.

"What's this?" Wayra asks. He opens the tissue paper, and grinning, he holds up my pink underwear.

"Pinky promise." *Debt paid,* I think.

Jax opens his, and seeing my pink bra inside, he laughs like I've never heard him laugh before. When Jax looks at me, I say, "I'm denying all knowledge of this transaction."

I sneak a sidelong look at Trey; his jaw is still tense. Ustus, arriving at our seats again, motions to me to follow him. The other agents have opened the doors to the trift, boarded it, and are waiting by the exit. "And as for you," I say to Trey in a teasing tone, rising from my seat and leaning down to whisper in his ear, "I want a divorce."

Trey's jaw tenses, like he finds no humor in what I just said. I straighten then and move to follow the soldier in front of me. "Kricket," Trey says my name, grabbing my wrist tightly. Seeing the grim expression on his face, my heart twists in my chest.

"Don't worry, your job is over now, and I've been here before—in this situation," I say softly, but his hand only tightens on my wrist. "I'm stone, remember? Nothing touches me." My smile is the plastic kind—fake. I say it more for me than for him. For some stupid reason, I let him into my world of one, but I'm better off alone . . . *I'm always better off alone.*

The pressure on my wrist eases as I pull my hand from his. Turning away and walking to the exit, I try really hard not to cry, taking deep breaths as my hands turn to fists. A dark-clad agent approaches me with a metal collar. My heartbeat picks up as he clamps it around my neck, snapping it into place.

"That's not necessary. She's not resisting—she's going with you willingly," Trey growls from behind me, his voice sounding deadly.

The agent ignores him, pulling out a gadget that looks like a garage door opener. Smirking at me with a glint in his violet eyes, he says, "Test in four, three, two, one . . ." He depresses the button, and the collar around my neck tightens instantly, squeezing my throat painfully while cutting off my oxygen. Wide-eyed, my hands fly to the collar, trying to pull it away from me, but it won't ease. I feel lightheaded and disoriented, and black spots form in my vision right before the collar eases, allowing me to breathe again.

As I take my first gasping breath, Trey's fist smashes into the face of the Regent agent holding the remote to the collar around my neck. Jax is next to me, demanding the code to release the collar, and Wayra is backing Ustus and his agents up so they can't get near me.

Chapter 12

Processing

Removing the collar from my neck, Jax holds me by my shoulders, looking in my eyes. "You knob knockers!" Jax says harshly toward the Regent agents being held back by Wayra. "She's smaller than us. She can't take the kind of pressure that a restraint exerts on a normal adult—is it even calibrated for a female? You need to recalibrate a collar for her if you plan on using it!"

I look over at Trey; he's holding the agent who had put the collar on me by his uniform, looking like he's ready to hit him again at the slightest provocation.

"You're violating our orders!" Ustus says from behind Wayra. "This is standard procedure."

"No, we're ensuring that our prisoner is protected. We didn't spend half a floan tracking her to have you kill her during the prisoner exchange," Trey replies. When he looks back at the agent he's holding immobile, Trey snatches the metal identification tag from the agent's belt. He studies the tag and says, "If she has one little scratch on her when you bring her to court, I will find you, Fex Theda, and we'll discuss it just as we have here."

"If we agree to take her unrestrained, will you turn over the prisoner now?" Ustus asks Trey.

Easing his grip on Fex, Trey lets go of the agent, who immediately backs away from him. "Why are we here?" Trey asks Ustus. "You said that you were taking her to the court for processing."

"And I will. We're here because she needs to see a physician before processing. She needs vaccinations before she can join the general population."

"Why here? Why not at a med station or a military base?" Jax asks. "She's going to be treated by the Regent's physicians?"

"Those are my orders." Jax's eyes shoot to Trey's. They're both surprised. "Now, can we remand the prisoner?" Ustus asks, looking huffy.

Trey nods curtly, his jaw tense and his eyes on me. Wayra looks devastated, as though he can't believe that the agents are going to be allowed to take me. Reaching down and picking up the collar, Wayra growls, "I'm keeping this! If you can't keep track of one little Etharian, then maybe you should find another line of work." When one of the agents frowns at him, Wayra steps menacingly close to him and asks, "You see something you want?" The agent quickly looks away.

"Fine," Ustus says, not looking at Wayra.

Straightening my shoulders, I wink at Wayra, who's watching me like his dog just died. I raise my chin a notch and look at each of the Cavars before saying, "Baw-da-baw, boys." Turning, I follow Ustus out of the aircraft and into the waiting hover vehicle that looks like an elongated Rolls Royce.

In the back of the vehicle, my new bodyguards surround me. I'm being patently ignored by all of them, which is good because my throat feels tight with unshed tears. Passing through guarded gates and along a winding, grassy boulevard with arching trees, we arrive at the cobblestone driveway that leads to the entrance of an elegant baroque palace. I think my mouth might have been hanging open for a moment while looking around in wonder.

Entering the palace, I'm led to a spa-like area with water cascading over a mosaic of blue and green glass-tiled walls. A tranquil examination room is set up with a view of the sprawling gardens outside the open French doors. Instead of an examination table, a chaise longue and elegant chairs furnish the space.

As beautiful as the place is, the next few hours are grueling. Two very tall, very smiley men conduct the medical examination. The one doing all the work is Tofer. He looks like he's in his thirties, with small, intricate braids in his hair on one side, making him look more like a sexy drummer from a hot band than a physician. I sort of like Tofer because he tells me everything he's doing as he does it. Every vaccination is explained to me, detailing its purpose and the symptoms to look for if one were to actually contract the illness. After Tofer finishes, diseases like Verdi Freckles and Dunder Sorrows can no longer harm me.

Yazer, Tofer's peer, is a bit harder to find likable because he asks me leading questions throughout my examination. Pacing the room with his arms crossed, Yazer asks: "Did you know that you'd be meeting me today?" and "Did you ever see me prior to today, in a dream, perhaps?" and "Can you tell me what I did yesterday?" and "Can you tell me what I'll be doing tomorrow?" I would have thought Yazer a complete lunatic if Trey hadn't told me about some of the precognitive gifts that Alameeda priestesses possess. Pretending that I have no idea what he's talking about, I simply shake my head to his questions, frowning at him like I think he's mental.

When Tofer is finished with the vaccinations, he picks up a visor and brings it to me. "Now, Kricket," he says, his violet eyes smiling at me, "I'm just going to check your vital signs and get a general picture of your health."

"Is that necessary?" I ask him, feeling nervous. "They already scanned me with those."

"Who did?" his eyebrows pull together.

"Never mind." I drop it because I'm not sure if I should tell him. I don't know who can be trusted. Allowing Tofer to put the "grandma goggles" on my eyes, I bite my lip as he makes a noise that sounds like he's choking.

"What is it?" Yazer asks, leaning nearer to see the readout. Then Yazer makes a similar noise to the one Tofer made.

"She's really—" Tofer begins.

"Yes, she is," Yazer agrees with satisfaction in his tone. "She can be taken for processing now. I'll advise the Regent." Yazer smiles at me again, looking thrilled while walking to the door. Opening it, he speaks to Ustus as he's invited into the room. "You can remand her to the corrective court now, and then . . ." he trails off, giving me the sense that there is a plan in play where I'm concerned. "You must stay with her—make sure she's protected."

"Those are my orders," Ustus replies. He gestures for me to follow him as he ushers me out of the palace and into the Rolls Royce hover vehicle with the other agents. Passing through guarded archways that have wrought-iron gates with blue beams of light coursing between them, I absorb as much of the outside world as I can. We're moving near the ground level, and there are several other levels of traffic over our heads that I see through a sunroof. But the speed at which we're traveling is fierce, making it almost impossible to see details as buildings blur past.

"Can we slow down?" I ask them, trying to look out the back window at the scenery because it's too hard to see anything through the side windows.

"This isn't a tour trolley," Ustus replies, typing something on his communicator as he smiles at his own joke. He's smaller than the other agents, but his features are more refined.

"No, just a ship of fools," I reply blandly, getting a smile from a couple of the agents while others frown at me.

"This does feel like a fool's errand," Ustus agrees.

"Why's that?" I quirk my eyebrow.

"You won't be staying there."

"I won't?" I wonder how much he knows about what's going to happen to me.

"Everything regarding your case has already been decided," he replies. "This is just a formality."

"What do you mean? I wanted to retain a wigg," I say, feeling my heartbeat pick up.

"Why? One will be appointed for you. You're a minor," he looks at me and frowns, like he's reevaluating the word he just used to describe me. His eyes linger on my breasts a little too long.

"Court-appointed attorneys usually turn out to be—how can I put this delicately?—oh, I know—*total knob knockers*," I reply with sarcasm, causing laughter to erupt from several of the agents.

"Please refrain from using that language. It makes you sound common." He sniffs prudishly. "What is an 'attorney'?" Ustus looks grudgingly amused now.

"It's a wigg, and stop pretending that you don't know what I'm saying."

"I doubt it will matter much, Fay Kricket," Ustus says, using my name for the first time. "I'm to stay with you while you're there. That means you'll be returning with me."

"But that's insane! I haven't had time to prepare a case! I don't even know what laws I'm being charged with breaking. I haven't been able to research a defense!" I panic.

"You're going to be taken care of—" He starts to assure me, but I cut him off.

"I don't want anyone taking care of me," I retort, frowning at him. "I want to make my own choices about what I do with my life!"

"Good for you," he says, smiling. "You'll just have to wait until you're twenty floans old for that day to come. Until then, I'm in charge of your case."

"What do you mean?"

"I mean, get used to seeing my face because I'm in charge," he says, just like a parent.

"*No!*"

"Yes." He dismisses my objection in a calm tone while typing away on his phone again.

"I was hoping my father had some family here. Someone who might help me get on my feet."

"I would not count on that." Ustus sighs quietly. "I read some of the Hollowell files. Your father's family has taken steps to disinherit any offspring resulting from the match of Pan Hollowell to Arissa Valke."

"Why?" I ask, not able to stop myself.

"I don't know their reasons, but the court documents shifted all assets to an uncle . . ."—he taps his communicator, scanning it—"ah, Farren Hollowell, Pan's brother. They couldn't take away the title though. That's still yours."

"The title?"

"Your father was Corinet, so the title falls to you. You're a coriness—making you 'Fay Kricket.'"

"What does 'Fay' mean?" I feel a stab of pain as I realize that I have family, but they think I'm trash.

"It's a title." The judge looks momentarily confused by my question.

"Like 'Miss'?"

"No, like 'Dame' . . . or perhaps 'Lady'?" he says, trying to relate it to something human.

"Will you notify the Hollowell family that I exist?"

"Yes," he replies honestly. I nod, dropping the subject as I kick around in my head what I was just told. I can only think of a couple of reasons why someone would go to those lengths to redirect assets: greed and shame. Neither reason is making me feel hopeful of meeting my long-lost family.

The car slows then, pulling into a drive and parking where the sign, posted clearly, says, "Restricted." Opening my door, Ustus and the other agents lead me to the brilliant glass building ahead of us. This place is so different from the palace that the only similarity is that they're both excessively clean and elegant. This building, however, is modern in a way that I've never seen before. It's all glass in the lobby, and the tiers of floors above our heads go on for at least a mile up. Glass walkways that are completely transparent rise above our heads, taking my breath away.

"Oh, I get it," I say, looking at Ustus's face. He raises his eyebrow, and I say, "It's a metaphor—a transparent system of justice." Ustus looks around then, as if seeing the building for the first time. "I prefer my justice to be blind," I say dryly.

"I never made the connection," Ustus murmurs, gesturing me toward a glass elevator.

"No, you just like it because you can see up all the girlies' skirts," I smirk.

"Does everything that you think come out of your mouth?" Ustus frowns. "If you will notice, the glass darkens to opaque when it is stepped on."

"Oh," I say. "I'm usually a lot more cautious about what I say. I just feel like maybe there's not a lot left for me to lose." Tears sting my eyes. I take a breath, choking them back down.

"You should really rethink that opinion, Fay Kricket. It will get you into trouble."

Getting off the elevator at the hundred and fourth floor, we walk across a glass causeway that gives me vertigo because we're so high up. When we pass through the threshold into a room, I realize that the outside is only an illusion of transparency, because inside the room is completely different than the façade has led me to believe.

"It *is* a metaphor," I murmur, because it's different from what it seems. Noticing the room has two walls that are pure glass, I walk toward them. As I get nearer to the window, I take in the panorama of Rafe. Several higher skyscrapers have glass enclosed skywalks that link buildings together. In the distance, there are more streams of traffic and in the sky above, there's a dome over the city, like a shield.

I move around the long, glass conference table to get closer to the window. "Fay Kricket, you'll remain here while I speak to the wigg and the mediator assigned to your case."

"Where are we—what city is this?" I ask absently.

"This is the Isle of Skye; it's the capital," Ustus answers.

"What's that?" I point to the sky before crossing my arms over my chest.

Coming closer to me, Ustus grunts, "It's a screen."

"What does it do?"

"It blocks some UV rays, it filters pollution before it can contaminate the environment, and it's a defensive shield," he smiles reluctantly.

"How does it work?" I watch the arch over the city glow like an iridescent bubble.

"Do I look like an engineer?"

"Why can't I be in the room while you discuss my future?"

"Because it's already decided."

"What's going to happen to me?"

"You'll live at the palace here in the Isle of Skye for now."

"Why?"

"Because you'll have gifts—gifts that will make you very valuable."

"How do you know that?"

"You're the daughter of an Alameeda priestess. It's a certainty. Had you been male, it may have been different, but genetically, female offspring always inherit the trait."

"Always?"

"Always," he replies, and I close my eyes, feeling like I'm going to cry. Seeing my expression, he says, "You may like the palace—"

"Don't." I hold up my hand. "I *really* don't want to hear it."

"Fine. I'm posting agents outside the door." He frowns at me before turning and leaving the room. When I'm alone, I sink into a chair, staring out the window, not really seeing anything at all.

It can't be more than fifteen minutes later when the door opens again. Glancing over my shoulder, my heart leaps into my throat when Trey closes the door behind him. He looks incredible in a long, tailored vest that's dark gray pinstripe with dark, tailored pants and very expensive-looking black boots. He looks thinner somehow, less muscular than he appeared in his uniform—or in the shower.

"Trey!" I say, bolting to my feet and grinning. "How did you find me? What are you doing here?" I rush toward him.

He frowns at me, and there's something in his eyes that makes me stop before I do something impulsive, like throw my arms around him. Searching his face as he's assessing me like he has never seen me before, I take a step back, realizing that he isn't Trey.

"You're not Trey." I say, confused and disappointed.

"No. I'm Victus," he replies, placing a communicator on the glass surface and taking a seat at the head of the conference table. "My brother asked me to come." He seems completely irritated with the fact that he's here now.

"You're twins," I say stupidly.

"He said you were smart," Victus replies in a derogatory way.

"Why did he ask you to come?" I wonder, feeling a blush creeping into my cheeks at his last comment.

"He said he's concerned about you," he answers, as he looks me over again from head to foot.

"Oh," I murmur, taking a seat as much to hide from his assessment of me as to sit before my knees show him that I'm shaking. "Why didn't he come then?"

"He wanted to come himself, but he's required to meet with Skye, and he could not refuse."

"What did he say?" I feel something stir inside of me at the knowledge that Trey is concerned about me.

"He sent me this." Victus holds up his communicator, showing me the picture of Trey and me together on the trift. "Do you know how damaging this can be to his reputation?" Victus asks me accusingly.

Shaking my head and feeling my face becoming redder at Victus's scowl, I find my voice enough to say, "No."

"Trey is practically engaged to a childhood *family* friend. This could end that, not to mention that the breach of confidentiality in his line of work could come with severe penalties." Victus seethes.

All my elation is crushed in that moment. Feeling instantly sick to my stomach, I look down. "Erase it," I say in a small voice, not looking at his face. "I won't tell anyone. I—"

"What do you want?" Victus sounds angry. "Are you blackmailing him?"

"What?"

"Why would he risk everything to send me this?" Victus scowls.

"I don't know," I murmur. "We're friends—"

"He has all the friends he needs. He doesn't need an Alameeda priestess for a friend. So, whatever you're doing to him, I want you to stop," he demands. "In exchange, I will help you with your case. What do you want? A reduced sentence? Currency?"

My eyebrows pull together in a frown. "Oh, that's so *gross.*" My lips twist into a scowl, feeling like he kicked me in the stomach. "You think I'm doing something to Trey? Like what?"

"I don't know. You're the priestess. You tell me." He glares at me again.

"Ugh, this is . . . too much," I mutter, putting my face in my hands. "You have no right—I'm not what you think I am. I'm just a human being," I stammer, feeling like I'm choking. "At least, I was last week—now I'm . . . some total freak."

"What are you talking about?" Victus asks in confusion. He looks so much like Trey that it hurts that much more to see scorn in his eyes. "You're not human."

"How much do you know about me?" I bite my lip so I won't cry.

"I didn't get details—just that you're an Alameeda priestess. Trey couldn't tell me about his mission. He just insisted I help you, and the picture he sent is telling."

"What do you mean?" I ask, knowing I won't like his answer.

"Are you lovers?"

"No." My heart twists again.

"You're lying."

"Why do you say that?" He looks me over again, and I straighten in my chair. "You know what? Get out!" I point to the door.

He straightens in his chair, like *I* just insulted *him*. "I'll leave when I'm finished," he says, narrowing his eyes.

"Ohhh, you're *so* finished, Victus," I state, getting up from my seat and walking back to the window.

"I want your word that you'll leave my brother and my family alone," he says, following me to the window.

"Done," I promise. "Goodbye."

"What?" he asks, looking surprised.

"I will leave all of the Allairises alone. I don't hurt my friends," I say. "Just tell Trey that I said I'm stone, and I don't need a babysitter. Then make sure he deletes all of those pictures. There are about six—no, seven. Oh, and his men, Jax and Wayra, might have a copy of a few. Make sure you get those, too. If someone leaks them, you can blame it on the mission. He had to pretend to be my consort in order to get me to Rafe from Earth. It was just a mission—you have nothing to worry about. He'll be on to his next mission soon, and he'll forget all about me."

"If you're not blackmailing him and you're not his lover, then why would he ask me to help you?" Victus asks, still unconvinced.

"Guilt. He thinks that since I was born and raised on Earth, and he was sent to bring me back, that I won't be able to survive here on my own, so he feels guilty," I explain, not looking at him, but raising my chin. "He's wrong, and you can tell him I said that his lack of faith in me is insulting."

"You're her," Victus says softly.

"I'm who?"

"You're the one. You're Hollowell! Of course!" he says, like he just put two and two together. Smiling, he looks just like Trey.

"Oh. I'm the urban legend—crazy priestess—run and lock up your sons. Freak on the loose—well, not really *loose*," I say sarcastically. "Listen, I'm kind of having a really bad day. Do you think you could just leave me alone before I say something I don't mean?"

"I apologize, Kricket. I have misread the situation here," he says in a quiet tone. "My brother was very upset when he spoke to me, and he couldn't tell me details. I rushed to the wrong conclusions."

"Don't stress, Victus. It's not the worst thing that's happened to me today."

"I may be able to help," Victus offers, now a total gentleman. "I was a wigg before I became an ateur."

"What's an 'ateur'?"

"A member of the House of Lords," he says, surprised that I don't know.

"You better not. It will look suspicious for Trey. He might get in trouble. In fact, you should leave before Ustus gets back. He might think you're Trey, and he's not happy with him."

"Why?" Victus asks, confused.

"Oh," I say, waving him off and touching my sore neck absently. Victus must've seen something because he walks over to me and his hand goes to my collar. Pulling it back gently, Victus frowns at me again.

"Why is your neck bruised?" he demands, just as pushy as Trey.

"That collar thingy was too tight," I reply, stepping away and feeling embarrassed. "It's okay. Trey made them take it off me."

"They used a restraint on you?" He sounds outraged. "You're a female, and you're so small."

Rolling my eyes at his comment, I sigh, "I'm not small!"

"Kricket, you're small," he states again, frowning.

"Whatever," I mumble. "I'm strong and I'm smart, and once I figure all of this out, I'll be fine."

"I insist that you let me help you," Victus says, using a superior tone again. "You should have proper representation."

"Oh, don't be a knob knocker, Victus," I reply, rubbing my eyes. "You can't bully me. This is bad for your family. The Regent is involved. They have a deal already." I gesture toward the door. "It's done. I'm theirs. I just have to figure out how to navigate in this world, and you can't help me with that."

"No one has called me a knob knocker in a very long time. In fact, Trey was the last person to call me a knob knocker," Victus says, fighting a smile.

"Yeah? Well, I learned that word from the Cavars on our way here. I need some more good swears for the Regent."

Victus sobers instantly, "No, you don't, Kricket."

"Don't worry, Victus. They went through a lot of trouble to get me. They'll want my cooperation, so they may play ball," I say, this last almost to myself.

"Play ball?" he asks, his brow wrinkling.

"Come to the palace some day, and I'll show you how it's done." I smile despite the situation.

"Is that where you'll be?" he asks, studying everything about me.

"For now."

"And you're sure that there is nothing that I can do for you?" He poses the question, and when I shake my head, he almost looks disappointed. "Do you want me to tell Trey anything else . . . other than you're a stone and you don't need to sit on babies?"

"I don't need a *babysitter*," I correct. Then, seeing his confused look, I murmur, "Never mind. Just tell Trey . . . tell him that honey is nectar that bees create, and it's very sweet and that I miss it . . . more than pizza."

"You don't have to miss it, Kricket. We have that here. We call it 'homitie.'"

"Oh. Just tell Trey what I said, okay?" I can't help holding my breath a little. He nods and I exhale. "Thank you for coming, Victus." Victus inclines his head. Picking up his communicator off the table, he walks to the door.

Victus pauses there before he says, "I don't think it's guilt." When I look back at him, he smiles. "No, it's definitely not guilt." He closes the door behind him, and I ponder his words as I stare out the window.

Chapter 13

The Palace

I don't even try to look out the window of the fast-moving hover car on the way back to the palace from the corrective court. "So, what's the verdict, Slim?" I ask Ustus, watching him tap on his communicator.

Ustus ignores me, probably because I called him "Slim." I try again: "Ustus?"

"You're a ward of the Regent until your twentieth birthday," Ustus states, not looking at me.

"The Regent?" I ask, wanting an explanation. "Is that normal?"

"It is unusual."

"You want to give me the odds on that one? Is it 'four-leaf-clover' kind of unusual or 'man-with-four-heads' kind of strange?"

"The latter, I think." He tries to ignore me again.

"Anything else?"

"Your wigg had the penance waived."

"Wow, what do you know? Maybe you guys have better public defenders than I'm used to," I mumble.

"No, your other wigg argued for the penance to be rescinded." Ustus's glare pins me to my seat.

"My other wigg?"

"Your court-appointed wigg was recused by Ateur Victus. He took over for him on what he claimed was your behest. He renegotiated the penance portion of your sentence, having it dismissed. Custody he could not wrangle, however, since he's not a family member. No, you are now a ward of the Regent."

This new information shocks me. Victus got involved, even when I specifically told him to step off. "You don't approve?" I watch Ustus's face. "You think I need penance?"

"Yes, you do need penance, but not as a punishment to you."

"What other reason could there be for penance?" I'm completely offended that he thinks I deserve to be punished for something I had absolutely no control over.

"Public image, Kricket. The crown has stepped in, instantly elevating your position by giving you its protection. They sought to counteract this political move by showing that you would still be responsible for what has occurred. Now, we will need to rethink how you are presented to society."

"How many wards does the Regent have?"

"One," he says, nodding toward me.

"Well then, giving me penance would be just like putting a hat on a spix to disguise its horns, Ustus," I reply.

"It's what?" He attempts to stop himself from smiling.

"Giving me penance won't distract anyone from the fact that I'm now the Regent's ward." I bite my thumbnail in agitation.

"Don't bite your nails; you'll ruin your teeth," Ustus says, looking at me. "A light punishment would have gone a long way with most citizens. If people thought that you had been punished, they might be far less likely to shun you," he says and then watches for my reaction.

"Some people will shun me? What are we, Amish?"

"Many will have a hard time with your Alameeda heritage. Penance might make you a little more . . . sympathetic to your peers." He is trying to be upfront with me, and I appreciate it.

"Ah, they want to see me put in my place, huh? Grovel a little, and then maybe we can be friends."

"Your grasp of the situation is impressive," he replies, forgetting his communicator for a second.

"What were you all planning—I mean, for my penance?" I ask with a sense of morbid curiosity.

"Nothing too tragic. A rotation in the public square."

"Huh?"

"You would've been made to stand in the public square for a rotation or so," he explains, shifting his eyes back to his communicator while I glare at him.

"Are you saying that I would've been put in a stockade or something and put on display for a day—a rotation——to be ridiculed?" Color floods my cheeks.

"You would not have been put in restraints if you cooperated with the court," he explains defensively, and his face flushes a little, too, as he avoids my eyes.

"That's archaic," I accuse, resting my head against the seat. "Would you have sewn an 'A' for 'Alameeda' to my chest and allowed people to throw rotten cabbages at me, too?"

"No—really your imagination is flamboyant. No one would dare throw anything at you. It would just cause enough embarrassment and discomfort to you to show everyone that you have paid your debt for violating our laws. It would also give everyone a chance to view you and get accustomed to you. It would make some citizens completely sympathetic to your cause because some would see the punishment as unjust."

"*I* see the punishment as unjust. I don't grovel," I retort, crossing my arms. "There will always be haters, Ustus. I can handle them on my own."

Pulling through the gates of the palace once again, we take a different driveway, heading to the west entrance. Complex lawns of intricately patterned hedges and water features drift by the window as we move at a more sedate speed along the outer drive. Turning and approaching the palace, I sigh, feeling small compared to the enormous fortress ahead of me.

After exiting the car, Ustus ushers me up the impressive stone steps to the towering front doors. Speaking quietly to uniformed men who clearly work here, Ustus inclines his head. In moments, a tall, willowy woman who is at least six feet four enters the foyer, approaching us.

"Ah, Ustus." She smiles at him and inclines her head. "This is Fay Kricket?" She turns her violet eyes on me, smiling again.

"Fay Kricket, this is Thea Moore—she's the chatelaine. She will show you to your room," Ustus says. "I will see you again at supper this evening."

"Can't wait," I reply absently, still studying Thea. Her hair is shorter; it only reaches to her shoulders, but it's dark like the hair of all the Rafes around here. She appears to be middle-aged, which probably makes her freakishly old, but with that age is an obvious air of sophistication and refinement.

"Please follow me," Thea says, and she waits for me to walk beside her. "We have put you on the west arcade. You'll be among other young females who are staying here for the summer solstice."

"The solstice?"

"Yes, you've arrived just in time for the swanks that take place at this time," she informs me, like I'm an invited guest. "Do you like parties?" She tries to make conversation while climbing a sweeping staircase that could accommodate a Humvee with no problem.

"Mmm, I live for swanks," I say, trying to be agreeable. "But I really have no experience . . . er . . . comporting in a venue such as this one."

"Yes, you were raised on Earth, were you not?" Thea asks, like it's not a crime.

"I was," I answer as we turn down a long gallery. We encounter a pair of really tall ladies, who both stumble to a halt just before we go by, becoming completely mute as their eyes follow me.

"I will mention this to Tofer," she says, pretending that didn't just happen as we pass tall, carved columns of etched marble.

"Tofer . . . the physician?" I ask, remembering the doctor who looks like a sexy drummer.

"Yes. He and Yazer will be instructing you on everything from the basics of our daily life here to the history of Ethar." *Yuck, Yazer,* I think, remembering his awkward questions.

Before I recover from my cringe, we turn into a substantial sitting room with an immense fireplace. A large, gilded mirror hangs above the mantel, reflecting the sunlight from the two sets of French doors that lead to a stone terrace. Tiffany blue silk covers the furniture. Wooden doors lead directly into a bedroom with blue silk draperies and a matching coverlet. The bed is insanely beautiful; the posters and headboard are made of white marble, carved to resemble creeping vines.

Going to doors on one side of the bedroom, Thea pulls them open, revealing a large array of clothing. "These just arrived for you. If you need help choosing something for dinner, you can ask Aella when she comes to dress your hair," Thea informs me before reaching out and touching with her elegant fingertips the pale fabric of a gown near the door.

"Uh . . . this is . . . I . . ." I try to think of something to say, but words fail me.

"The Regent is having a small dinner party this evening. He requested that you attend. You should rest; these things are known to be quite long. Is there anything that you need before I leave you?"

Shaking my head no, I feel panic rising in me. Thea smiles, turning to go. "A communicator," I blurt out. "Can I have one?" I hide my hands behind me because they're shaking.

"Let me inquire, and I will let you know," she replies smoothly before leaving me alone in my new room.

I unbutton my jacket and shrug it off before sitting down on the edge of the massive bed. I stare at the closet. *No one has that many clothes,* I think. *Bridget would freak if she were here. Bridget . . .* Choking fear hits me in waves. *Nothing is ever free. Nothing. They want something from me.*

I turn and crawl up to the huge pillows that rest against the headboard; I lay my head on one. Studying the room, I spot something that looks like an expensive cell phone on the bedside table. I scoot over and pick it up. Examining it for a second, I touch the display, and it illuminates. I run my finger over the screen, and the wall in front of me changes drastically, becoming a city scene where a couple of life-size Etharians are taking a walk. The holographic image of a woman is telling the man she is with, Rathis, that there are problems with her skiff, and how is she supposed to deploy all the underbits without a treston? "Yes, how will she do that, Rathis?" I ask, mumbling to the images on the wall. "You're her boo—you figure it out." Watching them, I realize that this is some kind of soap opera.

A light rap sounds on the door in the other room, and a moment later a very tall girl enters my bedroom. "Ohhh, is this *Violet Shadows?*" she asks me, laying down a tea set on the table near my bed. She's wearing a long, flowing skirt that accentuates just how tall and long limbed she is. Smiling at me, her violet eyes go to the wall as Rathis begins trying to talk sense to his emotionally overwrought girlfriend.

"I . . . don't know," I answer, wondering who she is. "I've never watched *Violet Shadows.*"

Her violet eyes widen as she studies me. "You really *are* from Earth!"

Nodding, I introduce myself, "I'm Kricket."

Sinking to her knee, the young woman says, "It is an honor to greet you, Fay Kricket. I'm Aella." And even on her knee, she's still really tall.

"Um . . . hi, Aella. You don't have to call me Fay Kricket. Just call me Kricket," I say, watching her rise.

"Oh, I couldn't do that. It's very familiar, and I'm to be your liaison," she replies with a blush.

"My what?"

"Your . . . assistant?" she falters, attempting to explain.

"Oh, then you *really* don't need to kneel. Why do I need an assistant?" I ask, seeing her eyes drift back to the wall where Rathis is showing all his white teeth as his fingers reach out to stroke his girlfriend's cheek.

"I believe they think I'll be helpful to you?"

"Oh." I scoot over and pat the bed next to me. "Here, sit down and explain what's happening here. Is this Rathis's girlfriend?"

Grinning at me, Aella climbs next to me, pointing at the girl on the wall. "That's Gizelle. She wishes she were Rathis's consort, but he's all but promised to Drea."

"So, Gizelle is a skeeza?" I take the cup of what looks like tea that Aella hands me.

"What's a skeeza?" she asks before pouring a cup of tea for herself.

"Boyfriend stealer."

"Yes," Aella nods adamantly, "she's a skeeza—we call her a lurker." I smile because she is so into it. "Don't let me watch too much of this. I'm supposed to get you ready for dinner." Then she inhales with a deep gasp. *"Look!"* She points at the wall, "Her skiff is not even faulty!" I try not to laugh, realizing a "skiff" is a type of hover car. Sneering disgustedly at the wall, Aella says, "Oh, turn it off. He's a nim."

"What's a nim?" I ask, handing her the remote.

"An annoying Etharian," she replies. Taking the remote, she speaks into it, "Stream melody—what do you like to listen to, Fay Kricket?"

"You mean, music?" I see her nod. "Do you have anything human?"

Shaking her head, she says, "No, it's illegal. But," she continues in a conspiratorial voice, "I know where to get some illicitly, if you'd like."

"You mean, bootleg human music? There are pirates even in Ethar?" I ask, seeing her nod again. "You better not. I'm sure they'll be watching me closely. Just put on something you like."

"You are not at all what I expected," Aella says, putting on some music that sounds like some sort of new age Celtic music.

"Really? Is that bad?"

"No, it's good." She smiles.

"How did you think I'd be?"

Shrugging and blushing a little, she says, "Well, you're part Alameeda. I thought you would be . . . mean."

"Are all Alameeda mean?"

"I don't know. I've never met one," she replies.

"How about a human?"

"I've never even seen a human before," she says, looking a little nervous. "What are they like?"

"Most of them are . . . crystal, but there are a few nims, too."

"I have a million questions about Earth," she says, looking excited again. "Maybe, when we have more time, we can talk about what it's like there."

"Sure," I say casually. "If you're going to be my assistant, we'll probably be together a lot."

"Mazi is going to be so annoyed that she passed up the chance to be your liaison," Aella gloats. "While you cleanse, I'll find you something to wear that will tell everyone that you've *arrived.*"

"Uh, okay," I murmur as she reaches out enthusiastically and ushers me to the lavare that is located next to the commodus in my room.

After showering, I'm given a long robe to wear while Aella weaves my hair into intricate patterns. Adjusting an automatic makeup artist, she hands me the box that looks like a viewfinder. "Close your eyes," she says when I put it to my face.

"Already learned that the hard way," I reply. Closing my eyes, I smile and hear her giggle as she clicks the button to apply a coat of cosmetics to my face.

"What do you want to project tonight?" she asks, walking into the closet and eyeing the clothes.

"Uhh . . . I want to project confidence," I reply, following her in.

"Okay, what else?"

Thinking, I add, "I want to say, 'I'm a boss; I don't get controlled—I control.'"

Aella's eyebrow rises as she gazes at my clothes, "Most of this is tailored to look your age—light colors and demure cuts, but you don't act your age—or look it. Let's try this. It's a little daring, but it will work for you, if you own it." Putting on the sleeveless, blood-red silk gown with an internal corset, I turn toward the mirror, seeing the gown hugging my contours in slim, elegant lines.

"This is what I'm supposed to wear to dinner?" Fear begins in the hollow of my stomach and creeps to my extremities.

"This is dinner with the *Regent*," she corrects me. "He's meeting with several ambassadors this evening, I'm told." Pulling out almost nude-colored heels with red soles, she hands them to me. "This outfit says, 'I own my destiny.'"

"Would Gizelle wear this dress?" I inquire as I study myself in the mirror and wonder again who I am.

"She couldn't afford it," Aella replies with a grin.

"Yeah, well, we have that in common then," I reply with a grimace. "Am I ready?"

"Yes, I'll take you down to Thea. She'll want to take you herself to the Gold Dining Room. It's in the amethyst passage where the Regent resides." Leading me out into the hall, Aella begins giving me a tour. "This is the west arcade, we call it the 'Lilac Crypt'; it houses the single females and is a restricted area. Everyone needs to have permission to be here."

"Why?"

"Because it's for royal females."

"So?"

"So . . . you're to be protected."

"Are you single?"

"Yes, I'm only thirty," she says, rolling her eyes like a teenager.

"You're thirty? Uh . . . of course." I try not to show my surprise as I attempt to cover up for the fact that I thought she was my age. She looks like a teenager, and she acts really young, too. "Do you live at the palace?"

"Yes, I have a small apartment in a separate building on the property. I've been working here as an undersecretary to the courtier's office—you know, doing correspondence and arranging accommodations for visiting royalty," she says, smiling.

I don't know, but I'm intrigued. "Really? Does it pay well?" I ask, wondering what I can do here.

"A liaison to you will pay really well," she says, grinning and nudging me with her shoulder.

Smiling back, I ask, "Who pays you?"

"The Regent's office," she replies. "We all work for the Regent."

Walking together down the grand staircase I had climbed earlier, I catch a glimpse of pale blond hair on the gentlemen milling around the area near the bottom of the stairs. I nearly stop, seeing Kyon approach the steps and wait for me to descend, but I raise my chin instead as my heart drums frantically in my ears.

Chapter 14
My Next Deal

Watching Kyon's eyes devour every inch of me as I move down the elegant staircase, I hear him say, "Kricket," when I reach the bottom step.

"Kyon," I murmur, inclining my head in a civil greeting. He looks tall and buff in a long, elegant coat and black, tailored matching trousers. His crisp white shirt is tied with a white neckcloth. His coat is belted at the waist, and if I didn't already know that he's a *total* knob knocker, I might've found him appealing.

Moving aside, he allows me to descend the last step before he takes my hand, placing it on his arm. To Aella, he says arrogantly, "I will escort Fay Kricket in to dinner. You may leave."

Fear shines in Aella's eyes as she assesses the massive enemy soldiers surrounding us. She shows some courage when she raises her eyebrow to me in question. Refusing to let Kyon intimidate me as he towers over me, I say, "I'm fine, Aella. I'll see you later." Appearing conflicted about whether she should leave me with Kyon, Aella gives the Alameeda a wide berth as she skirts them to head in the opposite direction.

Allowing Kyon to guide me down the marble tiled hallway, I keep my eyes straight ahead of me, but I can feel his attention on my face. "I'm surprised to see you here, Kyon," I say, noticing no less than six Alameeda fall in step around us.

"Is that so?" he asks, a note of irritation in his voice.

"Mmm. It's funny how you turn up in the most unexpected places. Night clubs, restricted airspace, here . . . Why are you here?" I ask, watching Rafe courtiers staring at us in outright disbelief as we pass them.

"I'm here for you," he says quietly, and the tensing in his arm increases.

"For me? What can you possibly want with me?"

"You belong to me, Kricket. I'm here to take you home," he replies, and he's not lying. He believes every word he just said. "I've come with ambassadors from Alameeda and Wurthem. We'll work out the terms for your release. It will be just a matter of negotiations."

"Hold up—can you go back to the part where you said I'm yours? Because that's where I stopped listening to you!"

"I have been awarded your suit by the Alameeda Brotherhood. You'll become my consort when we return to Alameeda," he replies, and my eyes flicker to his, seeing desire in his stare as his blue eyes rest on the cleavage above my gown.

I wrinkle my nose. "Yeah, that's not happening." We continue to walk together, and I feel him stiffen. His jaw tenses, too, making the planes of his face even more masculine.

"It will happen. You should never have run from me. We could have avoided all of this."

"Sorry to disappoint you, Kyon, but I'm not going to agree to be your consort in this or any other world that you try to drag me to."

"Your agreement is not required," he counters, a small smile gracing his lips.

"That's the most repulsive thing I've ever heard," I reply. "What's wrong with you? Can't you find someone else to haunt? Because I'm *clearly* not into you."

"You clearly need me, Kricket. Why are you allowed to roam around here without a proper escort?" he growls, glaring menacingly at everyone who passes us.

"What do you think will happen to me?" I blurt out, showing him my annoyance. "I can take care of myself."

"You're female. How can you possibly take care of yourself?" he asks in an equally annoyed tone.

"I've taken care of myself for years!" I'm completely offended.

"If you take care of yourself so well, then why are there bruises on your neck?" His look is deadly.

"That was a misunderstanding." Turning another corner, I almost stumble as I recognize the group milling around at the end of the corridor. My pulse quickens as Trey's handsome, violet eyes turn to meet mine. He looks incredible in a long, black, tailored jacket that is belted at his waist, just as Kyon's is, but Trey has a long stick, like a sword, holstered to his belt. It looks like some kind of weapon with a blunt, silver tip. Standing near Jax, Wayra, and Victus, Trey looks the most dangerous; his jaw tenses above his white, tied neckcloth as his eyes shift from me to Kyon at my side.

Feeling weirdly fragile all of a sudden, I blush as we approach the Cavars. They're staring at me like I've grown another head, so I incline my chin in greeting, saying, "Greetings, Etharians. Look who I found roaming the halls."

After inclining his head to me, Wayra says, "Kricket, you should just ignore the trash you see lying around. There are people here that will clean it up for you." He places his hand on the club sheathed in his belt to emphasize his words.

Feeling Kyon stiffen again, I smile at Wayra. "You never did give me a recurve, so diplomacy was all that was left to me." Jax and Wayra grin, but Trey and Victus don't. Seeing the brothers side by side, they are nearly identical, except Trey has broader shoulders than Victus, which is probably due to lifestyle choice. Trey also has military tattoos, which Victus lacks.

"Where are your Regent escorts?" Trey asks me, appearing as annoyed by my current escort as Kyon was when he found me alone.

I use a casual shrug as a cover for dropping my hand from Kyon's arm. I become almost breathless with relief that he's going to let me go for a second. "I don't know. Ustus said he'd see me at dinner. Is this the Gold Dining Room?"

Kyon's blue eyes narrow dangerously as he addresses Trey. "Are you responsible for the bruises on her neck?"

"I am," Trey replies, staring back at Kyon, and he's not lying—he must really think he's responsible for the restraint put on my neck by the Regent agents.

"I should've made sure you were dead. What did they do, regenerate you?" Kyon asks. He takes a step closer to Trey as his nostrils flare in anger.

"Something like that," Trey replies smoothly. He takes a step nearer to Kyon as they do that male stare-down thing.

My mind whirls, realizing that Kyon and Trey must've fought each other in the war between Alameeda and Rafe. "Trey is not responsible for the bruises on my neck," I state quietly.

"Is he responsible for bringing you here?" Kyon asks me in a tight voice.

"Yes," I answer, watching his frown deepen.

"Then he's responsible for your bruises."

"No, I'm responsible for what happens to me and what I do next," I correct him. "Now, if you'll excuse me, I'm hungry because I've been running through the jungle for the past few rotations and eating protein bars that taste like cat poop."

Dismissing Kyon and shifting toward Trey, I ask, "Do you think they'll be serving pheasant?" Taking his arm, I wait calmly for him to lead me into the Gold Dining Room.

Looking down at my hand on his arm, Trey seems to relax a little, losing some of the tension he had as he smiles. Kyon, on the other hand, looks like he's about to have a tantrum.

As Trey leads me away from Kyon, I whisper to him, "Why are you here?"

"We were all summoned by the Regent," Trey replies, his eyes focusing on mine. My heartbeat speeds up more when I see how lovely his eyes are.

"Oh," I murmur, tearing my eyes away from his and feeling disappointed that he didn't come here specifically to see me.

We enter the Gold Room together, and it doesn't fail to live up to its name. Every fixture in the high-ceilinged room is golden, not to mention the gold chargers beneath the dinner plates lining the long, highly polished wood table.

At the other end of the room, a group of three men are standing by the mantel of the fireplace. The taller, athletically built, commanding man is definitely Rafe, judging by his dark Rafeish-brown hair. This must be the Regent. The smooth skin of his face is unblemished and lightly tanned; he's used to being outdoors and active, but I can't tell what he does to make it so. His short hair doesn't cover his eyebrows and barely touches his collar in the back—closer to a military cut than I'd expected. His attentive violet eyes watch me. He smiles at something the man next to him says, but it seems more calculated than genuine; it also makes him extremely handsome and younger looking than I'd first thought—maybe late thirties in human terms. *He doesn't need to be a regent to get a lot of what he wants,* I assess. *He'd just have to employ that smile.*

He's dressed elegantly, just like Trey, except that his belt is larger, with a bigger, shinier, buckle in the front. The other two men he's with don't look Rafe, judging by their hair, blond on one man and light brown on the other. "His name is Manus. He's the Regent. You need to make him see you as a Rafe citizen—make it hard for him to treat you like a commodity," Trey coaches me. His mouth nears my cheek, and I shiver again as I react to him, remembering the taste of his lips against mine. Heat steals to my cheeks as I acknowledge his comment with a nod.

"How do I make him see that I'm not a commodity?"

"Just be yourself, but be respectful."

"Do you know the blond with him?" I murmur, tilting my face nearer to his and feeling a surge of desire for Trey plow through me.

"Yes, his name is Nark . . ." Trey trails off when I begin giggling. "What's so funny?" he asks me, his breath tickling my ear, causing crazy things to happen inside of me.

"Um, where I come from, a narc is someone who tells your secrets," I reply, seeing him smile.

"That's apt then, because he's an Alameeda ambassador—he has many secrets. You'll address him as Em Nark," he advises, and I giggle again. "Try not to laugh when you speak to him. He has *no* sense of humor."

"You've met him?" The Regent is still watching me during his conversation with "the Narc."

"We've met a few times. He likes to gamble; let's leave it at that," he says, making my eyebrow arch before I gaze back at them.

"The other?"

"Is Sam."

"Really?"

"Yes."

"That's too normal a name for one of you guys," I smile.

"He's Wurthem," Trey shrugs.

"Ah. Ambassador?"

"Yes, but he's an Alameeda puppet."

"I hate puppets—they're creepy," I reply softly, feeling his hand tighten on my arm.

"Yes," Trey agrees. "Let's make sure you don't become one."

Nearing the Regent and the ambassadors, Trey and I stop in front of them. I mimic Trey as we both kneel in a sign of respect to the leader of the Rafe clan. Em Nark immediately speaks up, as I begin to rise. "Kricket, you do not need to kneel before Haut Manus. You simply incline your head to him as a sign of respect."

Trey narrows his eyes at the ambassador while I watch Manus studying me. "With all respect, Em Nark," I say, smiling, "Manus is not only my Regent, he is also my guardian, and therefore I will show him my respect." *For now,* my mind whispers.

"You are an Alameeda priestess," Em Nark responds sourly, frowning at me.

"I'm a Rafe citizen," I say, keeping my smile in place, "and I've just returned home."

"We have been discussing your home," Em Nark says, his pudgy face jiggling. "We have not decided where you will reside."

"Is that so? Let me pull up a chair then, so we can continue the discussion." I watch his face go from pale to flushed.

"Perhaps there will be time to hear your thoughts on this matter after dinner, Fay Kricket," Manus says, his eyes softening in the corners as they take in everything about me.

"I will look forward to dessert then," I reply, seeing a real smile twist Manus's lips. Trey leads me away from them so that the others can be introduced.

"That was perfect, Kricket," Trey breathes in my ear, guiding me over to the table. A member of the Regent's staff indicates that I'm to sit on the opposite end of the table, facing the Regent. I reluctantly let go of Trey, and the security I felt at being by his side wanes with each step I take away from him. Trey is much closer to the Regent's end of the table. An attendant pulls my chair out for me, but as I begin to sit, another member of the Regent's staff rushes over and whispers in his associate's ear.

"Fay Kricket, please excuse me, but you're to dine next to the Regent this evening," he says in a formal voice, gesturing to the other end of the table.

"Oh," I murmur, and my eyes find Trey's as he stands by his seat next to Victus. His eyes widen in surprise, too. I thank the footman as he escorts me to the other end of the table. I take my seat beside the Regent, who's at the head of the table, and I smile at him when he takes his. Everyone else sits as well, and I cringe, realizing that Kyon is next to me, too.

A footman approaches my seat, carrying a mahogany box. As he holds it out to me, I gaze at the polished box that has two holes in the front of it. I have no idea what I'm supposed to do with it. Reaching out, I attempt to take the box from the footman, and the look of surprise that crosses his face as his grip tightens on it is almost comical.

"Fay Kricket," Trey says from across the table from me, "that is a basuess. You place your hands in the holes, and it will clean them."

"Oh, my bad," I reply, turning back to the footman holding the box. Tentatively, I place my hands in the box, feeling warm steam shower them. I smile as I glance back at Trey. "Who invented this?" I ask. "It's very clever."

Pulling my hands out, I examine them. When I glance up again, I notice every eye in the room is on me. Quickly, I drop my hands and hide them in my lap as the Regent chuckles next to me.

"I believe it was Esturn? Is that correct?" Manus asks, looking around the table.

"It was Dourreno," Trey replies.

"Yes, of course," Manus agrees, not at all offended at being corrected.

"We have much to do," the Narc says dourly, gazing tiredly at me, like I've already exasperated him beyond the limit of his patience. "Your training will need to be started immediately." I can't avoid his scrutiny. He's seated directly across the table from me between the Regent at the head of the table and Trey on his left.

"Yes, I agree," I say, before taking a sip of my water. "I need to begin applying to universities as soon as possible. Do they offer scholarships here, or do I need to apply for financial aid?" I ask the Regent. His smile suddenly becomes broader, like I made a joke.

"A public institution!" the Narc exclaims. "You will not attend a common—we have educators that will advise you," he finishes, looking scandalized.

"Home schooling?" I wrinkle my nose at him. "How am I supposed to make friends?" I watch the footmen delivering bowls of soup and placing them on the plates in front of us. "Thank you," I say to the footman, seeing him smile.

"You will make friends with the other priestesses," Kyon remarks.

"I prefer to choose my own friends. Anyway, I'll be here in the Isle of Skye, so it may be difficult to see Alameeda priestesses unless they come to visit me." My mouth waters from the aroma of the soup, but I wait for the Regent to pick up one of his spoons. He chooses the one located at the top of the place setting. I take that one, too, but wait for the Regent to dip it in his soup. Relieved to see that they eat soup like I do, I begin to eat.

"Fay Kricket is very independent," Trey says from across the table. "We had a difficult time convincing her to come home, but without her cooperation we may not have made it here safely."

"Yes, I read the report; it was fascinating," Manus says, looking me over again. "Did you really run from a saer?"

I shrug. "It was lucky for us that there were two of them." I watch as the Narc chokes on his soup.

Em Nark sputters, "Your Cavars put an Alameeda priestess at undue risk!"

"Oh, I'm fine," I reply lightly. "The saers ate the spixes." A round of coughing comes from the footmen in the room as they all struggle to keep their faces straight. Jax and Wayra are having trouble with the same thing.

"Did you know they would eat the spixes?" Em Nark asks me, his blue eyes narrowing slyly.

"Yes," I say, watching his eyes dart to Kyon's at my side, and then I add, "the saer had the spix in its mouth; its intentions were quite obvious." My comment causes the Narc's face to droop in disappointment.

"We appreciate that you were able to locate our subject for us. We're quite in your debt, Haut Manus," the Narc says, running his hand through his blond hair.

"My mother, I am told, was an expatriate of Alameeda," I say, before sipping the water in my glass. "Didn't she choose to live in Rafe for . . . political reasons?" I ask, watching him.

"She was never an émigré. Your father took her from us by force," the Narc lies.

"So you threatened Rafe citizens because she was being held against her will?" I shift my gaze toward the Regent, who's waiting for the Narc to respond.

"That is so," he lies again, looking a little sweaty.

I smile sweetly. "And now you are here to rescue her daughter?"

"Yes," he replies, his eyes meeting Kyon's before finding mine again. "You're Alameeda. You belong with our people. We . . ."

"You what?" I prompt him, taking another sip of water.

"We can take care of you properly."

"Am I not being properly looked after?" I ask him, a small smile on my lips. "My guardian is the Regent. I reside in a palace. I have Regent police for escorts."

"They cannot help you to utilize the gifts that you will develop," the Narc replies, looking to Kyon and Em Sam for help.

"No, I don't think that's it at all," I say, watching a footman take my bowl away and replace it with an entrée from a hovering tray that is gliding along in the air next to him.

"How do you see it, Fay Kricket?" Manus asks me, watching my look of fascination as the hovering tray continues to follow the footman around the table.

"Uh, well, if I remain here, wouldn't it be more difficult for the Alameeda to utilize my gifts?" I ask him innocently. "They can't let the rat escape the lab, can they? It could infect more rats, and then their other rats wouldn't be so very special now, would they?" Watching Em Nark's face redden as his eyes widen, I take a bite of the savory meat dish placed in front of me. "Oh, my gosh, Trey, did you taste this? What is it? It's sooo good!" I grin at Trey, and a smile crosses his lips in response.

"You don't want to risk another international incident," Kyon remarks softly to the Regent.

"Why would the international community be involved with the custody of a Rafe citizen?" Trey asks Kyon.

"She's an Alameeda subject," Kyon replies, his eyes narrowing.

"Ateur Victus," I say, looking at Trey's twin. "What are the extradition rights afforded to someone like me? Someone with a dual citizenship?"

"You're not a criminal," he says. "This is more a family court situation—it's custody because you're a minor."

"Your family in Alameeda will petition the court for custody of you. You have an aunt—your mother's sister—who would like to meet you," Kyon says.

"I'd like to meet her, too." Something lurches in my stomach at the knowledge that I have family that wants to know me. But if I go to Alameeda, I would belong to Kyon. "Victus, if I were a criminal, could I seek political asylum?"

"Of course." He looks puzzled.

"So, if I felt that I could be prosecuted in Alameeda for violating their laws regarding Earth, I could seek asylum here, in Rafe courts?" I ask.

A cunning smile creeps over Victus's face, making him look just like Trey, "Yes, I believe you could, Kricket."

"Crystal," I breathe.

Em Nark looks like he's eating sand as he chews his food, glaring at me across the table. Kyon is as stiff as a board, but the rest of the table is quite relaxed.

The Regent asks Trey, Wayra, and Jax questions about their time on Earth. I listen while Trey outlines their methods of tracking down my parents. They had used facial recognition software to scan news articles on the Internet. Their web crawlers finally located my parents' obituary in the *Chicago Tribune*. The same article had featured a picture of me. A well-intentioned neighbor had placed it there in hopes of locating some family for me, so I wouldn't become a victim of the child welfare system.

Trey watches me across the table as he says, "I infiltrated the Chicago Department of Social Services and located intake pictures of Kricket. I used those pictures along with facial recognition software to look for her on the Internet. I found her on Enrique's Facebook page."

I blanch. *Enrique and his stupid camera phone!*

"We located Enrique quite easily, and he led us to Kricket," Trey says, and for a second I think I hear a hint of guilt in his tone, but it doesn't show on his face.

"Have you been monitoring the situation on Earth?" Manus asks.

Trey nods. "I have the report from Skye detailing the latest developments. The authorities on Earth are no longer treating Kricket's disappearance as abduction. She's been ruled a runaway.

"Show us the report," Manus orders.

Trey glances at me, and I incline my head covertly. I want to see what's been happening with my case. I need to study everything about their methods of detection, so I can learn to avoid it in the future.

Trey says, "This was intercepted from Earth yesterday. Initiate hologram." He uses words and phrases that sound like complete gibberish to me. The only words I really recognize are "Enrique Rodriguez and Bridget Moreno." Instantly, miniature lifelike figures of Enrique and Bridget appear between Em Nark and me. As I look down the table toward the other end, the same six-inch figures appear at different intervals so that everyone seated has a clear view of them.

Bridget is next to Enrique, and Hipster Eric is behind her with his hand on her shoulder. They're standing near a small podium filled with microphones. Bridget looks like she's been crying a lot, but she's not crying right now. She's like me; she'll try really hard not to cry in front of strangers. A picture of me is on the front of Enrique's shirt beneath his black leather jacket. He must really like me because he'd never be caught dead in that shirt otherwise.

"I have a statement," Enrique says, and his face blanches as flashes strobe him from reporter's cameras. "The police may have ruled this as a runaway, but I'm here today to say they're wrong. All the evidence points to this being an abduction, and we're not gonna stop until this ruling is changed, the case is reopened, and Kricket is found."

A reporter's voice from somewhere in front of him asks, "Hasn't Kricket shown a history of running away?"

Enrique frowns. "Yes, but she was only running away from Social Services. She wasn't trying to hide from us."

"Are you her boyfriend? Did you two have a fight?" someone else asks.

"No! We were friends!" Enrique says. "She and I didn't fight!"

"Why do you think she would run away?" is the next question from the reporters.

Bridget's face becomes a mask of rage. "He just told you that she didn't run away, you stupid *rábo*! Don't you listen?"

Manus laughs. "Who is that one?"

"The roommate," Trey replies. I watch Enrique field a dozen more questions, each one tailored to make me look like I ran away. "She has been living with her boyfriend since Kricket disappeared. It seems like it may be a permanent arrangement."

"What about the other one," Manus asks. "Will he be a problem?"

"He's puny," Kyon says quietly to me in disgust. "What problems could he cause?"

My eyes narrow in anger. "You don't know anything. His heart is bigger than you."

"He won't be a problem," Trey assures Manus. "We left him no trail to follow."

The hologram ends and my friends fade away like they were never there. When the conversation turns to our time in the Forest of Omnicron, the Regent laughs heartily as Wayra tells them how I stood up to the Comantre Syndics.

"So, there we were," Wayra says animatedly, "all of us Cavars on our knees with blue beams dotting the front of our uniforms, and this tiny Etharian is facing down the entire unit, raging at us for losing her luggage and telling us that we ruined her holiday in the Forest of O!" The entire room erupts in laughter except for Kyon and the Narc who both look truly ill.

Leaning near my ear, Kyon asks, "You pretended to be Trey's consort?" He looks outwardly calm, but his tone is deadly.

"Yes, and I was quite good at it, too," I reply, seeing his jaw clench more. "Does that bother you?" I ask, my eyebrow arching.

"As your intended, it does," he utters softly, his eyes falling on my cleavage again. "If I wasn't aware that you're still a virgin, I might have had him beaten."

A severe blush flushes my face. "How do you know my status?" I take a quick sip of my water to try to cool the heat of embarrassment.

"I read your medical records provided to us by the Regent's physicians, who were quite thorough," he says, smiling at my apparent discomfort. "They did a body scan while you were with them. Everything is . . . intact."

Feeling violated, I want to wipe that smirk off his face. "The funny thing about that state is that it's easily changed," I reply. Seeing his eyebrows draw together, I smile.

"Be very careful, Kricket. Should that status change, I will kill the one who changes it." He's telling the truth. "You don't know what you're doing, do you?"

"I'm controlling my destiny," I say softly, looking into his blue eyes.

"No, you are sealing your fate," he disagrees with a sinister edge to his voice. "We don't let our rats go. We hunt them down and exterminate them if they fail to cooperate," he explains, reaching out and touching my cheek lightly. "I'd hate to see that happen to you, especially when I find you so appealing."

"What do you want?" I ask with fear threading through me.

"It's not what *I* want; it's what we *both* want. Think of this as the beginning of a symbiotic relationship."

"How is that possible when we are the same species?" I counter.

A grin forms on his lips. "Are we? That is debatable. I haven't the gifts that you possess. My hair doesn't grow back instantly after it's cut off. You are a mutated form of my species," he says, and his assessment of me is chilling.

"Maybe I'm just smarter than you—more highly evolved," I argue, not liking the word "mutated" because it makes me sound like a science experiment gone awry.

"There is no doubt that you are capable of many things. I can make it so that you achieve your full potential. Or I can achieve what I want by other means," he says quietly. "I could just drop you down a hole and keep you there until you learn."

"You say the sweetest things, Kyon," I murmur, pressing my sharp dinner knife threateningly into his ribs. "But you're really gonna have to stop touching me now."

A slow smile creeps over his face, making him look kind of handsome. "You are savage," he breathes, lifting his fingers from my cheek as his eyes all but sparkle.

"You have no idea how savage I can be," I reply, easing my knife away from him.

"I look forward to finding out," Kyon murmurs, looking me over like I'm dessert.

Our plates are cleared then, replaced with a pastry in the shape of a swan that tastes a lot like baklava. I force myself to eat the entire thing, even when I have completely lost my appetite. When the footmen take away our plates again, the Regent stands up, pulling my chair away from the table for me.

"Fay Kricket, would you care to join us in the next room for some fazeria?" he asks me, offering me his arm.

"I'll join you if you tell me what fazeria is," I smile, taking his arm and hearing him laugh.

"It's an alcoholic beverage, Kricket," he says, leading the way to the adjoining room. Everyone follows close behind, listening to our exchange.

"Is it good?" I ask, taking a seat on a silk-covered sofa.

"It is." Reaching out and taking a long-stemmed glass from the footman, he hands it to me. I take a small sip, and the amber liquid mildly burns my throat as I swallow it.

"Mmm," I smile at the Regent, who is watching me with an air of expectation. "It *is* good."

Appearing delighted, he takes a glass himself and sips it. "Em Nark, I have definite reservations regarding Fay Kricket. I need to consider the matter further."

The Narc joins me on the sofa then, making goose bumps rise on my arms. "Of course, Haut Manus. This is a delicate situation and we appreciate your reservations. Kyon is a ranking member of the Brotherhood. He will assume full responsibility for Fay Kricket as her intended consort . . ." he trails off because Wayra chokes loudly on his fazeria. Looking over at him, my eyes go to Trey, who looks murderous.

"We intend to aid in your negotiations with Wurthem for the Tectonic Peninsula," the Narc lies, ignoring the glares of the Cavars.

"Have you been in contact with the Peney clan regarding the Tectonic Peninsula?" Manus asks, pacing in front of the fireplace.

"No," Em Nark lies again, "but we would be happy to be the lead in the exchange there." Another lie.

"Are the Alameeda currently seeking a position in Peney?" the Regent asks, pausing and sipping his fazeria.

"We have no interest there," the Narc lies again. "Our interests lie in returning Kricket to her family." I'm finding it more and more difficult not to roll my eyes.

"We have heard some disturbing things regarding Alameeda troops pushing the borders near the Cape of Peney," Trey says casually. "You wouldn't happen to know anything about that, would you, Em Nark?"

"Your intelligence is faulty, there are no Alameeda troops near Peney." Em Nark is lying yet again. Trey's eyes shift to mine in question.

"How many troops do you have there?" I ask him, studying the glass in my hand.

"Excuse me?" the Narc asks with a scowl.

"More than a thousand?" I ask, studying his face.

"*No!*" the Narc lies.

"More than five thousand?"

"No, of course not," he lies, looking at Kyon, who is now turned away, facing the window.

"Is it more like ten thousand?"

"She is a soothsayer—a diviner of truth, Em Nark," Kyon says softly, causing every eye to shift to him. "Don't open your mouth again." Turning to the Regent, he says, "Write up your list of demands, and you shall have them. All we want is Kricket."

The room falls silent for several seconds as Kyon and Manus stare at each other. "Do you know what that was, Em Nark?" I ask, seeing his face growing pale. "That was a moment of silence for the death of your career."

"You don't know what you're doing," he sneers at me. "Mine will not be the only death to result from tonight . . ." he trails off as Jax and Wayra move closer to me, standing right behind our sofa.

Trey is less discreet, sitting down in the small space between the Narc and me, saying to me under his breath, "Down goes the bishop."

"You may leave now, Em Nark," Manus says in a dismissive tone. "Please take your trift back to Alameeda. Your things will be sent to you. I believe we should continue our discussion at the break of the rotation, Haut Kyon," Manus says softly, watching the Narc exit through the door. "There is much to explore in this matter."

"Do not think to keep her. We will not let her go. I will await your council, Haut Manus," Kyon says, while walking toward me. Taking my hand in his, Kyon brings it to his lips, kissing it. "Until the next rotation, Kricket, rest well." Releasing my hand, he leaves the room and leaves me to my fear.

Chapter 15

Come to Ruin

As I remain seated on the silk-covered furniture in the Regent's drawing room, I feel cold inside when Em Sam leaves the room behind Kyon. Trey's hand inches closer to mine on the seat, stopping a whisper of a breadth from it. His expression of concern makes me look away so that I don't cry. *I can't afford to be weak—not now, not ever.* Suppressing the impulse to touch Trey, my eyes shift toward the main threat left in the room: the Regent.

Seeing Manus's violet gaze studying me, I toy with the glass in my hand, trying to appear at ease. "Am I to understand by the exchange with Em Nark, Kricket, that there are Alameeda troops near the borders of Peney?" Manus asks me, his eyebrows rising. He is truly handsome in a dangerous way, with his five o'clock shadow cutting his cheeks at sharp angles. He looks like he could be in his late thirties, which probably means he's at least a half a millennium old.

Straightening in my seat, I reply, "At least five thousand Alameeda soldiers are there; there could be more, but Em Nark didn't answer my last question."

"How do you know this?" he asks, suppressing a frown while sitting in the seat adjacent to mine.

"I don't know—instinct, intuition," I say, feigning a casual shrug as my heart is pounding in my chest at the exposure of my secret. "I don't know how I know. I just do."

"You are a—what did Kyon call you—a diviner of truth? A soothsayer?" Manus asks, and he can't suppress the excitement in his tone.

"No," I sigh, shaking my head. "I can tell if someone is lying on purpose or bluffing, but truth is . . . harder to know," I reply, lowering my chin. "Just because someone believes something to be true doesn't make it so." Seeing his confused expression, I exhale another sigh, asking, "Jax, does fazeria taste good?"

Looking over my shoulder at Jax, he smiles at me before saying, "Yes." I nod.

My eyes shift to Wayra as I ask him, "Wayra, does fazeria taste good?"

He frowns at me, looking like I've put him on the spot. He begins to hedge, "Well, it's really sweet and I—"

"Just yes or no?" I ask, rolling my eyes at him.

"Well, then, no," he admits, looking awkward.

"You see? They both answered me truthfully, but their answers are conflicting," I explain, watching Manus absorb what I said.

"Yes, but if you were to ask the right questions, then you could divine the truth?" he asks me in a quiet tone.

"Don't get it twisted. I know if you're purposefully lying, but here's the thing—um, Trey, face away from me," I request. Looking confused, Trey faces away from me on the sofa. "Okay, Trey, I'm holding up three fingers. Tell the Regent that I'm holding up three fingers.

Not looking at me, Trey says, "Kricket is holding up three fingers."

"Ah," Manus murmurs, nodding. Trey turns to look at me and sees that I'm only holding up two fingers. "Trey believed you, and so he unknowingly lied to me."

"Yes, and I can't divine that kind of lie," I reply honestly, "because he believed it to be true."

"If your gift remains secret, then you have more of an advantage? Less of a chance that someone could manipulate the information?" Manus asks, and I nod my head.

"But now the Alameeda know to a certain extent what I can do," I say sheepishly.

"They may not know the limitations of your gift," he replies cunningly. "Kricket, you could be . . . an advisor to me. Sit in on affairs of state and foreign affairs as well."

"Uh, you know, I'm not that familiar with Etharian politics," I reply nervously.

"You'll get familiar with them."

"Are you planning on getting rid of our scene clinger, Kyon?" I ask. "We could talk business if I knew that this would be a more . . . permanent arrangement for me."

Manus's eyes widen in surprise, as a smile touches his lips. "Is that so?"

"Mmm," I nod, trying to look like I don't have a lot invested in this conversation. "You have unrest on the borders of Peney. They're not your allies, but if Alameeda is making a play for them, then you had better get in the game and find out who's really on your side."

"Had I?" Manus asks, watching me and looking intrigued.

"Yes," I nod. "And I can help with that in an advisory capacity for a fee, say . . . double what you pay your top advisors now." I toy again with the glass in my hands. "And if I knew that there would never be any . . . *seduciary* responsibilities for me where Kyon was concerned, then I would be more free to focus on the affairs of state."

"Seduciary responsibilities!" Manus hoots with laughter, as does everyone else in the room but Trey and me.

"You don't like Kyon?" Manus asks with an amused smile.

"In a word: no."

"You surprise me, Kricket," Manus says, almost to himself. "Kyon is very connected. He could be a strong consort for you. You shouldn't reject him without consideration. It would be unwise to turn him away just now. We will allow you both the opportunity of getting to know each other better," Manus says in such a way that I know that his decision is not up for discussion or contradiction. "Ateur Victus, you intervened in the corrective court on Kricket's behalf. On whose authority did you act?"

"Mine," I interrupt before Victus can answer him. "I hired him to help me."

"Since you have inserted yourself into Kricket's affairs," Manus says, ignoring me, "you will now be responsible for her entry into Rafe society. You will sponsor Kricket and accompany her as escort to every venue we deem important. This will help her by linking your family name with hers."

Glancing at Trey, I see his jaw tighten, but Victus is taking this all in stride, saying, "I would be honored to accompany Kricket."

"Good. You will attend a swank in her honor, announcing her arrival in town," Manus says.

"Oh, you know, I hate parties—all those people and . . . more people," I stammer, trying to slow down the propaganda train.

"Kesek Allairis," Manus says, and my eyebrow arches at the strange title that Manus uses to address Trey.

"Haut Manus," Trey replies in a military tone.

"You and your men will be reassigned in the capacity of personal protection for Fay Kricket," Manus instructs. "I want you to be discreet—no uniforms. You will lead the team. I need trained Cavars for this—Ustus and his men will answer to you. Expect retaliation from the Alameeda and their allies. You'll be briefed on what we know. Everything that Kricket does must be approved by you; is that understood?" he asks.

"Yes, I understand, Haut Manus," Trey agrees. Glancing at me, he doesn't smile.

"Is that really necessary?" I ask, rolling my eyes in exasperation, even as my heart picks up at the thought of Trey being here with me.

"Kricket, do not question my authority. I am the Regent and your guardian," Manus replies sternly.

"Yes, but I'm really not a child," I try to explain to him.

"You have enemies here and abroad. This can be a cold and violent world, Kricket. I will protect you from that . . . for now."

With an arch look at Manus, I ask, "And who will protect me from you?"

I see his eyes darken as he murmurs, "That will be left up to you."

"I'll have to rise to the occasion, then," I say, standing and recognizing that I need to quit now before this goes really, really badly for me.

Standing, too, Manus says, "I will see you at the break of the next rotation. You will dine with me and we will align our schedules." Lifting my hand, he squeezes it lightly while I drop my chin in a nod.

"I need to assess Kricket's quarters. I will escort her to her room." Trey says, rising next to me and offering me his arm.

"Mmm," Manus replies absently, watching me. Trey inclines his head to Manus and leads me to the door.

Once in the hallway, I sag a little, letting the mask drop as we continue walking. Glancing at Trey and seeing his eyes narrow at me, I try to smile, saying, "So, that went well, except for that *huge part* where it didn't. What does 'kesek' mean?"

"It's a military rank," Trey says stiffly.

"Oh, like captain?"

"More like major," he replies, pulling me out a side door and onto a lovely, lighted path leading away from the estate. He steers me into the hedge-enshrouded grounds. Stopping in front of a lighted fountain, he lets go of my arm and begins pacing in front of me. The dark evening makes his face look even more masculine as soft light near the fountain creates patterns on it.

"Kricket . . . you . . ." Trey begins in a frustrated tone, continuing to pace. "You can't—this is complicated, but you need to appreciate the fact that you're—and you can't expect men not to respond to . . . Manus is . . ." He stops pacing to glare at me.

"He's what?" I ask, concentrating really hard on what Trey is not saying.

"He's on a higher tier than you are and—"

"A higher tier?" I interrupt, narrowing my eyes at him because that sounds suspiciously like he's insulting me.

"He's the Regent, and you're . . ." He gestures at me.

"I'm what?"

"His ward," Trey says evasively.

"So?" I ask him, seeing that there's something he's not saying.

"So, that position could change," he replies sharply.

"Yeah, I know. I'm going to be his *crappy* advisor now, but what else could I do? I couldn't just sit there and let Kyon and the Narc make a play for me," I reply, crossing my arms defensively. "I had to get rid of the Narc, and that meant exposing my secret. It was a risk, but Manus could've been swayed by them. I could feel it."

"I agree. Until that point, you were like a beautiful piece of art to him, appreciated but easily bartered away. But you went too far, Kricket! Manus will never make you his consort," he says in a harsh tone.

"What?" I exclaim, feeling shocked because that hadn't even occurred to me.

"He'd have you as his *inamorata*, but do not expect him to commit to you." Trey's tone is bitter. "He's the Regent and you are half Alameeda."

"Hold up," I order, putting up my hand to stop him. "What is an 'inamorata'?"

"A lover," he says accusingly.

I blush. "You think that Manus wants me as his lover but not as his wife because he's on a higher *tier* than me?"

"Yes."

"Because *I'm* not good enough for *him*."

"That's the way it would be viewed," Trey replies, and my heart contracts painfully.

"Why are you telling me this, Trey?" I ask in a soft tone.

"I don't want you to be . . . disappointed." He looks away from me.

"Why would you care?" I ask, looking away too, toward the fountain so that I can blink back the tears in my eyes. "Aren't you supposed to be having a commitment ceremony of your own soon?" I stoop to pick up some small stones.

"Who told you that?" Trey asks, sounding sullen.

"Does it matter?" I toss a stone at the pool and watch it disappear beneath a lily pad.

"I've known Charisma my entire life. She's always been my friend."

"That sounds ideal. She comes from a good family?" I ask, forcing myself to sound normal, but my heart really hurts now.

"They own the estate next to my family's estate."

"In the Valley of Thistle?" The perfect place that I created in my mind begins to crumble.

"Yes."

"With the spixes?" I ask, my throat raw now, seeing the house where I had my fake commitment ceremony dissolve.

"Yes," he says again, but softer.

"I'm such an idiot," I breathe, squeezing my eyes shut.

"What?" Trey asks from behind me, sounding confused.

"Nothing. I wish . . ." I throw another pebble in the fountain.

"You wish . . . what?" he asks, coming closer to me.

Angry voices, speaking in hushed tones, stop me from answering him. Trey's arms wrap around my waist and pull me back into the shadowy edge of the hedge. I don't make a sound.

"She *is* the prophecy," someone hisses from the other side of the hedge. "We haven't had a diviner of truth for hundreds of years—and she can already do it—at her age with absolutely no training."

"That is an opinion, Nark. One you will not express again," Kyon's unmistakable voice responds while they continue walking by us on the other path. Trey lets go of me, following their voices.

I follow closely behind Trey, kicking off my shoes so they don't make crunching noises on the gravel. "This is not something that we should keep from the Brotherhood. If she is the prophecy, then she's more dangerous to us than just having a rogue priestess in Rafe hands. If she is the one, then a house will fall."

"I know the prophecy. You do not need to explain it to me! The house was not named. It could be Rafe that falls."

"Or it could be Alameeda . . . or Wurthem. Do you like those odds?"

"You want to maintain the status quo at the risk of greatness, Nark. That's why you'll always be where you are—at the bottom."

The bluster in the Narc's voice is unmistakable. "When I make my report, Kyon, I'll be sure to mention that to the Brotherhood. My trift is being made ready. You should join me. There's nothing here for you now."

"No, I'll stay. Don't be surprised if the information you impart does not throw you into a favorable light," Kyon says easily. "Safe journey, Em Nark."

"Haut Kyon," the Narc responds formally before feet crunch away on the path.

"What's the prophecy?" I whisper to Trey. He turns quickly and covers my mouth with his hand, pulling me back against his chest. I still and listen for a second for any sound that would signal this kind of reaction from Trey. A soft humming noise, like a low vibration, throbs near us.

Trey tenses for just a second, and then he lifts me off my feet, carrying me as he runs back the way we came. A static noise sounds behind us, and looking over Trey's shoulder, I see a shiny, long, bulletlike thing following us. It's emitting a green beam of light, scanning everything in the vicinity like it's looking for something.

"What the—" I breathe the words, and instantly, the green light flashes on my face. The silver metal thing turns as if it has locked on to me; it streaks toward us like a missile. Horrified, I can only clutch Trey's neck tighter and watch it near, emitting a high-frequency noise that makes every hair on my body rise.

Just as it's about to pierce Trey through the back with a long needle projection, he dives forward, carrying me with him head first into the pool beneath the fountain. Submerged beneath the lily pads, Trey's body holds me under, pressing me to him like an anchor. My lungs are burning. I try pushing him off me so that I can get to the top for air, but he's not letting me go.

Opening my eyes, I see the green light scanning the water above us. I stop struggling, trying to stay beneath the water as bubbles of air escape from my mouth. The light from above slips away, and Trey eases me to the surface of the water. Breaking the surface, I inhale air greedily.

Shouts and running feet pound on the gravel path behind the hedge near us. Someone yells, "Squelch tracker!" Then, the rapid fire of weapons erupts, and a huge explosion sends me back under the surface of the water.

Trey's hands wrap around me. He hauls me up again, pressing me tightly against his chest and stroking my wet hair. Shivering, more from trauma than from cold, I rest my cheek against his chest.

"Kricket, are you hurt?" Trey demands, pulling me away from him so I can look in his eyes.

"No," I say breathlessly, seeing water dripping down the sides of his perfect face.

His hand reaches up, cupping my cheek and pulling my lips to his. The moment his lips touch mine, I lose all thought of squelch trackers, prophecies, and Regent police. Wrapping my arms around Trey's neck, I press closer to him while my heartbeat drums in my ears. Trey's lips slip from mine, trailing a path of urgent kisses over my cheek to my neck. A coil of heat collects in my core and spreads to all of my extremities in an instant. My knees become weak, and a gasp of pleasure escapes me.

"Kitten," Trey breathes, causing shivers of pleasure to flow through me at the endearment.

Finding his lips with my own, I breathe against them, "Honey," before kissing him deeply and with a passion I didn't know could exist. I try to savor every moment of this kiss, only to groan as Trey pulls away from me, letting go of me completely.

"Trey." I say his name softly as footsteps sound on the gravel. Regent police burst forward near the fountain, training their guns on us.

Breathing hard, Trey says, "Lower your weapons. We were the targets."

Chapter 16
Tell the Truth

Splashing out of the fountain, Trey turns back to me, extending his hand and helping me out of the water. He picks me up off my feet and carries me toward the palace. The police fall in step beside us. I rest my cheek against his chest, relieved that I don't have to try to walk on my shaky legs.

Trey glares at the men near him, barking out orders, "I want to know where every piece of the squelch tracker was manufactured. I want to know where it was likely launched—check its heat signature. I want new rooms for Kricket in a private area that will be occupied by me and several soldiers of my choosing."

"You want her moved from the west arcade?" Ustus asks, appearing next to us. Looking at me, his face loses color, seeing that I'm soaking wet. "What happened?"

"Squelch tracker," Trey growls while glaring at Ustus. "How did it get in through your security?"

"Stealthily," Ustus replies, and his sarcasm causes Trey's scowl to deepen. Seeing it, Ustus quickly amends, "I don't know."

"Find out and look for more," Trey says through clenched teeth. "Where am I going?"

Ustus thinks about it for a second, and then he smiles. "There's the gaming lodge on the far side of the property. You'll need to take a skiff to get there—I'll also need to clear it with the Regent."

"Fine. Send me Wayra, Jax, and someone to drive us there while you clear it with the Regent." In minutes, Wayra and Jax round the corner, looking angry.

"Sir, what happened?" Jax asks while Wayra stares down everyone in our vicinity.

"I'll brief you later. We're taking up new quarters. I need you to secure them. Let's go." We follow the Regent agent who directs us to a skiff on the drive outside.

Trey opens the door and places me in the back seat, squeezing in next to me and putting his arm around my shoulders. Wayra sits up front with the driver while Jax faces us. No one speaks on the slow, winding drive, but Jax is taking in every dripping inch of us, trying to assess the situation. Pulling up in front of a dark, imposing mansion, which looks like an estate all by itself, I shiver, feeling cold and damp.

The place is beautiful, made of stone with a cedar shingle roof; it's a true, historic hunting lodge. Trey exits the skiff, extending his hand to me and helping me out. He doesn't drop my hand, but holds on to it as he leads me to the doors. Entering the mansion, Trey says loudly, "Illuminate hall, security—report respiration."

A fem-bot voice responds, "There are four Etharians present."

"Map voice recognition Trey Allairis."

"Greetings, Trey Allairis," the robotic voice responds.

"Kricket, say your name," Trey instructs. When I do, the robot repeats her greeting to me. Jax and Wayra do the same.

Trey orders, "Wayra, go room by room and do a sweep."

"Yes, sir," Wayra responds, pulling a chrome weapon that looks like a handgun from a holster under his pant leg and walking into the next room.

"Climate control to forty-two draks, ignite fire. Jax, find a blanket for Kricket," Trey says, leading me to the massive stone fireplace on the other side of the room. A fire has sparked and is now popping and crackling in the grate. The boom of a firecracker in the distance sounds, causing Trey to frown at Jax.

Wrapping a blanket around my shoulders, Jax says grimly, "I think they just found another squelch tracker. They should question that knob knocker, Kyon."

Trey shakes his head. "No. It wasn't him. He wants Kricket alive."

I feel myself pale. "So, that thing was meant specifically for me?" I ask. "Like a smart bomb or something?"

"Yes," Trey responds. "They're programmed to track a specific target for a surgical strike."

"How does it recognize its target?"

"Voice, optical, heat signature, heartbeat—depends on how it was programmed," Jax explains. "Someone wanted you to have a very bad night."

"Makes me feel so warm and cozy inside," I reply with a fake smile.

"You should be a Cavar, Kricket," Jax smiles admiringly.

Wayra enters the room, nodding to Trey before saying through his teeth, "I say we line up every one of those Regent police and interrogate them one by one. Someone knows something! Did you just hear another one go off?" he rages, pointing toward the window.

"We heard," Trey states in a calmer tone. He strips off his damp jacket and shirt, laying them neatly across a chair to dry. The firelight makes his wet skin gleam; it flickers over his muscled abdomen like a lover's tongue. Suddenly, warmth spreads inside of me as I imagine how his skin would taste if I were to do the same.

I shiver with a renewed awareness of him. His black, scrolling military tattoos do nothing to hide the deep vee of his hip bones above his waistband. My eyes travel back again to his powerful upper arms. Even if I wrapped both of my hands around one of them, his biceps are so big that my fingers would never meet. He'd used those arms tonight to pick me up and throw me over his shoulder as we ran from the squelch tracker sent to kill me. It could've torn him apart as well, but he'd done it anyway.

A deeper desire flares in me when I glance at his face and see that he's assessing me in quite the same way. Trey's violet eyes darken as they rove over my wet dress; the scarlet fabric clings to my breasts and my other curves like a second skin. My hair has fallen in loose, damp waves over my shoulders. I can still feel the place where he'd woven his fist into my hair at the base of my head and pulled me to him for an intoxicating kiss. I want him to kiss me like that again—like he needs me more than he needs to breathe.

Wayra clears his throat as he unbuttons his shirt and hands it to me. "It's dry," he says apologetically.

"Uh, thanks," I murmur in a daze, taking the shirt from Wayra.

"There's a commodus over there," he says, indicating a door to the right.

I find the bathroom and quickly strip out of my wet dress. Pulling on Wayra's long, formal shirt, it almost reaches my knees. I roll up the sleeves and drag my fingers through my damp hair before exiting the bathroom.

As I near the fireplace in the main room again, I pull the blanket closer, hearing the guys fall silent. Trey indicates that I should sit as he hands me a glass of water. I can tell by the look on his face that he notices my hand shaking when I grasp it. Sinking into the seat, I manage to say, "Thanks."

"Wayra, contact Dylan. He's the best at dissecting squelch debris," Trey orders in a clipped tone. "I want him here before morning."

"We need our own on this. Fenton and Hollis can be here in a few parts," Jax says. "That's only a few hours, Kricket," he translates for me.

"Get Drex and Gibon, too," Trey adds.

"Yes, sir," Wayra says, pulling a communicator from his pocket and speaking into it rapidly while pacing the room.

"Unknown Etharians approaching perimeter," the feminine robot voice says, startling me and making me stand immediately. Trey and Jax both pull chrome weapons from their belts, pointing them at the entrance.

Feeling the urge to hide, I take a deep breath as Kyon pushes the doors of the lodge open and walks in with a confidence I hope one day to possess. "Where is Kricket?" he asks, dismissing the fact that there are now three gunlike weapons trained on him.

Lowering his weapon, Trey responds, "She's safe."

"That's not what I asked," Kyon retorts, scanning the room and seeing me peeking from behind the chair. Lecto and Forester are with Kyon, trying to stare down Wayra and Jax. "Kricket . . ." he trails off when he takes in my wet hair and Wayra's shirt.

I pull the blanket closer to me and raise my chin, saying, "What's the prophecy, Kyon?"

"You're direct," he states, coming nearer, "and that is something that we should discuss privately." His eyes bore into mine. "I'll take you to my quarters. We'll guard you there until I can have an audience with the Regent. He'll see reason, and then I can take you home."

"Have you ever heard the sound a squelch tracker makes, Kyon?" I ask quietly, watching his reaction.

"Yes," he replies, his eyes never leaving mine.

"It's like . . ."—I pause for a moment, thinking—"it's like what I imagine a butterfly would sound like if it could scream." A shiver tears through me.

"I'll kill the one who is responsible for that," Kyon replies honestly.

"Em Nark?" I probe, trying to see what he knows.

"Is dead," Kyon replies in a calm tone.

"What?" I ask, stunned by his answer.

"His trift disintegrated as it passed over Violet Hill. That's Rafe territory, if you're unfamiliar with the area," he replies, watching me sink into the chair again and look at the fire.

"Come. I will take care of this," he urges me, extending his hand. Goose bumps rise on my arms as I ignore his hand.

"She stays," Trey replies easily.

"With you . . . half naked?"

"With me . . . half naked."

"She is my intended consort," Kyon states, clenching his teeth.

"She's so much more than that," Trey replies.

Kyon's eyes shift to me. "He cannot protect you, Kricket," he says, watching me struggle to keep my cool.

"Did someone kill him . . . the Narc?" I ask, my voice coming out in a whisper.

"You don't believe that his trift just blew up by itself, do you?"

"Why?" I feel ill.

"You're not asking the right question," Kyon replies.

"Which is?" I shoot back.

"Why let him live?" he responds in a cold tone.

"That's so harsh!" I say, looking at the calculation in his eyes. "What's wrong with you?"

"What do you mean?" He looks puzzled. "He was a threat to you, Kricket, and you act like you're sorry he's dead."

"Is he dead because of what went on tonight? Because of me?"

He smiles like I asked something completely lame. "Of course," he replies easily, "but proving that would be nearly impossible, since no one in the room tonight will be willing to discuss what was imparted there. If there is an investigation, it will be concluded as a tragic accident."

"What?" I choke, feeling responsible.

"No one here wants an international incident. Therefore, the death of the ambassador will be neatly explained away." Kyon watches my reaction.

They're all so powerful that they can murder people with no repercussions. That means he's not going away—ever. "I'm never going to be your consort," I state, hearing my voice shake.

"Your naïveté is so attractive," Kyon says with a slow smile. "Try to hold on to it."

My eyes narrow. "Your single-mindedness is creepy," I counter, clenching my fists. "Try to lose it."

"You're so passionate and resolute. How could I possibly let you go?" Kyon is still smiling.

Frowning, Trey says in a deadly tone, "I'll make you see that letting her go is the only option available to you."

Kyon's eyes shift to Trey's. "Don't tread where you don't belong, Rafe," Kyon says, his brows drawing together in a scowl, "or even regeneration won't put you back together."

"You can leave now, or you can remain and we'll see who'll need to be regenerated," Trey replies, looking calm.

Kyon's fists clench before he says, "Touch her, and I will make sure that not even your soul will survive."

"If I touch her, she'll have my soul," Trey replies.

I see Kyon's nostrils flare, and his eyes go to mine as he says, "Be prepared to leave in the morning." Fear makes my legs feel weak as I watch him leave with Forester and Lecto.

"Kyon is going to go directly to the Regent. I need to leave here before Manus gives me to him," I blurt out, seeing the shock on the faces of Wayra and Jax.

"We're not going to let that happen," Trey replies gently. "He won't get an audience until morning, and Victus will be there to argue for you." Even with his reassurance, I can hardly keep still. Letting the blanket drop, I pace in front of the fire.

"This is insane. Someone killed the Narc because of what I said," I breathe, knowing I sound as freaked out as I feel. "I didn't know they'd kill him," I admit, feeling choked.

"It's not your fault," he replies, staring into my eyes. "You probably saved lives by alerting us to the troops on the borders. Now a counteroffensive can be mounted." Trey reaches out and takes my hand. "You need to rest now. Let's find you a room here."

"But . . . Kyon knows where I am. I have to go because this has the *huge* potential of ending badly for me," I say, feeling my hand shaking in his. He squeezes it reassuringly.

"You're safe from him," Trey says, leading me toward the stairway to the second floor. "Jax, contact Victus and fill him in. Wayra, get the Cavars here." Taking the stairs, we make it to the second floor.

"No offense, but I need a plan B. Why can't Kyon take a hint? It wasn't even a hint! I flat out called him creepy, Trey, and it was like a turn-on to him," I rant, waiting by the door as Trey checks out a huge bedroom.

"What are you thinking for your plan B?" Trey asks quietly, going to the window and scanning the exterior.

"Hiding could be a plan—or heading back to the Forest of O could be an option . . ." I trail off when he frowns at me.

"Why would you need to hide when you have friends who'll help you?" Trey asks.

"How long will I get to keep you?" I counter, wanting to bite my lip as soon as the words are out.

"What do you mean?" He's clearly avoiding my question.

"How long?" I repeat, looking at my hands.

"I don't know. No formal plans have been made," he replies in a gruff tone. "I'll help to secure things for you. Once I know you're stable here, then . . ." He shrugs.

"Then it's on to the next mission," I finish for him, feeling very stupid. A familiar pain squeezes my heart. I know better than to let myself become attached to anyone like I've allowed myself to become to Trey, but it happened too fast to avoid it.

"I'll always be your friend, Kricket; that won't change," he says in a strained voice, seeing my emotions.

"Yeah, no, of course . . . friends." I nod with a contrived smile. My face flushes with heat and tears prickle my eyes. "Because I always kiss my friends like you kissed me tonight in the fountain. In fact, I should go and kiss Wayra and Jax goodnight before I turn in."

Trey frowns. "I shouldn't have kissed you," he admits. "We shouldn't have escaped tonight—squelch trackers don't miss, so it was like a rush when we survived." He looks into my eyes, trying to see if I understand what he's saying.

"Heat of the moment?" I ask, feeling my heart sink further.

"It's like you're some kind of charm against danger. Like you repel it. Saers don't ignore prey; squelch trackers don't lose targets," he says, watching my reaction to what he's saying.

"And that's the only reason you kissed me?" I ask and see him look away from me.

"I have . . . obligations that I . . . Friendship is what I'm offering you, Kricket. Don't look for more from me," he says softly, heading toward the door. I move so he can get by me. "Get some sleep. Tomorrow will be grueling."

"Okay," I murmur, feeling embarrassed and awkward. I close the door behind him and walk to the bed. Lying against its silky pillows, I allow tears to slide silently down my cheeks, feeling like I just lost something precious.

⸎

I awake to a blazing sun coming through my window. My arm comes up to shield my eyes. When my eyes adjust to the brightness, I pull my arm back and see food on a serving tray on the bedside table. I sit up against the pillows, rubbing my eyes. "Good, you're up!" Aella says, bouncing from the chair across from my bed. "I was told not to wake you. You sleep a lot!" She smiles, coming to my side.

"Aella . . . uh, hi. How long have I been sleeping?" I ask, feeling groggy.

She shrugs. "I don't know. Awhile, I guess. It's sixteen parts and the sun is in its zenith. I need to get you dressed. You're to accompany the Regent on a ride with some members of the House of Lords." She pushes a piece of round toast into my hand while making me get out of bed. "You need to wash and dress—hurry," she urges.

"Why didn't you just wake me up sooner?" I grumble, feeling annoyed as she ushers me to the lavare to shower.

"Because *he* said I couldn't," she states, nudging the toast nearer to my mouth.

"Who is *he*," I ask before stuffing the bread in my mouth.

"The really beautiful Cavar . . . um . . . Trey?"

"Oh," I frown, feeling a stab of jealousy that she thinks he's attractive, too. "Yeah, *him*."

Showering quickly, I walk out of the lavare, wrapped in a towel, to find clothing lying on the bed. I pull on the stone-colored pants that cling to my every curve and tuck a beautiful white blouse into them. Aella hands me an exquisitely tailored black jacket. I gaze at myself in the mirror as she loosely braids my hair. "Here, put these on and let's go," Aella says, handing me long black boots.

"What am I doing again?" I ask suspiciously while tugging on the boots.

"You're meeting with the Regent, Ateur Victus, Ateur Braedan, Ateur Gustoff, Haut Kyon—"

I frown as I interrupt, "Kyon is going to be there?"

"Yes." She wrinkles her nose like she smells something gross. "I don't know why they're letting him stay here. He's a scary nim."

"He wants to make me his consort."

Aella drops her brush as her mouth falls open. "But that's ridiculous. You're a Rafe citizen," she says defensively.

"I'm not thrilled about it." Seeing her confusion, I add, "I think he's a chester."

She gives a girly gasp. "Me, too!" she squeaks. "Stay away from him if you can. He's dangerous."

"That's the plan," I admit, smiling at her advice.

Following her downstairs, I find Wayra and Jax milling around with big, brawny Rafes that have to be Cavars, judging by their size.

"Kricket," Wayra says. "This is Gibon, Dylan, Fenton, Hollis, and Drex. They're part of our team."

"Hey, 'sup?" I say, lifting my chin in greeting. Immediately, I see them trying not to laugh. "I mean . . . greetings, Etharians," I amend, blushing and giving them a formal nod of my head.

Each one sinks to his knee in front of me saying, "Greetings, Fay Kricket."

"Yeah . . . you don't have to do that with me . . . we're good," I say, embarrassed.

Trey contradicts me. "Yes, they do," he says. Seeing him now after what he said to me last night is making my blush deepen. He's dressed like me and so is Wayra, but everyone else has on very chic, urban clothing that makes me want to change.

Straightening my shoulders, I ask, "Can't we all just be normal—on the same tier, or whatever you want to call it, without all this nonsense?" I feel prickly as they rise in front of me.

"No," Trey replies. "They're your guards. Not your friends."

"Where I come from, anyone who has my back is my friend. If they have my back, then I'll have theirs, too, and I don't need anyone to bow to me."

Trey's voice is calm, but he's stern as he says, "We're not on Earth anymore, and you will learn to adhere to the customs of the culture you're in now."

Trying not to roll my eyes at Trey, I murmur, "Fine. Aella, where am I supposed to go?"

"The stables." She hands me a riding helmet and a crop.

Looking at the crop and blushing, I say, "I'd hoped you were speaking metaphorically . . . like riding high or riding the wave of admiration."

"No, no, you're riding spixes."

"Nooo," I whine, panicking. "Can't we just go—I don't know—golfing?"

"What's golfing?" Aella asks me.

"Never mind," I reply under my breath, following Trey to the door. Wayra drives us in a skiff over to the stables, while I gaze out the window and try to ignore the fact that Trey is ignoring me, too.

"Fay Kricket," Manus says as I approach the stables. He's already mounted on a very large spix. It has horns that rise several feet from its head and are as sharp as daggers. "I'm very gratified that you made it after what occurred last evening."

"Oh," I say, giving a casual shrug, "you're referring to the dip I took in your fountain? It was . . . refreshing," I add, watching his face for any sign of malice.

Manus's look of concern remains. "That you can see humor in what occurred last night says much about your character, Kricket, not to mention your upbringing. I apologize for our lack of security."

"I had security. I had Trey," I reply softly, not looking at Trey.

"Yes, excellent work, Kesek," he says to Trey with admiration in his tone. "You both know Haut Kyon and Ateur Victus." Manus gestures with a smile as we greet them, inclining our heads. "This is Ateur Braedan and Ateur Gustoff."

Ateur Braedan is startling in that he doesn't have Rafeish violet eyes, but green ones like a Comantre. His dark hair is a little wavy, too. Ateur Gustoff is even more startling because he is the oldest looking

Rafe I've seen so far. He looks like he could be in his fifties, which probably means he's freakishly old. His hair is short, too, only just covering his neck, but still dark without a hint of gray in it.

"Greetings Ateur Braedan, Ateur Gustoff," I say while inclining my head. Then my eyes fall again on Kyon sitting on his spix, watching me.

"Have you ridden before, Kricket?" Kyon asks, looking me over.

"No," I reply with a grimace. "Where were you when I was ten, Manus, and I wanted a pony?" I ask, hearing them all laugh. But then a spix the size of a Clydesdale is led in front of me and my heart starts pounding against my ribs.

Manus grins indulgently. "A pony . . . that is a type of equine, is it not?"

"Mmm," I nod, trying to hide my fear, but I jump when Trey touches my arm. Leaning near my ear, his silky voice fills me with desire as he says, "I'll lift you into the saddle. Put your foot in my hands." I try to ignore the thrilling ache his nearness elicits. Resting my hand on his shoulder and lifting my foot to his hands, I resist the urge to let my fingertips linger on him as he lifts me into the saddle that has no pommel on it.

"Here are your reins, Kricket," Trey says, and I try not to focus on his perfect mouth. "Hold them in one hand, like this." He positions my hand on the reins.

"Okay," I murmur, not looking at him, but feeling myself blush stupidly from his touch. I wait as he adjusts the stirrups on the saddle to accommodate my shorter legs. Then, Trey mounts the spix next to mine.

"Are you ready, Kricket?" Manus asks, smiling.

"Yes," I reply, feeling sweaty.

"Just use your legs to apply pressure to its flanks," Trey instructs. I watch Trey as his legs squeeze the sides of his spix gently, and the animal moves forward easily.

"You mean I can't just put a token in it?" I ask quietly, seeing his lips twitch in a grudging smile as he pulls his spix to a halt, waiting for me to try it. "Okay," I breathe, squeezing the spix's sides gently with my legs; immediately the animal walks forward.

Smiling broadly at Trey, I ask, "What's this one's name?"

"What?" he asks with a crooked smile.

"Does it have a name?"

"A name?" Victus asks, grinning like I've asked a novel question.

"You know, like Sugar or Daisy—or Killer? Mister . . . Ed?" I trail off, looking around as they all begin to laugh again.

"It's a spix," Ateur Braedan says, like I'm an adorable idiot.

"How do you know which one is which then?" I ask curiously, not offended.

"They're numbered. That's twenty-two," Trey explains, pointing to the brand on the back of my spix.

I wrinkle my nose when I see the brand. "Number twenty-two, huh. That's lame."

"What would you name it, Kricket?" Trey asks me, trying to hide his smile.

"Er, I don't know," I say, patting the spix's neck softly. "She's very beautiful . . . maybe Andromeda."

That gets more laughter before Trey can say, "She's a he."

"Oh," I say, smiling at my faux pas, "then definitely Adonis." I walk my spix beside Trey's, and the conversation gradually turns to other topics. I listen while they discuss growth rates of pixelaries in the class five district.

"What's a pixelary?" I whisper to Trey.

Pulling his spix nearer to mine, Kyon answers me, "It's a plant that produces fiber to create material."

"Like cotton?" I ask, trying to show him that I'm not afraid of him.

"Yes," he says, smiling at me, "but it's more versatile than cotton. It doesn't leach the soil like a cotton plant does."

"Are you a farmer?" I ask Kyon, wondering just what he does in Alameeda.

"Not in the traditional sense. I own an interest in several agricultural ventures," he says, his blue eyes gazing ahead of us as we approach a wooded area. The path through the trees only allows for two spixes to walk side by side. Kyon maneuvers his spix to squeeze out Trey's, forcing Trey to fall back behind us with Victus.

"I'm sure the Brotherhood keeps you very busy," I say, not knowing anything about what I just said and realizing I'm his prisoner until the path widens again.

"It does," he agrees, "but I do spend most of my time on my estate near the Loch of Cerulean."

"What do you do there?"

"It's on the sea, so I sail, fish, walk on the shore . . . It's peaceful," he says, and I can't keep from giggling. "Why are you laughing?"

"Sorry," I reply, lifting my hand to cover my mouth. "I was just trying to imagine you walking on the beach, collecting seashells and the visual was . . . out of character."

"I underestimated you, Kricket," Kyon says softly. "You're so much more than I could have imagined."

"What?" I ask, startled by his compliment.

"Having to fight all your life for survival hasn't made you less . . . it has made you more." His blue eyes meet mine. "But wouldn't it be nice to no longer have to struggle for survival?" he asks, and my heart twists because he does see me.

"It would, Kyon," I agree softly, lifting an eyebrow. "But that's not going to happen any time soon."

"Not here. In Alameeda, things could be different," he replies, allowing his spix to come closer to mine. I glance behind me to see Trey frowning, but I doubt he can hear what Kyon is saying.

"Oh . . . right," I reply softly, "I should just agree to be your consort, and you'll take care of me. What did you call it? A 'symbiotic relationship'?"

"I'm sorry I said that. I propose a partnership between you and me. You need someone to advise you, Kricket."

"And that's you?"

"Who else will give you straight answers?" he counters, looking serious. "I know more about your gifts than anyone here. Though I have many questions . . . because there's no one like you."

"What do you mean?"

"You can just . . . do it, can't you? No preparation or trances you just . . . see."

"Pretty much," I admit. "Can I ask you something?"

"Yes."

"Precognition—is it possible to learn?"

"For you, yes. I am quite sure you will develop it."

"Really?"

"It was a gift your mother could do quite well—better than most," he replies. "I have a question. The day I found you, what did you do to bring me there?"

"What?" I gasp, feeling a burst of adrenaline course through me, and my spix prances forward in response to my knees tightening on its sides.

Kyon catches up to me easily, helping me slow my spix. "I didn't know where you were in Chicago, and then, I was walking by the nightclub, and I had an urge to enter. Trey found you at almost the same time. That was too big a coincidence to be random. Did you do something . . . special?" he asks, intrigued.

"No—I . . ." I trail off as my heartbeat increases. "I wished."

"You wished? What did you wish for?"

"Home," I reply, and Kyon's smile becomes almost radiant.

"You wished for us to find you," he says. "That's extraordinary."

"You're saying that I brought you there?"

"I am. Be careful what you wish for, Kricket."

"That's silly, Kyon," I murmur with a laugh.

"You're so naïve, Kricket," Kyon counters. "You probably don't even see what's happening here right now."

"What do you mean?" I have to lean nearer to him as I avoid a tree limb in the path.

"You don't find it strange that there are no other females here?" he inquires. I shrug, raising my brow in question. "It's because we're all potential suitors for you. Ateur Victus and Ateur Braedan are both unattached, powerful males. Ateur Gustoff has two unattached sons with a title from him and a title from their mother. You'll go into your first swank already sought after by several elite in Rafe society."

"What? You're wrong. Victus is—"

"Intrigued and the one with the title, Kricket." Kyon looks angry. "His brother is lesser royalty and already intended for someone else, and he *will* step aside."

"You don't know Trey," I say defensively.

"Ah, but I do know him," Kyon counters in a quiet tone. "He always follows the rules. He is kind and generous to his family. He'll make them proud of him. He may even encourage his brother to commit to you so that he can be near you . . . continue to protect you, but never touch you, never have you for himself."

"That's cynical, Kyon," I say, knowing he believes what he's telling me.

"And you won't commit to Trey," he says, "for one simple reason."

"Which is?" I counter, feeling cold.

"Because whomever you commit to here will be marked for death," Kyon replies. "No Rafe can be allowed to produce offspring with you as far as the Brotherhood is concerned."

"Do you have any friends at all, Kyon?"

"I hope that we can be friends. I don't control the Brotherhood. I'm trying to help you," he says, searching my face for understanding. "I'm not your enemy, Kricket. You're one of us. You're Alameeda."

"I'm both Alameeda and Rafe," I reply, looking straight ahead. "And right now, I wish I were human."

Seeing that the path ahead will widen to accommodate another spix, Kyon says quickly, "You should come to me with any questions that you have about your gifts—or the prophecy. If I can help you, I will."

"Why?" I ask, seeing that he's being honest.

I see a real smile, and he doesn't look like such a knob knocker when he replies, "Because I like picturing you in the Loch of Cerulean . . . on the seashore, collecting shells . . . with me."

Chapter 17

No Future

I remain silent while riding alongside Kyon for much of the tour around the grounds. As my spix wanders nearer to Manus's mount, I'm finding it difficult to listen to him speak to Ateur Gustoff about the Tectonic Peninsula. Trey is trying to make eye contact with me now. He has maneuvered his spix next to mine again, but I can't look at him. If I do, I might tell him that I think he's a *total* knob knocker for not warning me about what's really going on here. Hearing from Kyon that I'm being "courted" is like getting slapped in the face.

Squeezing my knees lightly, I urge my spix to step ahead, nearer to Ateur Gustoff on his mount. "I have spoken to several members of the House of Lords who believe that any bid for the Tectonic Peninsula will be seen as aggression toward Peney. This is a delicate matter," he lies to Manus.

"Who is expressing these reservations?" I ask innocently. Trey's spix nears mine again, but I ignore him.

Ateur Gustoff's eyebrows shoot up at my question. "It would be indelicate to say, Fay Kricket," he replies. "I was telling Haut Manus that I could use my sway in the House of Lords to smooth things over on this issue." His hollow cheeks have no smile lines, nothing to indicate that he finds anything amusing.

"That shouldn't be too hard for you," I smile, knowing he's fabricating the opposition. "How will you do that?"

"My son, Reven, could act as an ambassador to Peney, while I sway the Lords on our position."

"How good of you," I reply, wanting to roll my eyes but resisting the urge.

"I would like you to meet my eldest son, Reven," Ateur Gustoff says. Watching Manus smile, I resist the urge to grind my teeth.

"Fay Kricket, would you like to join us for a race along the riverbank?" Manus asks, gesturing to the stretch of land to our west.

"Nooo," I reply, shaking my head like he's insane. "I don't like the taste of dirt. This is a really good pace for me." I continue to plod along slowly on number twenty-two.

Manus tries not to smile as he says, "Well, then, we will see you tonight at dinner, Kricket." I incline my head, relieved that I'm being dismissed from the frat party.

"I'll ride back with Kricket. I have some things I need to attend to," Kyon says to Manus. Manus's eyes go to Trey's. Seeing Trey incline his head to his Regent, I know he's staying with me, too.

I follow Trey and am relieved when the stables come into sight. Number twenty-two must be feeling the same because he increases his pace toward his home. We stop at a paddock fence, and I look down, trying to figure out how I'm supposed to get off my spix.

"Here, let me assist you, Kricket," Kyon says, having already dismounted. He reaches up and plucks me off the saddle, holding me in his arms. "You're so little." Kyon grins while tossing me up and catching me in his arms again like I don't weigh anything.

Startled, my arms go around his neck. "Kyon!" I gasp, scared he'll drop me.

"Put her down," Trey orders, invading Kyon's space and eyeballing him like he'll take Kyon's head off the moment he puts me on my feet. Wayra is right next to him, looking like he could pounce at any moment, too.

"Why, Trey?" Kyon asks in a low tone, holding me closer to him. "I'm the answer to all your prayers. I'll take her far away from here where you'll never have to see her again, never have to wonder if she'll be at the dinner party you have to attend or the swank you're required to be at."

"Kyon, put me down please," I say softly, dropping my arms from his neck and seeing the deadly look on Trey's face. Kyon lowers me slowly to my feet, but now I'm sandwiched between them. "Trey . . . Trey . . ." I say with both my hands on his chest. Trey's eyes meet mine, but I'm not sure he actually sees me.

In an instant, Trey has me safely behind him, and Wayra takes it from there, leading me away from them. "Wait," I say, trying to see what's happening, but Wayra doesn't listen, ushering me to the waiting skiff. Wayra stuffs me in the backseat, shutting the door and climbing into the driver's seat. We wait for several minutes before Trey gets in.

When I glance at Trey's face, he looks like he could chew steel. "What did he say to you?" Trey asks stiffly as the skiff moves forward.

"When?" I ask, not liking his tone because it sounds more like an accusation than a question.

"Before you speak again, know that I'm not playing games. You're entirely too brilliant not to know what I'm asking you, so don't evade my questions with your own." Trey's hostility simmers just below the surface.

"Kyon said a lot of interesting things. He let me know what was really happening on our ride today," I reply with my own hostility. "Maybe you should've told me that I was being paraded around like a piece of meat. I like to know what I'm facing when I go into battle, and you didn't have my back."

"I had your back! I thought that if you knew, you'd feel awkward and say something off-color to make a bad impression."

"*So!* You did know!" I retort, my eyes narrowing at him.

"It's PR, Kricket! The goal is to help you fit into society. Being sought after by the elite means that doors will open for you."

"Do I look like I care about any of that, Trey?" I ask, seething. "I have a job—one that will pay me more money than I could ever have expected to make. I'm an advisor to the Regent. I can save my money, maybe buy an apartment in the city, and have my own life."

"Kricket," Trey says, rubbing his eyes. "You know that's not an option for you."

"So you agree with Kyon—that I either have to commit to some powerful Rafe jerkwad who can *try* to protect me from the Alameeda or accept the ultimate, blond jerkwad and whatever the Brotherhood has in store for me?"

"You will be protected from the Brotherhood! There's no way you're going to commit to Kyon, no matter how *cozy* you get with him!" he retorts, like he has the ultimate say in this.

"Cozy? Did you just say *cozy*?" I sputter, glaring at him.

"You had your arms around him!" Trey says, like I threw myself at Kyon.

"I was afraid he was going to drop me!"

After we pull up in front of the hunting lodge and Wayra stops the vehicle, I open my own door and storm into the manor. Jax rises from his seat with the other Cavars in the room near the fireplace. He drops his cards when he sees my face and asks, "Kricket?"

I hold up my hand, blowing by him and heading to the staircase. I just make it to the first step when Trey's hand wraps around my upper arm, ushering me with him to the second floor. Trey enters my bedroom with me and slams the door shut.

Trey points his finger at me angrily. "No matter what Kyon says to you, he's not your friend. He is smart and manipulative and he knows exactly what to say to get you to—"

"To get me to what?"

"To get you to trust him."

"Trey, you don't understand anything," I mutter. "He has information that I need—that I *crave*. He knew my mother—he knows about precognition—"

"You can develop your gifts on your own—in your own time. You don't need to learn anything from him. And the proof is that you're already more powerful than they ever expected."

I take off my riding helmet and toss it on the chair. "Kyon said I could ask him anything and he'll give me a straight answer. I have to find out what the Narc meant when he said that I'm the prophecy." I rub my chin.

"No," Trey says sternly.

"No? Why not?"

"Because Kyon is dangerous," Trey replies, like I'm a child.

"Well, so am I," I say, lifting my chin a notch. "I can handle Kyon."

"Handle him? Did you say *handle* him?" Trey asks rhetorically. "You're no stronger than a kitten. How are you going to handle him?"

"Uhh," I mumble as Trey comes closer to me, invading my personal space again. "I'm stronger than I look, Trey. Even Jax said so."

"You think you're strong? Handle me then, Kricket," he says, pulling me to him with his hands on my upper arms.

"I don't want to hurt you," I whisper, feeling my entire being light up at the nearness of him.

"How can you hurt me, Kricket, when I'm so much stronger than you?"

I gaze into his eyes, seeing his brows drawing together in anger. "If I lean in," I say softly, focusing on his lips, "close to you . . . so close that it makes my breath catch in my chest, and then I . . ." Closing my eyes, I brush my lips gently against his, feeling heat rush through me as Trey's hands slip to my back, crushing me to him.

I wrap my arms around the back of his neck and speaking against his lips, I continue, "Then I could just let the common symmetry that exists between us force you to see that you're mine . . ."—I kiss him—"and I'm lost without you . . ."

Slowly tracing my lips with his, he begins responding to my kisses with his own, before I pull back from him a fraction. I squeeze my eyes shut tight and say, "And then, I could tell you that none of that matters in this world . . . that because we share this common symmetry, the space between us will be filled with an undeniable gravity . . . pulling us toward one another. So that when you commit to Charisma, we can't be friends, because my heart won't understand the distinction. It won't understand that you'll be hers . . . not mine."

Trey's arms tighten around me as he leans his forehead against mine. Softly, he whispers, "Kricket . . ."

I give a humorless laugh. "As it turns out, my heart isn't made of stone . . . no matter how much I wish it were." My fingertips slip to his chest, feeling his rock-hard strength beneath them. "But it doesn't matter."

"It doesn't?" He lifts my chin so that I'll look in his eyes.

"No. I'm going to ask Manus to replace you as my bodyguard, Trey," I reply, feeling like I'm choking.

"*What?*" Trey scowls, like he can't believe what he's hearing.

"You can't stay here. Kyon isn't blind—it must be written all over my face when I look at you. Anyone I love is a threat to him, and he has the Brotherhood behind him," I say, feeling adrenaline ignite in my blood as the look on Trey's face goes from angry to deadly.

"What did he say to you?" Trey asks, his violet eyes narrowing.

"He just told me what you already know. Anyone I love will be marked for death," I whisper, feeling overwhelming sadness hit me.

"I thought you were a fighter, Kricket," Trey says. "You're just going to give in to Kyon because he will retaliate if you don't?"

"I am a fighter, Trey," I say, pulling out of his embrace and straightening my spine. "But I don't want you here!"

"That's not your decision, Kricket."

"I'm making it my decision."

"You need me and I'm staying here."

"Not if I insist that you leave," I reply, feeling instantly irritated with him because he's totally ignoring the fact that I just told him that I love him.

"How will you argue for my reassignment with Manus?" Trey asks me quietly.

"I'll just tell him that I've developed . . . certain feelings for you that make it hard for me to be around you everyday."

I see Trey try to suppress a frown as he glances away and says, "Manus won't relieve me of my duties because you have a crush on me."

"A crush? Did you say a *crush*?" I want to hit him as my cheeks flood with color.

"Yes. You're young and we've been in some very unorthodox situations together. It's inevitable that certain feelings would arise, but . . . they'll pass," he states, like he's a seasoned veteran when it comes to this kind of thing.

Closing my eyes, I want to die right here. My throat tightens. "You don't think that I'm capable of love?"

"You've only known me a few rotations . . . you're only a few floans old—you've been raised in the near absence of love, Kricket," he says softly.

"Trey, you can tell me you don't want my love or that you don't love me, too, but don't *ever* tell me what I feel or don't feel," I warn him, crossing my arms.

"You can't love me," he says seriously, looking like he's in pain now. "It's impossible."

"It's not impossible because I do love you," I reply heatedly. When he just stares at me and doesn't say anything, my heart throbs painfully in my chest. "Well," I say quietly, "at least it's just my heart, not yours. You should be relieved. Now you can be done here and go back to your life." I walk to the door and open it for him. Looking straight ahead, I wait for him to walk through it.

"I'm not going to step aside. You need me here, especially with Kyon in residence," Trey pauses on the threshold. "You're just confused right now . . . it will pass."

I raise my chin, feeling like he slapped me. "Lucky for me I have your wisdom to guide me."

"I'm not going anywhere, Kricket, so save yourself the embarrassing conversation with Manus. We can talk about this when you've had time to think about it."

"Can't wait," I reply, holding my breath until he leaves the room. Closing the door, I lean against it, wanting badly to pound my head against it for being so stupid. *What did I expect from Trey?* I ask myself. *A declaration of undying love? He loves someone else and I'm just a—what do they call it? A lurker.*

"You're pathetic," I whisper to myself.

❧

Unfortunately, I don't have time to wallow in my pain. I spend the next several weeks wading through social gatherings at the palace. I fake smile at dinner parties, teas, and luncheons with the Regent, Rafe officials, and foreign dignitaries from Wurthem, Comantre, and Peney. I try to listen to every word that might have significance as to what's happening within Rafe and outside its borders.

After each event, the Regent and I usually have a Q & A regarding who lied about what and what I was able to uncover covertly. And if that's not hard enough, these meetings always include Trey as my personal protection slash reminder that I suck at love. But I look forward to these meetings in a sick, pathetic way because they are the few times that Trey and I say anything to each other. He asks me questions and I answer him, but when we're alone, like in the skiff, neither of us has much to say.

That doesn't mean that the common symmetry between us has gone away. On the contrary, now that we don't talk, the attraction is all I can feel. I find myself counting when I am near him. I count how many times he glances at me or looks up when my name is mentioned. I count how rapid my breathing becomes when he walks into the room or how much it slows when he leaves it.

Kicking off my heels and tossing my wrap on my bed, I reach up to try to catch the clasp on the exquisite necklace the Regent wanted me to wear to the dinner party this evening.

"Here, let me do that," Aella says, swiftly releasing me from the heavy collar.

"Ahh, thank you," I sigh, feeling like I can breathe again.

"This came for you while you were at dinner," Aella says, handing me a card as she puts the necklace back in a box to take with her.

"Who is it from?" I hold still as Aella begins unhooking all the clasps on the evening gown of pale yellow satin.

"Ateur Braedan. He wants you to ride with him tomorrow."

"Oh, that could be fun," I murmur, having had a few riding lessons from my tutor, Tofer. "Is Victus going to be there, too?" Those two seem to always be together.

"No, he wants to ride with you alone," she says, helping me step out of the gown.

My brow wrinkles. "Why?" I ask, slipping into a pair of pajama bottoms Aella had made for me at my request. She also made up some thin T-shirts and tanks for me, but she always looks disapproving when I put one on, like now, because she says they make me look "human."

"Probably because he desires you," she replies, and I scoff, like she's making a joke.

"Yeah, no, seriously, does it say?" I glance at the card.

"I am serious," she smiles. "He's sent several notes to you requesting to be your dinner partner or to take a stroll on the grounds with him."

"He has?" I exclaim, shocked. "Why haven't I seen them?"

"Security screened them," she says, folding the gown in tissue and placing it in a box to be laundered.

"Security?" I ask, frowning.

"Mmm," she says absently. "You get lots of stuff that never gets through. I had to send back a mountain of things from Haut Nim himself. Jewelry, furs, clothes, scents—you name it, he has sent it."

"Haut Nim?" I ask.

"Haut Kyon," Aella replies with an ironic expression. "He couldn't get an audience with you if the entire Alameeda army shows up on the grounds, not that it stops him from trying everyday."

"I thought he left," I say honestly, feeling fear rush through me. "I haven't seen him around."

"The Regent agreed with Kesek Trey that Haut Kyon is too much for you to contend with while you're trying to assimilate here. He's been kept away for your protection," Aella states, picking up the boxes. "Do you want me to agree to the ride with Ateur Braedan?"

"Uhh, no. I don't really feel like riding," I say, feeling awkward. "Oh, here . . . I asked the footman tonight for an extra piece of that cocoa fantasy cake you love," I say, handing her the small box.

"You are my favorite Etharian, Kricket!" Aella says, happily taking the treat from me.

"Well, you're Sergen's favorite Etharian. When I told him that it was for you, he tried to give me the whole top tier of the cake."

Aella blushes, looking delighted. "I'll thank him tomorrow. Good night, Kricket."

"Good night, Aella." I smile, watching her place everything in a hover courier and program it to transport the cargo for her.

As I lie in my bed, I try to take my mind off the events of the evening by flipping mindlessly through the programs on the hologram vision. But I keep focusing on the fact that things are getting entirely too scary to ignore. Seeing the alarm in Manus's eyes tonight when I told him about the Peney ambassador's lie regarding the breakdown in talks with the Alameeda over their renewed interest in the Tectonic Peninsula has me worried, too.

I've learned that the Tectonic Peninsula is a strategic area of land owned by Peney. It would be integral for mounting an offensive against Rafe because it would allow Alameeda a staging point for their troops through its ports and airspace. If Alameeda secures it, then they eliminate the protracted resupplying of those troops.

After an hour of tossing and turning in bed, I throw my blanket aside with a huff. Getting up, I creep down to the first floor and head to the back of the house where the kitchen is located. I nearly collide with Drex and Fenton. They're patrolling the halls of the manor with large weapons that look like machine guns but can shoot projectiles, lasers, or electricity, depending on the need.

"What are you doing up, Kricket? Do you know what time it is?" Fenton asks, with a cheeky grin, eyeing my pajamas.

"I'm going to the kitchen . . . I mean the 'keuken' to see if there's any venish left or if Wayra ate it all," I say, smiling at him.

"He ate it," Drex and Fenton say in unison.

"Oh," I sigh disappointedly, "figures. Can I bring either of you back something?"

They both look at each other and grin. Drex says, "Ah, no. We have to patrol the perimeter, but we're playing fritzer later, if you're interested."

"Didn't I already take all of your money, Drex?" I grin, backing down the hall.

"Yeah, you knob knocker, she already skinned ya. You want to keep bleeding coin, keep trying to beat a priestess," Fenton insults Drex. "She can probably see right through your cards."

"Can you?" Drex asks, looking intrigued.

"I'll never tell," I reply, putting my finger to my lips before turning and walking toward the kitchen.

Going directly to the commissary unit, located on the kitchen wall, I browse through the pictures of entrées still available.

As I pick up the plate of savory pheasant, I nearly drop it when I turn and see Kyon sitting at the long black soapstone table with his feet up on it. "Kyon!" I gasp, "You scared me! What are you doing here?"

"I had to see you. You've been ignoring me," he replies, looking relaxed as he pulls his feet off the table. He sees me look toward the entrance to the kitchen and says, "Please sit. I came to talk to you."

I set my plate down on the table across from him and sit down. "How did you know I'd be here?" I ask him, suspicious.

Kyon's blue eyes meet mine. "Em Quinn said you didn't eat much at dinner this evening. I took the chance that you'd be hungry later," he says, smiling at me. His blond hair is pulled back from his face, and the soft light makes it look darker—more golden.

"That's interesting. Does the ambassador of Peney often spy for you?" I ask, feeling uneasy that Em Quinn is passing information about me to Kyon.

He relaxes in his chair; his massive shoulders block the seat back from sight. "When the need warrants it and it costs him nothing."

I grasp my fork more tightly. "Interesting. So, why are you here?"

"I've come to talk to you about the growing tension between the houses. There is unrest. We're on the brink of war, Kricket," he says honestly, watching my reaction.

Fear threads through me with icy fingers. "Can it be avoided?"

"No."

"Why not?"

"Alameeda is meant to rule Ethar," Kyon replies. "You're a part of that, Kricket. You're of Alameeda, too."

"Do you know how ridiculous you sound?" I see Kyon's eyebrows draw together. "That sounds like comic book crap. Only complete morons want to take over the world."

"The Brotherhood has a vision, Kricket. They want a peaceful world for their people." His words chill me.

"Their people, but not *all* people," I say. "What happens to everyone else?"

He shrugs, "I don't know, but I'll protect you when that day comes."

Goose bumps form all over my body. "I can't be a part of any of that, Kyon."

"You'll feel differently when the house of Rafe falls. I came here tonight to tell you that I have to leave Rafe. I want you to come with me."

"I'll take my chances here, thanks," I reply, feeling myself growing paler by the second.

"You know that they're just using you for your gifts."

"And it would be different with you, how?"

"It *would* be different with me. I care for you," he says, looking annoyed—but honest.

"I'm staying here. My friends need me," I reply.

Kyon leans toward me calmly, setting his enormous hands on the table. "He doesn't need you, Kricket. He's going to commit to someone else, and when he does, you'll be dying to be anywhere but here." The truth of his statement knocks the breath out of me.

"That's not your problem," I say, looking away from his piercing blue eyes.

"It is my problem," Kyon replies with menace in his voice.

"I don't want your help."

"With your upbringing, I'm sure you've already seen that want and need are two very different things," he states, rising from his chair at the table and pacing the room. "Rafe and Comantre can't possibly hold out against us this time. You're on the losing side."

"What makes this time so different from last time?"

"Last time, there was a neutral house."

"Peney? Peney is siding with Alameeda? Are they going to relinquish the Tectonic Peninsula?" I breathe, feeling panic rush through me.

"They will," Kyon replies, frowning. "It's war, Kricket, the likes of which you probably can't even imagine yet. Alameeda only needed a sign to rally around to get us here, and that's you, Kricket."

"Me?" I feel ill.

"Yes. The Brotherhood believes that you are the one spoken of in the prophecy—the priestess born of two houses that will bring about the demise of one, leaving one house to rule Ethar," he replies grimly.

"Who—"

"Your mother was prolific, especially in the realm of precognition. She saw many things."

"Which house will fall?" I ask, not sure if I can trust what he believes to be true because it sounds like a bunch of freaky nonsense. But even if it is nonsense, if the Alameeda believe it, it could become a self-fulfilling prophecy.

"I was hoping you could tell me that, Kricket," he replies speculatively. "Come with me now, and I'll work with you to develop your gifts."

"I don't think I want that gift, Kyon. Especially when it can be used to pinpoint future Rafe positions and predict their next move."

"Ah, so you've learned what some priestesses can do?" he asks. "You'll participate, either way. You just need to choose a side—unless you want to play for both sides."

"What?" My hands begin to shake beneath the table.

"You're a survivor. Maybe you don't have to choose a side but can play for both teams. A little information here, a little there . . ."

"You know, you remind me a lot of a foster father I once had, Kyon."

"Is that so?"

"It is. His name was Daniel—'Dan the man.' That's what all his friends called him at the bar on our street. They'd all shout it, too, whenever he walked through the door. I loved him as a kid; I *actually* loved that man," I say shaking my head. "He taught me a lot. He showed me how to hustle so I'd never go hungry on the streets of Chicago. He was educated and he spoke well; he taught me to speak well. He also taught me scams that kept a roof over our heads. He was great, until I turned fourteen and Dan thought he knew a new way for us to make money. One night, he came home drunk from the bar. He brought some friends with him. He offered me to them for money. When I fought them off with one of their broken beer bottles, he nearly killed me before he passed out. You're a lot like him, Kyon. It's there in your eyes. You'll do anything to survive. I've made my decision. I'm Rafe, screw Alameeda."

Kyon's expression is grim. "I'm nothing like that human! I'm offering you a way out, Kricket," he says defensively. "The Brotherhood will begin a smear campaign against you if you stay, making it look like you're the real reason they're going to war. You'll be reviled wherever you go—in Rafe, in Comantre, in Peney—"

"I'm used to that, Kyon," I reply. I lift up my shirt a little and show him the shank scar on my abdomen. "What else you got?" I ask, dropping my shirt and crossing my arms.

"He's got a few circas of vista to drug you into going with him, Kricket. Don't you Kyon?" Trey says from the doorway of the kitchen.

Chapter 18
One of Us

Kyon scowls at Trey as he enters the kitchen and stands next to my chair, pulling it out for me. "Kricket," Trey says in a gentle voice, "go back to bed now." Reaching down he takes my hand, helping me up. As I stand beside Trey, I squeeze his hand tighter, refusing to let go of him as I glare at Kyon.

"Why did you let me get past your security, Trey, if you didn't intend to let her go with me?" Kyon asks, zeroing in on my hand in Trey's. "I was beginning to believe that you intended for me to take her away so that you wouldn't have to have her here anymore. No more reminders of what you can't have."

Trey scowls back at Kyon, looking insulted. "I wanted to let Kricket choose her allegiance—Alameeda or Rafe. Everything that she has encountered thus far has been thrust upon her," Trey says. "She has handled it with grace, but we both know that war is inevitable now. If she had decided that she would be better off in Alameeda, then I would've let her go with you."

"You know that she'll be safer in Alameeda with me," Kyon says with a smug smile. "You don't like your odds, do you?"

"Maybe she would be safer, but I believe her exact words were 'screw Alameeda,'" Trey replies, and he can't hide the pride in his voice.

"Sir," Wayra says from the doorway behind Kyon, "I think her exact words were, 'I'm Rafe, screw Alameeda.'" He's holding a tricked-out automatic weapon pointed straight at Kyon, and the grin on Wayra's face is priceless.

"Yeah, that's definitely what I heard," Jax agrees from the doorway behind me. "Now can I shoot him?"

"You would risk her life because she doesn't *want* to go with me?" Kyon asks them angrily. "You can't win this war. We'll annihilate every last one of you, especially you, Kricket. Traitors die horribly in Alameeda; the torture will go on for several rotations before it ends."

"Can I shoot him now?" Jax's face is dark with suppressed rage.

"Fenton, Drex," Trey barks in a tight voice, "take Haut Kyon to the Regent police and have him restrained until Skye decides what to do with him. Wayra, Jax—go with them and make sure no one kills him. He has information we need."

Fenton and Drex come in through the doorway behind Trey and me, searching Kyon and throwing several weapons and a couple of vials of what must be vista on the table. Seeing it, I shiver.

Kyon watches me the whole time, his face livid. "Kricket," Kyon says in a soft tone, "the next time you see me, know that I'm not coming to take you home."

"I'm already home, Kyon, but thanks for the warning," I reply, raising my chin as his blue eyes narrow at me.

"Here," Trey says, tossing a communicator to Jax. "This is a recording of the conversation between Kyon and Kricket. Make sure the Regent views it tonight: then we turn it over to Skye along with Kyon."

"Yes, sir," Jax grins. Turning to Kyon and hauling him toward the door, Jax says, "How much do you want to bet that this is your ass, and before you ask me what an ass is, let's just talk about what I think yours is worth."

As the door closes behind them, I stand frozen in my spot by the table, not sure about what just happened or what it all means.

"Kricket, are you okay?"

I shake my head. "No . . . you were going to let me leave with Kyon?"

"Yes," he answers, watching me struggle to remain calm.

"But that goes against all of your orders. You could've been incarcerated—treated like a traitor. You're supposed to keep me from the Alameeda, not let me go off and join them."

"I know," he agrees, looking at our hands tightly clasped together.

"So, if I wanted to leave—"

"I'd help you escape."

"Because . . . ?"

"Because we're going to go to war," he replies, looking grim.

"You were allowing me to choose my own side: Rafe or Alameeda."

"Yes, but I have another option for you, Kricket," Trey says softly.

"What option?"

"You can choose to be human—at least you can go back to Earth." He eases his hand away from mine.

"What?" I ask, seeing he's serious and feeling cold now that I have nothing to hold on to.

"I can have you taken back to Earth—hide you—keep you safe while we fight the Alameeda. If we win, you can remain there, or come back if that's what you want. If not, Earth may be the best place to hide from Kyon," Trey says, like he's choking on his words. "Maybe by then you'll develop a way to stay ahead of him—precognition . . . something."

"You'd help me get back to Earth?" I feel my heart pounding in my chest.

"I'm sure both Wayra and Jax would volunteer for the mission," he replies. "I'll order them to stay with you and help you dodge the raindrops."

"But you'd stay here?" My heart sinks.

He nods. "I have to stay. I have to protect Rafe from what's coming." He looks grim.

"But if I stay, too, I could be really helpful to Rafe. Interrogations alone would make me invaluable," I struggle to think logically and figure out what's happening here. "And if I can develop precognition, then I can see what the enemy is planning."

"You don't know what you're saying," Trey says with conviction. "War sounds romantic, heroic even, until everyone you know starts dying."

Nodding numbly, I hold on to a chair. "You're right. I don't know what it will be like here. But I've seen what one human can do to another—things that have made my spirit ache." Looking up at Trey's face, his eyes soften a little in understanding.

"How am I going to keep you safe here?" he asks, looking solemn. "I'm a soldier. I lead men into battle, Kricket. I don't know if they will allow me to stay with you much longer."

"You'll have enough to worry about with your own family. I can look after myself." I pick up my plate and take it to the compost chute. Placing my dish in the receptacle, I turn to see Trey watching me.

"You can't be left alone here, Kricket," he says quietly.

I rub my eyes tiredly with my hand. "I'm not your problem, Trey."

"You're my responsibility," he insists.

"Why?"

"Because I brought you here."

I laugh humorlessly. "If it weren't you, it would've been someone else. I don't need your pity, Trey. I don't need anyone. I do my best work alone."

I drop my hand from my eyes and turn away from him because I don't want to see his face when he explains his reasons for leaving; it might break me. A part of me knows this has to happen. I should be doing everything I can think of to make him leave. The Alameeda will begin their smear campaign soon. The dirt they plan to throw at me will spatter onto anyone standing near. The problem I have now is that my heart is no longer stone; it feels like paper, ready to be shredded at any moment.

"This isn't pity. You can't survive here without help."

I turn and quirk my eyebrow at him, pointing my finger at myself as I say, "Chameleon, remember? Anyway it's clear you're done with me. We don't have to drag this out—"

"Done with you?" he asks incredulously. "How in Ethar did you come to that conclusion?"

"You just tried to pawn me off on the enemy."

Trey frowns. "I wasn't trying to *pawn you off*," he says defensively, "I was trying to let you choose. I'd like to think that I would've let you go, Kricket, if that was what you wanted, but the truth is that I don't know if I'm capable of letting you go."

"What?" I feel like the world just moved around me, while I remained still. I glance at Trey; he's wearing a grimace that says that he may have just said too much.

"Kricket, I—"

"You know—stop right there"—I hold up my shaking hand—"because you can't say stuff like that to me. You can't just kiss me in fountains and then say you only want to be my friend," my voice cracks as my throat tightens. "You can't just tell me that it's impossible to love me while you treat me like I'm some kind of *lurker*, and then say you don't know if you can let me go!" I shout angrily, trying to see him through my tear-blinded eyes. "Because it hurts me too much when you do things like that, Trey. It makes me hope that you could love me some day, and that kind of hope for someone like me is just . . ." Feeling tears rolling down my cheeks, I turn toward the door, hoping he'll have the decency to let me walk away and hide for a while.

Before I can make it to the door, Trey's arms wrap around me, pulling me to his chest. Trying really hard not to cry is only making me cry harder. "Kricket," Trey whispers in my ear, rubbing my back soothingly.

"What am I to you, Trey?" I whisper.

His arms tighten almost painfully around me. "You're . . . my friend."

I stiffen, pushing hard against his chest so that I can see his face. "Your friend? That's all I am?" My throat aches from choking back tears. I hate crying in front of him. I never want to cry in front of him again.

He averts his eyes from mine. "Yes." His jaw tenses.

I pause, and then my eyes widen. "You're lying!"

"Kricket," Trey warns, "don't."

I dry my eyes with the back of my hand. "Don't what? What else am I to you, Trey? Tell me!" I demand.

Trey lets go of me and walks toward the other end of the table. "You're someone I'm paid to protect," he says with his back to me. I'm gutted. It's true and it hurts more than I thought it would to hear him say it out loud.

There it is. He doesn't want you. He's doing his job, just like everyone else in your life. "Oh," I mumble. "That's it?"

"Yes."

"No . . ." I frown, reading him. "You just lied to me again. Why?"

Trey's hands ball into fists. Then he turns around and his eyes stare into mine. "We can't do this now."

"Do what, Trey?" I growl. "You're lying, and I want to know why! Am I a burden to you or something? Is that it?"

"No!" he barks, like I said something utterly absurd.

"Then what is it? It's not like you love me, right? We've established that much," I say derisively.

"Right," he lies.

My eyes widen in shock as I become breathless. "What did you just say?" I ask slowly. "Did you just lie, Trey? Do you love me?"

Trey doesn't answer me, but his jaw grows tighter with each passing moment.

"Do you?" I demand—and then hold my breath.

"No," he lies again.

I exhale sharply. "You love me!" I whisper in near disbelief.

Trey exhales deeply, too. "I'm not allowed to love you, Kricket," he says honestly, watching my reaction. "By loving you, I put you at even greater risk than before. It would come from all sides—from every angle—not just from the Alameeda."

"You said it was impossible to love me," I go on, ignoring him. I feel almost as hurt now as I had then.

He shakes his head slowly. "No, I believe I said it was impossible for *you* to love *me*. Almost as impossible as hiding the fact that I love you."

"I told you I loved you, and you said it was just a crush." I feel my face flood with color again.

"I'm not the one who inherits, Kricket, Victus is—"

"You think I care about that?"

Trey takes a step toward me. "No one will want to see us together."

"I know," I shiver. "Kyon said the Brotherhood will try to kill anyone I love—"

"I'm not afraid of the Brotherhood."

"You aren't?"

"No." He stops only a breath away from me so that I have to look up to see his face. "I'm trying to protect you, Kricket. If we tried to be together, we wouldn't be able to trust anyone but each other."

"I'm already there."

"You're only seventeen—this is your whole life—"

"My age is irrelevant," I frown, "and I'm eighteen now. My birthday was last week."

"Your birthday was last week?" Trey asks me grimly. Seeing me nod, he asks, "When?"

"Wednesday—I mean, Fitzmartin . . . that's Wednesday, right?"

"Yes," he nods. He takes my hand and leads me away from the kitchen to the unoccupied drawing room. The carved wooden furniture in the room is the same rich, dark stain as the exposed mahogany beams of the high ceiling. Chandeliers hang down from above like melting stars in a night sky. We pass chairs with soft, cream-colored cushions facing a low, oval, glass-topped table. Crossing to a sofa in front of the enormous stone-carved fireplace at the far end of the room, I wonder, and not for the first time, why they have such large fireplaces when the entire estate is practically climate controlled by the use of advanced technology.

Nearing the hearth, it dwarfs us with its graceful symmetry. I glance away from the unlit grate to study my hand in Trey's; it's tiny in comparison. For a second, I lose myself as I imagine his rough hands on me, running the length of my body. The thought makes my knees weak and my abdomen tighten. I reach out with my other hand to steady myself, touching the carved armrest of the sofa. It's a replica of a saber-toothed saer from the Regent's coat of arms; its legs and feet comprise the legs of the sofa as well. Its mate is on the other side with its ferocious mouth agape in a fire-breathing display of royalty.

Trey waits for me to sit on the silk-covered cushion before he joins me. "Ignite fire," he orders. The grate roars to life with fiery orange tongues.

The heat of the flames is seductive. I lean my head against his shoulder, feeling his hard bicep flex beneath my cheek. He moves his arm so that my cheek shifts to rest against his chest. His arm wraps around me to lie gently across my shoulders. He strokes my arm softly; warm fingers raise goose bumps on my flesh. I inhale deeply. His scent causes my paper heart to flutter and riot; a thousand folded airplanes made from its scraps soar within me.

"I missed your birthday?" he asks in disappointment as his hand pauses on my arm.

I shrug. "It's not a big deal. I didn't tell you my birthday."

"That doesn't make me feel better," he mutters. His arm tightens. He pulls me even closer to him to stroke my hair. I hear his heartbeat beneath my ear—calm, steady—the opposite of mine. "What did you do on your birthday—on Fitzmartin?" he asks in a silky voice.

"Uh, Fitzmartin?" I repeat stupidly, feeling every fiber of my being come alive at his touch. "We went for a boat ride on the lake with Em Quinn and his sons, remember?" I ask, feeling him brush my hair back from my neck, causing a sensual shiver to run through me. "Uh . . . we had to listen to Em Quinn tell us that long story of how he once saw a wild saer near the border of Comantre," I remind him, before biting my lip as Trey's thumb caresses my nape absently. I don't even know if he knows he's doing it. It seems unconscious.

"Golden bathing suit," Trey says softly near my ear in an intimate whisper, "which was actually just circles of gold linked together with golden-metal hoops . . . black wrap skirt that exposed your thigh with every step you took . . . black shoes with gold nail polish on your toes . . . I almost killed the little one."

"You almost killed the little what?" I ask him, my eyes widening as I lift my head to look at him.

"The one that touched your—"

"Oh, you saw that?" I ask, surprised.

"Yes, I saw that."

"Then you saw me smash his toes with my very sharp black heel?" I arch my eyebrow in a questioning look.

"Yes." His perfect lips spread in a wide grin. "But it didn't save him from the black eye."

"You did that?" I gasp. "I thought he was thrown from his spix."

"He was thrown, but he was nowhere near a spix when it happened," Trey replies; then he adds, "I want to make it up to you."

"Make up what?" I ask.

"Your birthday," he says.

"Why? It's just another day."

"Because it's *not* just another day—because I should've known it was your birthday."

"That's not your job to know."

"It's what friends do."

He's back to putting me in the friends zone. I stiffen. "I'm good, Trey. I don't want to celebrate it."

"Why not?" he asks, like the idea of someone not celebrating her birthday is ludicrous.

"Because it won't be for me."

"Whom would it be for?" he asks in confusion.

I wave my hand in a dismissive way. "Manus. You tell him it was my birthday, and he'll throw some outlandish swank—he'll invite all his enemies and expect me to spy on them for him. He'll make a big production of giving me some outrageously expensive gift—I won't know what it is, thereby reducing me to a foolish-looking nim."

"Is that what you think? That you look like a foolish nim?" he asks me, his violet eyes searching mine. I feel fragile under their scrutiny.

"People always laugh."

Trey's eyes soften. "They laugh because they're delighted by you—you enchant them. You're cunningly naïve—vulnerable, yet fierce. But the party I had in mind wouldn't involve Manus—it would be with your friends—"

"That would be a *very* small party," I smile in an attempt at levity.

"I'd be there."

I look away from him, resting my head against his chest again in an attempt to hide the tears that brighten my eyes. *He means just as friends, you idiot,* my mind whispers. "You're going to be far too busy for that," I reply.

His arm tenses around my shoulders. "What do you mean?"

"The Alameeda are in Peney. You'll be leaving."

"Nothing has been decided yet." His heartbeat beneath my ear becomes rapid.

"True, but you'll probably be busy with your other swank."

"My other swank?" he asks in confusion.

"Don't you have a commitment ceremony you have to plan?" I close my eyes briefly. I didn't intend to say that—I just blurted it out like a well-honed survival instinct. All the paper airplanes of my heart nosedive and crash, coming to rest in a heap in the pit of my stomach.

Trey sighs, saying, "My commitment to Charisma has always been the expectation for both of us. Our families have pushed for it for as long as I can remember."

"Then you should do it," I murmur, dying inside. "There's nothing more important than family."

"Isn't there?" he asks softly.

"I can't think of a single thing."

He lifts a piece of my hair and absently plays with it between his fingers. "What if what they want for me isn't what I want for myself?"

My cheeks flush and I become breathless. "What are you saying?"

"I spoke to Charisma. She and I both agreed that we aren't right for each other."

"You're not?"

"No." I feel him shake his head. "I don't love her the way I should love her."

I can't move. "How should you love her?"

"I should love her like there is an ache that won't go away unless I'm with her."

I know the ache he's talking about. It's the one I carry around for him, but mine doesn't go away anymore. It's always there; it gets even worse when I'm with him, like now. "When did you figure that out?"

"Hmm?" he murmurs, and I become fully alert. He's stalling.

"Trey, when did you call off your engagement to Charisma?"

"I—" He pauses. He looks like he's about to bluff before he exhales deeply. "The night the squelch tracker attacked us. I spoke to her that night after I spoke to you, and I ended it. Deep down, I knew I was going to end it before I kissed you in the fountain."

"How did you know?"

His soft groan rumbles his chest. "This would be so much easier if I could lie to you."

"Trey?" My eyebrows knit together in confusion.

"I knew because I can't stop picturing a very different ceremony, one performed in a gazebo adorned with wildflowers . . . with a bride in a white gown, who commits to the most enticing of promises . . ."

Something that feels disgustingly like hope begins to paste small bits of my paper heart back together. "So, you're not going to have a commitment ceremony?"

"No."

"Because you love me?"

"I told you before, I'm not allowed to love you," he says with conviction. "I'm not supposed to have any feelings for you. Your guardian will never allow it."

"You're right. It doesn't matter. I'm not allowed to love you either. The Brotherhood will kill you," I state with equal conviction.

His warm hand cups my cheek, forcing me to meet his eyes. "I told you before, I'm not afraid of what the Brotherhood would try to do to me. It's you I'm worried about. You're Manus's ward. You're at his mercy until you're of age. He has the power to make your life excruciating with very little effort."

"Manus? You're worried about Manus?" I ask, surprised.

"Don't underestimate him, Kricket. You're a coriness, not to mention a priestess, and Manus's favorite toy. I'm minor royalty, a dreykar; it's hardly a favorable match for you," he admits. "There's nothing for Manus to gain in it."

"He has a lot to lose, though, if I were to stop cooperating," I reply.

"You can't afford to alienate Manus. He has the power to hurt you. I'm here at his request. That could change if he knew how I feel about you." Trey reaches out and touches my cheek, like he can't help himself. "If he were to decide that you should be handed over to the Alameeda, no diplomacy on our part would prevent it. I'd have to make you disappear—somehow convince Skye to intervene."

"What does Manus want from me? I feed him every bit of information he asks for." *Could I have missed something with Manus? I wonder. Maybe. I've been so distracted lately by Trey that I haven't been as diligent about my surroundings as I should be.* That fact alarms me.

"I've been watching him, Kricket. I don't like the way he looks at you lately."

"How does he look at me?"

"Like you're his inamorata," Trey says honestly, gauging my reaction.

"His lover? You have to be wrong!"

"I'm not wrong."

A shiver of fear erases every other emotion inside of me. It's like my foster father, Dan, all over again. "What can I do to make him not want me, Trey?" I whisper.

"Nothing. There's nothing you can do."

"We have to make the stars align for us now—find a way for us not to get burned for being together."

Something about what I said triggers a reaction in Trey. Maybe it's the panic in my eyes, or maybe it's that I said that I want us to be together. He leans forward and cups my cheek. "I'm working every angle I can think of to align those stars for you, Kricket. I promise," he admits. "I'll find a way out of this for you."

"What if I were to change my status?" I ask.

His eyes search mine. "I'm sorry? Your status?"

"Kyon's gone now—he won't be able to get to you—we could keep it from him—from the Brotherhood."

"Keep what from them?"

"What if I were to change my status from virgin to . . . other? Maybe Manus wouldn't want me then. What if you became my inamorata?"

Pulling his hand back from my face, Trey tenses. "Inamorata is feminine. I would be your *inamorato*, your *male* lover."

I bite my lip, blushing, before I continue my argument, "It wouldn't have to be a permanent arrangement for you. I would just need someone to . . . um . . . be with me, so Manus gets the idea that I'm not his plaything."

"And you'd rather be my plaything than his?" he asks, his eyes growing dark—and I can't really tell if it's with anger or desire.

I nod, but I'm beginning to see by his frown that maybe he doesn't like my plan. "It's my body and my life. I'd rather my first time be with someone I care about than someone I don't."

"This shouldn't be a forced choice, Kricket! I don't want you to be with me because I'm the lesser evil!"

"You're my first choice, Trey. My only choice," I state quietly. "There's no one else I'd want but you."

"Your plan will never work, Kricket."

"Why not?"

"There are so many reasons that I don't know where to begin."

"You don't want to be with me?" I ask in a small voice. The scraps of my paper heart blow away in my chest, leaving a barren, gaping hole.

"You could never be a temporary situation for me, Kricket. I know that once I have you, I'll never be able to let you go." He looks concerned as he scans my face. "I want you as my consort . . . 'until death do us part, and then forever after that,'" he quotes what I said on the transport plane to Comantre.

His words do something to me. A flood of warmth begins in my belly and spreads throughout my body. "So you do want me?" I ask.

I shift on the sofa, moving to straddle his legs and sit on his lap so that we're face to face. "I'm right here."

Trey stares at me like he's never seen me before. Reaching up, he tucks my loose hair behind my ear. His hand lingers there before his fingers entwine in my hair, gripping the back of my head. He leans forward, while his hand in my hair gently pulls me closer to him. My heart has found its way back to my chest and now pounds in it like it had never been torn apart.

Trey covers my lips with his firm, enticing ones. I feel his other hand on my back; he pulls me to his chest. I melt against him. My arms slowly encircle the back of his neck while my mouth opens to taste him against my tongue. The most delicious pleasure I have ever felt winds it's way through my veins. I want this; I want him so much that I ache from it.

My hands cup his cheeks. He hasn't shaved since this morning; my fingers revel in the feel of new growth, like sandpaper against my skin. He groans as his tongue strokes mine; the sound he makes sends a hunger through me that I've never experienced before. I want to find a way to make him groan like that again.

"Kricket," he whispers against my lips, "I'm not about to deflower you as a means of keeping you away from Manus. It would never work anyway. The minute he finds out about us is the exact moment that he gets rid of me, and you become well and truly his. The fact that you're untouched is the only thing keeping him from you."

"Oh," I say as I shift on his lap to meet his eyes. "But if I were your consort, then he couldn't separate us, and it would be okay if I did this?" I lean forward and nuzzle his neck just below his earlobe.

"Yes," Trey breathes as his hands rest on my hips, "if you were my consort."

"And this would be okay, too?" I whisper, nibbling on his earlobe and feeling his fingers tighten on my sides when my teeth gently graze his skin.

"That would be required," Trey replies in a strained voice.

"And this?" I touch my lips to his as the flushed heat of intense desire builds between us.

"At least a hundred times a rotation," he replies against my lips.

"At least a hundred a day?" I ask with a growing smile.

"You're right . . . at least a thousand." He smiles, too, and then it fades. "But you'd need Manus's consent to commit to me. He'll never give it to us."

"You don't know that. We just have to find something he wants more than me."

"There's nothing he wants more than you."

"How do you know that?"

"I know it because he has the same look as must be on my face every time you enter the room."

Trey's lips turn down as his expression becomes grim. I lower my lips to his, gliding over them and feeling them soften their hard line. Tugging his bottom lip between mine, I nibble on it. He kisses me hard, like he can't get enough of me. It goes on like that until I'm breathless with the need to consume him and be consumed by him.

"I wish I knew a way for us to always be together, Trey," I whisper to him in his ear. "I would do it, no matter the cost."

"I'll find one," Trey promises. His voice is rough as he grips me possessively.

Suddenly, something deep down inside of me feels very wrong. Pressure builds from within my head, like it's an overblown balloon ready to burst. "Uhh," I exhale, a deep breath as searing heat, like sparks of molten dust from a white-hot sun pass over my skin. Fear and pain erupt in the core of me. I pull back from Trey to look in his eyes. As I gasp to take a breath, I whisper, "Trey, help me!" The world whirls around; something rips me away from Trey and thrusts me forward out of my body. I see myself from above as my body slackens in Trey's arms. I feel cold in a way that I've never felt before.

"Kricket!" Trey shouts, shaking my body that I have left behind, as the walls of the lodge crumble around us in flakes of ashy embers.

In seconds, I flash forward into the starry night. The sky bleeds above me like tears of black, and the pinpoints of light streak horizontally with the speed of eternity. Instantly, I'm in stasis in front of the gates of the palace; the blue beams of the security fences illuminate the dark sky.

A military-style skiff is pulling up to the security gates, attempting to exit the palace. Inside, Drex and Fenton are seated in front, while I can just make out Jax, Wayra, and Kyon in the back. An instant later, I move from beyond the palace gate to the side of the skiff, standing by the open window as it pulls next to the security checkpoint.

The palace security detail moves forward to speak with Fenton through the window of the skiff. The guard has his weapon strapped to him, but lowered away from the interior of the vehicle.

"Prisoner transport to Skye—authorization Indie, Mega, Preston, one, seven, two . . ." Fenton trails off as the guard grasps his neck, pulling out a silver dart from his skin with a groan of agony.

To my horror, the guard begins to swell up, his hands and face inflating to grotesque proportions, before his eyes pop out of his head and his body explodes all over the side of the skiff. A vapor trail of blood hangs in the air where the guard had stood. Fear, like a paralyzing drug, roots me in place.

From the security house, a squelch tracker streaks to the vehicle, emitting a humming scream, while its green laser flails around it. Its long, silvery, razor-sharp point passes right through me, like I'm made of air, as it locates its target ahead.

"Squelch tracker!" Fenton shouts, before the weapon penetrates his door, entering the cab and stabbing his side. Once it enters his body the lasers tear and cut Fenton to pieces in seconds, leaving no more than a pile of flesh on the front seat.

"Ambush!" Jax shouts, pulling his machine gun up and pointing it out the window. *"Reverse, reverse, reverse!"* he orders Drex, as metallic, mechanized spiders tumble from the security house, scrambling toward the vehicle.

A second later, I'm inside the vehicle with them, sitting across from Jax in the skiff while it's wildly careening over the manicured grass of the palace's geometric gardens. Hearing a scurrying sound of metal tapping against metal, two mechanized spiders have forced their way through the hood of the skiff, disabling the engine. Our vehicle immediately falls to the ground, with a bouncing, jarring crash. Sparks fall on us from the roof before the metal groans as it's pulled back like the lid of a tin can.

Wayra points his weapon at the sky, dispersing several bursts of electricity from it. The energy flashes out around a spider, frying its circuitry and rendering it useless. *"Ahhh, I hate those chrome-plated chiggers!"* Wayra shouts. *"Don't even think of moving, you blond knob knocker, or I'll push a sanctum amp down your throat!"* he screams at Kyon, who's struggling to try to remove his neck restraint.

The ominous sound of rapid gunfire splinters the air around our skiff. Glass shatters and sprays the interior of the vehicle, cutting through me as if I don't exist. *"I'm hit!"* Jax screams, the spray of his blood peppering the seat beside him. Blood is spilling unchecked from the gaping hole in Jax's chest, as his eyes close in agony and he writhes in pain.

Light shines down on us; the powerful beam blinds me as the eerily quiet sound of an E-One helicopter hovers above us. Shielding my eyes from the light, I can just make out the growing smile on Kyon's face as he's plucked off his seat like iron to a powerful magnet and is gone from the skiff.

The ping of metal hitting metal draws my eyes to the floorboard.

"Sanctum amp!" Wayra shouts. He moves to cover it with his body to save Drex and Jax. An instant later, the loudest *boom* I've ever heard

in my life blows out of the grenade. Shrapnel cuts through Wayra as a fireball consumes the vehicle.

The blast forces me from the skiff, launching me through the starry night.

"*Noooo!*" I scream, but it only comes out in a cracked whisper.

"Kricket!" Trey breathes, holding me tight to his chest while he rocks me back and forth with his body.

My arms feel heavy and limp as I stare at the fire in front of me. "Burning . . ." I whisper weakly, still feeling the eerie coldness within me.

"Burning? Kitten, you're freezing—your skin is like ice," Trey says frantically, rubbing my arms.

"Ambush, Trey," I say in a raspy voice, breathing heavily as I try to force more of the words from me. Trey's hands still on me and his eyes meet mine.

"What?" he asks in a tense voice.

"Ambush—retreat . . . Jax is dead . . . Wayra—sanctum amp, chiggers, squelch—reverse . . . Kyon gone—" I say in a frantic stream of words, my voice oscillating with a need to scream when I can hardly speak.

"Did you see something?" Trey asks. The pressure of his hands on my upper arms causes pain.

"Palace gates—*ambush*—*palace gates!*" I shout at him, my eyes opening wide as I try to make him understand me.

"There's an ambush at the palace gates?" Trey asks in a military tone, his jaw tensing as his eyes search my face.

"*Yes! They're all dead!*" I sob, feeling my body shaking with cold and trauma. Trey checks the pockets of his pants and exhales with a grim expression.

"*Hollis! Gibon!*" Trey roars, while letting go of me gently and getting up from his knees on the floor in front of the fireplace.

"*Sir!*" Hollis responds, running into the drawing room.

"Hand me your communicator," he says, holding out his hand. "Tell Gibon to contact the Regent police. We have enemy infiltration at the palace gates."

"Yes, sir," Hollis responds.

Accepting the communicator, Trey barks words into it and waits a few seconds.

"Hollis, you knob knocker, what do you want?' Jax asks in an amused tone.

"Give me your position," Trey orders curtly.

"Sir! Uhh . . . I didn't know it was you—" Jax begins.

"Position!" Trey barks again.

"We are en route to Skye, approaching the palace main gates."

"Halt! Ambush ahead at palace gates! Fall back—everyone on alert!" Trey says, his jaw tense as he scowls at the room around him.

"Halt!" I hear Jax yell to the occupants of the skiff through the communicator. *"Ambush. Fall back! I repeat: Fall back!"*

"Do you see the enemy?" Trey asks Jax.

"No, we're fifty dicrons from the gates," he replies.

"They have squelch trackers and sanctum amps and chiggers and an E-One to transport Kyon!" I say, trying to relate the information to him quickly.

"Is that Kricket?" Jax asks.

"Yes, and she said they have squelch trackers, amps, chiggers, and an E-One," Trey replies.

"How does she know that?" Jax asks, sounding tense. "Wait. One of the guards just stepped out of the guard house."

"Get back!" I yell. "Tell him to get to a safe position!" I order Trey.

"Ahhh! Mother of all Wackers! The guard just vaporized, sir!" Jax says, his voice heightening with tension.

"Fall back!" Trey barks.

Entering the room, Gibon stands at attention and says, "Regent police have been dispatched to the gates, sir." He stares at the communicator in Trey's hands as the sound of rapid bursts of gunfire and explosions issue from it.

"Dispatch Rapid Ascenders—there's at least one enemy E-One nearby that has cloaked itself from detection. Destroy it," Trey demands.

"Yes, sir," Gibon responds grimly, before pulling out his communicator and barking orders into it.

The sounds of yelling and gunfire go on for several minutes while I wait in tense anticipation next to Trey. Then, Jax says, "Enemy E-One brought down. Prisoner secure. Returning to base."

"Good work, Cavars," Trey says, lowering the communicator.

Exhaling a deep sigh, I sit down on the sofa by the fire, feeling exhausted and physically beaten. "Kricket, that was . . ." Trey trails off, looking like he's searching for the right word.

"Freakish?" I mumble, half in shock.

"Amazing," he counters. "You saved my men."

"But first, I had to watch them die," I reply, still shaking from trauma.

"How did you—"

"I don't know." I rest my head against the cushion wearily, listening to the sound of my teeth chattering.

Trey plucks me off the sofa and sits down on it, pulling me onto his lap. He strokes my hair while holding me close to his chest as he whispers in my ear, "Everything is okay. You saved them . . . you saved them . . . you saved them . . ." He keeps repeating it softly, like a mantra, until my teeth stop chattering.

Chapter 19
Bend or Break

After waiting for Jax and Wayra to return from transferring Kyon to another unit, I'm greeted in the drawing room like a hero by them and the rest of the detail. I answer every question that Trey and the other Cavars put to me about what happened— what I saw. When we compare the two scenarios with the guard at the gate, my version is reasonably similar to how that guard was actually murdered. I'm dizzy with fatigue when the Cavars begin discussing strategy regarding my security.

Seated on the sofa near the fire, I lean my head against Trey's shoulder.

⁂

I open my eyes to the darkness of my bedroom. Disoriented, it takes me a second to realize that I'm in my bed. As I sit up, I glance around in confusion, seeing an odd shape in front of my bed that I don't recognize. I bend forward and rub my eyes before remembering everything that went on tonight like a blur of unreality. Pushing back the thick blanket, I'm about to get up and make sure that everything's all right, when Trey's voice stops me.

"Kricket," he says softly.

"Trey?" He moves closer. Reaching me, Trey's hand strokes my hair soothingly. He touches my cheek, making my heart leap in my chest. "Is something wrong?" I rub my eyes again, realizing he must have carried me up here at some point during the night. I glance at my clock on the nightstand; it's been hours since the Cavars returned. I must've been sleeping for a while.

Trey's voice is hushed, "I need you to get up now—change as fast as you can into something you can travel in. We have to leave before morning."

I reach out and take Trey's hand in mine. In a rush I ask, "What's wrong? Where are Wayra and Jax?"

"Shh," he quiets me softly, "they're here, downstairs—they're fine, everyone is safe."

"What is it, Trey?" I squeeze his hand, sensing something is extremely wrong. Trey is in my room in the middle of the night. He'd never normally do that because he'd be afraid of risking my reputation.

Letting out a sigh, he says, "We have to go now. I'm getting you out of here."

I crawl out of bed and face him. "What has happened?" I'm starting to panic.

"The fight over you has begun, Kricket," Trey says in a strained voice.

"The fight? What fight? You mean with the Alameeda?" My heart is throbbing painfully in my chest.

"No, this time it's domestic. You've heard me speak of Skye, right?"

"Yes," I reply in an apprehensive tone.

"Skye is the military branch of our government, and they're as powerful, if not more powerful, than the Regent and the ateurs in the House of Lords put together. And now, they want you." He watches my reaction.

"Skye wants me?" I ask, trying to figure out what he's saying. "For what?"

"For what you can do. For what you did tonight—predicting the Alameeda attack."

"How did they find out?"

"They intercepted everything we said on the communicators—everything," he replies.

"But I don't even know if I can do any of that again!"

"I know," he says gently, trying to calm me down. "They want to help you develop your skills—"

"What about Manus?" I ask in confusion. "I'm his ward and his adviser."

"Yes, and he'll fight to keep you," Trey agrees. "He won't want to relinquish you to the Cavars or the Air Brigade."

"The Cavars? You mean I'll be enlisted? That I might have a chance of being with you?"

"We'll make it work to our advantage. You'll probably be assigned to a special unit—intelligence," he replies. "That will keep you off the front lines."

"Will we be assigned to the same base together?" I feel desperate all of a sudden.

"If you're drafted into the Cavars, there's more of a chance of that happening. I have people working on it right now."

"You do?" He nods. "When will you know?"

"Soon," he replies, trying to reassure me, but I can see that there's more.

"What aren't you telling me, Trey?" I search his face as best I can in the dark.

"Manus has ordered our reassignment. He wants all the Cavars to leave in the morning," Trey says in a tense tone.

"*What?*" I whisper-shout, not able to control my reaction.

"Manus has assigned his police to guard you," Trey replies, trying to remain calm. "They're downstairs now—they don't know I'm up here. They think I'm gathering my gear. With Skye demanding that you be turned over to them, Manus sees us as a threat. Skye wants you, and he no longer trusts us. We're Cavars—we follow orders from Skye. He sees the conflict of interest and has replaced us. By morning he plans to move you back to the palace."

Stepping forward, I wrap my arms around Trey's waist, hugging him fiercely.

"I'm not leaving without you, Kricket. We'll go to Skye; I'll find a way for us to stay together. I promise."

Finding Trey's lips, I press mine against his, and what begins as a desperate act, slowly becomes something quite different. Returning my kisses, his hands slide from my waist downward toward my lower back. I fit against him like I was made to be there. "They won't keep us apart, Kricket," he promises. "We won't let them."

"How will we stop them?"

"When Skye enlists you, you'll no longer be the Regent's ward. You'll be emancipated with all the rights of any other Rafe citizen." Trey kisses me tenderly.

"So, I'll no longer need Manus's permission for . . . anything?" I ask. Warmth spreads through my body as Trey runs his lips over the soft skin of my shoulder. "And if I'm no longer his ward, then I can commit to anyone I want?"

"I love the way your mind works, Kitten. Have I told you that?" Trey's words cause shivers of desire to dance over my skin. "But there's only one person you'll commit to."

"Do I know this person?" I ask innocently, feeling the strap of my tank top slide over my shoulder and rest against my upper arm. I bite my bottom lip when the rough stubble on his cheek follows the strap's descent, causing my breath to catch at the intense desire it creates.

"I don't believe that you were ever formally introduced to him, but he's very tolerant and understanding . . . perfect for a saer like you."

"He does sound perfect," I agree, my fingers entwining in Trey's thick, dark hair. "I think I know this Etharian . . . did he travel all the way to another world just to find me?" I tug on his lower lip with my teeth.

Trey groans and then smiles. "He'd go much farther than that for you," Trey says against my lips, holding me and pressing me close to him.

"He doesn't have to." I trace my finger down his chest and see the growing darkness of desire in his violet gaze. "I'm right here."

He captures my finger in his large hand, and bringing it to his lips, he kisses the tip of it. "You have to change now. We'll slip out your window. I have Drex and Fenton outside. Wayra and Jax will run interference."

Trey leads me to my closet and I look for something to travel in. He turns his back as I hurriedly drag a sweater on over my cami. I whisper, "Talk to me Trey. I'm starting to freak out a little."

"You live up to your name, Kricket," he says softly.

"Are you calling me a bug?" I smile at his broad back.

"Your father was definitely a soldier. He understood the power within your name," Trey murmurs. "And it takes another soldier to understand just what it means."

"What does it mean?" I ask as I shed my pajama bottoms and pull on dark, tailored trousers.

"Pan knew about war. He spent a lifetime outside under the stars, in trenches or bunkers, when the only sounds at night that will bring you any comfort are the songs of the crickets."

"Why would that bring you comfort?" I ask, scurrying around in my closet and finding black boots with a low heel. I sit on the closet floor to put them on.

"When the crickets are singing, their music drowns out all the other noises in the night sky. You can have faith that the enemy isn't moving because they'll warn you," Trey replies. "It's when the crickets stop singing that you know the enemy is near and the battle is about to begin."

"You're a philosopher." I smile up at him, lacing my boots.

"No, I just recognize what he was saying," Trey whispers.

"And what's that?" Despite everything that has gone on tonight, unbelievable happiness is creeping into my soul.

"He was telling us that your voice will give comfort when the night becomes its blackest," he replies. "And I'll protect that voice with my body, my mind, and my spirit . . . because without it, I'm alone in the dark."

"Trey." I say his name, not realizing that I have tears in my eyes until one slides down my cheek. "What if I just told Manus that I want to be with you?" I ask.

"Kricket, he's obsessed with you," Trey says. He turns toward me and reaches down to help me to my feet. Cupping my chin, he uses his thumb to brush away my tears. "He wants you for himself. I don't believe that he'll ever give you his permission to commit to anyone, even a perfectly acceptable match."

"Trey, all of that is meaningless. The only thing that matters is how we feel about each other. I love you, and that's never going to change," I promise, leaning forward and placing a gentle kiss on his cheek. "I'm yours," I whisper, shifting my lips to his other cheek and kissing it, too. "And you're mine," I continue, looking in his eyes before touching my lips to his.

Groaning and collecting me in his arms, he murmurs, "I'd break every rule for you." Trey breathes, watching a grin slowly encompass my face.

Ustus's voice startles me. "That's quite a lovely sentiment, Trey," he says from the doorway of my room. "But I'm afraid you're never going to have her."

"Ustus!" I gasp, tensing. Trey shifts me behind him. "Get out of my room!" I order, appalled that he overheard my intimate conversation with Trey.

"Kesek Trey, you and your men have overstayed your welcome here," Ustus says, eyeing Trey cautiously as he raises his automatic weapon. "You are to return to your base. I've been instructed to inform you that you're to have no further contact with Fay Kricket." The last is said with no small amount of satisfaction.

"Ustus, don't be stupid." I scowl at him. "I'll talk to whomever I want."

Trey walks toward Ustus menacingly. Ustus, in turn, points the gun at Trey's chest. "You'll have no one to speak with if Trey continues to move," Ustus barks out, fear creeping into his tone.

Grabbing Trey's wrist, I try to step in front of him, but he brushes me aside. "Wait!" I plead, afraid that Ustus will pull the trigger. "It's okay, Trey!" But Trey doesn't stop.

Ustus swings the gun in my direction, pointing the blue laser at my chest. Trey stops dead; he stiffens. "Lower your weapon, Ustus."

"Not until she walks down those stairs with me and we depart," Ustus says. "I have orders to take her back to the palace. I cannot have you leaving with her, Kesek. She can survive a bullet if it keeps her here."

"*Sir!*" Wayra says from the door, training his weapon on Ustus.

"Tell him to lower his weapon," Ustus orders with sweat slipping down his face as he continues to train his gun on me.

"Wayra, easy," Trey says. "Lower the gun." Wayra complies slowly, not making any quick movements. "We're going to allow Ustus to escort Kricket to the skiff. It will take them back to the palace without incident."

"Let's move," Ustus says to me, using his head to indicate the stairs.

My eyes flicker to Trey's, and I see him nod. Wringing my hands, I walk forward, moving toward the stairs. Ustus falls in behind me, never letting his weapon waver from me. Passing Jax and Hollis, they both reach for a weapon before Trey orders them to stop. I walk out the front door and to the hovering skiff. Several Regent police surround us.

Silently, I get into the hover car and remain mute all the way to the palace. I refuse to even look at Ustus. When we arrive, Ustus doesn't use his gun, but merely gestures me to follow him from the vehicle. We head straight to Manus's personal arcade on the north end of the estate. Once in the Amethyst passage, we quickly arrive at the Regent's sitting room.

Ustus leaves me with the attendants who offer me a drink from the bar. Accepting a glass of water, I try not to gulp it down. I walk around the room and absently touch the small statuary on the tables. I've never felt more awkward in my life.

"You've put me at a disadvantage, Kricket," Manus's deep voice sounds behind me, startling me because I didn't hear him come in.

"How so?" I ask, trying to recover my cool. Looking up, he's by the door of his bedroom, dressed in an elegant, black robe. His hair is a little less meticulous than usual, and his violet eyes are trained on me.

"I was not aware that you were . . . lonely," he replies, accepting a fazeria from his attendant and then waving him out of the room.

"I'm not lonely," I say, trying to figure out what he means.

"Then why was Kesek Trey in your room this evening?" he asks, and I almost choke on my drink. I set it down on the table.

"It's been a frightening evening for me, Manus. I was afraid, so I asked him to stay with me to guard me," I lie, knowing that I have to protect Trey.

"Mmm," Manus says in a noncommittal tone. "You won't mind putting these on for me then . . . just to see?" he asks, holding out a pair of the grandma goggles to me. Knowing that the visor will scan my entire body, I grit my teeth. Walking to him, I take them from his grasp. Placing them briefly on my eyes, I wait for only a few seconds before handing them back to him.

Analyzing the data that I'm sure is telling him that everything is still "intact," I watch his expression, seeing a small smile creep to the corners of his lips. "What was the point of that?" I ask.

"You know what the point is. I needed to know if you were still a virgin," he replies, smiling.

"Why?" I shoot back. "That's personal. It's my choice."

"No, Kricket, it's *my* choice," Manus counters, losing a little of the satisfaction he was sporting. "Things are changing quickly. I have many decisions to make, and you seem to be at the center of them all."

"Am I?"

"Mmm," he nods. "It would seem with your new ability that you are even more valuable than before. Unfortunately, I was not able to keep this ability from Skye, like I have your other ability. No, this one is more . . . overt."

"I'm not loving it either, if that's what you're saying." I take a sip of my drink and walk toward the double glass doors that lead to the private terrace.

"You can see the future?" he asks me point blank.

"I don't know. I saw a version of it that didn't come to pass—"

"Because you changed it."

I shrug. "I don't know. It all happened so fast. But I'm sure you heard the communication. What do you think?" I ask, curious to hear his interpretation of the event.

"I think you intercepted an event in the future and changed it."

"I have no idea how I did it or if I can ever do it again. I can't tell you what triggered it or even how to re-create the event, so . . ." I see his smile broaden.

"You're so humble. It's an endearing trait, Kricket. Do you know that?" He approaches me and lifts a piece of my hair, letting it slip through his fingers.

"Okay," I say, feeling uncomfortable with him this close, touching me.

"When you first arrived here, I was astounded by you," Manus admits. "You're such a beauty, but it's as if you're not even aware of it. And the way you speak to me, like we're friends, but you never overstep, and you never underplay. You just glide effortlessly along."

"You like my flow?"

"Yes," he gives a small laugh, "your flow. You have such a colorful vernacular, it makes me want to sit with you for hours just to listen—not only to what you'll say but how you'll say it." His hand lands lightly on my shoulder.

"You're a 'best behavior' friend, Manus," I say, moving away nonchalantly. "I walk a fine line around you because you have the authority to affect my life adversely."

"Yes," he agrees. "That you can do it so seamlessly is what is so intriguing, Kricket. Most females your age are playing at seduction, but you don't need to. You can intellectually spar with my top advisers and then leave them tongue-tied, watching you walk away."

"I have the advantage of knowing when they're lying." I try to deflect his compliment because he's making me more and more uncomfortable.

"I had decided to give you to Kyon before I met you. Did you know that?"

Turning to look at him, I can see he's being truthful. "You changed your mind."

"Not at first. I merely wanted to see just how much I could gain from Kyon in exchange for you. But then, not only did I begin to enjoy the information that you could glean from every conversation to which you were privy, I also enjoyed being with you more and more each rotation."

"In a paternal way?" I ask in a hopeful tone.

"Hardly," he replies, smiling. "So, now I have some decisions to make."

"Which are?" I ask, quirking my eyebrow.

"I'm in an inconvenient position. On one hand, I have the Alameeda who will begin to smear you if I refuse to turn you over to them. I've been in meetings all evening with ambassadors from Alameeda, Wurthem, Peney, and Comantre. Each is urging me to give you away to avert a war."

"Nice of them. Let me guess: Em Sam is involved?"

"Quite involved," Manus replies. "And on the other hand, I have Skye who is insisting that you be turned over to them for intelligence purposes."

"Are you asking for my input? Because I'm all for saying 'hi' to Skye," I reply, knowing he's really telling me something completely different.

"Yes, that would make you an emancipated minor, wouldn't it?" He comes nearer to me.

"And that bothers you?" I stand my ground as he stops in front of me. "I can take care of myself."

"I'm sure you're quite capable of that, but I have grown attached to you, and I'm unwilling to part with you," he says, touching my cheek lightly. "I had thought to make you my inamorata after you were of age, of course, but now all that has changed."

"What has changed?" I ask, feeling dread creeping over me as fast as the flush of red in my cheeks.

"Word will spread about the attack on our soil and how you thwarted it," he replies, seeing the blush staining my cheeks and giving me a sensual smile.

"So?" I try to shrug.

"You have elevated your tier. You're a hero."

"Only for the moment," I counter. "When the Alameeda attack, I'll be the mutant that brought war upon our people."

"No, you'll be my consort, the royal who is attempting to protect her people." He touches my hair gently.

"*What?*" I grasp his hand and push it away from my hair. "Are you insane?" I ask in shock.

Frowning, Manus says, "I believe I'm speaking rationally."

"No, you're not," I reply, crossing my arms over my chest. "You're like my parent!"

"I've never treated you like a daughter—a pet maybe, but never a child," Manus replies, amused by my reaction. "Do you know that what I'm offering you is a great honor?"

"So, it's an offer? I can say no?" I watch his frown deepen.

"You may not refuse," he counters, somewhat shocked by my reaction.

"Of course I can refuse. I'm not in love with you!"

"You're young. Love may come—"

"And it may not," I retort, pacing.

"True, but that's hardly relevant."

"It's relevant to me!" I argue, stopping in front of him again.

"You love him," Manus says accusingly, a scowl beginning to grow on his face. "Kyon warned me that you were falling in love with your guard, but I thought you were too intelligent for that. He is not even on the same tier as you."

"What does that *mean*?" I ask, completely disgusted. "If by *tier* you mean honor, then, yeah, he has more of that than any of us."

"You will forget Kesek Trey. He is lust, nothing more. You will be my consort, and together we will take down the Alameeda. You may work with Skye, in an advisory capacity only, but at the end of the day, you'll be here with me," Manus states in an even tone, just like he's discussing the way he expects his table to be set or his spix to be saddled.

"I'm not a bobblehead, Manus. I'm not going to agree to commit to you just because you order it."

"Yes, you will," he says adamantly, "or I'll crush Trey and his family."

"What?" I breathe as my knees weaken.

"I'm not letting you go, Kricket. I'll give you to the Brotherhood before I see you with Kesek Trey."

"*Why?*" I ask, unable to stop myself.

"Because there is nothing in that for me."

"That's *so* sucky," I retort.

"You will be my consort. Please refrain from using words that demean your stature," he warns me.

"You're a knob knocker!" I growl at him. Instantly, he backhands me in the mouth, causing me to fall against a small table. Catching myself before I fall all the way to the ground, I lean against it heavily. Then, straightening, I look into his eyes, seeing his anger as I touch the back of my hand to my mouth while tasting blood. Reaching into the pocket of his robe, Manus pulls out a handkerchief and hands it to me.

"Our new relationship is off to a rough start," I murmur, refusing to cower while touching the linen to my lips.

"As long as you are aware that it has started," he replies evenly. "We'll announce our engagement at your coming-out swank. It will be awkward with Allairis in attendance, but it will be gossiped over if your Cavar is not there to wish us well. Do not embarrass me, or he pays for it."

"You're hurting me," I whisper, deciding that maybe honesty will sway him.

He touches my hair gently, saying, "I'll make it up to you. Give me a daughter and you can do as you please."

Too shocked to say a word, I just stare at him in confusion. "I had hoped that you would want to stay with me in my room to celebrate our engagement, but I can see that you will need some time to adjust to the idea." Manus watches me. Pressing a button on the remote on the table, he summons one of his attendants. "Please make the room next to mine ready for my intended consort, Fay Kricket, and have all of her things moved."

"It has already been made ready. Shall I show her to her room now, Haut Manus?"

"Yes," Manus turns to me. "You need to get some rest, Kricket. You look tired."

Straightening my shoulders, I nod to Manus before following the attendant. I don't see anything as I'm led to the bedroom that adjoins with Manus's room. As soon as I'm alone, I crawl into the enormous bed and cry myself to sleep.

Chapter 20
Swanks and Tanks

I stay in my new room for most of the next rotation, feeling fragile and upset about my forced engagement to Manus. But hiding is not my style, so the following morning I dress in a riding outfit and ask Aella to cancel all my scheduled meetings. Walking through the halls of the palace, my guards trailing me, I have to contend with the well wishes and congratulations of the staff. Manus must've already announced his intentions to them, so I grit my teeth and plaster a crocodile smile on my face.

I head to the stables where number twenty-two is saddled for me. Riding out with my guards, I ignore them, trying to concentrate on finding a strategy to get out of committing to Manus. Several options come to mind, everything from sneaking out and joining the Cavars to escaping back to Earth, but all of these options have desperate consequences for Trey.

"I wish I knew a way out of this," I mumble to myself.

"What?" Ustus asks, riding next to me.

"Nothing," I sigh. Then searing heat, like sparks of molten dust from a white-hot sun, passes over my skin. Fear and pain erupt in me as I try to clutch the reins in my hand tighter. A part of me ascends into the air as my body slips from the spix and falls limply to the ground. Thrusting forward, I travel ahead in time while my guards scramble off their spixes to crowd around my body on the ground.

⚜

Waking up in Ustus's arms, I shy away from him, feeling deathly cold in body and spirit. "Fay, Kricket! How do you feel?" he asks anxiously.

My hands tremble along with my entire body as I just shake my head mutely. His expression changes to one of determination. Standing up, he hands me up to Fex, who holds me on his spix while wheeling it around and taking me back to the stables. Once there, they transport me via skiff to the palace.

Tofer and Yaser meet us at the entrance, hovering over me while I insist on walking to my room. They do a complete physical on me, listening to the details that Ustus provides.

"Was it a seizure?" Tofer asks Yaser, puzzling over what just occurred.

"It wasn't a seizure," I say at last, finding my voice. "I need to speak to Manus. Please, just—can somebody get him?" My throat sounds gravelly.

Waiting impatiently for Manus to arrive, I try to think of what I can tell him about what I saw in the future. I have to make him believe me, or he's dead. "Manus!" I say in a rush as he enters my room. "I have to speak with you."

"I was informed that you fell from your spix. Are you well?" he asks. Putting his arm around my shoulder, Manus pulls me to his side.

Yaser rushes to reassure him. "She is quite well—"

"I have to talk to you. Alone," I say, my eyes going to Yaser and Tofer and the attendants in the room.

"I would like to speak with you as well. Leave us," he orders. Watching everyone in the room clear out, I pull away from Manus's side, wringing my hands. When they're gone, Manus sits in the high-backed chair by the fireplace. I take the soft chair across from it. Manus frowns, "I've had time to think about our last conversation. I lost my temper with you . . . I'm not used to anyone saying no to me, and I could have been more persuasive when I told you that you will commit to me—"

Holding my breath through his dissertation of the events of our last meeting, I finally interrupt him, "I don't care about any of that right now, Manus."

His eyebrows rise in surprise. "You don't?" Manus asks, watching me shake my head no. "Then, you've decided to comply willingly with my wishes?" His face lights up with pleasure.

"Manus, if I comply with your wishes, Kyon will kill you."

"How is that possible when Kyon is currently in a military prison near the Comantre border?" Manus asks me softly, his face falling a little.

"I don't know, but when he gets here, he's gonna be really annoyed with you."

"And when will that be?" Manus asks in a calm tone, looking stony.

"Tomorrow night, at the swank. He knows about it—it's been planned from the first day I arrived here," I explain, watching his face.

"And he will—what? Show up and kill me?" Manus sounds doubtful.

"You, your guards, your friends, your enemies, your staff . . . everyone standing around," I reply, remembering the bloody terror of the future.

"And you? Do you survive?" he wonders, raising his brow.

"Yes," I nod. "He has special plans for me." My face grows pale.

"Kricket, really, this is absurd. I know that you have a special talent, but to try to lie to me like this is really beneath you," Manus says, rising from his seat.

"I'm not lying!"

"By tomorrow morning, Kyon will be executed for his escape attempt and his subversion against Rafe," Manus informs me coldly. "He cannot kill me if he's dead."

"He's not dead yet," I point out, feeling ill. "You and I know that his escape is possible. It nearly happened the other night. I'm begging you to stop this. Committing to me makes you and everyone around you a target."

"You're very convincing, Kricket—such passion. I cannot wait to taste it." He smiles, reaching out and cupping my chin. "I'll move up Kyon's execution. He dies tonight instead. Does that please you?"

"No," I answer, my voice cracking as I cover his hand with my own. "Manus," I plead, "he kills everyone—none of you get away. They have people everywhere. It's an invasion."

"Alameeda is in no way ready to invade Rafe."

"They're more than ready. Peney must've sided with them, like Kyon said."

"Peney hasn't sided with the Alameeda. Kyon was playing you. He understands your gift."

"What if you're wrong?"

"The events can't happen as you describe because Kyon will be dead," Manus says, like it's a foregone conclusion.

"That's too simple of a solution. Someone else could lead the invasion—you can't take that chance."

"This is about my plans to announce our engagement, isn't it?" Manus says sourly, dropping his hand from my face in anger. "That plan isn't going to change, Kricket. I admire your ability to manipulate others; I find it to be your most attractive quality, but don't think to ever manipulate me."

With my hands in fists, I nearly growl at him, "I'm not trying to manipulate you! I'm trying to save you! If you make this announcement, you're dead. This is called survival, Manus—yours and mine. We need to inform Skye so that they can protect the city—"

"I'm not bringing Skye here. This is about your Cavar," Manus says, like it all makes sense to him. "He's already forgotten about you, Kricket. You know soldiers—they do their jobs and then they go home . . . to their families. I meant to tell you before the swank that ours will not be the only engagement announced that night," he says, looking into my eyes.

"What do you mean? Who's the other lucky couple?"

"Trey. He has agreed to commit to his love after all. What is her name . . . Charisma Foster?" he asks, making my heart twist painfully because he's not lying.

"Let me speak to him," I demand, holding out my hand for his communicator.

"Let him alone," Manus says softly. "You'll only cause him pain." Seeing the truth in that statement makes my eyes brighten with tears, but I blink them back, refusing to cry in front of Manus. "Don't be sad. I'll provide the kind of life for you that you could not have dreamed possible. This is your home," he says, lifting his hands and indicating his opulent palace.

"Just do one thing for me, Manus." I look up at him.

"What?"

"Make sure Trey and his brother, Victus, don't come tomorrow. I don't want them here. Will you do that for me?"

"Of course," Manus agrees, a smile touching his lips. "I don't want this to be painful for you. I'll advise my staff to make the appropriate calls."

"Thank you," I murmur, feeling my throat closing. Turning my back on him, I walk toward my closet. "I haven't even picked out anything to wear tomorrow. Isn't that silly of me?" I look over my shoulder. "What does one wear to an invasion?"

"Something has already been made for you," Manus replies dryly.

"Pretty?" I ask through my clenched teeth because he's completely ignoring my warnings.

"Exquisite," he replies, but I get the sense he's not talking about the gown.

"Well, I'm sure it'll be perfect for the massacre," I reply mockingly.

"Kricket!" Manus barks my name in warning.

With my back to him, I say desperately, "You have to believe me, Manus. I'm not playing you. This is real."

There's a long silence between us. I look over my shoulder at him. "Kyon dies tonight. I'll go and witness it myself," Manus states with a frown, approaching me from behind and hugging me to his chest.

"Manus, don't," I say, struggling to pull away from him. His arms tighten around me.

"Fight me, Kricket, and I'll make sure that Trey comes tomorrow night. I'll make a production of announcing his engagement. You can meet his intended consort."

I still and the sound of my heavy breathing is loud in my ears. Manus pulls my hair aside and kisses the nape of my neck. "I'm sore from the fall from my spix," I murmur.

"This is going to happen, Kricket. You know that, right?" Manus asks. "I'll give you until tomorrow night, but you will be mine."

"Tomorrow night then," I murmur, as I cringe over the two possible scenarios for my future.

Turning me in his arms so he can see my face, he says, "Until then." I tense as Manus kisses me tenderly on the lips. I don't kiss him back—I can't. He doesn't seem to notice my lack of response as I catch the gleam in his eyes when he pulls away. "I'll leave you to rest. If you should need anything, you'll call for me?" All I can manage is a nod as I look down. Manus lifts my chin with his finger. "We'll be happy together. I'll make you happy, Kricket," he promises, believing every word he says.

I just nod, feeling empty and afraid. After watching Manus leave, I hold my head in my hands. I have no sense that I've changed anything regarding the events about to unfold. I fall back on the bed, staring up at the ornately carved ceiling. *At least I saved Trey,* I think, feeling an ache in my chest, thinking of him. *Now I have to figure out a way to save myself.*

⁂

There isn't much time to compose myself the next morning. Aella ushers me out of bed early, going straight to work on making me into a debutante for the swank. By the time my gown arrives, I'm ready for Aella to be gone.

"Now, when you're done here, you promise that you're going to take Sergen and leave for the night?" I ask her for the hundredth time.

"Yes," Aella says. I can see her rolling her eyes in the mirror in front of me, so I try a different tack.

"I hear that there's a hot club downtown that has thumpin' music," I say, holding still while Aella fastens the intricate hooks on the back of my strapless, floor-length, lavender gown.

"You heard that from me," she says, grinning at me in the mirror.

"Right, so everything is set. Don't even think of coming back here tonight. I can manage without you."

"I bet you will," Aella replies with a smug smile. "Haut Manus will make sure this dress comes off tonight."

"Yes, well . . . just as long as you know not to come back here," I say evasively, my cheeks flushing with embarrassment. "I have something for you," I say as she finishes the last hook that attaches the long train to the gown. "It's on the dresser."

Going to the dresser, Aella picks up the envelope on it. She opens it, and her eyes go round and her mouth drops open. "What's this?" She stares at the wads of fardrooms I've stuffed into it.

"A bonus," I say, "I want you to celebrate tonight. Buy a bottle of the best fazeria and invite as many of your friends from the palace as you can."

Amy A. Bartol

"But this will buy more than a bottle of fazeria," she breathes.

"The rest is for you," I say softly, feeling choked up.

"Why?"

"Because you're the best liaison I ever had," I reply, feeling my eyes blur with tears.

"Well, thank you, Kricket," she says with a teary smile.

"You're welcome." I wipe the moisture from my eyes with a tissue. "I think I'm ready."

"You look stunning." Aella exhales the words, her eyes going to the tiara woven into my hair.

"Such a difference from the jumpsuit I used to wear. If only my friend Enrique could see me now. He'd be so jealous of my tiara."

"He probably couldn't wear it like you can," Aella winks, handing me the small jeweled clutch. "Oh! You should go. The Regent will be waiting for you by the grand staircase in the ballroom! Remember, you're to enter from the third floor, like we practiced."

"I know—it's like a hundred and fifty stairs or more. I should just slide down the banister."

Her eyes flare wide and she puts up both her hands. "No! Don't do that!" Aella warns, looking appalled.

"It wouldn't be the worst thing to happen tonight," I mutter grimly.

"What?"

"Nothing."

"Well, at least Haut Nim won't be there," Aella says absently.

"Excuse me?"

"Oh, I wasn't supposed to mention it. They were going to execute him last night, but he killed himself instead," Aella says with a shiver. "Can you believe it? He doesn't seem the type, you know?"

"He killed himself?"

"Yes."

"Kyon?" I ask in disbelief.

"Yes."

"They're sure he's dead?"

"Well, yeah . . . I guess so," she says, shrugging her shoulders.

"How do they know? Did they do an autopsy of—they're sure it's him, right?" I ask, latching on to her upper arm and searching her face.

"Yes, I'm sure they would've checked. I heard the body was burned badly, but it was in his pod so—I'm sorry, I shouldn't have told you this right before the swank. Manus thought we shouldn't say anything about it."

"No, it's fine. I'm fine. You should go now . . . have fun," I reply, feeling cold inside as I let go of her arm.

Nodding, she walks with me to the sitting room where Ustus and a few other agents are waiting to escort me to the ballroom. My hands are trembling by the time I arrive near the stairway of the ballroom. It's virtually empty up here on the third floor because it's been cordoned off so that I can make my debut in a grand style. But now that I'm here, fear has my arms feeling heavy and my knees weak.

Breathing heavily, I'm finding it hard to catch my breath. Ustus, seeing my fear, asks, "Nervous?"

"I feel like I'm walking into an execution," I reply, trying to breathe deeply.

"Just do as you're told and there won't be any problems."

"Would it make a difference if I told you it was your execution?"

Ustus considers what I said for a moment. "Kyon is dead. Whatever you saw, or you *think* you saw, can't happen."

"What if you're wrong? It feels the same, Ustus." I wring my hands because I know that I didn't try hard enough, or this wouldn't be happening. "What if nothing has changed? If you make me go down there, people will die."

"We have orders to drag you down the stairs if necessary," Ustus replies, but he pales as he looks over the balcony to the reception area far below.

"Ustus!" I say his name like a plea and see him stiffen.

"Manus is waiting for you." He lifts his hand toward the stairs. "He won't like it if you're late. Are you going on your own, or do I need to guide you down?"

I take a deep breath and compose myself. "I'll go by myself, but if I don't see you again, enjoy your flight. Baw-da-baw." Straightening my shoulders, I walk beyond the sweeping curtains to the top of the staircase.

The scene below reminds me of the elaborate miniature ballroom I saw in one of the picture windows at the Water Tower in Chicago. It featured regal figurines gliding along an exquisite floor, dancing in rings from the mechanized magnets beneath it, while the crowd looked on in admiration.

Chamber music begins to play, and as I stare at the hundreds of elegantly attired people below, I realize that this is real. I'm now trapped within the display, and there's no way out. Composing myself for a moment, I see Manus step to the bottom of the staircase, waiting for me.

Descending the stairs on shaky legs, I search the crowd and the upper balcony. A terrifying sense of déjà vu is settling in because I've already experienced all of this a little more than a day ago, with grim consequences. *One thing is different, though,* I think, taking the last few steps to meet Manus. *I can't find Trey in the crowd, like I could before.* Holding on to that difference like a lifeline, I greet Manus with a formal nod. Extending his hand to me, I take it, walking with him to the center of the room as it clears for us.

Casting his gaze around, Manus announces to the assembly, "May I present Fay Kricket, Coriness of Rafe, Priestess of Alameeda, and in less than a fortnight, my consort." Applause erupts from the assembly, and heat stains my cheeks at the bitter pill I have to swallow. Gathering the train of my gown, I sweep it up over my arm.

"You look breathtaking," Manus compliments, holding me in his arms as the music begins again. Leading me in the waltzlike dance that I've practiced with Tofer, I feel numb, like I'm still in the future, not the present.

"Thank you," I reply softly. My eyes meet his briefly before darting back to the floors above us.

"You seem worried—you shouldn't be," Manus comforts me. His hand at my back presses me closer to him as we dance.

"Really? I look worried?" I ask, meeting his eyes again. "Because I feel terrified, so I guess worried is a step up."

"Why?" Manus asks, his eyes widening in surprise.

"I told you, I saw you die here," I reply, frowning at him for not taking this seriously.

"Yes, but you also said that Kyon killed me," he counters with a smile, gliding effortlessly with me around the floor.

"I did. That's how I saw it when I was here before," I reply, feeling off kilter because even the scent of him is the same as I remember.

"I took care of it—there's no cause to worry. I want you to enjoy tonight. It's our celebration!" Manus says, relishing the moment as he wheels us closer to the staircase again.

"Yes, you said that, but everything still feels the same to me," I reply, tensing as we pass the steps.

"How was I killed?" Manus asks, sounding entertained. "Before, I mean."

"Kyon's snipers were up there," I say, indicating the second and third floors with a flick of my head. "He was up there, too."

"So, he shot me from above?" Manus asks, looking around at the floors above us, amusement in his raised brow.

"No." I shake my head slowly. "First, he killed your agents, but we didn't know that they were dead until he threw Ustus over the railing. His head shattered like glass on the floor in front of us." I pale, feeling ill. "Then, Kyon casually walked down the staircase, spraying the crowd indiscriminately with forty-caliber shells that tore some of them in half."

I see Manus's eyes narrow as he says, "Kricket—"

"When Kyon got to us, everyone who could run did, but they didn't get far because Alameeda had infiltrated the palace and were going room by room, slaughtering everyone they could find, so running wasn't really an option. But you didn't run . . . maybe you thought he wouldn't kill you, but you were wrong. Kyon stuck the gun in your mouth and when he pulled the trigger . . ." I trail off, unable to continue.

A frown touches Manus's face briefly. "I'm sorry that I didn't take you more seriously. I see now that it must have been frightening to witness something like that, but you don't need to be afraid. I will protect you. Kyon is dead."

Before I can answer him, Ustus's body hits the floor just in front of us; the blood from his crushed skull spatters in scarlet patterns on the bottom of my gown. Halting near his body, the look of shock on Manus's face is as disturbing as the screams and gunfire that erupt all around us.

"You should try to run this time," I say, watching his face lose color. When he doesn't react, I shout, *"Now! Go now!"* Pushing him hard in the chest, I try to get him to move. He just stands there with the look of disbelief still on his face, so I backhand him on the cheek. *"Run toward the garden!"* I yell at him, pointing away from where I know the gunmen to be.

Manus begins backing away from me, like I'm the devil. Then, he turns and runs toward the side doors, leaving me to watch Kyon descend the grand staircase, the muzzle of his gun igniting as it spews bullets like raindrops over the crowd in front of him.

Seeing him coming toward me, I wait patiently by the bottom of the steps for him. He stops firing when he nears me, but the clinking sound of the empty shell casings, rolling down the stairs, follows in his wake. Gunfire continues around us. It radiates from rooms far and near. Forester and Lecto are killing anything they see move around us.

Raking me with his eyes, Kyon searches my face as I meet his blue stare. A slow smile creeps over his lips. He reaches out and touches my cheek. "You knew I was coming, didn't you?" he asks softly. "You didn't even flinch when his body hit the floor."

"I knew," I reply, feeling icy as the odor of the hot muzzle of his weapon assails my nostrils.

"They didn't believe you?" Understanding grows in his eyes along with a sense of satisfaction. Shaking his head, he adds, "They have no vision, Kricket. They cannot see, even when they're told!" He gazes around at the carnage he has created, but I refuse to look, keeping my eyes on him instead.

Kyon's eyebrows pull together ruthlessly as he fires at a body not far away that is still moving. "You've turned my whole world upside down, do you know that?" Kyon asks me in a tense voice. "I came here to kill you!"

"I know . . . but you won't." I watch him stiffen. "I think your exact words the last time I was here were 'I came here to kill you . . . but where is the passion in that?'"

Kyon lets go of his weapon, allowing it to hang loosely at his side by the strap around his chest. He reaches forward and grasps me by the back of the neck, pulling me to him. He lowers his mouth to mine and kisses me ruthlessly, bruising my lips. "I waited too long to do that," he breathes against my mouth. "Knowing you were mine and having them keep you from me . . ." He kisses me again. "Do you know how special you are?" His eyes practically gleam. "You can see the future—"

"I can affect the future," I correct him softly, watching his eyebrow rise.

"Yes, and you used it to thwart my rescue attempt," he retorts with his eyebrows slicing down.

"That was just an opportunity for you to show your resiliency, Kyon," I counter and then tense, knowing what's coming.

In the next instant, Kyon slaps me hard in the face, sending me to the ground by the twisting marble railing of the staircase. I reach out and sweep the metal hilt under my dress before palming the knife that I had stashed there when practicing my entrance.

"Why do guys all insist on hitting me in the face?" I ask while looking up at Kyon's twisted lips. "Do me a favor next time and hit me in the stomach or something because it's really hard to hide bruises on my face." I hold out my hand for him to help me up.

A slow smile creeps back to the corners of Kyon's lips. He murmurs, "It's difficult not to respect you, Kricket," while he reaches down to help me up. Locking hands with him and using the momentum of his own force, I pull myself up as I arc the knife in my other hand toward his chest with all my strength.

Feeling the knife embed in the left side of Kyon's chest, I watch his blue eyes widen in surprise as he staggers back. I stumble away from him on shaky legs while my mind screams for me to run. Instead, I continue to watch in horror as Kyon grasps the handle of the knife, pulling it from his chest. It clatters on the marble floor, as he grimaces.

"Kricket," he says my name grimly, panting and raising his gun, pointing it at me. "I apologize if this disappoints you, but I'm not human . . . I'm Etharian. My heart is on the right side of my chest."

"How stupid of me," I reply, balling my hands into fists as I wait for him to shoot me.

I flinch and squeeze my eyes shut as gunshots puncture the air. My knees go weak, waiting to feel the pain of my body being ripped apart by bullets. When I open my eyes, I see Forester dance like a marionette as slugs riddle him. Another short burst from an automatic and Lecto is on the ground, too.

Looking toward the wide archways of the ballroom, I see Trey entering the room with stealthy military grace, his automatic weapon drawn up to his shoulder and trained on Kyon. Jax and Wayra flank him, while Hollis, Fenton, and Drex come in through the sides, surrounding our position. They're all yelling at Kyon to halt and drop his weapon. But Kyon hasn't moved, the blue beam of his automatic is trained on me.

Gigantic booms, like mortar blasts, sound outside, causing the ground to tremble and the chandeliers to chatter and sway above us. I look up, thinking the roof may come down at any second.

"Drop your weapon!" Trey yells again at Kyon above the din of warfare from outside.

Kyon blinks a few times, swaying on his feet; he looks like he's trying to keep his focus on me while blood continues to seep out of his chest wound. Narrowing his eyes, Kyon's fingers tense on the trigger of his gun, but then they ease again. He is breathing heavily, and sweat runs down the side of his face. "She is meant for me," Kyon says in a quiet tone. "Do you think she's yours, Trey? You couldn't even keep her from Manus."

"Put your weapon on the ground!" Trey retorts, but Kyon doesn't move.

"Why?" Kyon smirks. "She'll be the death of us both. I'd be doing you a favor by pulling the trigger. Don't you know that you should eliminate what you can't have? She's a priestess. She's in your head, Trey."

"My head, my heart, my blood," Trey responds immediately.

"That's unfortunate for you, because she belongs to me. I *own* her. I can end her now," Kyon says, and the blue beam of light sways a little as Kyon does.

"Gamble to win, Kyon. Kill her now and you lose," Trey replies, his eyes narrowing as his fingers tense on the trigger of his automatic.

"Is he telling the truth, Kricket?" Kyon asks me with a slow smile. "Will I lose more if I kill you now or more if I don't?"

"I don't know," I whisper.

"You don't know?" Kyon's face twists in anger. "Pay attention, my love, because I'm tired of repeating myself. If you're not with me, then you won't be with anyone," he says, his voice sounding a little slurred. "Which will it be?"

"Kyon, please . . ." I breathe, feeling like I'm choking.

Another booming mortar shell shakes the ground just as the roof begins to splinter. Spidering cracks creak along the plaster, looking like dark, wildly growing vines. Big, thick chunks of the ceiling fall around us, while pillars of marble crash to the floor, fracturing and sending clouds of dust into the air. The lights flicker, and I bring my hands to my ears to block out the tremendous noise.

"They're extracting!" Trey yells to Jax and Wayra, as the lights all die around us.

The only illumination now is the laser on my chest and the searchlights swirling above as the ceiling of the ballroom is torn off, exposing a shadowy outline of an E-One in the starry sky. In the next instant, bright white circles of light lock onto Kyon and me from the belly of the hovering helicopter, blinding me. The blood in my feet feels as if it's being forced upward into my head. My tiara flies from my hair and makes a rapid ascent toward the black metallic vehicle above. I begin to follow it as I lift off the ground into the air.

As I rise quickly toward the ceiling, I suddenly change direction when someone tackles me to the ground, knocking the air out of my lungs. Tumbling along the floor and too stunned to move, I'm dragged beneath the arching staircase and wrapped in someone's arms as the eerie hum of the E-One still radiates above us.

Struggling to breathe, I'm being gently rocked against the chest protecting me as someone strokes my hair. More yelling and gunfire erupts around us, but it soon wanes. Then everything is quiet. Small beams of light, from flashlights mounted on guns, hit the walls and floors, as Jax's voice yells, *"Sir?"*

"Here," Trey's voice says behind me, his arm loosening a little around my waist. The flashlights swing to us and cause me to squint at the Cavars wielding them.

"Is she okay?" Wayra asks in an anxious tone.

"Kitten, are you hurt?" Trey asks softly in my ear, before kissing my temple and running his hands over me to see if he can locate any obvious injury.

Numbly, I shake my head before turning and burying my face against his chest, trying to hold tightly to the front of his uniform, but my hands feel weak. Approaching us, Jax and Wayra both crouch down and reach out their hands to me. Jax gently rests a hand on my shoulder while Wayra's hand goes to my back. Hollis, Fenton, and Drex follow suit, touching me lightly for several seconds before they move back.

Trey whispers in my ear, "That's a sign of respect, Kricket. We do that after a battle if someone shows particular valor." He squeezes me to him tighter. Rising from the ground with me in his arms, he asks Wayra, "Did anyone tag Kyon?"

"We tagged him, but they still got him out through the roof," Wayra reports, sounding frustrated.

"Can he be regenerated?" Trey asks Jax.

"Possibly. He'll need several sessions—at least half a floan, best case," Jax replies, "If he survives the transport. We have rapid ascenders en route to cut off their trajectory," Jax reports. Looking at me, he frowns, "We need to take a look at her. She's really pale."

Trey barks out orders, "Hollis, Drex, Fenton, make sure the perimeter is secure before we go for transport. No one approaches us, not even the Regent. Treat everyone as hostile until we have Kricket secured."

Everyone snaps into formation around Trey and me, weapons drawn to their shoulders while they scan the surrounding balconies.

In moments, we're in the geometric gardens. Big, hovering machines with beefy, tanklike cannons are wreaking havoc on the aircraft above, pulsing huge beams of light into the sky and fracturing ALVs extracting armored Alameeda troops from the palace.

Trey moves toward several vehicles that look like oversized motorcycles without wheels. They're shrouded from view by an ivy-covered stairway, and when we reach them, I notice that they've got sleek, bulletlike exteriors. Speaking to a bike, Trey says, "Unlace compartment, engage ignition." The lid opens to reveal a long seat as it rises from the ground with a soft hum. Setting me gently on the seat, Trey pries my arms off his neck and mounts the bike in front of me.

"Hold on to my waist," Trey says gently, putting my hands on his hips. Nodding my head, I rest my cheek against his back, smelling his scent through his combat armor-plated uniform.

"Wait," Jax says, coming up behind me and tearing the train off my lavender gown with a grimace. "Forgive me," he says, but I don't respond; my arms just tighten on Trey.

"Diamond formation. Stay on the coms—any static and we disperse in teams. Jax and Wayra, with me," Trey orders before leaning forward as the compartment door encloses us in the tight space.

Using his hand to cover my clenched hands around his waist, Trey murmurs, "Kricket, I should've been here sooner."

Squeezing him tighter, my voice is weak when I whisper, "You saved my life."

Trey's voice is less than benign when he says, "No. He chose not to kill you. Kyon was just buying time so he could try to get you both extracted."

Fear cuts through my feeling of numbness. "What do you mean?"

Trey tenses as he says, "Kyon wanted a priestess—that's all you were to him when he first went to find you. But now, he won't be satisfied with anyone else. He'll only want you, Kricket." Trey revs the engine of the vehicle, and it purrs beneath us. "I'm certain that he was under orders to kill you if he couldn't extract you. He had the opportunity to do it, but he didn't."

"What are you saying?"

"I'm saying that I failed to kill him," he growls with regret. "He'll regenerate."

The taste of fear on my tongue makes it hard for me to ask, "And then he'll come looking for me?"

"And then I'll kill him," Trey promises.

"Where are we going now?" I can feel the bike rocket forward at a dizzying speed.

"Somewhere safe."

"Where's that?" I ask, not lifting my cheek from his back.

"Our new home. Skye."

Something like hope sparks inside of me for the briefest of moments. My curled arms around Trey's waist ease a bit as I lift my cheek from his back, and unable to stop myself, I whisper the word, "Home."

Chapter 21
Never Enough

Streaking through the dark night on the back of Trey's hovercycle, we avoid Rafe troops as they scurry to rout the Alameeda extraction. We soon exchange the chaos at the palace grounds for the eerie dead silence of the unlit city streets of the Isle of Skye. Having only been here for my court appearance, I'm finding it unnerving to see the absence of anyone on the streets as we cruise through them. They're on total blackout mode, but the city ignites with bursts of colorful light as the firefight near the palace wages on.

At this accelerated speed, the cool air streaming in the shark-gill vents of the protective hood is like water over my exposed skin. The farther from the palace we get, the darker it becomes. With the only light coming from bluish headlamps mounted on the hovercycles, we could be in a submarine on the ocean floor, exploring the pristine remains of a submerged city. Steely, wavering buildings rise like sea grass out of the dark and force us to circumvent them. Around every corner, I expect some leviathan-like Alameeda ship to intercept us. I lose my sense of direction the further into this metropolis we travel, and try to hold on to time instead: I gauge it to be only a score or so minutes since we left the palace grounds.

We slow when we near a blue laser wall; it reaches far above our heads, all the way up to the arcing, protective screen that covers the city. I tighten my grip on Trey. The light from the cycle's display illuminates his face with ghostly shadows that are mirrored on the hood. "Don't be afraid—it's just a checkpoint, Kricket," he murmurs. "We have authorization." Trey's hovercycle emits a pulse of light, which disconnects the blue beams. An arching gateway opens directly in front of us. Trey pulls the cycle through the pathway. I glance over my shoulder at the Cavars with us. They're following closely behind.

Passing beyond the wall, the hovercycle changes, deploying wings on either side. We lift further off the ground, rocketing up and winding our way through the towering buildings until we're swimming in a dark pool of stars. As we fly through white-capped cloud banks high above the city, the shadowy outline of a floating fortress's hull blots out the moon. It cuts across the moonlight without the benefit of sails, and the sight of it tightens my throat like the taste of saltwater.

It drifts through the Isle of Skye's dark airstream, its anchor weighed, and at first it looks like just a planetary shadow against the night. As we near it though, the shadow pixelates. Blocks of different-colored blacks and grays hide the stars behind them like the intentional censoring of a deviant film image. The hovercycle sends out a pulse of light; it strobes the shadow. Then, a pulse of light from the desaturated night sky engulfs us. The cycle reacts, lurching as it's drawn forward.

I squeak in fear, and Trey immediately reassures me. "Shh, it's okay." He rubs my hands with his. "It's a tractor beam. They're bringing us in."

A shimmering, scrolling line etches in the sky; it carves an elaborate Victorian keyhole opening. As we pass through the keyhole and beyond the shield, the camouflage recedes, and the tractor beam disengages. The light from a massive cityscape is visible on top of an elliptical, metallic base. Trey flies us closer, and it's clear that Skye's headquarters is a world unto its own—a world encased in a floating transparent bubble. Inside this shield, Ethar's moon is visible and so close that I can see the dark blue craters in its surface.

As Trey takes us closer to the bottom portion of the fortress, we're dwarfed by the etched hieroglyphs of modern-looking warriors. These massive carved soldiers with a myriad of deadly weaponry conceal the very real cargo doors, gun slits, and other defensive weapons that track us as we pass.

My head spins as we travel upward and pass elaborate, vine-covered terraces with living quarters, and still more cannons, whose barrels could swallow us whole. Finally, we reach the top of this massive orb, flying over a city of jutting skyscrapers with causeways that run between the towering structures. Ships of every size and shape scramble near us at dangerous speeds. The unfamiliarity of it all is doing nothing to ease the shock of this night.

Bypassing this city on top of the world, we descend to the other side of the ellipse. The surface of the round landing deck illuminates as we approach it. Trey quickly opens the hatch of the hovercycle. As he rises, he takes me in his arms and holds me to him for a moment. Then he kisses my temple before he crushes me to him again. I'm grateful for his arms around me because he's the only thing keeping me from falling.

"Kricket." Trey says my name, betraying his raw emotion. He touches my face as it rests against the hollow of his neck. The backs of his fingers caress my cheek before his large hand slips behind my neck, tugging me to him so that our lips meet. His kisses are pure emotion, filled with a savage urgency that's brought on by anger and fear. They speak to me with an unrestrained truth: *I can't lose you.*

My heart, that I have tried so hard to make stone, beats furiously. *All I want is to be in your arms,* my lips convey as an answer to his. I cling to him as if someone might try to tear us apart.

The sound of the other hovercycles arriving makes Trey lift his lips from mine. "I love you," he whispers quickly before his men come nearer. Unwilling to let me go, he picks me up. He strides along the terrace to an arching portico, with Jax and Wayra close behind us. At the end of the hallway, sleek, glass-paneled doors disappear into the ceiling ahead of us as we enter a glass enclosure. Gridlike patterns of light shine on me from above, scanning every inch of my body. Next, the opaque glass wall in front of us dematerializes. This allows me a view of the bustling crowd of Cavars within the floating city.

Jax and Wayra speak to the armed Cavars stationed near the entrance as Trey lowers me to my feet. Gazing around, I'm amazed by the vastness of the fortress. It's like some sort of elegant mall with interconnecting walkways above and podlike vehicles that move through transparent tubes, fast enough to make them just a blur of color.

"This is . . ."

"Skye," Trey finishes for me.

"I should have known."

"Why?" Trey asks.

"Because you guys are always so literal."

A smile touches his lips, the first that I've seen tonight. It causes his eyebrows to lift a bit. "Yes. Is that bad?"

"Depends."

"On what?"

"On what they want from me."

"Agreed. I'm working on aligning those stars we talked about, but for the moment, the stars are still hot enough to scorch us," Trey replies, leading me through the twisting luminous hallways.

I'm already lost in this labyrinth. "Where are we going?" Every passageway looks exactly like the last.

"My quarters," he replies, and my heartbeat drums in my chest in anticipation of seeing where he lives.

The passageways abruptly become posh, with wider portals, alcoves, and soft lighting. Coming to enormous double doors at the end of an elegant hallway, Trey says, "Gennet Allairis."

Immediately, the doors lift, allowing us to enter before they close again. My mouth drops open when I see an entire wall of glass on the other side of the room, with an unimpeded view of the brilliant moon. I hold Trey's hand as I walk over the black marble floor. Descending a few stairs to a sunken seating area in front of the glass, I peer down at the skyscrapers below.

"What is 'gennet'?" I ask absently, not ready to look at him yet.

"It's a rank—like general," he replies, reaching out to touch my cheek.

"You were promoted? No more kesek?"

"Yes, that's right. It means that I can decide the missions I lead."

"So, tonight was—"

"My first official mission as gennet," he replies. "I received your message."

"Message? I didn't send you a message," I frown, looking into his violet eyes.

He brushes my hair back from my face and smiles down on me. "I was uninvited to your swank. Manus let me know that it was by your insistence that I not attend. You wouldn't have done that unless something really bad was going to happen." His fingers trail over my cheek and down to my neck, making me shiver.

"How did you know that?" I ask breathlessly with my eyes on his lips.

Leaning near my ear, he whispers, "I know you."

"You do?"

"Yes."

"Then what am I thinking?" I try to stop the tears from clouding my eyes.

"I had Victus lie to Manus—I'm no longer engaged to Charisma."

"You're not?"

He shakes his head. "No, I'm not. I knew things were bad for you. I knew that Manus was forcing you into the engagement. I was trying to make things easier for you by letting him think I was still engaged until I could find a way to get you out. You didn't believe that I'd walk away from you after everything we've been through—after the promises I made to you when we were last together?"

"I didn't know—"

"You can trust me with your heart, Kricket," Trey says as if he's speaking directly to the organ in question. "I won't allow Manus near you. All the wealth in the world won't keep us apart, I promise you," Trey says. He takes me in his arms and hugs me again.

"What about your family? Manus told me that he'd crush you and them if I didn't agree to be his consort," I explain, feeling desperate.

"I'm a gennet of Skye. I'll crush *him* if he tries."

"Of Skye? Not the Cavars?" I ask, my eyes going wide.

"I'm still a Cavar. I'll always be a Cavar, but now I'm a ranking member of Skye as well. Skye controls all branches of the Rafe military: the Cavars, the Armada, the Air Brigade, Infantry and all the distinct branches of intelligence."

"Like a defense department?" I ask.

"That's right. I've been assigned to lead the Special Operations Command in our defense department—in Skye."

"So what will your job entail?"

"It's covert ops, Kricket, but because it's part of Skye, I'll have every branch of the military and intelligence community at my disposal—not just Cavars—it's joint component command."

"Interservice coordination?" I ask.

"Yes."

"Where would an Alameeda priestess fit into all that?"

"Special reconnaissance, counterterrorism, unconventional warfare."

"Which all fall under—"

"Special Operations Command."

"Which you help lead?"

"Which I help lead," Trey affirms.

A little of the fear I've been harboring dissipates for a moment until I remember Kyon. His eyes had been filled with pure malice after I stabbed him. I know that look—it promised revenge. "You don't think Kyon is dead? You're sure that I didn't kill him?"

"You didn't kill him." Trey answers slowly. "You were so brave, trying to face him on your own—with a knife. What were you thinking, Kricket?" Trey's face is a mixture of pride and distress.

"I saw what would happen. I tried to warn them, Trey, but Manus wouldn't believe me," I explain, my voice cracking. "He thought I was lying to him when I told him that Kyon was coming tonight to kill him."

"Shh, it's okay." Trey rubs my back soothingly.

My throat feels raw. "No it's not! Those people died tonight because of me."

"No, they died because the Alameeda want to start a war and will go to any lengths to do it." Trey wipes the tears from my face with his thumbs. "You were caught in the middle of that, and the valor of your actions speaks volumes."

"No, I did everything wrong," I whisper.

"Aella told us what you said to her—how you practically begged her to leave for the night and take as many people from the palace with her as she could."

"Aella said that? When?"

"We tracked Aella, and she told us what you said to her. That information warranted the immediate mobilization of troops, mechanized weapons, and constant surveillance of the palace as well as the airspace surrounding it."

"How did they get through your defenses?" I ask, overwhelmed by what he's telling me.

"They have priestesses, Kricket," Trey says softly. "They can find holes and make holes with misdirection and the power of persuasion. But they didn't realize that we knew they'd be there. We were able to engage their troops the moment they hit the ground. Otherwise, it would've been a complete massacre."

Seeing that I'm on the verge of an emotional breakdown, Trey picks me up again. He moves toward a door on the far left of the room.

"I need you to say your name," Trey murmurs in my ear.

"Why?"

"Because I can't open this door to your quarters, only you can do that," he answers, kissing my forehead.

I frown in confusion. "This is my room?"

"Yes," he smiles.

"It's attached to your apartment," I state the obvious.

"It is." His smile gets broader. "I hope you don't mind, but I gave you my personal liaison's quarters. I want you close to me. "

The thought that he wants me near chases away some of the chill I feel inside. "Kricket Hollowell," I say in a strained voice. The door immediately opens for us. As we enter the other room, it looks almost exactly like the one we just left, only on a smaller scale. Turning toward a metal staircase, Trey carries me up to the loft above; it has a balcony overlooking the same view of the moon as the floor below. Laying me on the enormous bed, Trey snuggles up beside me, pulling my face against his chest and letting me cry my heart out to him.

ॐ

Waking up in bed, I look over and see Trey asleep on the pillow next to mine. My heartbeat picks up as I memorize his perfect face looking so peaceful. I watch him for a long time. At the first blush of dawn, I lean forward, brushing my lips gently against his.

When he opens his eyes, he pulls me closer. He leans down to kiss me, and my heart pounds against the wall of my chest. His lips meet mine, teasing my lower lip with his. A soft gasp comes from me as his fingertips skim along the bare skin near the curve of my breast. Heat coils in my belly at his gentle caress.

"How come I'm naked and you have clothes on?" I murmur against his lips, smiling despite my disadvantage.

"Your dress looked uncomfortable, so I took it off you." Trey is completely unapologetic.

"How did you get it off without waking me up?" I gaze into his violet eyes. "There were, like, a hundred clasps on it."

His large hand comes up to cup my cheek, stroking it with his thumb. "I noticed . . . so I cut it off you," he replies, his lips deepening our kiss.

"Was it hot?" I ask between kisses. "Cutting it off me?" I stroke his rough cheek with my hand, feeling the growth of the last few hours.

"Hot?" he asks, his brows drawing together like he's confused. "I wouldn't describe it like that. It was . . . hazardous and delicate. I've had easier times disarming explosives . . ." he trails off for a second, kissing me and causing thrilling heat to creep through my entire body. "All that lace and . . . skin . . ." he mutters against my neck in a tortured groan.

"You don't like the undergarments that I ordered?" My smile grows by the second. "You should know that trying to describe garters and stockings to someone is really difficult, and bras are almost impossible . . ."

"Undergarments . . . is that what you call those polar little monsters?" He nibbles on my earlobe.

"Mmm," I nod, more to cover my shiver of pleasure caused by his lips grazing my shoulder than to answer his question.

"They're cruel, Kitten. They creep into their victim's soul and make it almost impossible for him to get any rest. Just remembering what they looked like on you will occupy whole rotations of my time."

"Before you cut them off? Because they had hooks . . ."

"Yes, I studied them afterward. We should send for your other undergarments, for later, and then you can demonstrate for me how they work," Trey says thoughtfully, his finger tracing my collarbone.

"Instruction?"

"Practical application," he replies, his smile growing.

"That sounds like dangerous work." I nibble on his lower lip. "You might put in for hazard pay," I smile.

"I might . . . something for after our commitment cere-mony . . . Baw-da-baw."

A fem-bot voice from above startles me, causing me to flinch a little as she says, "Kricket Hollowell, your presence is requested by Skye in the High Council Arena."

"What was that?" I ask Trey, my eyes narrowing as I look around the room for hidden cameras.

Trey groans and scrubs his face. "Say, 'I will attend. Estimated time of arrival one part.'"

Repeating what Trey told me to say, I ask, "What did I just agree to?"

"I gave the council a partial report last night after you were asleep, but we have questions to answer before we can move forward."

Wrapping the sheet around me, I ask, "What's the plan?"

Frowning, Trey says, "We need to make sure that Skye allows you to join my unit, because all of the different branches of the military are clamoring for your service."

"So, I could get put in the Air Brigade or the Armada?"

A look of disgust crosses his lips before he says, "I'm going to make sure that doesn't happen. I'll negotiate to get you assigned to me permanently."

"And then we can be together?"

"That's one way. I was able to explain to Skye the friendship and trust that exists between us. It's the reason they allowed you to have quarters next to mine temporarily. They want me to help you get acclimated to this environment."

"Do they know about us?"

"No," Trey says, his eyebrows lowering. "I kept that part quiet. I don't know what they'll do with that information, and I don't want them to have a reason to keep us apart."

"Do you think they'd do that?"

"Once you are emancipated, you have the right to choose a consort. No one can interfere with that decision." He strokes my cheek.

"Fine. Who do I have to convince, then?" I ask, watching his lips twitch in a smile.

"That is the question, Kricket," Trey sighs.

He rises from the bed and walks across the black marble floor to an automated panel. When he touches it, a virtual hologram of clothing appears in front of him. As he flicks his hand, the clothing moves along, rapidly changing in color and style. Trey presses virtual buttons on the hologram screen. Soon a long, black jacket with black leggings appears in the virtual closet.

Pressing more buttons, a package drops from a chute near the automated panel. "Here," Trey says, handing me the package. "These should fit you. Get dressed and meet me in my quarters."

"Are you going to teach me how to use the instant mall?" I rise from the bed with the white sheet wrapped securely around me. "Do I need a credit card or—"

"It's requisitioned, and you'll have access to whatever you want under my rank," he replies, amused, before leaning down and kissing me softly.

"Ah, thanks, honey," I murmur under my breath, watching him pull back and walk to the stairs.

Locating the lavare, I wash and dress quickly. The clothing Trey gave me is chic in a very urban, military kind of way. The package comes complete with long black boots that give me more height.

Walking to the stairs, I take them down to the main level. I pass the window, glancing at the amazing view of the sun rising near the skyscrapers below. When I come to the adjoining door between my quarters and Trey's, I say, "Kricket Hollowell."

A fem-bot voice announces, "Kricket Hollowell requests admittance of Gennet Allairis."

A moment later, the door opens, and I see Trey with Jax and Wayra. "Kricket!" Wayra says when I enter the room. "A knife—a dinner knife?" he asks me, not waiting for me to come to him, but meeting me halfway and picking me up off my feet, swinging me around. "I'm going to tell that story to every new git that enlists in the Cavars. That kind of courage you have to be born with; it can't be taught."

"I didn't kill him though," I say, looking into Wayra's grinning violet eyes.

"Next time," Wayra says with the assurance that there will be a next time. "I'll make sure you have a bigger knife. Ah, but you saved the Regent . . . at least most of him. He got tagged a few times by the forty-calibers and received burns from a poorly thrown sanctum amp. We won't see him for a few specks while they regenerate him."

After Wayra puts me on my feet, Jax picks me up. "You need an anatomy class. We're different from humans," he says, grinning at me and giving me a giant hug.

"You think?" I ask, smiling reluctantly. "Well, just add it to the growing list of things Trey will have to teach me. Swimming, climbing, weapons, anatomy . . ."

"I'll teach you anatomy," Jax sets me on my feet.

"At ease, Kesek," Trey frowns at Jax.

"Kesek?" I ask Jax, my mouth dropping open. "You made kesek?"

"Yeah," Jax grins wider. "Working with you is like a fast track to good fortune. Even Wayra got promoted to venteur—uh, that's like captain—and with his knack for insubordination, we know it has to be our good luck charm that's influencing the decision."

"I'm hardly good luck, Jax."

"You're wrong," Wayra interrupts. "You're going to give us the edge we need to win this war the Alameeda are bringing to us. We routed them last night. We destroyed nearly all their ALVs because of you."

"Not me, Trey," I stutter, feeling anxious because they're putting their faith in abilities that I can't control. "I just made a mess."

"If what you did last night was a mess, Kricket, then I want to be around when you get it right," Trey replies with a slow smile.

"Here, here," Jax agrees.

"It's a whole different world when we know where they'll be and when, like they do with us," Wayra says with grim satisfaction. "It evens the field—well, it puts them at a disadvantage. Their troops are sloppy because they've never needed much skill to take us when they have surprise on their side. It was like taking out gits last night."

"It won't always be like that, Wayra. They'll adapt," Jax says, his eyes on me.

"And Kyon knows me. He knows what I can do," I say softly, with ice in my veins.

"They'll have to put him back together first," Trey replies in an even tone.

"How long will it take to do that?"

Trey frowns. "Half a floan."

"Six months," I say absently. "Then it'll be on."

"And we'll be ready. Gentlemen, we have our navigator for our next mission. Let's make sure she comes home safe."

"Baw-da-baw," Wayra and Jax say in unison.

"Home," I murmur softly, before walking beside Trey to the door to face Skye together.

Acknowledgments

God, all things are possible through You. Thank you for Your infinite blessings and for allowing me to do what I love: write.

To my readers and bloggers: Thank you, thank you, thank you! The outpouring of love that I receive from all of you is mind blowing. Your generosity toward me is humbling. You make me want to write a thousand books.

Tom Bartol, you're my best friend. I cannot imagine my world without you in it. I love you.

Max and Jack Bartol, I count myself as the most fortunate person in the world to have you both in my life. Thank you for knowing when to let me write and when to rescue me from my computer.

Gloria Lutz, your unwavering support and unconditional love are a guiding light in my life. Thank you for using your wicked editing skills on this project. I love you and I'm very grateful.

Tamar Rydzinski, one of the best days of my life was when you agreed to be my agent. Your tireless work and incredible perspective and insights on this manuscript were integral to making it what it is. What you've already taught me about writing and publishing is invaluable. I'm truly grateful for everything you've done for me. I can't wait to work with you on more projects.

Janet Cadsawan. You. Are. Brilliant. Thank you for introducing me to Tamar. Without your help, this book would not be what it is today. You're a creative genius, and I look forward to seeing the heights to which your talent will take you.

Aaron Draper, when I first saw your photograph of the girl in the water, it gave me goose bumps. Your picture told a story. You captured something so delicately beautiful and undeniably vulnerable through your lens that I had to try to find you to at least tell you how much I loved it. Thank you for agreeing to allow a version of it to appear as the cover of *Under Different Stars*. I could not have found anything else this perfect to represent Kricket and the story.

Regina Wamba: Thank you for using your exceptional experience and artistic talent to create the cover of *Under Different Stars*. You married the genre of the manuscript with Aaron Draper's photograph and created a perfect representation of the story. You've exceeded all of my expectations. You're a rock star.

Cristina Suárez-Muñoz, I couldn't have found a more generous and thoughtful friend if I scoured the world for her. Thank you for beta reading this story and giving me your opinion. Thank you also for all of your hard work and dedication to this project. Your skill with marketing has helped me tremendously. I'm grateful for all that you have done and continue to do to make this novel a success.

Trish Brinkley, you're a very powerful person. I don't think you realize it yet. Over 2013, you've managed to carve out a very serious niche in a cutthroat market with the launch of your organization: The Occasionalist. I'm extremely grateful to you for what you have done for my career, beginning in Boston with help from the amazing Megan Ward O'Connell, and now as we head into the future. I can't wait to see what you'll do next.

Amber McLelland, your wicked wit and savage sense of humor keep me laughing every day. Thank you for being such a good friend to me and for beta reading *Under Different Stars*. I'm so lucky to have found you.

Janet Wallace, you're amazing! Thank you for including me in your insanely creative world. Your generosity toward me knows no bounds. I marvel at what you have accomplished in such a short period of time. I'm eagerly awaiting your next jaw-dropping feat of awesomeness. See you in utopYA.

To my lovely Hellcats: Georgia Cates, Shelly Crane, Samantha Young, Michelle Leighton, Rachel Higginson, Angeline Kace, Lila Felix, and Quinn Loftis. Thank you for allowing me to turn myself loose in our chat room every single day. It has not gone unnoticed by me that I often sound like a degenerate sugar addict set free in a candy factory, but I love you all for humoring me. Clearly, you're the reasons why I've been able to maintain control and haven't had to be soaked down with Mace on a daily basis. I love all of your guts. Always.

About the Author

Photo © 2013 Georgia Cates

Amy A. Bartol is the award-winning and bestselling author of the Kricket Series and the Premonition Series, the latter of which includes the books *Inescapable*, *Intuition*, *Indebted*, *Incendiary*, and *Iniquity*. She lives in Michigan with her husband and their two sons.